# BUTTERFLY MORALS

## SEDUCING MOSES AND CHARLES

BOOK Nine

*of the*

**SECRET BUTTERFLY SERIES**™

A NOVEL BY

Rosemary Lightfoot Ness-Bitner

Copyright©2025 Rosemary Lightfoot Ness-Bitner. All rights reserved. Published in the United States of America. No part of this book or its audio book may be reproduced or used in any manner whatsoever without written permission, except in brief quotations embodied in critical reviews or articles.

"SECRET BUTTERFLY™" and "THE EYES BEHIND THE BUTTERFLY™" design are trademarks of Bifster One Publishing, LLC. For more information, please contact: rosemarylightfootnessbitner@aol.com.

To order, wherever books are sold:

ISBN 978-1-961850-20-0 for eBook

ISBN 978-1-961850-19-4 for Paperback

The eBook and print version layouts of BUTTERFLY MORALS were done by eBook launch. I am Minna Morinette, your audio book narrator.

## A caution and disclaimer

All characters, events, and conversations in this book are fictional, the product of the author's imagination, or used fictitiously. Any resemblance to actual characters, living or dead, events past or present, localities, or conversations, is entirely coincidental.

If you are offended or stressed by characters' offensive behaviors and expressions of strong opinions about controversial subjects, you are advised and cautioned to not purchase this book or listen to this audio book. If you are a child under the age of eighteen, do not purchase this book or listen to this audio book as it contains erotic adult content. Sexual activity may cause diseases.

THIS BOOK CONTAINS SADISM, MURDER, AND EXPLICIT EROTIC ROMANCE CONTENT. IT IS INTENDED FOR MATURE READERS AND AUDIENCES OVER THE AGE OF EIGHTEEN ONLY. IT MAY BE OFFENSIVE OR STRESSFUL TO SOME READERS.

CHAPTER FOUR, 'PRINCE MOSES,' CONTAINS PARTICULARY MACABRE, GRUESOME, AND DEPRAVED CONDUCT MATERIAL. IT MAY TRIGGER A STRONG EMOTIVE RESPONSE IN SOME READERS AND LISTENERS. IF YOU ARE SENSITIVE TO EXPLICIT SCENES OF SEDUCTION AND CARNAGE, YOU ARE ADVISED TO NOT PURCHASE THIS BOOK OR THIS AUDIO BOOK.

OPINIONS, VIEWS, AND ADVICE GIVEN IN THIS BOOK BY ITS CHARACTERS TO OTHER CHARACTERS, AND BEHAVIORS EXHIBITED AND ADVOCATED BY ITS CHARACTERS DO NOT REFLECT THE OPINIONS, VIEWS, OR ADVICE, OR ADVOCATION OF BEHAVIORS OF, OR BY, THE AUTHOR OR PUBLISHER, OR OF, OR BY, ANY ORGANIZATION OR ENTITY TO WHICH THE AUTHOR OR PUBLISHER ARE AFFILIATED. NEITHER THE AUTHOR, THE PUBLISHER, NOR ANY OTHER PERSONS ASSOCIATED WITH THIS BOOK SHALL BE HELD RESPONSIBLE FOR ANY CONSEQUENCES ARISING FROM THE OPINIONS, VIEWS, ADVICES, BEHAVIORS, OR INTERPRETATIONS EXPRESSED BY THE CHARACTERS IN THIS BOOK; OR, IN ANY OTHER WAY, EXPRESSED IN THIS BOOK, OR BY ITS COVE

This book is dedicated to lovers and their dreams.

*Marty knows she's in a bizarre predicament. In LOVE AND LOV-ERS, our eleventh book of THE SECRET BUTTERFLY SERIES™, we will find Marty sitting on hay bales, waiting for David to do whatever he's going to do next. Hallucinogenic mushroom extract and chloroform will have induced their semi-trance. Her mind will become transported to a magical other world where reality and imagination become blurred. Past events that have already happened are yet to come; and events yet to come will appear as vivid in Marty's imagination as if they happened yesterday. But first, here, in our ninth book, BUTTERFLY MORALS, we must look inside the soul of a murderess. We need to understand why she is the way she is; and why she loves to murder. Marty brims with pride. She has recently murdered Bertie and George. Now, she vividly relives events from her soul's past, from lives she lived before her present life, as if she were living them now, in the present. In BUTTERFLY MORALS, we will visit with Marty's mind as it travels down a dark rabbit hole to find its semi-conscious, mentally expanded state. Her mind vividly reveals details of her spirit soul's past that she had previously hidden from David; and even she, herself, had forgotten that these events had ever happened.*

*But, you see, dear readers and listeners, in our biocentric cosmos, where life is permutated, reconstituted, and reincarnated; where butterfly spirits guide human ones and where all people are good people; and where even bad deeds can be considered good deeds, the spirits, not we mortals, decide good and bad; right, and wrong. And everything and everyone has a purpose.*

*There, in eternity, it doesn't matter when something happens, or whether humans witnessed it happening. It happens merely because we believe it did or because we believe it will. This must be true, because that's what the butterflies tell us! And the butterflies surely know, because they are born and reborn through metamorphosis. They've lived in the spirit world as well as in our physical world. And they have witnessed historical events as they really happened; not in the homily versions given to us in religious scripture.*

*The butterflies have merrily fluttered through all of it. Their spirits have mingled with our spirits and their spirits have learned our secrets. And the butterflies always tell us the truth! So, of course, we must believe what the butterflies tell us! Come flutter with me, Minna Morinet, as I narrate BUTTERFLY MORALS, the ninth book of our SECRET BUTTERFLY (tm) SERIES. And, together, we will discover Marty's greatest love and her greatest reveal.*

# CHAPTER ONE

*Let them look upon virtue and pine that they have lost her forever. (Persius: Satires)*

*Reimagine morality. Reimagine a world without strife or wars. Imagine all temples and churches replaced by shrines to intimate artistry; and all religious books and texts replaced by Rosemary's SECRET BUTTERFLY SERIES, in every home and library. Imagine a return to ancient prostitution worship; and elevation of today's porn stars to esteemed goddesses. Imagine human intimacy and connectivity teachings replacing childhood religious instruction. Imagine humanistic love and intimacy as forces that drive our species' colonization of the universe. Imagine seeing the world through a whole new lens. (Rosemary Ness Bitner, author)*

## ADIEU VIRTUE

Marty's head nodded and her smile widened. She was on the hay bales. David had done something to her. Her drugged subconscious remembered her glorious past life. She had a rush of warm feelings. They brought forward her great accomplishments; her conversion of Cecilia; the Temple's fornication rites; her many orgies; and the spectacular tribal murder rituals of her past pagan life. Her fuzzy memories coursed anew through her blood. By reliving her memories, the eternal rightness of her whoring ways was reaffirmed. Miss Iniquity gave her the inner confidence to advocate that more women embrace immorality and shamelessness. Marty had decided. Now it was time she took her rightful place as the leading spokeswoman for the erotic film industry. She recalled her memories as they appeared in her mind.

She remembered her recent interview with Consuelo Lovely, the editor and respected columnist of Porn World Magazine. Consuelo was asking Marty whether she had some tips she'd care to share with young women considering a career in pornography. Miss Iniquity spoke to Marty's mind, helping her form her answers:

*'Very good, Marty, simply bring forward your confidence and training methods from seven thousand years ago. Adapt them to the present. Do not equivocate or hold back your feelings. Speak plainly. Do not use imprecise circumlocution.*

*'Tell them that the world they live in now with its stable institutions, social etiquette, high values, religious gathering places and accepted dogmas are not the true and natural state of human existence or nature. Tell them that instability, uncertainties, social predations, wars, pestilences, and commonplace horrible deaths are the normal experiences of the human condition.*

*'Explain that those who live in high minded morality are not living in a normal human condition, but in a resistance to it. Explain that immorality, iniquitous debauchery, homicide, and whoring are the trusted sacred glues that bind the gravitas of humankind; and that all humans secretly crave to experience the delicious tastes of evil and sin.*

*'Tell them how rewarding it is to be an unrepentant pagan whore; to be as free as a butterfly. Remind them that prostitution is the world's oldest, most honest, and most honorable profession. Tell them to be proud of prostitution as their chosen profession. Tell them to have faith in its eternal righteousness. Let thousands of young*

*women hear your wisdom. Speak to them with authority and confidence from your own experiences.*

*'Introduce the fabulous career opportunities that await them as intimate film artisans. Dispel their fears and equivocations. Explain that morality is a merely an arbitrary, subjective standard that fluctuates widely, depending upon who rules society at any given time. And assure them that human needs and desires are the only true, constant, and natural forces; and that they are driven by the spirits we hold within ourselves. Assure them that those are the true forces we must heed; that those forces alone are compelling us to choose our own morality. And acquaint them with the glory, honors and satisfaction that accompany prostitution's financially rewarding lifestyle.*

*'Remember, Marty, I am always here for you. I am the steady voice within you.'* Miss Iniquity's voice kissed Marty on her cheek. Marty now felt prepared to speak with confidence.

Marty remembered her response to Consuelo:

*"Oh, sure Consuelo, of course I can give you some tips. If a young woman is thinking about making an erotic film, she should go ahead and make one. She can learn for herself whether she enjoyed making it. The very first thing she should ask herself is: Does she love having sex? By that I mean does she find herself feeling she'd like to continue having sex, after her performing partner has come inside her? Does she find herself wishing he had stayed harder inside her; and stayed longer for her so she could have had more pleasures? And, if after making the film, does she find herself wishing she could have sex more often than she does now? Does she wish another partner would join with her; quickly penetrate her; plunge his shaft deeply into her, and make love with her; giving her continuing pleasures, after her first partner has ejaculated?*

*"Does she feel there's a stifled someone inside of her that craves freedom from the life she has? Does she feel a yearning for a certain handsome man, even though he may be a fellow office worker or*

her best friend's husband? She needs to assess herself; reflect and consider that she may have different needs than the needs she was raised to believe she should have. She must ask herself whether she's ready to accept that her different needs are completely normal; and nothing to fear or feel ashamed of. I mean, can she accept the fact that we humans are polygenetic; and that there's a nymphomaniac gene profusely proliferating through many women of our species? Can she accept that there is an epoch happening taking place; and that it is a healthy one? She needs to ask herself why she should fear it? And, why not simply accept it and embrace it?

"Does she find herself saying 'to hell with it?' more and more often when feeling confronted with impossible demands? Does she feel imprisoned in a life that's ordered by everyone else? If so, she needs to face it. Are the demands of living a proper responsible, respectable life crushing her spirit and smothering her? Then, she needs to ask herself: Would making love with her co-worker or her best friend's handsome husband make her feel liberated? Would that tumble for a delicious hour make her feel like she climbed a mountaintop and ascended into heaven? If her answer is yes, she knows that it would, then a career in adult entertainment may be a wisely considered choice for her.

"And that's okay. It's nothing to feel embarrassed about, or be ashamed of, either. It's natural. She is a normal woman with normal needs and normal urges. She has normal DNA that needs to express. It's there, living inside her. It's telling her it wants to be let out of its closet. It wants the nympho within her to be free and running wild. She needs to be assured that there are great venues available to her. They allow her all the freedom she ever wanted. She should also be informed about the important roles prostitutes, courtesans, and erotic actresses have played throughout human history. The Roman empire in its declining centuries comes to mind. Prostitutes were esteemed and revered by the nobility and upper classes; welcomed to *live in their palaces and join them in social events. America's future is unfolding in a way that extolls similar values.*

*"How will she know if intimate film creation is a good full or part time career choice for her? Can she imagine she'd like to make love several times a day with handsome male partners; and make love with them as often as five or six days a week? Would she prefer a sensuous lifestyle to changing dirty diapers and driving a van load of screaming kids to soccer practice? Would she prefer getting pampered and caressed to staying up nights with a sick kid; waiting anxiously for her husband to come home late or maybe not come home at all? Would she rather be escorted to fine dining and theater shows than waitressing snacks from the kitchen to her sofa planted husband, while he watches football all weekend? She needs to know she has the right to choose her life. If she thinks she'd prefer frequent sex to eternal drudgery, while getting well paid for her sexual escapades, then intimate adult film art is a career choice she should explore.*

*"Before she goes to an established studio for her first professional audition, I suggest she confide in three to five of her most trusted male friends and tell them what she's considering. Assuming they'll agree to help her, my advice is to practice having sex with them while watching some erotic films that feature top ranked actresses. She needs to ask herself:*

*'Does receiving extensive foreplay stimulation and sensual, uninhibited erotic sex please her?'*

*"Hopefully she'll experience a wonderment feeling and a lack of shame or inhibition while her initial experiences take place. She needs to ask herself:*

*'How do I feel about sucking my partners' penises and fondling their balls; then making love with them in several different positions?'*

*"If the films and her partners stimulate her and cause her libido to crave even more sex, that's a strong, reliable indicator that erotic films are a viable career choice for her. She should discover, quickly,*

whether she's craving nympho sex. If she feels her thoughts often returning to sexual encounters, that is a positive indication that natural promiscuity is taking hold of her career choice decision. It means the nympho seed is taking root inside her mind. She should nurture that seed and encourage it to grow. The beginnings of a career in porn are happening for her. And, that's great! Remember, her initial inclinations towards nymphomania are completely normal. They can lead her to a healthy addiction to sex. She doesn't need to feel embarrassed about her feelings; and, she should keep in mind that a career as a top porn star can compensate her very well.

"She needs to be sensible about her health. She must make sure that she is totally and completely clean, everywhere, if you know what I mean; and, she should also be well rested before she has intercourse. Being rested helps lift her spirit and get her into the mood for sex. She needs to frequently test herself and her partners for diseases. Should problems present themselves, early detection and treatment usually knocks them out.

"She also needs to try different positions and different foreplay experiences. She should ask herself:

'How did I feel when that penis first presented itself? Did it frighten me, or did its presence thrill me? When it first found its way into my mouth, did its presence on my lips and in my mouth terrify me; or did I feel excited about the fellatio I would be giving it? Did I feel focused on it? Did I feel a kind of admiration and love for it? Did it whisk away all my other thoughts and make me feel wonderful about the time I was about to have, sucking and having intercourse with it?'

"And she needs to ask herself some basic, honest questions about how she feels the first time a new partner's penis first penetrates her outer vaginal lips:

'Does having this unknown penis entering me thrill me? Does it make me feel like I'm desirable and wanted by it and the man who is attached to it? Does it frighten me or does it make me feel awe and wonder and splendor over this new experience? Do I feel guilty about what I'm doing, or do I feel emancipated and excited about a whole new world opening up for me? Am I fearful that it might hurt me or am I thrilled that it will soon be giving me stimulations and passions that I have yearned to have?'

"Being hurt by a penis is unlikely if you properly lubricate your-self before it enters you. I thought I should mention that to your readers, in case they didn't know, Consuelo. Also, during and after her sex with her new partners, she should get her partners' opinions about how she reacted and expressed herself during her make-believe on-camera scenes. She should remember their best reactions and her best talking lines and giggles and laughs that her partners told her she had while they made love with her; and then she should practice making those reactions part of her repertoire, so they become auto-matic while she's having sex on an actual film set.

"She needs to concentrate on expressing how wonderfully plea-sured she feels while she's making love; and she must never, ever allow any distractive thoughts about stealing another woman's hus-band or boyfriend to enter her mind. Those are irrelevant bunny trail thoughts that bring out facial expressions that detract from her expressions of pleasure. She should learn to immerse her thoughts in her limbic mind and think only of her own pleasures and the plea-sures she is giving her partners; and become fully invested in fully expressing them. And, she should have no thoughts of anything or anyone else while she is making love with her partners and perform-ing fellatio with their penises.

"I confess that limbic immersion and concentration is sometimes hard to do. I am guilty of occasionally letting my own thoughts stray. Sometimes, when a lady has a wonderful, exceptional lover, it's very difficult to not imagine that she is with him when she is with a new partner; but it's very important to a film's success that she tries her very best to focus on enjoying her love making with the man she is with. She must try to keep her thoughts always focused on the present moment. Always think pleasure! Enjoy your present lover's thrusts and his touches. If he feels you enjoying your sex with him, that tends to make your partner more loving and caring. And that helps create a better film overall. And, she needs to forget about other women or porn stars' experiences with her partner. If any other woman has issues with her having pleasure with her partner, those are that other woman's issues, not hers. She must never, ever feel guilty about having sex with any of her partners.

"She must practice, and practice more to fine tune her love making in all sorts of positions, until she's certain her reactions are realistic and evocative of her most passionate feelings. She must remember to always be a loving lady. At its core messaging, the porn industry is about delivering the message of love to its viewers. She should practice having sex until her male partners become more enthused with her love making each time they practice with her, than they were the time before. She must bring her partners along until they become wildly enthusiastic and thrilled to practice her sex acts and positions with her.

"She must perfect her sensuality and her copulation performances until her partners beg her to keep going. This happens when she captures their limbic minds and they become overwhelmed with desires to please her. It's when their love for her intensifies and consumes all their consciousnesses. It happens with one lover and also with multiple lovers during an orgy session. I call these phenomena in male sex partners the adoration times. It's where they express their love in terms of adoration. It's when, in her partners' minds, she becomes their goddess. They'll say things like how they worship me, how they'd die for me, how they'd leave their wives and their wealth for me, those sorts of things. She can aid and abet these emotive transformations in her partners by using scented oils to enhance the *mental impressions of her natural pheromones. But in truth, there is no substitute for her own mental attitude during her performances. She must lose all her inhibitions and all her other thoughts in complete totality. In other words, she must completely immerse her mind and all her passions into her natural, inner love of fornicating. And she must be attuned to her partners to reinforce their expressions of delight. She needs to listen for those male expressions of love and lust. Once she hears them, and responds to them with ever greater heights of passion, her partners will reward her with similar outpourings of endearment. Those emotive tells will show on her films. Once she masters this limbic capture, she'll see it when she reviews her film work and her confidence as a porn star will skyrocket. Her partners see it too. They will crave to perform on set with her in her future films. Once she masters emotive limbic capture, she'll make highly successful films. She'll notice that her fans are responding by buying more of her films. Advertisers will notice the increase in her views. They pay for eyeballs and clicks. Her cash flow will rise.*

*"A big key to successful erotic film making is communication. This encapsulates where society is heading. Traditional films and erotic adult films are in the transition phase of blurring the lines that separate them and blending the two genres into one widely acclaimed film genre which I prefer to call 'Intimate Artistry.' Successful actresses in this new, evolving genre will be completely at ease and uninhibited with intimacy while the cameras are rolling. A budding adult actress must practice. It's necessary to become comfortable and natural while performing these scenes. She must practice talking to her partners' penises and balls, their faces, and lips, even their nipples, while she's having has sex with them. Practice praising partners' penises and their sexual attributes. If her partner's penis is hitting her clitoris in a way that sends her emotive urges skyward, by all means, tell him. Tell him she loves what he's doing. Tell him she wants more of that. Tell him she loves the way he holds*

her and touches her while he's having sex with her. That personalizes the explicit nature of a porn film and helps engage the viewers in the feelings she has while creating her scenes. It makes for sensually engaging film art. It draws viewers into her scenes and helps them empathize with her.

"Producers will quickly recognize whether she entices viewers into her scenes, so I can not emphasize enough how important it is to practice lovemaking often. It's like going to piano or violin lessons. The more she practices having sex, the less inhibition she will have; the more accomplished she will become and the better her film craft will become. Importantly, she must ask herself whether, by creating porn, she enjoys herself while having sex more or enjoying sex less than before she began creating porn. If she enjoys sex more, the more often she has it, then she's ready to audition. If she has a warm, glowing, satisfied inner feeling after she's performed an orgy scene with three or more men; if she feels like she wishes she could continue with the orgy after all her partners have ejaculated inside her, rather than stopping the orgy; and if she has the sense that her lovers were happy to be her lovers and they'd like to have orgies with her more often, then absolutely, she's ready to studio audition.

"This is a small thing, but it's not inconsequential. If a wife of a practice partner becomes outraged or unruly, or files for divorce because of his practice sessions, then she must evaluate her feelings about the episode. If she feels embarrassed or ashamed, she is not ready to become an adult film star. She will carry her guilt with her onto her sets and that will detract from her performances. If, on the other hand, she is inwardly, deeply pleased that she caused a split up or divorce; and if she has zero pity or compassion for the scorned woman; then, absolutely, she has reached the point where she is ready to do films. She must inwardly enjoy knowing that men are leaving other women and choosing to join her erotica filled world, *which venerates sinning and whoring. She must feel no guilt whatso-ever about the choices men make to perform with her.*

*"If she enjoys oral sex with other women; and if other women enjoy her too; and there are feelings of shared love with female partners, then she's ready to audition as a well-rounded performer. Essentially, she must experience a mental transition. Her mind must reach the place where she rejects or ignores the religious and moral teachings she was subjected to since childhood. She needs to think of those teachings as outdated idol worship and mentally smash those old idols.*

*"Her mind needs to get into that place where she absolutely loves making love and having pleasure as often as possible, with many different partners for her sheer pleasure and sexual joy. She must think of her vagina as a beautiful vessel that gives and receives pleasure, that her life's purpose is giving and receiving pleasure; and that pleasure giving is a desirable, shameless, honorable way of advancing human connectivity and the fulfillment of human life. She should feel cradled by warm, loving arms of like-minded sisters, congratulating, and blessing her for the beauty of her love making.*

*"Frequent sex may possibly become her addiction. That is nothing to be feared. Sex can be no less addictive than cigarettes, alcohol, or drugs; but it's a different sort of addiction. It is not destructive like the others. It's inclusive. It expands sensitivities and awareness. It can be the cornerstone upon which she can build loving, lasting relationships. She must perceive her film artistry as beautiful and fulfilling. She must never resent herself for becoming addicted to her sexual cravings, as many smokers and alcoholics resent themselves for their addictions; instead, she must celebrate herself and feel proud of her sexuality.*

*"She will pass through a mental transition of sorts. She must make a serious assessment of her own mind, especially it's subconscious yearnings. For instance, when she's not performing, when*

she's away from the set or away from her practice partners, where are her thoughts? If she's in a movie or at a party, is she focused on the here and now; or, do her thoughts drift back to her porn experience? Does she keep recalling a certain male's penis when she first held it and when she first brought it to her lips or guided it into her vagina? These are important indicators. If her mind constantly drifts back to her times with penises, then it's likely that she's comfortable in the world of porn. And, there's nothing wrong with that. She shouldn't try to suppress those thoughts or feelings. She should embrace them.

"If she's a natural for performing porn, when she's not having sex, she will dream and daydream about having sex. Sex will essentially become her 'Raison d Trey,' her reason for living. She should embrace her life. She should imagine her next partner, whom she will meet for the first time, will be a fabulous lover. She should be able to imagine herself naked, loving his touches while he kisses her neck, shoulders, back and between her thighs to stimulate her; loving his nipple kisses; feeling aroused; anticipating her joyful abandon while his penis probes her outer lips, before it enters her.

"She should feel her sex getting moist, her mouth salivating and her anticipation building at the prospect of making love with and experiencing different sex acts with each exciting new partner. Visualizing herself on set beforehand is a wonderful way to prepare for the actual film shoot. I do that every time I'm about to make love with a new partner. It helps me to imagine myself lying naked beside or on top of my partner; French kissing him fully in his mouth while I'm fondling his balls and stroking his penis makes me anxious to perform with him.

"She should imagine, as I do, how wonderful she will feel when his huge penis penetrates her for their first time and how wonderful she'll feel as it slides deeply inside her. Then, when she's about to walk onto the set before the cameras start rolling and the lights go on, she *should feel thrilled and eager to meet him and make love with him; and not have the slightest timidity about this new experience or have the slightest reluctance to pour out her love to him. She should think she'll be with the truest and greatest love of her life, because for the next few hours that will be her reality. Her imaginings should blur with the realities of her life; that is that she is no longer like other women; or even like her pre-porn self. She has emerged from her everyday world cocoon into the bright wondrous world of endless love making. She will transition from caring how others tell her she SHOULD think and feel to how she DOES think and feel.*

*"When will that magical moment come for her? It could happen during her very first practice session or it might come months after she's auditioned and become a paid performer. It happened for me when my first film partner's eyes told me that he loved me. In those fleeting seconds I knew he would remember and cherish our love-making forever. It might happen while she's on set having coitus and realizing she's hot and juicy inside because her lover's penis feels so wonderful inside her, or it could happen one day when she's holding a beautiful hardened penis in her hands about to suck it or guide it into her vagina; realizing how blessed she is to try different touchings and kissing techniques with a new, marvelous penis that is about to erupt in an ejaculation because of its intense yearning to fuck her; and not feel in the slightest bit of inhibition about those feelings; or it could come one day during an orgy scene while a vibrator is stimulating her vagina's crown while her partner's penis is thrusting inside her and tapping her uterus while he's penetrating her from behind; while she's enjoying multiple fantastic orgasms; or while her mind is exploding with pleasure from her multiple orgasms and she's feeling completely natural and wholesome about the entire experience. Whenever that moment of her epiphany occurs, and it will occur, she will suddenly realize that there's no other career choice or lifestyle that could come anywhere close to the complete satisfaction*

*and joy of having those expansive feelings that she experiences while she creating adult films.*

*"At that moment she'll know she absolutely loves the sex, the glamour, and the feeling of being loved and admired by so many men. She'll love hearing different men telling her how beautiful and sexy she is. She'll love hearing them tell her how wonderful her vagina tastes and how much they love the intimate feelings they are having while their penises are inside her. She'll become fascinated by the different feelings she has when different partners make love with her; and she'll marvel and appreciate that no two penises feel the same or perform the same inside her. She'll be able to discern how her partners are communicating their different feelings and emotions to her through their penises. She'll become an afficionado of partners' moods and methods; all in the realm of intimate artistic creation.*

*"More and more, she'll desire to discover new ways of love making. She'll become a connoisseur of intimacy; never able to get enough of it. She'll discover that she loves to experiment with partners, positions, methods, moods, and settings. She'll feel an expansive sense of freedom that she never thought was possible before. She'll become hooked on her career choice; wildly enthusiastic about her performances and the challenges of attaining perfection in her expressions; and unable to imagine what held her back from starting sooner, unable to imagine any other career choice. Once she's 'into' her career and fully immersed in it, she'll never look back or feel regrets about her choice. Like me, she'll become addicted to the sex and the lifestyle, because it's truly a beautiful, wholesome, and honest lifestyle. She'll realize she'll never be able to get enough of it. It's hard to say when it will happen, but when it does, absolutely she will know it. She will feel a great unburdening from the stresses of her past life.*

*"When that moment does come, she will have become a sexual, loving, uninhibited woman. Like a glorious butterfly, newly freed*

*from her cocoon, she will have transitioned. Now she dances and dazzles carefree before the entire world; flutters freely from one lover to the next; and appreciates that she is revered, adored, and worshipped by her many legions of followers. She feels a warm glowing pride within her bosom, knowing that she is exalted, idolized, and praised. She feels glorious and omnipotent, knowing she has arrived; knowing she is the world's greatest, most awesome gift to all mankind. She is a sensual woman; a porn star.*

*"Yes, she is a star; and a star with a purpose. A star that lifts the spirits of those who are downtrodden by the dullness and conformity that imprisons them. She is freedom to these multitudes who inwardly can no longer stomach the hypocrisy of their political leaders; to those who revile at the mind-numbing freedom-robbing advance of socialism. She is, after all, a capitalist, trading a service for money. What can be more helpful to those captured millions than to witness the divine beauty of a woman in the throes of her orgasms? What can fire their imaginations more than the spectacular glory-freeness of two lovers enraptured with each other's sensuality while in their intimate act of love making?*

*"She becomes revered in the hearts and minds of millions as an artisan, a forceful expressionist of independent thought and beauty; and that makes her and the art she creates priceless. She becomes beauty, glory, art, and love personified in the flesh. She is adored. Her film art is cherished. Millions dream of consorting with her. In their minds, she is setting them free.*

*"So, you see, Consuelo, there is a certain noble purpose that drives the human craving for ever more erotic film artistry. When making a film, while taking her lover's penis into her mouth or vagina, she must know in her joyful heart that, silently in their innermost hearts, a million freedom starved minds are being unchained and released from bondage. Their silent hungrily thirsting tongues will be shouting out in unison, quietly, from the depths of their souls:*

'Bravo! Beautiful! We love her! We adore her! We want more of her! We will gladly give everything that we have in order to make love with her, if only once, just for one, wonderful, awe- filled moment of time.'

"That longing she creates in the minds of these enraptured souls persists for days, months, even years. They fantasize and pray in unison to her image impression:

'Some day those will be my balls she holds in her hands; that will be my penis she is having sex with and sucking. I will experience the warmth of her body while we lie naked together and make love. She will dig her fingernails into my back and thrust her sex hard against my shaft as it glides over her clitoris; and her eyes will stare in wonder into my eyes as she releases another of her beautiful orgasms. I will feel her lips kissing mine and I will know the pleasure of having her iniquitous tongue, her beautifully naughty, gloriously immoral, educated, sensuous tongue, which has tasted the semen from a thousand penises, finally entwined at last and forever with my own tongue. I will know that delirious feeling of total abandon, as I lose myself and my very soul in her sin lust. And I will love her! I swear I will love her forever!'

"She must understand what her films will do to men's minds. Her lips, breasts and vagina will cease being mere mortal manifestations of her sexuality. They become metaphysical avenues to eternal nirvana. Her vagina becomes a mystical portal which a viewer's mind enters. He imagines himself riding atop his penis as it probes the depths of her passage, passing its steamy slippery delicious walls until it finally communes with her in holy ejaculation rapture. His mental images of her intimacy scenes become catnip pictures that drive him towards madness. Her films will cause him to snap free from his moral moorings. She must accept that some men will obsess over her and she must be prepared to deal with the obsessed as a cost of business.

"I have another important perspective that I hope will encourage and give confidence to any woman who is sitting on the fence about beginning her career in intimate film work. Maybe she is not the most beautiful girl on her block or college campus; but she should not let that hold her back. There are many women who are actually not very beautiful, who make fabulous, insanely serious money by making sex films part time and servicing their private clients. And they have a wonderful, sociable time in the business, while getting to know their partners and their film crews.

"Many women absolutely love making the films. It's like any-thing else. She will develop a fan base and loyal men who will want to partner with her. She'll communicate with them through her pri-vate service, Emails, and web site; and she'll build her following and partner loyalties with every film she creates. Her fans will follow her anywhere because they will fall in love with her. It's an intimacy thing. It's about what's in her heart when she's making love on that set. If she is sincere and loving, the camera and her fans will know it. And they WILL ABSOLUTELY LOVE her!

"Remember. Love happens in the mind. There will be something about her that makes some men fall in love with her. They'll love everything about her; her smile, her eyes, her hair, her voice; perhaps the sight of her vagina or her tush. Many men will desire her. Many will obsess over her. They can not help themselves. It's all very natu-ral. ABSOLUTELY, FOR SURE, THAT WILL HAPPEN.

"She'll become the woman they dream about and want to take home to their mothers. Through her service or agent, she'll get invita-tions to dinner, the theater, social and awards events, sporting events, offers to accompany her admirer on trips, and offers to endorse prod-ucts and services. Some will try to learn her schedule so they can glimpse her in person; or even touch her or the clothes she wears.

"She'll need to learn ways to politely love her followers back; but still set firm boundaries or else she'll get herself into situations where *a man might go crazy and hurt her, himself, or some other man or woman; and she never wants that to happen. If she feels she can't control her own feelings or those of her male followers, then she'll need to have a private service that provides her with protection, as in muscle.*

*"I encourage all women who create intimate films to feel good about their work and themselves after they leave the set. When she walks along a sidewalk or through a mall, she should feel complimentary about how blessed she is. She should think of her vagina as a precious and beautiful asset. When I'm alone I often remind myself how wonderful my clitoris felt while it received tongue strokes from a loving tongue and how sensational if felt when its tentacles flamed hot with lust for more, while I gushed and pulsed with pleasure from my orgasms.*

*"Never ever feel ashamed or regretful about your chosen profession. Always think about what you might have done better on set that last time you performed. Did you feel uncomfortable in any way? Did you always feel you were in the optimal position to give yourself the greatest pleasure? Were you ever feeling that you needed lubrication but hesitated to stop? Never, ever allow yourself to be made uncomfortable. As you walk down that sidewalk or through that mall you need to feel absolutely wonderful about who you are, what you do, and how you're going to have even more pleasure while making an even more sensuous erotic film the next time. Think of yourself as a modern-day temple goddess; a prostitute who is loved, worshipped, and adored by millions, because you are!*

*"My last thought is that a woman can enter the intimate film business at almost any age, from age eighteen and older. There are growing demands for mature women to make films, and there's a genuine shortage of women ages thirty to sixty who are willing to enter this growing field; so, if someone is interested in creating intimate film art as a career, she should not let age deter her without*

*first exploring her opportunities and at least giving herself a chance. There's really no way of knowing what the demand will be for your films unless you make a few and see what sorts of results and feedback you get.*

*"Do not be afraid to try and fail, either. It's a lot like professional sports that way. You will never know how far you can go and how much you can earn unless you work hard at it and give it your honest, best try. There's no stigma to failure, either. Failing is part of the American experience. It's not a disgrace to fail; not anymore. People will understand if you try and fail. No one will blame you for trying. If you do try and fail, just shrug it off and go on to something else. It's really okay. This is modern America. We're not living in the Victorian age anymore. Lots of men would be thrilled out of their minds to date a woman who took a chance at being an adult film star. Many would jump at the chance to be on set with a porn star, taking turns kissing your mouth while you are in the throes of performing your inspiring, sensational, loving fellatio; in a real sense, sanctifying your carefree immorality and adoring your uninhibited pleasuring. Their kisses on your mouth will be their acknowledgement of you as their goddess. They will worship you and love your carnal ways. Many will admire and love you for expressing yourself in your many loving ways. Believe it. It's true."*

Consuelo posed the question she thought would surely be on the minds of the girls who were listening to Marty's rosy portrayal of life as a porn star:

*"Marty, I'm sure our listeners appreciate your advice and opinions. And I'm equally sure that the advice you are giving them is from your own experience; but let me ask you what I'm also certain is on the minds of many girls who are considering a career in adult films. What about when they become older? And what about after they die? How will they explain their life choices to others and to their creator?"*

"Consuelo, those are excellent questions. As far as explaining her choices when she is older and her children or her friends' children ask her why she chose to perform intimate artistry, the answer should be obvious. At the pace things are moving in our world, the last vestiges of Victorian morality are slipping beneath the surface of our collective dust bin. I foresee in the next twenty years, adult film actresses will have their own hall of fame, kind of like football players do today. They will appear as cause célèbres at film premiers and galas. They will be invited as paid opinion guests on influential talk shows. They will be hailed as liberators of thought and human expression; even lauded for the many marriages they may have played a role in ending. You see, Consuelo, humanity is moving forward. It's better to lead than to lag.

"And I do not believe she will ever have that dreaded conversation with her creator. Those of us who believe in the Modern Morality Standard do not believe there is a judgement throne occupied by a bearded old white man who may send you to hell for being human with human limbic needs. No, I think he simply does not exist. But I do have a belief in an afterlife. I often feel it and momentarily relive it in my own flashbacks to my past lives. It's unknowable what your next reincarnated life will be like. Speaking for myself and recalling my flashbacks, I can tell you with certainty that I have lived many past lives as a pagan goddess. I have presided over many sacrifices which were conducted to honor and revere my promiscuity and my insatiable appetite for sex in all its methods of expression. Many men, women, and children were also sacrificed to me because my tribal members regarded me as the divine presence among them who enabled them to succeed in war upon other tribes. I have also witnessed and participated in sacrificing many victims who were given up to me in the belief that their sacrificial deaths would help insure the fertility of my tribe's crops and animals. Perhaps humanity will reassert those tribal worship practices and she will be a goddess who presides over life and death in her next life. Perhaps her soul will rebirth I another world and she will be a tribal goddess there. It's unknowable. But she does know with certainty that humanity is always progressing. And it progresses through the creation of life. Humans need to have sexual intercourse to progress. It's a natural, undeniable truth. Believe in it.

"Whatever happens, my belief is that she will, like all of us, reincarnate into a new body in the flesh and with a new spirit soul; and that she will live, free of any guilt for whatever she may have done or not done in this present life. And if her spirit soul is anything like my own, she will live endless happy and pleasure filled lives throughout all eternity, joyfully fornicating and performing delightful, stimulating fellatio; happily receiving reciprocal stimulations, erotic touches, and cunnilingus from her many loving partners. I believe that will be the essence of life after this life. And I think she should look forward to enjoying herself in this life and all her next lives; and not trouble her mind with religious clap trap. And whenever she hears religious dogma or suggestions that she is a 'Bad Girl,' she should just tune out that criticism; tell herself that she has moved on and turned the page on male misogynism; and remember that she has First Amendment Rights, including the right to freely express herself; remember that she has a right to life, liberty, and happiness; and that, as consenting adults, she, and her partners in film making and in their private liaisons have no one they need to account to or fear. Guilt should never be her motivation for living. Joy should give her that motivation; and she should live her life to the fullest."

# CHAPTER TWO

*The demand for sex is limitless. That's why there are more of us now than there were a million years ago. (Rosemary Ness-Bitner, author)*

## DEMAND

*"Thank you, Marty. That was an inspired answer. You don't believe in religion or a god, do you?"*

*"No, of course not. Life itself is God. Procreation and worship of human intimacy gives homage to Life. Intimate artistry celebrates the divine art of love making and the joining of spirit souls. When I perform my intimate artistry, or porn, if you will, I feel the rapture. I feel the presence of the divine. I believe I participate in the most holy expression of reverence to Life.*

*"From the beginning of human existence, men have been fascinated by women's sexuality. You see, Consuelo, when a man sees a woman engaged in copulation, a hormonal flood takes place in the male amygdala. That hormonal flood results in limbic control of the male brain, shutting out rational thought. But when the male brain sees intimate artistry, or pornography, a secret little door opens inside the male limbic mind. Inside that door is a room which contains a male's prurient thoughts. There, in that room, the male sees the female porn star as a woman who is divinely inspired to perform erotica. She may be performing a threesome with two male partners.*

*"The male viewer sees her actions as other worldly; beyond the behaviors contemplated by more placid women. He sees a divine*

*force emanate from inside her which compels her to engage in all manners of self-pleasuring. In his mind she is transformed into Goddess; his desired and sought after God. In ancient times she became abstracted as an idol and images were made in her likeness. Her name was Ashera.*

*"And her carven images exaggerated the size of her vagina, because that's where the male obsession fixated. That female vagina is what the males and the entire tribe worshipped. It gave them unity, because they all worshipped it. It gave them fertility and the continuation of their lives. And it gave them motivation to succeed in their hunts and their wars. They prayed to their tribal prostitutes. They worshipped their female vaginas. Prostitution worship is returning to humanity once again. It comes in the form of the porn star.*

*"So, Consuelo, since legions of men already see me as their God, why should I believe there is a higher power than myself? Why should I place some imaginary white haired old man on an imaginary throne chair before me?"*

*"Very good, Marty."* Consuelo was flummoxed. She had no response to Marty and quickly changed the subject. *"Now, I have another question: Are you seeing an increased demand for intimate film art in general, Marty, or just a greater demand for your own work?"* Consuelo sought to know whether her magazine continued to serve a growth industry.

*"Well,"* Marty replied, *"many performers I work with have commented how it's becoming harder to keep up with the demand for new films and fresh performance themes, as well as keeping up with their private service demands; so, I believe demand growth is widespread. And, as I look inside myself, Consuelo, I often feel that I and my body of work are central to a theme sweeping the nation and much of the world. It's partly a realization that religion no longer serves the same societal purposes it once did. We no longer need those rigid controls and that policing of our thoughts and bodies.*

*I see humanity's departure from religion as similar to a horse that realizes for the first time that it has been freed from its hobbles. It can run free and enjoy the world around it. My work and the works of other porn stars are also the new theme of humanity's liberation. It embraces what humanity desperately craves, which is intimacy and love; and at the same time, it's a rejection theme. It's making old entertainment genres passe. It's the demolition of the Hollywood Studio model. It's box office rejection of high budget special effect films, and the disdain for the insane political apparatus that Hollywood has become. My world is entertainment. That's me; that's what I feel; and it's what I love doing. And that's what drives my industry. It's not geek world ego trips smacked onto mind-numbing films; and it certainly is not politics.*

*"That brings my precious friend,Dom, to my mind. He's smart and innovative. He knew society at large was starting to embrace what we formerly called pornography. He knew perspectives were changing and that people were recognizing our genre as beautiful, expressive intimate art. He recognized that people were relating to our work and emoting with us as we performed it. He studied the evolution of the industry from tawdry films to the latest evolutionary works of intimate art.*

*"Dom correctly assessed that society was about to idolize its adult film stars. He learned his friends' preferences and dalliances. He knew we'd be more successful by involving his influential friends. So, Dom used his contacts and got them involved. He understood how to expand the market for my work. He was careful to bring them in on the ground floor of his marketing plans. He intended to use me and my film works as backgrounds for product endorsements and our expansion into merchandise venues with our own product lines. I paid close attention to what he was doing. He cleverly created the background buzz for the announcements he would make later. Dom shook the trees and the coconuts fell down. Reporters, journalists,*

and product sponsors were suddenly made aware that Dom and I were going to create a special kind of magic.

"Quickly, word got around that the world's number one ranked adult film star was at a Cannes' casino craps table with Dom. A crowd gathered around us as I threw the dice. A cheerful roar went up whenever my throw produced a win for me. Dom put up a million dollars that day. He ate all my losses. So, speaking to aspiring actresses, it helps expand your demand if you can get someone to back you. As more stars get that sort of backing, expect the growth of adult films to accelerate.

"So, you really did take Cannes by storm, just like the newspaper accounts said, didn't you?"

"Yes. And, by the way, my Premium Service demand has skyrocketed as has the growth in requests for my endorsements. The Cannes trip succeeded wildly. It was surreal. It seemed the entire casino floor wanted to rub shoulders with me, run their hands over my ass; kiss my hand or cheek; touch and kiss my vagina. I felt I was the second American invasion of France; except I didn't wade ashore with a mighty military force. I flew in on a jet delivering my sex appeal. My sexcapades at Cannes would not have happened five years ago. That tells me intimate adult films are coming on strongly in the marketplace.'

"Well, let's talk more about your Cannes trip. What did you do there before you and Dom flew to Las Vegas?"

"Sure. Dom walked me to the baccarat tables. He bought three million dollars worth of chips from the croupier and piled them on one of the tables between the shoes. He arranged for a photographer to take photos of me lying on the table on top of this huge mountain of ten-thousand-dollar chips. The shot where I've pulled away my bikini bottom to display my naked vagina on top of millions of dollars in chips is the photo that made the covers of all the sex culture magazines. I had my vagina all plumped up, freshly waxed and *oiled. It appeared to viewers as an irresistible creamy white morsel, anxious for sex. That photo sold a million copies of your magazines."*

*"Yes, we remember it and we thank you."*

*"You're welcome, always, Consuelo. Anyway, Dom's subtle messaging was to inform marketers that I was the world's most beautiful and most expensive whore with a most delicious, eager to please, vagina; and that I was available, for a price. I thought my stomach looked perfectly flat in that photo, didn't you? Did you happen to see it?'*

*"Yes, I did, Marty. You looked ravishing, positively gorgeous. You're doing wonders for the intimate film trade with all the promotional work you do. My publishers wanted me to tell you that and encourage you to keep going. They know when you appear on our cover and when they run feature stories about your escapades and peccadillos, our street sales jump. They appreciate that you give us so much access to you."* Consuelo stoked Marty's ego. Marty continued her story.

*"Dom let me keep all our winnings. After I cashed my chips, we left the casino. I had a half million-dollar check in my purse. As I walked out of the casino, I knew that I had just become the most exclusive, most sought-after prostitute on two continents. I knew that Dom was giving me a fabulous opportunity. I appreciate that. I'll never let him down."*

# CHAPTER THREE

*Have thoughts that you keep to yourself; but when you are alone with the object of those thoughts, express them. (Rosemary Ness Bitner, author)*

## SWEET TREACHERY

As Dom and Marty strolled toward the Cannes beaches, a battle of her inner voices broke out. Miss Iniquity started it:

*'Look, you now have the entire world eating from your hand. What more could you possibly want? You have Dom now. You MUST get rid of David. It's time to leave him, forget the murders and go off on your own.'*

Miss Lust, a deep narcissistic voice whom Marty feared to offend more than any other, spoke:

*'DON'T be a fool. Your position with David gives you access to huge money. You just bagged a sheik and his two sons. There's more of those. You can have them. Besides, there's much more to life than money. You do have it all; and you CAN have it all. You SHOULD have it all. You DESERVE to have it all. And you CAN manage both. Just pay attention to your scheduling. You know you can not live without your blood lust. You know there is NOTHING that feels like the divine ecstasy of murder. Don't let your other voices ruin what you have going with David.*

*'Think how complete you feel while you have orgy sex in your victims' blood after you watch them die. Remember the beautiful*

power surges you feel inside your mind and vagina. You KNOW nothing gives you greater pleasure. David LOVES watching you murder, too. You KNOW you tingle with joy when you please David.

'DON'T listen to your other voices. Ignore them. They're fools. Murder IS the ULTIMATE bliss. You need that. You know it's true. You love watching the headless body twitch while blood spurts spastically from the severed neck. It amuses you knowing the blood will spill onto the table, and you will frolic in it while the horrified head realizes its body's blood will never reach it.

'You love feeling strong and alive while your victims' bodies grow weaker as their hearts die. You love seeing their jaws gape, while they try forming words without lungs to force air passage over their tongues and lips. Where else can you feel that same smugness of superiority while their eyes widen in horror realizing they can only think for another moment before their brains shut down?

'When you kiss their lips while their eyes glaze and dim, you know they bond with you. You know they know that you are all they have left. You are their last link to life. You know they'll love you forever. They hang onto that last link to life for every precious last second. They hope you have power to give them more life, although you know you don't; but that struggle you see in their eyes before they surrender all their love to you in their last-ditch hope amuses you. It warms your heart knowing you are their last hope. In a very real sense, they pray to you; beg you to help them, as if you are their god. Such power you have in those moments! You KNOW murder is your ultimate thrill. Money and fame can't hold a candle to the thrill of it. You know it's true. NEVER, EVER even THINK about giving up murder again.'

'But everyone believes it's immoral to murder. If I'm caught what will people think of me?' Marty's mind raised the objection her other voices often expressed.

'Are you STUPID?' Miss Lust became angry. 'There's no such thing as morality. You already know that. Murder is perfectly *normal. It's cathartic. It helps you relieve tensions. It's good for your self-esteem. Look, humanity is evolving. Murder is becoming more commonplace and accepted. Inner cities are no different than insect colonies where murders are routines of daily life. Humanity isn't all that far removed from the insect world, anyway. The only real difference is we have endoskeletons and insects have exoskeletons. We got up-bred by the giants that Enoch wrote about in his book that predated the bible; and the insects simply didn't. They got left behind. That's all. Your evolved DNA is almost the same as an ant's. An ant has no guilt over murdering, and neither should you. It's an everyday fact of life. It's normal. Don't get hung up over it.*

*'But why does everyone say it's wrong to murder?'*

*'Marty, Marty, Marty, it's time you got out of your fantasy bubble. You like your lifestyle, don't you?'*

*'Yes, of course I do.'*

*'Good, Marty. Then it's time you accepted a basic reality. Fame, wealth, and power do not just fall from the sky and land on you because you are cute.'*

*'But I am cute.'*

*'Of course, you are; but in order to have the fame, wealth, and powers you have you must do whatever it takes to have them. Surely you have heard the saying that the end justifies the means, haven't you?'*

*'Yes.'*

*'Well, then don't have qualms or misgivings about what you must do to be the world's number one porn star; and bask in all the wealth and power you have. Famous and powerful people routinely commit murder or do whatever else they need to do to advance their power and wealth. That's how the world works, Marty. Do you think Bathsheba or Salome had misgivings about murdering? No, of course they didn't. They were both very practical women. They got rid of people who stood in their way of getting wealth*

and power; and they were well rewarded for their lack of morality, weren't they?'

'Yes, they were. Weren't they?'

'Of course, they were. Listen, Marty, it's honorable to murder when it helps you achieve a broader acceptance of your immoral ways. Bathsheba knew what she wanted. She knew what she needed to do to get what she wanted. She didn't hesitate or feel any guilt about it. She purified herself after her period. Then she displayed her sexuality to entice King David. He invited her to come to him and sleep with him. When she placed her fragrant vagina upon his face, it was as if he was tasting the softest petals of the most delightful, fragrant rose. He could not resist her charms. He was smitten with lust for her. She then persuaded King David to have her husband murdered, so that she could marry King David and become his most favored bride. She wasn't about to let her inconvenient marriage or guilty thoughts about her immorality stand in the way of what she wanted, was she?'

'No, I guess not.'

'Of course she didn't. And while her husband was being speared to his death by the defenders of Rabbah, concubine Bathsheba was reveling in the fruits of her treachery; savoring the tastes of King David's penis in her mouth and her vagina; contemplating her glorious future as the King's favorite wife. Despite having many previous wives, King David indeed preferred Bathsheba; so much so that as her terms of marriage, she had him promise her that he would leave the throne of Israel to her son.'

'She had him do that?'

'Yes, she did. Thus, instead of leaving his throne to Adonijah, his son in natural ascension to his throne by Haggith, after the death of Absolom, his first borne son, King David ignored the tribe's conventional line of succession. He loved Bathsheba and her immoral whoring that much. His passions for her knew no bounds. She was *the most beautiful, most glorious whore in all of Israel. She bedazzled her King and showered him with her favors. He kept his promise to her. He honored Bathsheba and her fabulous, incomparable, immoral whoring.*

*'Thusly, he had Adonijah, his own son by Haggith, murdered; once again rewarding Bathsheba for her ruthless, unconscionable treachery. And he gave his throne to Solomon, the second son of unprincipled, adorable Bathsheba, history's most calculating, magnificent whore; then King David also had unfortunate Haggith murdered so she could never seek revenge for her son's murder upon King David's beloved whore, Bathsheba. So, you see, Marty, being an unapologetic immoral world class whore rewards you with immeasurable love, honors, esteem, respect, power, fantastic compensation, and lasting benefits.'*

*'So, I am not the only whore who murders, am I?'*

*'No, Marty, not at all. Salome was another fabulous whore of biblical times. She had the preacher man, John the Baptist, decapitated because he had openly criticized her sensational public displays of open whoring in the King's court. He had called upon the King to turn away from Salome. But the King was smitten by Salome's beauty and her sensuous dances of seven veils. He adored her deliciously lascivious, carefree, immoral ways. He greatly preferred Salome's delightful pleasure offerings to the preacher man's criticisms.*

*"When the King informed Salome that, as she requested, he had sent his guards to decapitate the Baptist, Salome took the King into her arms and led him to her bed where she expressed her pleasure with his decision. She placed her coveted vagina upon his face, promised him he could partake of her whenever he pleased, and made passionate love with him. He afterwards honored her conspicuous whoring with treasures of gold and power. He glorified her sinfulness and her role in the murder of the Baptist. He introduced*

her to visiting Kings and encouraged her to whore with them, receive their gifts and good will. The King championed Salome's insatiable, immoral lusts. He rewarded her unscrupulous, wicked promiscuity by lavishing great riches upon her. He seated her at his right hand in his court and favored all her wishes; demonstrating, once again, that immoral, conscience-free whoring can gain a woman fabulous power and immensely rich rewards.'

'Oh, it can, can't it?'

'Yes, certainly it can. And you've already murdered so many people, why stop now? So, Marty, just ignore those naive men and women who condemn you for your whoring. They're just way behind the times. Never let their opinions or affronts to moral sensibilities concern you. Be you, Marty. Place you own needs and pleasures first, always. David honors and rewards you handsomely for your murders, just as King David honored Bathsheba and as King Herod honored Salome. David loves watching you enjoying yourself while you commit murder. Never feel shame when you murder to advance your prestige, wealth, power, and pleasure. Be proud of your glorious deeds and your magnificent whoring. Concentrate on perfecting your skills.

'When you murdered Bertie, you prevented others from learning the secrets she taught you; plus, you silenced her screaming tongue. That greatly pleased your partner, David. Whenever murder helps you advance your immoral ways, it's always good, Marty. Trust me. As humanity evolves, the murder of undesirables by a whore will be reestablished as a venerated and honored tradition. It will again be accepted and glorified as it was during biblical times. Pagan lust worship will reassert itself, for it is the natural inclination of people to express their lusts. Execution by a top porn star will even become revered by the public, just as the barbarity of the Romans' gladiator games once were. It may even become a new Olympic sport. The porn star who excels at decapitation competitions will be rewarded with orgy celebrations in her honor as well as Olympic Gold. She might even be a reincarnated you.

'So, Marty, be true to your character. Never listen to others. Never let morality confuse your thinking. Your sixth finger is all the proof you need. Your DNA is closely related to an ant's DNA with its six legs. Yes, you can think abstractly; but who can say an ant cannot? Your instinct for the pursuit of your own pleasures is merely your finely tuned abstraction. Always assume your immorality will serve you well, Marty. Never be afraid. Always do those things that make you feel pleasure.

'While you are on set making beautiful porn with your partners, keep your thoughts focused on the pleasures you are feeling. Think only of their spectacular thrusts into your vagina and your tushie, and the pleasures you feel. Think about how much you love kissing the heads of their gorgeous penises and how thrilled you are to lick and suck them. Remember to give your winsome smiles to the cameras; remember to say how much you love being fucked this way and how you want to fuck like this all day and every day.

"And remember to kiss your partners' mouths and ask them to please come inside you. Tell them that you love feeling their hot come shooting inside you and how you always want them to come inside you because you feel more like a beloved whore when they do that. Remember to smile and show your triumphant semen pool to the cameras; and to take some semen and swallow it; and to smile while you tell the cameras you loved being fucked that way and that you want to fuck your partners again, and soon; and tell those viewers who want to come and play with you to call your Premium Member Service. And, completely forget your murders while you are making your porn films. Block them out of your mind.

'Forget Bertie. Forget George. Forget all the others that you murdered. They are in the past. You don't need them anymore. You don't need to think about them. There's no reason to think about them. All *you need to think about is the beautiful loving porn you are creating. All your mind needs to imagine is the millions of men who will watch the film you are creating and all your future films. Imagine every man in the world is watching you while you perform; wishing, praying he could be the lucky man whose thrusting penis is in rhythm with the thrusts of your insatiable vagina; and kissing your welcoming mouth with soul kisses; and squeezing your breasts and licking your delicious nipples. Imagine what your fans are thinking. Imagine how countless men wish they could be thrusting their tongues into your deliciously profligate, thoroughly immoral, pleasure crazed nympho vagina; licking and lovingly caressing your clit and savoring the hot, juicy tastes of you.*

*'Then, relax. Enjoy your orgasms and your triumphs. Laugh! Giggle! Roll over and over and run your fingers through your hair while you smile with the thrills of your shameless, spectacularly immoral pleasures. Be shameless. Flaunt your immorality. Express your joys at being pleasured. Remember, countless men will be revering you for your unbridled immorality. Never concern yourself with your treacheries. Feel proud of them. Imagine morality is an old coat that you no longer need. Throw it in the trash and walk away from it. Forget it ever existed. Your new garb suits you better.*

*'Relish your sensational immoral whoring. Know that you are unique; the most sexual, most promiscuous woman in the world. Feel no guilt or shame in that. Feel pride. Be jubilant. You are beautiful. The world loves you. Murder and prostitution are simply a normal, healthy part of you. The more porn films you create, the more orgies you have, the more men's limbic minds will be attracted and addicted to you; and more of them will desire and adore you.*

*'When a new Premium Member first consorts with you, know that he is spellbound in awe of you; feeling privileged beyond ability to express his wonderment that he is blessed to pleasure the world's most profligate whore. Know that, for him, it is the singular moment*

*he will treasure all his life. Yes, it's true. Not the moment he kisses his first love. Not the moment he makes love for the first time. Not his wedding night. All those milestones pale in comparison to adoration's passion lust flames that ignite when you take him into your arms and kiss him and guide his shaft's first touches to your outer lips. That is the memory he will cherish all his life. That is the moment he became one with his ultimate dream goddess.*

*'Remember, every man loves watching you flaunt your immorality. They love you for that. They love seeing you shamelessly copulate with different lovers. Your lack of inhibition makes their mouths water. They pine over every scene; and love you for who you are. So, feel no guilt whatsoever. None! Murder becomes you; completes you as a vessel who is entitled to love. You are our modern day, Ashera; our divine, conscious free Goddess! Your followers wouldn't care if they discovered you murdered. That revelation would only bring joyous approval to their pagan hearts. Murder is incidental and irrelevant to why they love you. They will always love you for the joys of who you are and the wonderful, breathtaking porn you are creating.'*

*'But I know I should give murder up. Murder is risky.'* thought Marty to Miss Lust.

*'Marty, Marty, Marty. Remember how you were taught in school that America was the greatest country in the world?'* Miss Lust began her challenge.

*'Yes, I remember.'*

*'And, do you remember that you were told America was great because it was the one country that had all its freedoms and those freedoms allowed each individual to become the best that they could become; and that's how we got innovation and progress and our vast material wealth?'*

*'Yes, I remember all that.'*

*'Well, Marty, times have changed. Because of fiat money and the dupes that espouse it and benefit from it, America is dying. America*

is disintegrating right before your eyes. The institutions and belief systems that people once held dear are failing them.'

'I know. I see that, too.'

'Very good, Marty. It's good that you see that because that is giving you a great opportunity. Just because America disintegrates does not mean that you must experience America's fate. America's demise is your opportunity to ascend. You will rise up above the demise of America. You will profit and gain immense power from America's demise. You will be praised and glorified. Naked, you will be seated upon the highest throne of the New Morality Standard Religion, with your leg over its chair arm, your lustrous vagina exposed for all the world to worship. The masses will flock to you. They will abide by your teachings. They will praise you as their savior and they will pay homage to you, showering you with riches of gold and jewels. Millions will adore your spectacular intimate artistry. They will prostate themselves before you. They will discard their past moral beliefs for the chance to kiss your profligate insatiable vagina; because their old beliefs have failed them.

'And, you will give them the sustenance their souls so desperately need. They need you, Marty. They need to believe in you and your new morality. You will show them the way to cope with their changed circumstances and flourish. You will enable them to overcome America's ruin.'

'And, how will I do that, Miss Lust?'

'By being you; and by being more and more of you. Your work is unfinished and ongoing. You must not rest from your calling until you have shredded every remaining remnant of religious' ordered society. Drive the wedge of your immorality into every American family. Search out every fissure. Probe with your tendrils until your immorality gains its foothold. Nurture and strengthen your initial breach forces. Then, separate fathers from their children; and children from their mothers. Plant your thought seeds. Disparage and demonize religious leaders. Laud criminality of all sorts. Proclaim whoredom normal and unpunishable. Rend the moral fabric that binds every marriage together and replace those marriages with the binding ties of loving human intimacy, the immoral love-lust that reaches into every human heart.

'Continue your quest to have every church and temple scraped from their foundations and replaced by shrines that glorify Paganism. Assert that the female vagina is the true source of creation; humanity's only true god. Create more and more of your spellbinding porn films. In your intimate artistry, venerate the venal; shatter social taboos. Demonstrate that heretofore forbidden relationships and mores are now cherished and accepted. Create educational programs that acquaint young women with the fabulous opportunities available in prostitution and pornography.

'Be innovative. License your life's story and all your related characters to developers who will recreate your world in the metaverse. Offer licensed non-fungible tokens to people. Help their minds become you and your character lovers in the metaverse, complete with wardrobe offerings in exchange for your tokens. Your new immoral lifestyle will sweep the world. Displace all existing religions. Sweep them aside.

'You will be worshipped. Your glorious vagina will be venerated as the new God. The masses will pray to you and your vagina for guidance in their troubled lives. You will assure them that immorality and honest feelings are beautiful and good. You will become the goddess of every heart. You will replace America's failed institutions with your limitless passions and love. You will restore hope and faith in humanity's love and acceptance to millions of lost souls. Your immoral ways and teachings will become the foundation for a new, more loving, more accepting, reborn America. Your whoring, your insatiable, marvelous vagina will bring new light and hope to all mankind.'

'Yes, Miss Lust,' whispered a newly inspired Marty, 'I see your vision for the future. It enthuses me. And, absolutely I wish to continue creating new and more enticing porn films. And, I fully intend to continue my whoring ways while I'm away from the porn sets. And, yes, your vision of expanding the venues for my immorality completely agrees with my own goals. But should I not give up murdering? What happens if I get found out and caught? Is my risk-taking worth it?'

'I understand you believe that you should give up your murdering's, but understand: Why can't you?' answered the voice of Miss Lust. 'Forget humanity's evolutionary reasons. Forget the commandment that: Thou Shalt Not Kill. Those reasons are easily dispensed. Tell me your real reason. Why can't you give up murdering?'

'Because, murdering is the only thing that eases my pain.' Marty's thoughts whimpered her anguish to Miss Lust.

'Ah! Yes! And, what pain is that, Marty?' Miss Lust's voice taunted Marty's thoughts. Her most immoral evil voice knew it had the upper hand.

'You know what it is, Miss Lust. It's my endless pain. It's the pain I carry around inside me because Daddy left me. It's the pain that I was abandoned as a child. It's the pain that Mother denied me my childhood.' Marty's soul begged Miss Lust for understanding.

'And what does murder do for your pain, Marty?' The taunting voice pushed Marty toward her reality.

'It takes away my pain for a while.'

'Why does it take your pain away, Marty?'

'Because, after I murder those men, I kiss their lips and their faces and I talk to them while they still have some life in them.'

'But what else, Marty? What else do you do with them?' The voice was forcing Marty to confess her deepest secret.

'I pull their noses deeply into my vagina and I hold their noses there, inside me, so I can impress my unique scent signature upon them.'

'*And, why do you do these things, Marty? Why, Marty? Tell the truth to yourself!*' The evil spirit of Miss Lust had brought Marty at the point of her ultimate truth.

'*So, when their spirit souls enter the spirit world they will carry my sight, my touch, the sound of my voice, my kisses, and my unique scent with them. They will meet Daddy's spirit soul and his senses will recognize my senses; and my senses will tell Daddy that I love him and that I miss him and I want him to come back to me. Then, maybe he'll come back to me. I miss my Daddy. I want my Daddy. I want him to come back to me. I love him so much!*' Marty's voice sobbed its confession to the evil voice. Her insane mind confessed to its psychological dominatrix.

'*Very good, Marty, now tell me how you feel after you commit a murder.*'

'*I feel free and wonderful and released from my pain, like my brain becomes warm, happy, and good again. I feel peaceful; free, like my brain is orgasiming. I feel a renewed sense of hope. I need to feel that hope. My heart feels uplifted and wonderful because I did a good thing. I pretended I punished Daddy for leaving me; and then I pretended my spirit would find his spirit. It would make him desire me enough and love me enough to come back to me.*'

'*And if he did come back to you, would you fuck him?*'

'*Oh, yes, Miss Lust. I would. I know I would like that. I have always wanted to fuck Daddy since I was a little girl.*'

'*But you know you can't do that; so, you transfer your desires to your assistants, right?*'

'*Yes, Miss Lust. That's exactly what happens. I have to have sex then; more than at any other time. After the decapitations, my vagina becomes wet and hot. I'm anxious to fuck my assistants. I know I'll soon have fabulous sex with them. They are David's men, his strongest, most handsome, and virile. He bought them for me. Their penises stay huge and hard for an hour or more. We always have spectacular sex. It's an erotic experience like no other. My brain, heart, and vagina all orgasm at once, because I have hope that I'll be with Daddy again and he'll love me again, like he always did. There's no way I can experience that bliss without murdering.'*

*'But, tell me, Marty, and this is important. Why is it necessary for you to have those feelings?' The voice of Miss Lust wanted Marty to get all her feelings and all her truths out.*

*'Because I'm a hopeless nymphomaniac with serious abandonment issues.'*

*'That's right, you are. And you're never going to tell anyone about these feelings of hurt, or about the murders you do to make them go away, are you, Marty?'*

*'No, I can't tell anyone. I know I can't tell. I'd go to prison for the rest of my life or to one of those insane asylums where the other inmates would drive me nuts.'*

*'Very good, Marty. So, only David and the assistants know, right?'*

*'Right.'*

*'Very good, Marty; and we're going to keep that our innermost secret from everybody aren't we?'*

*'Yes, we are.'*

*'And why are we going to keep that secret Marty?'*

*'Because I fear David, that's why. If I ever displeased him, I think he might kill me. I don't think I could get away from him if he wanted to kill me. He has his ways to control my mind and my life. I can't leave him. He knows everything about me. Everything I am and everything I have is because of David. He gave me my career. I can hide behind my career and pretend I'm a legitimate businesswoman. That security gives me protection for my prostitution and my films. I owe him and he knows that I know I owe him. He terrifies me; and yet, I also love him in this odd way. It's a very deep-seated feeling. I can't explain it, but I could never separate myself from David.'*

'And, you are going to continue to commit murders, aren't you?'

'Yes, of course I will.'

'And, you love committing murder, don't you?'

'Oh, yes, Miss Lust, I do. I love it. I know I love it. I love murdering more than anything.'

'And, you'll murder anyone David tells you to murder, won't you?'

'Yes, of course I will.'

'Very good, Marty, now stop thinking foolish thoughts and put away any notion that we'll leave David. Relax. You will never be caught. David will always protect you. We are not leaving David. We both love the blood lust that he gives us. We both know we can't live without that, don't we? We both know that all the money and all the sex in the world could never replace that wonderful feeling, don't we? We love doing the murders, don't we?'

'Yes, we know all those things.'

'Good, Marty. Now I want you to reach way back into your spirit memory; way back to the time your spirit was brought to Earth; back to the time when your spirit was with the Anunnaki. Can you do that?'

'Yes. It was a splendid time. It was the beginning of my feelings.'

'Yes; but even before that. Tell me what you remember, Marty.'

'Yes, I'll try. I'm remembering. My spirit was in this bright white light. The light was going to many different stars and picking up other spirits; and all of us spirits were together in the light. And the light moved instantaneously from planets around the different stars to other planets until the light came to Earth. That's where my spirit needed to leave the light. And my spirit went into one of the Anunnaki.'

'And what were the Anunnaki doing, Marty?'

'They were making the light cut huge rectangular boulders from a stone mountain and they were directing the light to move the stones into place to create a huge, elevated platform. And they were commanding the males of Earth to build this huge staircase up to the platform.'

'What were they doing on this platform, Marty?'

'They were changing the Earth people.'

'How were they doing this?'

'They were murdering the males and taking the females into the light and unzipping the DNA of the females and splicing into their DNA the DNA of birds and reptile snakes, and foxes; and then they were fornicating with the females. And this went on for thousands of years. And the females gave birth to a new hybrid race of people who were more beautiful and more promiscuous than the original Earth people.'

'And why did the Anunnaki do this, Marty?'

'They needed to create a human species that could populate the entire universe. This new species needed the new human DNA to be quick, alert, promiscuous, ruthless, and cunning. And the new race needed Anunnaki DNA to be resolute and strong. It needed to destroy all other human-like species' competition for Earth's resources. They were creating today's modern humans.'

'Why only modify the women, Marty?'

'Because they knew that the women would give birth and their new DNA would continue in their offspring. And the light of creation could go easier and faster to more places, if it carried with it a hundred of the new human women for every human male. The Anunnaki are now with creation's light, populating the universe's distant galaxies with these new humans.'

'And what did the Anunnaki do with the original human males, Marty?'

'They murdered them. They had these huge swords. The light brought the males to the platform and the Anunnaki severed their heads with their huge swords.'

'But not the women? They left the women alone, didn't they?'

'Yes, after they modified the women's DNA, they left them alone.'

'And the Anunnaki treated you differently from the other women, didn't they, Marty?'

'Yes. I was the woman that they singled out.'

'And why were you singled out?'

"I do not know. They never told me. All I remember is they said that they wanted to instill promiscuous lust and passion into my spirit soul; and they said that my altered spirit soul was to attach to my human body, all through time; forever.'

'So, what did they do?'

'There were twelve of them; all males that were twelve feet tall. They were giants with extremely huge penises. And they took me up from Earth with them, into the light. We were in the light for a very long time; I think we were in the light for possibly years of Earth time. It seemed like an eternity. And I was floating in the light in many different positions for the entire time. I was weightless. There was no gravity. And, one after the other, the twelve Anunnaki males came to me and spread my legs and inserted their penises into me. And their huge penises felt glorious and wonderful; filling my vagina as they did. And the twelve all took turns ejaculating into me. And their ejaculations were like this steady stream of refreshing coolness that flowed steadily over my clitoris, giving me this warm, glowing inner sensation. I heard the Anunnaki say they were taking eggs from my ovaries and sending my seeds all over the universe. This magical orgy continued for what seemed like forever. I began to orgasm. My stream of orgasm fluids flowed and combined with the ejaculations of the twelve Anunnaki men. I came to feel that fornicating with the twelve Anunnaki was the natural state of things. I wanted for nothing. I was not hungry.

'All my bodily functions ceased, except for the fornications. I felt serene and wonderful. I loved it. I was becoming conditioned to understand that fornication was the natural and unapologetic order of my life; and my new way of living my spirit life. I didn't want the Anunnaki's' fornications to ever end. But then, they did end. And I was brought back to the Earth. And the light and the Anunnaki left. But I knew then, that my spirit soul had been changed; and that my spirit soul had become the spirit soul of a whore who always wanted to make love. Yes, I remember now. That's when my spirit came to believe that, for me, making love was my natural way of life. From that experience onward, making love has always been the desire of my spirit soul.

'But you did not leave with the light and the Anunnaki when the creation light left Earth. Why not?'

'The Anunnaki wanted the most beautiful women, the most promiscuous among us, the whores, to remain here, on Earth, to create a worship order for the people. Our spirits from creation's light attached to these women's bodies and we became the temple whores; goddesses of the people. We fornicated with the people and gave them order in their lives so they could build great civilizations on Earth. They worshipped us.

'We created and ordained Baal worship; and it was very good, very progressive, and successful. We created rituals of ceremonial sacrifices to us. We murdered and sacrificed those peoples whom our warriors conquered and whom would not accept us. We even sacrificed our own children who were not considered exceptionally beautiful and strong. We threw them into fire. And the Anunnaki showed us how to abort our wombs when we learned that we had conceived a baby that we didn't want to have and raise. We intro-duced progressive civilization to the Earth, a civilization ordered by progressive women; led by female prostitutes.'

'And what was the purpose of this civilization, Marty?'

'To progress; to move humanity forward; to make humanity more perfect and more able to propagate and move throughout the universe and colonize it, especially our Milky Way Galaxy, carrying the DNA of the Anunnaki and the DNA of the new hybrid females.'

'And was not murder a necessary part of this movement forward, this great progress that took place, even before the Noahide laws were given to the tribe that would later become the Hebrew tribe?'

'Yes, murders were necessary. When the Anunnaki came, they introduced murder as a method of creating progress. The Anunnaki murdered the other nearly human hominids, but not the women of the human species. There was constant ritualized murdering. The Anunnaki were very tall and strong; and they wielded huge swords with very sharp blades. They easily swiped heads off those whom they chose for murder. It was our accepted culture and our righteous way to murder all those who opposed our rapid human progress. All who were not like us and all those who clung to their old ways were murdered by the Anunnaki. The Anunnaki celebrated their murders by fornicating with us and by impregnating many thousands of human women. The Anunnaki wanted a pure human race with a craving for sex, that was committed to progress and to whoring. They wanted many women to become whores so that those women would inspire men and other women to change and become promiscuous; and to accept progress. The Anunnaki told us that we needed to prepare ourselves to go into our galaxy; to visit the planets of many stars and propagate ourselves.'

'And why do you think the Anunnaki wanted that?'

'They said they loved human women; that human women have a unique propensity to make love even when we are not in estrus; unlike the other humanoid species or the other animals. And they said that they loved making love with human women; and they wanted more and more of us to make love with, for themselves and for the other Anunnaki who were not with them on this journey that had come to the Earth with the light. They enslaved legions of human men and made them build a huge pyramidal Zigaroths. That's a pyramid with a flat platform top and a long step ramp leading up to the platform on the top.

'Then the Anunnaki had their slaves build smaller platform stations on the top of the Zigaroth platforms. And upon our tribal pyramid, upon these smaller elevated platforms, the Anunnaki placed me and a few of the other human women. The Anunnaki then ordered all the assembled people to worship us, the platform women; and to whore with us. They declared that we were the peoples' new gods; and that any among them who disobeyed their decrees would be put to death.

'The Anunnaki ordered the assembled peoples to work the gold mines for them. They needed the gold because it enabled them to move through space and made them live longer. They also worked Earth's men to death while they fornicated with the Earth women. They declared the new variation of promiscuous human women to be their new goddesses and developed our new human race. And they declared that fornication rites with their new breed of human women were beautiful and desirable. And these fornication rites continued every day for many months. In their own way, the Anunnaki introduced pornography to humanity and they declared pornography to be desirable and beautiful. The Anunnaki told us that they wanted to create a species of humans with promiscuous women who loved sex, because the Anunnaki, themselves, loved sex. They explained to us that the more sex a woman has, the more beautiful she becomes.'

'Very good, Marty. So, you know that you now have the hybrid promiscuous, ruthless reptilian female and the Anunnaki DNA within you; given to you from many millennia ago.'

'Yes, Miss Lust, I do understand that; but there is something I do not understand.'

'And what would that be, Marty?'

'Well, Miss Lust. It's you. You are different from all my other voices. I hear them speaking to me in my head. I know them very well. I feel I can trust what they are telling me when they talk with me. But that is not at all how I feel about you, Miss Lust. You are very different, somehow. I do not actually hear your voice talking with me. You're different. I feel you talking to me. It's like your feelings are speaking, but not your voice. Why is that? Can you explain that to me?'

'Marty, my sweet darling, I thought you knew!'

'Knew what?'

'I thought you knew you were insane!'

'I'm insane?'

'Yes, you are. We are!'

'We?'

'Yes, we! I'm your spirit soul. I'm your mirror image of yourself. Didn't any of your shrinks explain this to you?'

'No. Well, maybe Mrs. O'Dell talked about my spirit soul sometimes. But she never told me it was you. She never said you lived inside of me and I could feel you talking to me like this. I always thought you were just a mysterious presence; not a living presence like this. I mean not someone I could feel talking with me.'

'But you are, Marty. We are. We are the same person.'

'But you are not like me; not always, anyway. Only during those times when I'm having sex or committing murder. Help me understand why that is. Please! I need to know.'

'Okay; okay. Relax, I'll explain everything. Remember those times when you are sleeping and you have dreams and flashbacks?'

'Yes. I have a lot of those.'

'Okay. Well, that's when you can know me. That's when the Great Spirit of All Living Things has your spirit soul; that's me, merge your soul with Poon's soul.'

'Poon? Who is Poon?'

'She's a butterfly. She's a beautiful Monarch butterfly. She's spectacularly beautiful; and very sexy; very driven to procreate. Her spirit soul unites with me, your spirit soul. You see, Marty, your soul, while you are in limbic mind mode and while you murder, becomes Poon's soul.'

'What does this mean, Miss Lust?'

'It means you become a person whose soul is Poon's soul. It means you have the same feelings Poon has when she mates with her lover, Tang.'

'Wait! What? I have this butterfly's feelings inside me while she's mating with another butterfly? Am I going to be okay? Is this why I'm insane?'

'Yes, you have her feelings inside you. And you will be okay. You are okay. All of this is very natural. It's just that you cannot think like a human or be like a human when you are aroused for sex or when you murder. You are more like a human butterfly.'

'How? What happens to me?'

'Well, you lose all ability to think or feel like a human. Your mind can't concern itself with other persons' feelings, for example. You can't concern your feelings or thoughts about other women whose boy friends or husbands you are making love with. You cannot think about religious or secular laws because you only feel natural law. You only feel Poon's natural urges to mate. I'm sure you feel that way. Don't you feel like wrapping your arms and legs around your lover's body while you are having sex?'

'Yes, I do.'

'Well, that's what a butterfly does. And isn't that a very intense feeling?'

'Yes, it is.'

'And don't you feel like you absolutely must feel your partner's penis with its semen sperm shooting inside you; feeling it's hot flows coursing over your clitoris and filling your vagina? And don't you *find yourself feeling that you absolutely must get enough semen shot into you so that some of it gets through the opening in your cervix and enters your fallopian tubes to swim upstream to fertilize your eggs?'*

*'Yes. Miss Lust. I do feel all that; but I only ever have one egg in my womb at any given time.'*

*'I know. But Poon's spirit soul doesn't know that. She feels like she must copulate with Tang above the canopy of the Mexican rain forest, and she must hold his body tightly against her body and squeeze him and love him until he's exhausted from shooting every last droplet of semen sperm that he has in his body, into her body. You see, Marty, I, as your true spirit soul, believe I must have your partner fertilize hundreds of your eggs when I'm in the rapture of intimacy. I'm like Poon, then. And you are my mirror image. You are me. So, you feel that same spiritual insect intensity when you mate, just like Poon does.'*

*'And that explains why I feel so manic while I'm making love and while I commit murder? Even though I'm on the birth control pills and even though I only have one egg, I get that same manic intensity about making love that this Poon butterfly lady gets? And I also feel it while I commit murder, right? Am I hearing this correctly?'*

*'Yes, and it's all true, Marty. It's also why you become lust obsessed while you make love with Marshawn.'*

*'Oh, no, Miss Lust. That happens because I feel I need to save him from Alayah.'*

*'But you have 'saved' many married men. Why such intense lust for him?'*

*'Alayah. I told you. I'm taking him from Alayah.'*

*'But when he's inside you, we're not thinking about Alayah, are we?'*

*'No, I guess not. So, what is it, then?'*

*'Think, Marty. Think back in time closer to your first reincarnations. Remember to the times before you were Sara; before you and*

Abram left Terah and went to Egypt. What can you remember about Egypt, long before Sara's time?'

'Oh, yes, I remember now. I was Hathor, goddess of fertility. The Apis Bull God, my sexual companion in the fertility ceremony; the fertility ceremony itself, the flutes and drums and the beer and wine; my sacred copulation with the bull, taking the seed of fertility from the Black Apis bull; the bull's massive semen flood into me that ushered in the flooding of the Nile into Egypt; the rituals when the high priest of Thebes kissed my whoring semen filled vagina to bless it as the living vessel of god's fertility on Earth; the taking of the bull to drown it in the Nile and then mummify its body; the slaughtering of first-born children, as the peoples' sacred fertility offering to bless and deify my fabulous whoring cunt. And then, the fortnight of sacred orgies to celebrate our possession of eternity's life creation forces. Oh, yes, Miss Lust, I remember now. So many lovers; and endless time of glorious lovemaking and delightfully, endless fornications. We, the people, were happy beyond words to express. We were delirious with our communal love and our lust cravings.'

'Yes. The people worshipped you as their goddess. You inspired the Pharoahs to conquer the world for you. But what specific lust memories do you have, Marty?'

'Oh, now I see what you ask. Yes! The bulls' penises were so huge! The stretching. The filling of my vagina until I overflowed with my juices. All my clitoral tentacles went berserk. I became mad with sex lust. I could only think of fornication. I couldn't control my nympho rage state. I didn't want to control it. I wanted to release it.'

'And, later, when you reincarnated with the Hebrews at Mount Sinai, while Moses was away on the mountain, do you recall yourself then?'

'Yes. The people wanted to go back to Egypt; return to the fertility rites. They made a golden calf. Then the men placed me beside *it and they copulated with me, trying to recreate the fertility rites. But the men could not recreate the stimulus I felt from the Apis Bull.'*

*'So, size matters, doesn't it?'*

*'Oh yes, Miss Lust. It does.'*

*'And that's why you and I, your mirror, are so much like Poon when she couples with Tang. Tang has the greatest penis size of all Monarchs. The Apis bulls had spectacular penises. And Marshawn has a spectacular penis. That's why you and I become raving lust crazed when you and Marshawn make love.'*

*'I do, don't I?' Mmmmm. I feel excited just thinking about Marshawn.'*

*'I know you do. It's okay. It's healthy. It is why you are the way you are. It's also why you feel the urge to display your semen pools in your porn films. That's you DNA memory, displaying your semen pools during the Egyptian fertility rites. You are laying the foundation for the return of fertility worship to our modern era.'*

*'Tell me, Miss Lust, why did Moses stop our orgy by the Golden Calf? I didn't want to stop. Does that make me a bad girl?'*

*'No, Marty, you were not being a bad girl. You need to understand what happened in context. Remember when you first met Moses? Remember when you were a hottie from the captive Hebrew tribe who was on a mountainside gathering firewood; and Moses, one of Pharoah's sons, saw you; desired you; and made love with you? He described his experience with you as his burning bush moment where he met his true God. Remember how he kissed you that first time?'*

*'Yes, I remember. He started kissing me and he continued kissing me. He could not stop.'*

*'Yes. His amygdala was aflame. His blood ran hot with fires of limbic lust, remember?'*

*'Oh yes! I remember that, too. He squeezed me tightly. He never wanted to let go of me.'*

'Yes. That's a good memory. Then, do you remember when he first went down on your vagina to perform cunnilingus with you?'

'Oh, yes, Miss Lust. I remember. That was our first divine moment.'

'Very good, Marty. That was when your vagina became his true God. He left his wife and kids for you. Remember?'

'Oh yes, I do remember. He began spending his nights with me. He was a wonderful lover.'

'Then, when you were selected to be consort to the Apis Bulls, and Moses celebrated that you had received the power of divine procreation and fertility from the bulls into your vagina, he became smitten and nearly insanely obsessed with lust for you; he cheered and applauded you wildly. Do you remember?'

'Of course I remember. I saw the lust in Moses' eyes. I saw him wet his lips and mouth me kisses. I knew he wanted me. That's when I seized my moment. I was Pharoah's favorite concubine. Of all the whores in his harem, he consorted with me the most often. So, unashamed to reveal our closeness; after doing the huge black Apis bull, I pranced over to Pharoah's throne chair. I sat upon his lap, placed my arms around his neck, kissed him, and stroked his penis. I knew he would not refuse my request.'

'What did you request of Pharoah?'

'That he add the names of Zeporah, Gershom, and Eliezer to the list of departed's.

'But she was his daughter in law!'

'Yes, but I was his favorite whore. Besides, she was not true Egyptian. She was a Midian; Prince Moses's vassal property from a vassal country. I was naturalized Egyptian from centuries of service to the Kingdom. In truth, Pharoah couldn't stand her or her two brats. But he loved me and my delicious cunt. He would do whatever I asked. And, when he commanded his scribe to inscribe their names on the parchment, I straddled his penis into my vagina and kissed him boldly on his mouth.'

'Zeporah had no idea?'

'No. I wanted to see the surprise on her face when their names were called. I wanted to see her eyes plead to Moses. I wanted her to see my smile while I captured her precious status and took her place as the wife of Moses.'

'You can be devious and cruel, Marty.'

'Yes, sometimes. I find it useful to think ahead of my enemies.'

'So, that's how you set up their demise? And then you went about performing your pornography, as if there was nothing planned? Nothing out of the ordinary?'

'Yes. I did not look at her. I gave no indication that her fate was sealed.'

'I see. And then it came to the part of the ceremony where Pharoah wanted you to help him assimilate the newly conquered Nubians into Egyptian society. He wanted you to show by example that Egypt was welcoming and inclusive. Can you recall what you did to please your Pharoah?'

'Oh yes! I remember it vividly, like it happened yesterday. The temple guards brought these eight strikingly handsome black Nubians before me. They were naked, tall, and muscular. The first among them was their leader. He kneeled before me and kissed my feet before he stood. That's when I beheld his gigantic penis. It was an unnatural oddity; a freakish thing; even much larger than the penises of the Apis bulls. It was extremely long and very thick. I smiled when I first beheld its presence; partly because I was taken by surprise at such a monstrous sized organ brought to me for my pleasures, and also because I felt honored by Pharoah to have been chosen to demonstrate our welcoming openness to our new allies from the south.

'I remember how enamored I felt about performing with it when I first held it in my hands. I realized it was so huge I could not possibly get my mouth around it and take it into my mouth. So, I simply began kissing it and licking it while gently stroking it with both my hands. I remember feeling myself falling in love with it; and feeling excited about having it penetrate me. After I had kissed it and licked it for a considerable time, it became extremely hard. I sensed the moment had come. That's when I bid the Nubian to stand over my while I positioned my vagina over the edge of my platform bed and spread widely my legs.

'He seemed very timid about doing what I invited him to do; but I nodded to him and smiled, indicating that it was all right and that I wanted him to enter me. I reinforced my assurances by taking his penis in my hand and guiding it to my outer lips and rubbing it up and down along my lips. He seemed to know everything was all right after I did that. He smiled. I then moved my hips in a slight upward thrust to capture the very tip of his monster penis head within my outer lips.

'Then, ever so gradually, I patiently took in more and more of the gigantic penis until I had it nearly completely inside me. He responded to my efforts by placing his massive torso onto my chest and kissing me on my lips. I held him close to me and rocked him like a baby while we found our rhythm together. He fucked me so beautifully and so gently. Mmmmm. We had beautiful love making. It was such an ethereal, other worldly experience. The court musicians were playing their flutes and lyres; the slaves were fanning me with their palm fans to keep me cool and pleasured.

'Realize, this was the very first time in all my lives that I had experienced the joys of having sex with a fabulous black penis. And I enhanced my pleasures by inserting round balls carved from smoothed ebony in my vagina. My loins tingled as the tentacles from my clitoris erupted in hot flames while those huge black penises repeatedly plunged and probed my vagina. It was my first foray into heightened BDSM pleasuring; and I loved it. I must have screamed: 'Yes! Yes! Yes! And Fuck me! Mmmmm. Yes! Fuck me harder!' at least twenty times while I proceeded to fornicate with all ten Nubians.

'The Nubians' wives were gathered around me, witnessing the spectacle. As I fornicated with their husbands, I chortled. I could not help myself. I knew that, if I wished, I could steal away their husbands from them. And that gave me a sense of ribaldry. My carnal lusts were heightened more than ever. Looking back upon that orgy scene, I now realize that was when I first understood myself as a destroyer of relationships. I could feel my sexuality was causing my partners to desire the breaking of their relationships with their Nubian women. In their culture, I was prized as a relationship trade up. In front of their wives, the Nubians were telling me that they loved me; adored me; revered my whoring; wished to worship my vagina; and wanted to copulate with me more; that they wished to have me often.

'I knew, had I given them the slightest encouragement, they would obliterate their relationships with their Nubian wives and consorts. They wanted me. They thirsted with carnal lust for me. My sexuality and my whiteness had flooded their limbic senses. They had become obsessed with me; touching me; and pleasing me in every way. But I didn't want them as husbands. I wanted Moses, only Moses. But I absolutely wanted the Nubians for my sexual pleasures. And I laughed and smiled and giggled like the true fuck crazed nymph I was, that entire time we cavorted in our unapologetic revelry. In a very real sense, my nympho soul was discovering its insatiable addiction to uninhibited, shameless sexual pleasures for the very first time.

'I think Moses must have noticed how enraptured I felt with those gigantic Nubian penises inside me; observing those magnificent penises exploring the deepest reaches of my vagina; titillating me with pleasure; bringing me to orgasm after orgasm; hearing me moan my Mmmmmm and Yessss sounds:

'Yes! Oh yessss! Mmmmm. Mmmmm. Yessss! Fuck me. Oh Yesssss! That's it. Ohhhh. Please, please, fuck me! Don't stop! No. More. I need you to fuck me more! Mmmmm. Oh, yes! I'm coming. Yes! That's soooo wonderful. Mmmmm.'

'Moses watched me and heard my sounds of pleasure. He heard them ravishing me. I could tell, as he watched Nubian after Nubian lick my vagina; and as he heard me squeal with pleasure from their cunnilingus, he became overwhelmed. His limbic mind flooded with obsessive desire to harness my profligate fecundity for himself. And he loved everything about me; all of me; the unapologetic whore that I am. And he loved me. He fell hopelessly into love with me, the most glorious whore in all of Egypt. And he saw how I loved what I was doing; loving the heavenly sensations from my orgasms, as those loving Nubian tongues plied my vagina with absolutely delightful oral sex. I intuited that my revelry was causing Moses to lust after me and to fall into love with me. It was a beautiful moment. I loved my ravaging. I didn't want to ever stop. My breathing became very heavy:

'Ha; Ahhh; Whoa; Whaaa, Oh my God! I'm gasping for breath. Oh, I'm feeling him thrusting into me, so hard; I can hardly breath! Yes! So beautiful. Mmmmm. Yes. Yes.'

'I panted breathlessly from the exultation of my heavenly fornications. I knew I was making history; bringing our two races together; and I loved the experience of those monstrous black penises plunging deeply inside me. I could have gone on this way for hours; but I could tell my newest partner prince of lower Egypt was excited and anxious to have me. He was ready to release. I whispered to him to come into me and to go ahead; release his pent-up flood of semen into me. I could tell he wanted to, but he seemed hesitant. I nodded to him, assuring him that I wanted him to. I smiled to him and blew *him a kiss and I said: 'Come to me. Come. Place your penis head into me. I want you to fuck me. I want you to release inside me. Yes. I really want you to. I want all of it.'*

*'Then, the handsome prince ejaculated this massive semen flood stream into me. I felt like I was being hit with a stream of heat from a fire hose. Mmmmm! I loved being fucked this way. I held him tightly. I felt myself falling in love with him. My clitoris erupted with a wildly frenzied orgasm. I gushed wildly! I screamed: Yes! Oh Yes! That is so wonderful! Semen and orgasmic juices overflowed and spilled from me. The crowds went crazy. They applauded us wildly. Moses shouted his enthusiastic hurrahs. I became the living symbol of fertility; true Goddess of the Nile. I knew I was revered and adored.*

# CHAPTER FOUR

*No man can serve two women. At least not completely and simultaneously. Rosemary Ness Bitner, author)*

## PRINCE MOSES

Humanity has progressed through three eras of worship experience; and is now entering its fourth. The first era encompassed the period from about four hundred thousand years ago until about twenty thousand years ago. During the first era humans bonded together in tribes of hunter gatherers. In these tribes the men and women consorted freely with one another. The males hunted. The women gathered food roots, savaged meat from dead animals, collectively raised the tribe's children, and provided fornication services to the tribal males. Women's sexual favors were the cohesive glue that bonded each respective tribe and held it together. Worship of any deity did not exist, per se; however, the males needed the women and the women needed the males in order for the tribe to function. Males and females revered each other in a sexual sense; and sex, per se, was considered vital. Fornication was respected. Couples engaged in fornication were respected. And the act of fornication was considered beautiful and necessary. A group sense of reverence towards fornication took root.

Humanity's second worship era occurred from about twenty thousand years ago until about ten thousand years ago. Individual tribes banded together to form larger tribal collectives and nation states. This was when humanity began to cultivate fields and husband animals such as sheep and goats and cattle. During this period when like tribes of peoples with similar physical features, collective attitudes, and common goals joined together, the concept of deities arose. Deities would safeguard and advance the interests of the various tribes. They would ensure that a tribe would prevail against rival tribes in contests over territory. Fertility rites came into prominence and deities dedicated to fertility assumed a vital role that ensured the continuity of the tribe. A prominent deity was Ashera. She was envisioned as a kind of super-sized goddess of sexuality and fertility. Many men wore and carried with them amulets of Ashera to give them confidence in their own sexuality and to remind them of their allegiance to the imaginary goddess who looked over them and guaranteed their manhood. Ashera was often represented as a female figurine amulet with huge boobs and a supersized vagina.

Humanity's third worship era occurred between around ten thousand and six thousand years ago. During this period, living females replaced Ashera amulets as objects of worship. This period heralded the birth of prostitution worship and the introduction of pornography as divine artistry. Exceptionally beautiful and promiscuous human women were deified during this critical period. This was the period that presaged the birth of man made abstract fictitious deities such as God, Jesus, Budda, Allah, etc. It was a kind of tug of war period that straddled prostitution worship and abstract fictitious deity worship.

Humanity's fourth worship period is the one we have entered now. It is the time that has come to humanity after humans have given up on the artificial concepts of God, Jesus, Allah, Buddha, and the like. Humanity is currently experiencing great stress. Secular governments with fiat currencies are failing as a viable governing concept. Risks of massive human annihilation abound due to the presence of terrifying weapons of mass destruction. Humans have never possessed a weapon that they failed to use on other humans. Think about that! It should scare the crap out of you.

Our current worship period is a type of retrograde period. We are reverting away from what is not working and returning to what was once working. We are leaving organized religion and returning to prostitution worship. And pornography is leading our way forward into this new revision period. Our modern-day porn stars are displacing organized religion. This is a trend that will only accelerate until religious practices as we know them today cease to exist. We must understand why humanity feels driven to embrace pornography and its porn stars in order to understand where we are going. That way, we might possibly be able to make sense of the chaotic events that surround us.

Existing orders change. It matters not what form of governance we have, or what form of money we use, or what God or prophet we worship. Whatever once served us well, inevitably ceases to do so. And the old ordered structures of our lives must be replaced. The individual human mind has a rational component and a limbic component. Collective human thought also has this same rational and limbic component.

When the established order begins to fray, people notice. First, in our rational minds, we see that society is becoming less stable; crime has become more commonplace and more serious offenses are on the rise; inflation has gained a foothold and has begun to erode stability; acceptable moral standards become relaxed and immorality becomes more commonplace; and doubts about the viability of the established order begin to seep into our collective rational mind. Questions about where society is headed and by what methods it will get there are expressed more openly and more often. The political order becomes more fragmented and dissent from the status quo becomes more vociferous.

As our rational collective mind senses greater frustration with the established order's flagging ability to provide stability, our collective's limbic mind seeks ways to escape the reality of advancing change. People 'tune out.' They seek escape through attendance at sporting events, theater shows, and motion picture films. Gradually, almost imperceptibly, the spectre of moral decay begins to gnaw at the established order. Prostitution becomes more commonplace. Once only confined to dark alleys and seedy upstairs brothel cubicles, whoring becomes more mainstream. Ordinary housewives become available to perform fellatio and quick fornication services because they 'need a little extra money to make ends meet.'

Prostitution, previously condemned, is quietly tolerated. Prostitution laws are laxly enforced or not enforced at all. Once shamed in the pulpits, the clergy becomes silent on the subject of moral decay. And where prostitution is known to exist, our collective persona no longer confronts it. We choose to quietly look the other way.

Pornography, once confined to dirty magazines and grainy films shown in seedy theaters to people who sneaked there during off hours, becomes more mainstream as well. Our collective limbic mind welcomes pornography as just another venue to assuage our anxieties. Those who pay attention to trends notice that pornography, or explicit erotica, is the fastest growing genre in book, audio book, and film sales. Adult film festivals and awards ceremonies spring up to pay homage and give acclaim to the most viewed, most creative, and most newly noticed performing stars in this new genre.

This is the transition phase of societal reordering and humanity is now in the midst of this reordering. Humanity is in the process of turning its back on the established religious order we have lived under for the past five or six thousand years. Why? Because it is no longer working! We are transiting into a period where humanity is returning to its pre religious historical worship practices. We are becoming aficionados of pornography. We are identifying and glorifying individual porn stars; ranking them; collectively weighing their individual attributes; identifying with and empathizing with them and their lives' choices.

We are gradually, almost imperceptibly, making the lives of porn stars an everyday part of our own lives. This gradual acceptance is not unlike daily indoctrination of religious practices. And it is growing; steadily gaining in market share of our collective belief system and taking in more and more of our money. Pornography's cash flows are increasing while collections in churches are dwindling.

In the not far distant future, we should expect humanity to make its full transition back to its pre religious worship practices. We should expect our illustrious, much ogled porn stars, to gain far greater influence over our societal, cultural, and political norms; not less. After all, money talks and money buys influence; and our top porn stars are doing well. We should expect that prostitution worship will gain tax exempt status. We should also expect that individual porn stars and their profligate whoring practices will become deified and worshipped as our true Goddesses, as they were in humanity's pre religious era.

Prostitutes and porn stars, once stigmatized, are much less so today. More and more, women who have performed penetration and fellatio scenes in erotic films are accepted and welcomed in our 'polite' societies. Presently, non-disclosure agreements such as the ones used by our U. S. congress and by President Trump keep their private matters private.

But with the advent of social media, a more mature attitude about liaisons with sex providers will ascend. And acceptance of such relationships and the women who provide them will likely become mainstream normal fare. Much like the ancient Romans, we, too, will welcome prostitutes and porn stars into our homes and social circles. So, what revisions should we expect to experience as humanity moves forward? No doubt, for a few, like the wife and children of Moses, this reversion change will be traumatic.

But for our collective society, this reversion process will be a welcomed change; for it will bring with it a return to social order. Morality will adjust to a more open, accepting standard, at first. But like a pendulum, this process of realignment of our mores has a long way to swing before this new realignment is complete. It will only be completed once pornography has become deified and tax-exempt status for pornography worshipping religious services is incorporated into our tax codes. Society will adjust to the concept of pornography's 'life cult' messaging replacing religions' 'death cult' messaging, and our new social order will 'work,' again, as it has 'worked' before, during our fifteen thousand pre religious years.

There is no better place and time to examine and understand this profound human need to reorder society and gain a sense of how it will be ordered afterwards than to look back upon the cultural and religious practices that governed ancient Egypt. Let's now return to those good old days of the Pharaohs. Let's look closely at their religious practices, so that we may glimpse our own future.

Ancient Egypt, in the era before any concept of western religious thought had been born, the people and their leader Pharaohs, princes, and priests believed that celestial deities determined their fate. They believed in reincarnation and the transit of the human soul in its afterlife to a new realm where it joined with the souls of other souls which had departed from life on Earth and where it communed with the celestial gods for all eternity; or something like that.

A most important Egyptian god was the Goddess of Life and Death, which swept away the remnants of the old and used up, such as the withered shafts that remained after the grain harvests. This important Goddess also heralded the renewal of fertility and life. The Goddesses name was Sopdet. She is known as Sirius to modern day humans. She appeared to us and presented herself to us as a star; the brightest star in the sky. Every year she predictably appeared. She presented herself to the ancient Egyptians by lifting her brilliant light above the eastern horizon. Her sparkling luminescence denoted the changing of Egypt's seasons. Sopdet arrived precisely at the end of Egypt's winter season and the beginning of the season of warmth, fertility, and new growth. Coincidently, when Sopdet appeared, the great Nile River began rising from the run off of snow melt from the mountains in the lands of the Nubians, south of Egypt.

The ancient Egyptian culture felt the need to curry the favor and continued good graces of Sopdet in order that they might live and prosper. The custom of fertility worship evolved around the rising of Sopdet. This custom celebrated the sweeping away of all things that had died. Shocks from withered grain stalks were gathered, bundled, and burned; their ashes returned to the fields. The old and infirm were consecrated to the eternal Nile where crocodiles disposed of their bodies. That customary clearing away of the old to make way for the new was the somber part of Egypt's Sopdet worship.

But the portion of the annual ritual which all Egyptians longed for was the fertility worship ceremonies. These were a time of over indulgence, over imbibing, ritual sacrifices, and glorification of life's creation processes. In this time before Abrahamic religions, prostitution worship was humanity's way of paying homage to Sopdet for the gift of fertility, food, and life.

In one of her previous lives, Marty, in the ancient personage of Baaleezebelle, was chosen to personify the Goddess Sopdet. She was humanity's original sex symbol. Being chosen to lead the fertility rites was a great honor for Baaleezebelle, or Belle. She was born a Hebrew slave. Her parents were murdered because her father had transgressed against one of the Kingdom's high priests. The matron of Pharoah's harem took notice of young Baaleezebelle and decided to raise her in the harem.

As a child of five; and until she was eight years old, Belle, did chores for the harem. She swept floors, took out trash, served food, cleaned tables, and changed bedding for the harem women. When she reached the age of eight, the matron decided it was time for Belle to learn fellatio. Belle was introduced to the male penis and trained in the ways her mouth and tongue could pleasure it and bring it to ejaculation.

Many of the priests and princes became intrigued with Belle. She was Hebrew, and unlike the other harem girls and women, her skin tone was not swarthy, but white; creamy, lily colored white. Often, men would request that the matron give them time with the 'white' one. Belle didn't mind that she was called upon to perform fellatio more often than the others. She developed a liking for the males' penises. She became carefree and nonchalantly matter of factly accepting that performing fellatio was a normal part of her everyday life.

When Belle reached the age of twelve, she came into her maturity. The matron noticed. Belle was introduced to vaginal penetration by the males' penises. This function, too, became part of Belle's daily routine. She enjoyed the feeling of having a penis inside her. And, after about three months of experiences with the different priests and princes, Belle developed a craving for fornication. She found that, much more than the other women, she looked forward to being the one selected by the matron to provide sexual pleasures. More and more, the matron's clientele asked to be paired with the 'white girl.'

Belle, at age eighteen, was the most desired woman in the harem. Her favors commanded the highest price; and priests and princes gladly paid the matron for Belle's favors. Belle noticed that one prince in particular, Moses, had begun seeing her; first weekly; but now every other day. Moses was more loving toward her than the other customers; and Belle noticed. She also noticed that, after Moses ejaculated, he lingered long by her side and kissed her lips tenderly; and he seemed reluctant to leave her. And Belle noticed that her heart and spirits lifted when she heard that Moses had arrived at the harem and had asked for her.

Pharoah noticed Belle and the effect she had on men. It was not by random lot that he chose her to perform the fertility rites, by personifying Sopdet, Goddess of Fertility, Life, and Death.

Belle arrived at the altar platform on a palanquin, carried by six slaves. She was shrouded by a transparent blue silken sheet. She wore none of her customary rubies, diamonds, or gold jewelry. This day she was naked; her hair beautifully braided; her eyes taupe shadowed with touches of lapis fleck dust; her lips invitingly red. And her body was slathered with almond oil and perfumed with scents of lilies. Her up lilted, lily-white breasts presented her cherry bright protruding nipples. Her smile was contagious. Hearts warmed to her. Penises became erect as men beheld her sexuality. She was the most beautiful creature in all of Egypt.

Having stepped away from her palanquin, Belle stood at her appointed place. Then, at the appointed time; and as the trumpets sounded and as harps and flutes began to play, her slaves lifted her up and held her legs apart. As if on que, the star, Sopdet arose from below the eastern horizon and appeared. It's dazzling blue-white brilliance shone brightly between Belle's legs.

Beneath her, on the floor of her altar throne, the priests had laid down polished obsidian. The shiny mirrors captured the light of heaven's stars and moonlight and reflected their focused light onto Belle's vagina. An obsidian blade in the delicate hands of a temple priest had shaved her mons pubis completely smooth of all pubic hairs. Her vagina was then anointed with almond oils, and perfumed with the scent of lily.

The effect was mesmerizing and other worldly. It appeared to the assembled masses that the Siris Star's brilliance emanated from Belle's vagina. The illusion was breathtaking. Sopdet's brilliant light and Belle's vagina had suddenly become one, united as a single Goddess; bringing illumination to humanity's greatest need; the need to procreate; as well as being Egypt's deliverer of fertility and life; and its arbiter of death.

As if on cue, Pharoah himself ascended her throne and knelt before Belle to pray to her vagina. He spoke to the assembled masses:

'We are gathered here today to mark the passing away of old life which has served us; but is now used up and of no further use. We are also gathered here to worship new life. And to honor the great Goddess Star of Sopdet, who has now come before you from the Gods, in the human presence of Baaleezebelle, the most desirable whore in my harem and in all of Egypt.

'It is meet, right, and fitting that we rid ourselves of the old and celebrate the blessings of fertility and new life. Baaleezebelle represents all that is good and righteous and glorious. She personifies the wonders of destruction of the old order. She, through her glorious fornications, illustrates for us divine nature's procreation wonder.

'Her divine fornications and her glorious pornography have been sent to us from the Gods; for us to honor, pay homage, and give thanks for these wonderful blessings she bestows upon us, the living. May the Gods appreciate and bless her sacred fornication rites as she leads us into a new year of bountiful fertility and new life. I present to you, my loyal subjects, the guiding light of our lives: Baaleezebelle.'

After offering his homage to the most magnificent whore in all of Egypt, Pharoah arose and stood before Belle's openly splayed vagina. Belle smiled widely, thrusting her vagina upward and skyward to receive Pharoah's kiss and his blessing of all the fornication acts she was about to perform. She pinched her nipples with her forefingers and thumbs and lifted them outward and upward, indicating that she was eager to commence the fornication rites celebration.

Then, Pharoah whispered to her:

*'I know you will make all of us proud. Remember, I fully support you in all you are about to do. Enjoy the festivities and be proud of all you do. And fear no retribution from anyone whom you may offend.'*

Belle smiled to Pharoah, indicating she had read his mind; and acknowledging that she was about to upend the established social order of the kingdom. Pharoah returned her knowing smile. A die was cast. Her rival for the affections for the man she loved would die today. Pharoah understood women and their ways of achieving their ends through their prowess in lovemaking. His knowing smile assured Belle that he was fully supportive of everything she wished to accomplish.

To signal the commencement of these most sacred of days in the Egyptian calendar; to officially open their High Holy Days, the Pharoah clasped Belle's buttocks firmly in his hands, while he leaned forward and kissed her vagina; after which he turned to face the multitudes, raised his hands heavenward and proclaimed:

*'And now; let our sacred festivities commence!'*

The masses oohed and aahed. They loved the effect of the starry bright light, magnified, and projected from the obsidian mirrors; brilliantly magnifying the glistening sheen of the body oils that slathered Belle's naked body; and illuminated her dazzling vagina. To the awed crowd of worshippers, the mirrors acted like a hologram, causing the image of her vagina to appear twice its normal size. And it was an iniquitous vagina, thirsting to create new life. It glistened and shined and pulsated, signaling its insatiable cravings for the males' penises. Belle's fuck hunger vagina would not be denied a moment longer. It was eager to fornicate.

The masses shouted out their approval of the glorious whore's shining lips and glistening mons pubis. They thirsted to see Belle kiss the penis of her first lover; take it lovingly into her hands; stroking it while guiding it past her outer lips; smiling broadly and with confidence while guiding it into her delicious, heaven-sent pleasure place. The crowds screamed their approval. They cheered and clapped for her. They could not have waited another moment for her to commence her pornographic performances. They salivated in anticipation of her wonders; eager to witness the ejaculations of her suiters; ready to be uplifted by her exclamatory squeals of delights from her pleasuring's.

Their Goddess! Receiving pleasure! To sanctify their sweeping away of the old and expired! And to usher in new life! To sustain them and protect them from famine during the uncertain year ahead. She was performing her sacred fornications for them!

In their religion of celestial and nature worship, Belle was not an evil presence. She was a divine presence; a force for all that was natural and good. She was a celestial sent Goddess; a presence here on Earth, to be honored and glorified. In their reference of faith, they fully believed that Belle had blessed them with her presence. They believed she had been brought to them by the celestial gods; to lead them; to show them the way forward in life; and, by her exemplary pornographic performances, lead their fertility rites.

She would show them the natural ways of communal love. She would bless them by whisking away the old and the withered and the undesirables. Belle would purify them and bring them fertility and new life. Belle was their Goddess on Earth; theirs! They were fortunate that she bestowed her holy continence upon them; for she was a Goddess; and they were merely the great unwashed. And they would honor her! They would spare no effort; hold nothing and no one back from their offerings to her majestic and all glorious, all consuming, penis craving vagina.

She was their very own Goddess to worship and love! And to fornicate with! Her wishes were to be honored and obeyed. There she was! Presented by the Gods and by Pharoah as a divine blessing to them! This beautiful, ravishing Hebrew girl, born of slaves and now become their divine Goddess! Soon, she would be joined on her platform by her adoring consorts. Soon, she would delight the gathered masses with her breathtaking pornography with multiple partners. The adoring masses were about to witness her every blessed fornication and marvel by their approving gasps at every ejaculation into her sacred mouth and vagina.

Rave excitement overcame the crowds. They pressed forward towards the altar to better see, close up, comely Belle's sacred stroking and thrusts and the workings of her heavenly mouth and tongue with her partners' penises. Many sought to touch her flesh while she performed her sacred rites; but the temple guards kept them at a near distance. People jostled with one another for a chance to see Belle fornicating, up close. This woman was their living God! The peoples' excitement was palpable.

Moses watched Belle as she smiled and waved while presenting her raised, glistening vagina; showing off her semen streams to the multitudes; and blowing her heart felt kisses to them. The world's first porn star would lead Egypt's fornication rites for the next fortnight; performing all sorts of lascivious acts with men and women; and with the Apis bulls.

This was the role for which the harem matron had groomed her since her childhood. Sex acts were the natural mainstay of Belle's harem life. She enjoyed performing them. She was a tireless performer; always willing to do more than expected. She had long expected to be chosen to perform these sacred rites. Today, she reveled in her role. She was shameless and enthused about being chosen to lead these sacred rites; immensely proud that Pharoah had entrusted her with this great responsibility. She knew she was expected to fornicate and perform fellatio several times each day for fourteen days. And she warmed enthusiastically to the task before her.

Seeing Belle in this way, as his Goddess, Moses knew his life was about to enter a passage that would forever change him. He knew he was about to become hopelessly addicted to her spellbinding pornography. And he knew he would be among the privileged males who were chosen to consort with her. And after consorting with her, he also knew that his old life would leave him; and that he would never be the same man he was before he made love with her. Within his bones and the deepest depths of his soul, Moses immediately understood a profound, undeniable truth:

He loved her.


Marty shared with Miss Lust her experience, as Belle, with Sun God Ra:

'*Suddenly, an unexpected force took hold of my spirit soul and lifted it from my body. My soul was spirited heavenward and brought before the Great God Ra. My soul was placed upon his lap. Ra held me in his arms and kissed me while he slipped his penis into my soul's vagina. Ra's penis was unlike any other I had ever known. It was alive with a kind of radiant glow that warmed me, all through my insides. I knew what was happening was a good thing. It was a divine blessing for my soul to be chosen for intercourse by Ra.*

'*After a long few moments, Ra finally spoke to me:*

'*I have seen the wonders of your magnificent whoring and I am well pleased. You are a divine example and spiritual guide to all women who desire freedom and independence. I am proud of you.*

'I am particularly pleased that you have shattered the racial barriers which stand in the way of human intimacy and understanding. You have helped move human enlightenment forward. You represent progress toward godliness.

'Moses, a man who pleases me, has found his limbic dreams in you. He adores you. He will seek to make you, his wife. I command you to become his wife. Together, you will create a tribe of people to be favored over all other peoples. Your tribe shall enlighten all the peoples of the Earth and rule over them; and use them to create great wealth for your tribe and for all peoples of Earth. Your tribe shall be much like you, Baaleezebelle, a catalyst change agent on Earth. You shall inspire Moses. Your ethos shall become his ethos. Your tribe shall propagate change and disorder; always advancing humanity; always advocating for the disadvantaged.'

'Yes, Ra. I understand. And I will do as you say. But what about family values? What about the children and wives I am about to displace? Should they not be my concern And if not mine, whose?'

'Your only concern is your lovemaking and your spectacular, adorable pornography. It inspires humankind to be more openly honest and shamelessly immoral. I command you to perform more and more of it.'

'But, Great Ra, the wives, and children? Whose concern shall they become?'

'The Nile crocodiles can concern themselves with the wives and children. Those magnificent reptiles are also creatures of creation. They also need sustenance. It is my way and my wish that they deal with wives and children. But you, my dear, are a spectacular, magnificent pornographic artisan. You must only trouble your beautiful mind with pleasuring yourself in new and creative ways.

'Before you leave me, I must caution you about Moses. He wants you. But he also has strange thoughts about some imaginary invisible God. Such thinking causes him to believe this God created everything; but that is not so. Everything that is has always been; and all life has always been alive in the force of life. The way Moses thinks leads to control impulses and that leads to feelings of superiority and that is the cause of strife. Remember, no one can control you or your body. You are your own person and you are free to make your own decisions.

'Think about what I just said. And know that I will be watching you. I very much enjoy enticing sketches of you performing your intimate artistry. I love seeing the streams of semen flowing from the penises of your partners onto your eager tongue and into and from your welcoming vagina. I love watching your pornographic performances in the evenings after I surrender the sky to the moon. And, I have immensely enjoyed fornicating with your spirit soul. You please me. Now, divine soul of the whore I adore, you need to remove yourself from me and rejoin your Nubian consorts. Go forward. Make love. Fornicate. Unite humanity!

'I awakened from my dream state as my soul returned to my body. Then, to complete my performance, I called upon the handsome muscular Nubians to come to me and fuck me with their magnificent penises. I openly, joyously fornicated with and performed fellatio with these seven newcomers to our kingdom. My mouth and vagina soon became semen filled. The Nubians ejaculated onto my breasts and my vagina. I was literally drenched; soaked in semen. I loved the orgy. I loved the attention and adulation I received from the gathered masses. I did not want to stop. I was very successful at integrating our kingdoms and spreading my promiscuous good will to our newcomers.'

Miss Lust joined Marty's thoughts:

'And Moses? Can you remember, as I do, how he responded when he took in your abject wantonness? How his eyes bulged and his mouth gaped open as he beheld your beauty and natural promiscuity? My dear child, he saw what I and all men see. You are a woman who may take whatever she wishes from a man. You may have your way with men. They will do as you ask to please you.

'Your face was irresistible to Moses. It melted his will and all his resolve for any other thoughts. Your eyes were taupe shadowed with purple green malachite kohl. They devoured men's hearts and souls. Your body glistened with the sheen of rosehip oil. Your skin beamed vitality. It begged to be caressed and kissed. Your henna-tinged hair had been washed sparkling clean, beautifully braided, and scented with the essences of sandalwood and lemon. Your reddened lips parted when you smiled to reveal your perfect white teeth. You were irresistible. You personified lust.

'I observed the face of Moses when he first beheld you. I could read his mind. He was enraptured and completely smitten. Never had he imagined any woman so stunningly beautiful and capable of such debauchery; and so enthralled and cavalier about wantonly pursuing her natural cravings; and being so unashamedly proud to flaunt her unbridled promiscuity. He desperately wanted you as the femme fatale you are. He loved the whore that lived inside your soul. He wanted that elixir of shameless sinfulness that dwells inside you. He wanted to surrender his very soul to that core essence of your being. He wanted you to subsume him and for your soul to devour his. He was beholden, spellbound. Of that much, I was certain.

'What I could not know then was that he was willing, from that moment forward, to give up his position as Pharoah's most favored prince and leave Egypt so that he could have you all to himself. Nor did I realize then that he would acquiesce to your condemnation of his wife and children to the crocodiles, so that you would not need to trouble your prurient thoughts with their needs. He would rather you had your beautiful mind on the giving and receiving of inti-macy and pornographic pleasures; carefree of any detractors while you fornicated and performed your exquisite fellatios; and while you gloried in your pleasuring's from cunnilingus. Moses became a man transformed in that moment; a man given over to your devilish charms; beholden to your open defiance of all things moral; rejecting godliness and family; and even Pharoah's social order. He wanted a new world; the world of Baaleezebelle.'

'Oh, yes, Miss Lust. Moses did want me, didn't he? We must remember Moses. He clapped and cheered my intimate erotica like a man crazed with lust adoration. His eyes widened with awe as I squealed:

'Mmmmm! Mmmmmm! Yessss! Yesssss! Fuck me! Ohhhh! I love having all your beautiful penises inside me.'

'My eyes became alive with lust fires as I shamelessly screamed:

'Oh! I'm panting like a sex crazed animal in heat! Mmmmm! Mmmmmm! That feels soooo wonderful! And You! What a splendid penis you have! I love it. Here, let me suck it. I love all your penises. Here, let me caress your testicles. Let me lick all your beautiful penises. Yes! All of them. I want to suck all of them. Oh! You! Yes, you! Fuck me now. That's it. Yes. Come inside me. Push harder now. Faster! Yes! That's it! Oh! You are doing me so beautifully! I love what you are doing to me. Mmmmmm.'

'I nodded my head and smiled joyously, as every one of the Nubians, one by one, fucked me and ejaculated inside me:

'Oh! You're coming! How beautiful. I love feeling you come. You all have such lovely large penises! And you are all so firm and hard! Yes! I want each of you. Give me all of you; every one!'

'I assured each man as I kissed him that I loved the pleasures he gave me. And Moses thoroughly loved and approved of my performances. He appeared spellbound; a man transformed. I noticed he was staring at me. I decided it was time to join our souls; so, I willed that he should have a vision of our future together and our eternity:

'Time stood still for Moses that day while he beheld my soul. I opened my mouth as if to impart a kiss to him. And while he fixated on me, transfixed, my soul took the form of a large black snake. It's head peered out of my mouth and its eyes stared at Moses; then, it slithered free of my body and ascended into the air above my head. It became rigid, displaying its full eight-foot length. Then, another, smaller, white snake appeared. It was the spirit soul of Zeporah. And it slithered towards my black snake, as if to chase my snake away; as if to tell my snake that it did not belong in the presence of Moses.

'But then, my black snake raced to the white snake. My snake opened wide its jaws and devoured the white snake, thus swallowing the soul of Zeporah. And my snake smiled her pleased, comely smile to Moses, as if to tell him she was proud of what she had just done. Moses was dumbfounded by what he saw; but he also seemed pleased to be free of Zeporah's soul. It was then that my black snake slithered to Moses and lovingly, seductively, entwined herself around him. When her head reached the head of Moses, she kissed his mouth. When he returned my soul's kiss, I felt warmth in my heart. This inner warmth assured me it was time to include Moses in my destiny.

'But I needed to be sure about Moses. I had heard many speak of his greatness as a leader. It was said that he had conviction; that he believed in himself and in his own judgment. But how could that explain his marriage to Zeporah? She was a Midianite progeny of her father who lived Midianite ways; not Egyptian! She was a very plain and stupid woman. Had Pharoah's sister, her mother, pressured Moses to marry her? Had mighty Moses bended to the will of a woman? Why had such a great prince; a man with such great promise, married Zeporah? She detracted greatly from his great potential; yet he had married her! Was Moses unable to know his own mind? Unable to control his own destiny? Could it possibly be that he loved her? I could not imagine it. She was so inferior to me. And he clearly signaled to me that he loved me. He even spoke the words! I bid the snake of my soul to learn more about Moses. I needed to learn the truth.

'My snake then slithered into the ear of Moses and entwined herself lovingly around his mind. It's tongue then split into two parts and her split tongue engulfed the mind of Moses; brought it to her mouth; and whispered into the ear of his mind. While Moses watched, fascinated by my pornography and beholden to my debauched sinfulness, I reveled in my fornications with the black Nubian penises. When my spirit soul black snake knew that Moses was smitten by my ribaldry, it revealed my intentions to him:

"Moses, hear me. I am the spirit soul of Baaleezebelle, the grandest whore in all Egypt. I know your thoughts and wishes. I know you intend to fulfill Akhenaten's vision, that mankind should worship only one god. I am here to help you in your grand quest. I will pledge my allegiance and my followers to your cause. Together, we shall lead the Hebrews out of Egypt. You shall succeed in forging a nation of Zion from the Hebrew tribes; and all our united peoples shall worship your one god.

"And your people will believe you when you tell them they are the chosen people of God; and that they are destined to dominate and reign over all other peoples on Earth. Your leadership and the laws you give them will forge them into a willful tribe, capable of inflicting bitter defeats upon their enemies. My spirit trusts you to lead us, Moses, for you are a tall, strong, handsome, and willful prince. You were born to be a leader of men.

"And I will be with you on this journey, my prince. I will lavish my womanly favors upon you every day and night. I will comfort and satisfy you and keep you steadfast in your pursuit. Embrace me and kiss me, Moses. Affirm to me that we are of one soul, united in our singular purpose to dominate all humankind."

'And the soul of Moses took the black snake, the soul of Baaleezebelle, into his arms and kissed her mouth. And the snake-soul wrapped her hundred pairs of arms around the soul of Moses, and clasped his soul tightly to hers. Then, after she had drawn his soul

*"You must know, my love, that this is only our beginning."*

*"I don't understand,"* replied Moses.

*"Our souls are eternal, my prince,"* explained the snake. *"They cannot die and they will never die. And we shall be entwined as lovers forever through all of time. After this life, my soul shall fly away to the great eternal wheel of lust. Upon this lust wheel I shall stay until time passes and the wheel turns. And when this turning comes, your soul will come again to discover my soul; and our souls will then reenter human bodies and we shall love again. You see, my prince, soulmate love is forever and never ending."*

*"But you and I will be dead,"* asserted Moses.

*"Yes, of course. But that does not matter. Our souls will live forever. We will reappear and assume the human bodies of Bathsheba and King David; Salome and King Herod; Cleopatra and Anthony; Isabella and Ferdinand; Susan and Marvin; Marty and Bob; Sheila and Hud; Connie and Paul; JoAnne and Gibby; Jen and Thor; and millions of other pairs of eternal lovers. Love is eternal. It endures after all else is gone. Our love will never leave us."*

*"So, this is my soul's price for your love?"*

"Yes. My love is special. It is priceless. Do you reject my offer? If it is Zeporah you want, you must speak now."

"No, my love, the soul mate of my soul. I accept. And I understand. And I do love you. And I want to have your love for all eternity."

"Good. Then you must know that Zeporah and her sons are a mere distraction from our grand purpose. You must not concern yourself with how the gods deal with them."

"I understand, delicious soul of Baaleezebelle, and I accept all that you do and all that you cause to be done."

"Then we have become one. Prove your love to me."

'While the Nubians were still on my performance platform, Moses came away from his soul. He stepped onto the platform and from us. That's when he, as a man, confessed his love for me, as a woman:

Moses:

*'I adore you and I love you. You are my Goddess. I want you for my wife and life partner.*

Belle:

*'But Moses, you already have a wife and you have children with her.'*

Moses:

*'But it is you whom I want. I speak from my soul.'*

Belle:

*'I understand. But you must know my soul. I am not an ordinary sort of woman. I am completely; and without reservation, an unrepentant, immoral whore; raised and trained in the artistry of whoring; grown accustomed to my whoring and my pornographic performances; being carefree and naturally comfortable and guilt free about who I am and what I am and with the things I do with my partners.'*

Moses:

*'I understand that about you. But you are my true love. My soul has met your soul and it knows that is true. I crave to be with you always. I want you. It does not matter to me that you are the most incorrigible, profligate, immoral whore in all of Egypt. I must have your profligate, glorious vagina. I must have your soul and your flesh with me always. You are the metaphor for Egyptian fertility. I cannot settle for anyone or anything less. I want to take you up in my arms and love you and hug you and adore you and make love with you. I wish to give my life to you. I wish to commit my soul to your soul. I wish to marry you.'*

Belle:

*'I understand that you know my true essence; yet you wish to give your life and your soul to me, a thoroughly unrepentant, profli-*

Moses:

'Yes. It is true. I swear it.'

Belle:

'But do you fully understand this soul you say you want? I am a demanding whore. I take. I take men's lives away from the women they are with. I take their love and possess it. And I take their wealth. I am the whore who takes everything, and all of everything, my dearest Prince.'

Moses:

'Then you shall have me; my life, my soul, my wealth as well; all that I am and all that I have. All for you. All of everything; only to have you.'

Belle:

'But you are already married, my sweet love. Do you know that I cannot share my life or my bed with your wife and children?'

Moses:

'I know that. I would never ask that of you. I would send them away.'

Belle:

'Those are only words, Moses; they are not deeds.'

Moses:

'I would never go back to them. I swear it.'

Belle:

'More words, Moses. You would have me give up my love of whoring to be yours, alone; yet you could return to your wife and children?'

Moses:

'How can I prove to you that I would never return to them? Would you have me murder them?'

Belle:

'Ahhh! You have said it, Moses. Again, I hear you speak your words, Moses. I could love a man if only he were a man of deeds!'

Moses:

Belle:

'Do my mouth, my breasts, my vagina, my touches, and my passions affect you this much? Do I mean that much to you? Do I, really? And would you have me, forever?'

Moses:

'Yes, I swear it. You have captured my heart and my soul. You are the only woman for me. You are all I ever wanted in a woman. And I love everything about you; your beauty; your profligacy; your shamelessness; your pride in who you are and what you do. I adore you. I must have you. I accept all your terms, without reservation of any kind. I will remove those who would distract you from my life. I will remove them from life itself, so that I can never return to them.'

Belle:

'Then, are you telling me that they are like Kamatz (Yiddish for crumbs lying on the floor) to you? Are you saying that you wish them to be swept from your life; be gone forever; never to be seen again'

Moses:

'Yes. I am saying that. They are my past. And I wish my life to be only with you; to give my life and my soul to you; to dedicate my life and my soul to pleasing you and making you the wealthiest, most pleasured woman in the world. I wish to free myself from all things in my past. Nothing and no one can stand in my way.'

Belle:

'But your wife and children are living humans. They are not mere crumbs to be swept out the door.'

Moses:

'The plains of Egypt are as a floor which must be swept clean of old and withered detritus stalks this time of year, to make way for new life. Your performances at the fertility rites, your exquisite pornography, have convinced me that it is also time for me to sweep clean my life; and begin my new life with you. Having now known *you and your irresistible charms; they are as Kamatz to me. I wish to make my life swept clean of them to make way for you; just as the plains are swept clean to welcome the fertility of the eternal Nile.'*

Belle:

*'I do not understand. The fields are burned and the ashes scattered; made ready for the Nile floods. Tell me, my sweet, darling prince: By what method? How would you sweep your life clean? How will you make ready my way to become your fertile wife and your only soul mate? Will I take pleasure in knowing your preparation? Will I see it for myself to be certain that my way is made ready?'*

Moses:

*'Yes. You may observe it, my love. You will know my allegiance to you and your glorious whoring soul. I shall surrender my detritus to the mighty Nile and its voracious crocodiles. You will be free of mind and feel freedom to flood me with your glorious lovemaking. Our souls will flood each other's souls. We shall enjoy our rapture and create a new life. You will see and hear all. You will know it is you; and you alone, whom I love.'*

Marty shared her most intimate thoughts with Miss Lust, the soul of her bones:

*'That's when I knew that Moses wanted to give his soul to me. It was when that special moment came, when I had revealed my true essence to him. And he recognized it; appreciated it; understood it; and, despite my incorrigible nymphomania, he knew that I was the only woman he wanted. And he confessed that he completely loved me for the woman I am.*

*'It was during that time in human history when humanity was struggling to understand its way; trying to know what it could trust and believe. On the one hand was Baal worship and Pagan fertility rites; on the other this nascent concept of monotheism had reared its*

head in the thoughts of mankind. Moses and I became swept up in this grand dilemma. I had heard that this was a subject that fascinated him. And I, too, fascinated him. I believe he felt the solution to his puzzlement lay, somehow, within me.

'And I observed how he watched me performing my pornographic acts. My eyes glimpsed his eyes while I was being pleasured with cunnilingus by one partner and simultaneously receiving semen onto my tongue, from performing fellatio with the penis of another partner; and while also being simultaneously caressed with soft touches and kissed about my face by yet two other partners. I was laughing, giggling, and chortling from the ribaldry of my wantonness. I was thoroughly enjoying myself and feeling sublimely confident in my role as the featured whore of Pharoah's fertility rites. There's something wondrous and magical about letting myself go; surrendering all inhibition to my limbic mind's possession of my will; defying all things moral and decent.

'Spitting in the face of his one God. Yes. That's what I was doing. I represented the opposite of the abstract God concept, which Moses was brewing in his mind. I was me, in my dreamlike, limbic state. I love being there. When I am there, I have no cares about who thinks what of me; or even about what I may think of myself, afterwards. It's such a wonderful, wanton place, all my thoughts apart from this mental state become meaningless. I only care about my pleasure. And that's when Moses' eyes met mine. My eyes had already captured his; but now, his eyes captured mine. They looked deeply into mine. They saw my soul. And they wanted it.

'Suddenly I knew our souls were fated to join together. His eyes were telling me that his thoughts and soul had traveled far away from our fertility rites. They were seeing my soul. They were seeing me as a whore, thoroughly committed to my whoring and my pornography. Yes, of course they saw that. But they were now seeing a deeper me. They were seeing my boundless capacity to love all of humanity; my *determination to unlock mankind from all inhibitions and fears of death; my willingness and determination to perform my pornography to advance humanity's appreciation of life for the living. My role in the Egyptian fertility rites was my way of letting the People know that there is hope for humanity's future; that our Pagan gods and our blessed Nile would never forsake us; that they could trust and believe in Pharoah to lead them; that they could trust in themselves that their faith in humanity was a goodness, and not something misplaced; and that our communal love and human intimacy was the wholesome and natural order of humanity.*

*'Moses could see that I represented all those wonderful things about life and love. That's when I knew that watching me having orgy sex and performing fellatio had made Moses, Pharoah's most favored prince, fall crazily into love with me. He no longer saw me as a mere temple whore. He now saw my pornographic acts as divine messages from our spirit gods. And he saw me as human divinity; an all glorious, wondrous divine goddess, there before him, live in the flesh. And he wanted me more than he ever wanted anything or anyone; even more than his abstract god. I became certain of it.'*

*'Good, Marty. That's when you realized how powerful your pornographic performances are; how your intimate erotica can capture a man's heart; and cause him to forsake all others. Isn't that true?'*

*'Yes. Absolutely true. And it was also the moment when I realized that murder in the furtherance of humanity is justifiable. Although, at that point in my soul's journey, I had not yet personally committed any murders. But I was deeply pleased that Moses was willing to commit murder in order to have me all to himself. It was a new kind of feeling. I felt loved in a way that I had never felt loved before.'*

*'Good. Then, can you also remember when it came to the part in the fertility rites ceremony where the people sacrificed their babies to the Nile, to reward the Nile for giving them sustenance; thusly, returning some fruits of their existence back to the Nile?'*

'Yes, of course I remember that. Pharoah and Moses had both become obsessed over me. It was my very first live pornographic performance. And everyone loved it! I was so excited to perform it! And I remember how the people adored me. And how I had excited all the gathered people into a frenzy.'

'Indeed, you had! Pharoah observed that the people adored your whoring so much that he ordered one hundred babies to be sacrificed in your honor. He wanted the people to express their gratitude to the eternal Nile for your talented mouth and vagina, which had milked the semen streams from the Apis bulls and from a dozen princes. He wished to pay homage to your fabulous, insatiable, fuck-crazed vagina. All the gathered people sang their heartfelt songs of praise to you, Sopdet Goddess of both New life and Death; and they sang praises to their Nile God. They sang that they were tenfold grateful for your sensational, glorious whoring skills; your boundless, insatiable whore lust; and our determination to fornicate with the same wild abandon as a female dog in heat. Your rapacious, whoring vagina represented the divinely expressive, ever bountiful, eternal fertility of the Nile.

'They believed the Star of New Life and Death, and their Nile Gods had delivered you to them as a blessing to them. And they were immensely grateful that you came to consort with them. They then, to honor you and your spectacular whoring, sacrificed one hundred babies to their Nile God of Fertility that day, instead of their customary ten babies. They wished to show their extreme gratitude to the Nile for your adoring, insatiable, mouth and vagina.

'They adored your performances with the bulls. They cheered and wildly roared their frenzied, enthusiastic approval as you stroked and sucked the penises of the Apis bulls and relieved them of their sacred semen. Their frenzy heightened to a fever pitch while they witnessed how carefree, joyful, and proudly unashamed you were while copulating with them. Their hearts adored and loved *you for bringing forth the vital life semen from those bulls. Your spectacular fertility performance assured them that their animals were healthy; that they could reproduce; and that they would enjoy the Nile's bounty for another year. You personally guaranteed the fertility of their fields and cattle. Remember?'*

*'Yes, I remember. I had no inhibitions. None. I enjoyed doing the bulls; the eroticism of it. I loved hearing the frenzied enthusiasm of the crowds. I was their dog star; the center of attention; and I carried the hopes and future of Egypt in my whoring soul. I held the masses spellbound, in awe of me. I glistened and glittered like my dog star namesake. I felt wonderful about who I was and what I was doing. I loved everything I did.'*

*'And, do you remember how the chosen mothers placed their sacrificial babies upon the reed rafts and sang their blessing songs to their babies as they pushed their rafts into the waters to thank the great Nile? They were making their thank offerings to the Nile for blessing them with your deliverance of fertility through the fornications of your fabulous, ecumenical vagina.'*

*'Yes. I vividly remember that, too. I was deified and exalted. I felt exhilarated and venerated. My pornography was praised. The people loved me. I had come down from the heavens to become their savior. I was there with them to resurrect new life from death. My love of lust and life's creation forces overpowered all my other thoughts and all other aspects of my life. It was a grand and glorious time; a profoundly religious time. The people were paying homage to me; sacrificing their most vulnerable in honor of me.*

*'I was their creation goddess. I was massaged and attended to with creams and oils while I fornicated with partner after partner throughout that sacred fortnight. My smiles and lips welcomed lover after lover to the pleasures of my mouth. And my pink outer lips glistened with oils and creamy white semen from the hearts and souls I stole away to join my soul in capitulation to my eternal desire. Every*

*partner sought to have his penis pay homage to me, their fertility goddess. With their semen flows they reposed their respect for life in me. Even into the evenings, when the night shadows and darkness fell, I continued my honor services to the fertility rites. In those dimming times, my vagina, slathered with its oils and white semen cream, exquisitely captured the moonlight and the starlight. It appeared far larger then, because its brilliant luminescence seemed even more glorious amidst the surrounding darkness.*

*'It was in these moments that Moses stayed close beside me; his eyes adoring me. I began sensing that he was accepting me; not as a wife who sells her life to a man; not as a whore who rents her body and soul by the minute or the hour; but as a sacred goddess who symbolized the essence of life; and as a life companion who could bring a tribe of people to him and help cement them to his teachings. Moses intuited that the peoples' belief in my powers would naturally accrue to him and his 'One God Fits All' concept. From that moment on I sensed that his interest in me was deeper than my womanly favors.*

*'And in those moments, while I was capturing men's hearts and souls to my carnal ways, I began to not care what Moses or any man thought of me. I was learning the truth about myself. I came to realize that I loved performing my pornography not only to please Pharoah and the people; but that I loved performing my pornography, for me. I felt wonderful about myself while performing. It became my joy. I found myself loving myself more than I ever had before. I loved being able to admit to myself that I loved the pleasure aspects of performing all my pornographic acts; the excitement; the variety; the orgasms and semen flows; the touches and kisses; and the debauchery that comes with the romantic aspects of it; and the intimate loves that formed between me and my partners; all of it. And I have loved all of it, ever since, in all my following lives.'*

*'Yes. And while the sacrificial babies were crying out, while they were being dismembered and devoured by the crocodiles, Moses then*

*performed exquisite, loving cunnilingus with you. He was accepting all of you, for you. And he was signaling to the gathered masses that you were life's true creation force; and that all that was in the past needed to be swept away and forgotten; and that you and your pornographic acts were to be honored and glorified, for you were their divine goddess, the creation force, and the future of all the People. Remember?'*

*'Oh yes. Mmmmmm. Of course, I remember. I remember his loving tongue strokes over my clitoris; how they warmed my body and made me feel adored as a complete woman; and my long orgasm flows while hearing the crocodiles thrashing and tearing apart the bodies that had been sacrificed to them. And I remember appreciating the salutary effects of the Nile's cleansing as the reptiles roiled and splashed the waters with their death rolls. It was all so natural and necessary; the price the people gladly paid for the privilege of living. My amygdala resonated with the amygdala's of the Nile reptiles. We were as one. And all that we did and were doing was a natural and necessary part of life. And we were beautiful in performing our deeds. And I was beautiful. I became reptilian in body and soul; feeling nothing for those who were being dismembered and devoured.*

*'Mmmmm. It was such a beautiful, divine time. I was ecstatic; completely content with myself. I'd never felt more alive and appreciated as a sexual woman than I was then. I loved how Moses's hands touched my body; the ways he hugged me tenderly and pressed his flesh against mine; how his breaths inhaled my scents; how he kissed my eyes; how he nuzzled his face against my neck and between my breasts. I received more than his passions. I received our first shared love.*

*'Yes! I knew it! At that instant moment, I knew it! We had fallen in love! I was even beyond ecstatic. I knew I had become deified, as the true God of Moses. I experienced this surreal feeling. I was bringing life and death to the people. My power was unbounded.*

Death and life had become as one in my mind; and within me, in the minds of the people. And this magnificent man loved me. And, I knew it then. I also loved him!

'I was being glorified. There, in the midst of our ardent love-making, lives were being sacrificed to honor me and my profligate whoring. Mmmmmm. I felt so alive in the midst of so much death. Mmmmmm. It was the first time I felt sublime and blissfully proud of who I am as a complete, unapologetic whore and woman. It was the precursor to the feelings that I have often had in my present life, when I have displaced a married woman from her home and bonded her husband and his wealth to me through my whoring. This was my awakening time. My star as the living personification of Sopdet became true to life, in me. I realized how important I was in the lives of those men who wanted me; but especially, Moses. I was experiencing the greatest pleasuring of my life. I was whispering my love messages to Moses amidst hearing the desperate death cries and wailings of the forlorn and helpless:

"Love me. Only me. Love me always. Mmmmm. Yes! Oh yes, my darling love! Fuck me. Yes, fuck me. Mmmmm. Oh, yes. I'm coming. So sweet. So lovely. Mmmmmm. Moses, slide your penis over my clitoris. Slowly. Yes, Mmmmmm. Now, press it hard against me there. Mmmmm. Yes. That's wonderful. I'm coming again. Mmmmmm. I could do this forever. Oh, how much I do truly love you! That feels soooo beautiful!"

'And how did you feel; what did you feel about your own persona while you orgasmed?'

'Divine. Unashamed. Powerful. Sinfully wicked. Glorious, and proud of my performances that day. Secure in my whoring. There I was, being pleasured by Pharoah's favorite son, before all the temple priests, ministers, and gathered throngs of faithful Egyptians. I repeatedly pushed my mons pubis hard against his penis; determined to relieve him of every droplet of semen he had within him. I felt profoundly privileged to be recognized and exalted as the supreme Goddess Whore of Egypt. I was not only proving myself as a worthy lover to Moses; I was also demonstrating to the people that I was the most exemplary whore in the Kingdom of both Upper and Lower Egypt, all of Egypt; and the most deserving of all women of Egypt's finest, most noble prince. I imagined my vagina was winning a contest for his love. I was in the throes of triumph while all other contestants for his favors became horses who were racing to catch up with me.

'But they couldn't come close to my passions or my lust fires. One by one, they strained a tendon and hobbled away from this race. His wife, too, had become a horse. And she collapsed and fell away from me. And, there I was; the winner! I was left alone with him then, making sweet, passionate love, with no other cares about anything or anyone in the world; making Moses mine; all mine; only mine.

'My mind then entered in its limbic, ethereal dimension. I felt immense pride in my profligate wantonness. While I again orgasmed, this time into my Pharoah's Prince's mouth, I knew Pharoah whole-heartedly approved and blessed all my pornographic acts. He loved me because I was had assured fertility and continuity of his dynasty. Moses needed me to be a whore. He could not love me and commit to me otherwise. Only by being a whore could I be immoral enough to set him free from the drudgery of his family life. And Moses needed that freedom to pursue his destiny. He was fated to reshape human morality.

'The crowd sensed this historic happening. They sensed I was freeing their prince to reshape the course of humanity; to do great things. They knew his wife and children could not be part of his great calling. And they loved me for being the one; for helping this historic happening to blossom. They loved me as the whore I was. They revered me as their exalted whore. And I felt their love. I responded to it with my passion thrusts. I became sublime and glorious in my revelry. I knew I was revered and accepted by all'

'All?'

'Well, no. Not all. I rolled my head during my cunnilingual pleasuring from Moses. And out of the corner of my eye I glimpsed the face of Zeporah, his wife. Her mouth was quivering and her eyes bespoke her true feelings. Tears rolled down her cheeks. She was not enjoying the ceremonies like the others. She was horrified. She knew she was losing her husband to me.'

'And did that give you pause? Make you want to stop?'

'Oh no. Nothing like that. I only gained more confidence; and complete certainty that I was intensely loved and adored by Moses. In those precious moments, I felt his love becoming part of me; his soul was becoming absorbed into my soul. While her eyes communicated her impending terror, his eyes communicated his steadfast obsession for me.'

'And do you remember the final part of the fertility ceremony?'

'You mean when the deplorables and the unwanted had their hands and legs bound; when they were loaded onto the barge and floated out onto the Nile and fed to the crocodiles?'

'Yes. And who was on that barge? Do you remember?'

'Yes, I arranged it. How could I forget?'

'You arranged it? How?'

'I made their deaths part of the fertility ceremony.'

'How? Tell me!'

'Remember the beginning of the festivities, before Pharoah kissed my vagina and proclaimed it to be the brilliant earthly presence of Sopdet, star Goddess of fertility?'

'Yes.'

'It was then that I had a premonition, a seeing of my future. I knew then, instinctively, that this day would be the day of my emergence. My metamorphosis was about to complete; and I was to shed my cocoon, leave the harem and become the wife of Moses. Pharoah's kiss would bless my fornications and make sacred my immoral morality. I knew that I could captivate Moses with my flutter; and my fornications would be the death curse for Zephorah.

'I only dimly perceived the gruesome, mordant costs my winsome performance would exact upon Zeporah at that time. Her fate was an opaquely veiled decision in the hands of others. It was only to be revealed to me should I choose to flutter onward and embrace my destiny; if I chose to be undeterred from my purpose; if I chose to neglect my moral conscience.

'I then exhaled deeply and smiled the smile of a resolute temptress, determined not to allow anything of being or thought deter or dissuade me. Within my soul's depths I vowed to take leave from all morality expected of virtuous women. I then inhaled fresh new air and breathed in my new morality, my Butterfly Morality. My new morality would guide my flight from all probity. My butterfly wings would transport me through that opaque veil of uncertainty and alight me upon the next chapter of my life. And I would enter my new world of Moses.

'Would I be the instrument of Zeporah's fate? Perhaps? But I could not know her future and I refused to assume a mantle of guilt. After all, who was I, a mere harem girl, to control whatever fate the gods had planned for her? These matters are all preordained by the gods. I decided not to trouble my head about her or her two brats. I reminded myself that I was Baaleezebelle, a harem whore. And I was chosen by Pharoah to perform before the assembled throng of fertility worshippers during the height of our festivities. I needed to concentrate on pleasing my Pharoah, my partner pornographic performers, and my gods. I needed to be uninhibited and proud of my profession. And I would be. My audience would see the glee in my face and eyes as I kissed and licked the penises of the Apis bulls and fondled their testicles. They would witness my revelry as I brought forth the semen streams from the bulls into my mouth; thus, assuring fertility of the lands and our people.

'And the great god, Ra, would shine his continence upon me and warm me, beholding my salacious pornography, and cherishing me for the radiant life affirming whore that I am. And Sopdet, goddess of fertility, will chorus my praises; blessing me as I fornicate with a hundred penises; thus, affirming that the males' seeds of life are forthcoming to perpetuate our people. And I shall kindle within the heart and mind of Moses such lust passions that his own eyes will speak to him:

'See her? She is spectacular! And her whoring surpasses that of every other whore in Egypt. She is even more desirable than the finest whores of Babylon! See how she kisses and licks the penises of her partners? See how she lavishes her ardor upon them? See the glee in her eyes? Her mirthful mouth? She loves the male penis! Unashamedly! Proudly! And without reservation! Seeks more than one! One for her mouth and one in each hand! An amazing whore! Never before have you witnessed such splendid enthusiasm for fellatio! She loves to mouth the testicles while she strokes the shafts until the semen spurts forth and surrenders to her welcoming tongue and mouth. She chortles now; so shamelessly; so boldly confident in her craft. Hear her, Moses? She wants you. And she is yours for the taking! Listen!

"Mmmmmm; Mmmmmmm. Come, Moses, join me. I wish to please you. Discover my mouth. Discover all of me. Come to me. Mmmmmm. Please! Hurrrrry!"

'She moans her incorrigible ribaldry; urgently invites you to come to her and consort with her; join your pleasure lusts to hers. She wishes to please you with her passions and her pleasures. She's offering you an eternal abyss of sin and debauchery; and you know that is exactly what you seek. Her whoring is unrivaled on this Earth; the very finest of female flesh. You know you need her. You know you want her. You know you desire to clasp your hands to her tush and bring her vagina onto your shaft. And you know she wants that. She seeks to have you taste her vagina and sheath your penis inside her.

'You must not give thoughts to those who would control you and

*Zeporah. She is younger; fairer skinned; softer, silkier hair; so, inviting of face, mouth, and eyes. And so anxious to please! Her very orientation is to please with her lovemaking. Through her pornography, she openly proclaims that her very reason for living is pleasuring by fornication and fellatio. And she takes immense joy in it.*

*'You know you need her. Do not deny yourself. Open the window to tomorrow. You need who and what she is. Be with her. Take Baaleezebelle as your mistress, your wife, and your ally. Go to her, now! Give your urges their head! Forget Zeporah! Zeporah is your past! Baaleezebelle is your future! Embrace your future! Welcome it!*

*'Take Baaleezebelle in your arms. Hold her, kiss her, and love her. Give your heart and soul to her. And love her completely; and with wild abandon. Never look back. Never regret. Let her plant within you her seeds of desires; and let those seeds grow into ever more desires for her. Drink in her delicious flows and savor her lusts. Surrender your soul to her soul. Lie down beside her. Discover humankind's true god between her legs.'*

*'With those perceptions of the thoughts in Moses' mind, I resolved myself that the happiness of Moses should be my sole concern; and that considerations for Zeporah's life and her fate should not cloud my thoughts, confound my better judgement, or detract, in even the slightest way, my seduction efforts. I became clear of mind and purpose. If Pharoah and Moses deemed that the fate of Zeporah and her children should be entrusted to Sobek and his crocodiles, then who was I, Baaleezebelle, to doubt their wisdom? I needed to focus all my thoughts and energies on seducing and pleasing Moses; and place my trust in my Pharoah and my gods to deal with such unimportant matters as the life of Zeporah and her children.'*

*'And then, after Pharoah could see that you were at peace with your thoughts and that you were enthused about your forthcoming pornographic performances, he asked you if you were ready?'*

*'Yes, he did. And I confirmed to him that I was ready and anx-*

'And the Pharoah then kissed your vagina, blessing it and its god-like qualities; and he praised you to the cheering multitudes; and he then held his arms high and said his blessings over your coming sacred fornications?'

'Yes, he did. Then, he hugged me and kissed my lips. I felt his warmth come into my soul. I wished to please him. I then climbed onto Pharoah's throne, wrapped my arms around him; kissed his lips fully and warmly to consummate his blessings; and I guided his penis into my vagina.'

'Yes, I remember you doing that. You gave him your first honors.'

'Well, yes, Miss Lust. Of course I did. A girl must never forget her sponsor. But then, you must not have heard what I whispered into Pharoah's ear! I revealed my deepest desires to him.'

'Oh, please, do tell me! Let me hear all of it.'

And Baaleezebelle recanted her secret conversation with Pharoah:

Belle: 'Pharoah, dearest, sweetest man, and mighty ruler of all of Egypt, I bear upon my tongue the voices of both Sopdet, the Goddess of Fertility, and of Sobek, the God of Death. My spirit is possessed by both Gods. And they wish that you heed them as they speak through me.'

Pharoah: 'Speak freely, my beautiful love child. How do these Gods instruct me?'

Belle: 'Sopdet requires that Moses, First Prince of Egypt, become my husband at the customary conclusion of these fertility rites.'

Pharoah: 'Ah, I see you hunger for him, my sweetest one. But if I should obey this command of Sopdet, what would become of you? Would you leave my harem? Would I never know your delightful favors again?'

Belle: 'I would leave the harem, Pharoah; and I would make my bed with Moses. But I would never leave you, my dearest Pharoah. Whenever you summon me to come to you, I would come to you, *immediately, even if I was with Moses. I would immerse you with my favors. My lips; my tongue; and my vagina would always be eager and willing to serve you above all others, my lord.'*

*Pharoah: 'And Sopdet would always approve of this arrangement?'*

*Bella: 'Yes, my lord. Sopdet knows that your penis is the most highly prized in all of Egypt. And I would always be most highly honored to entertain my Lord in every way, and always without fail. My vagina would be more pleased than ever should you obey the commands of Sopdet.'*

*Pharoah: 'No doubt you would, you clever minx! But what am I to believe? Would you share the bed of Moses with Zeporah, my sister's daughter?*

*Bella: 'Sobek now wishes to speak to you through my lips, mighty Pharoah.'*

*Pharoah: 'Speak, Sobek. Speak to me through the lips of this lovely, irresistible nymph. Let me learn of her desires.'*

*Bella: 'Mighty Pharoah, Zeporah and her brood brats are to have no place in the dwelling of Moses. Sobek commands you to purge them; cleanse the kingdom of them ; and offer them up to him as sacrifices, so that the mighty Nile will again flood over Egypt.'*

*Pharoah: 'Surely Sobek knows Zeporah is my sister's daughter? And her sons are young. Their lives lie before them. The morality of this……'*

*Bella: 'Oh yes, my Lord. Sobek knows all matters concerning death. And Sobek sometimes chooses to take the innocent and the young. Sobek's ways are sometimes sudden and harsh but they are not for us to judge. But Sobek wishes to remind Pharoah that Pharoah's sister married a Midianite; and she begat Zeporah, who then married a Midianite. And Sobeck speaks to remind Pharoah that Midianites are an inferior race of people. They are short, swarthy, unkept peoples; and they are not beautiful when compared with*

*Egyptians. Midianites sleep with their animals. They even smell like them! Midianites are not clean, like we Egyptians, my Pharoah. Midianites live in squalid mud huts made without adequate straw. They do not have glorious temples and funerary chambers like we Egyptians. Sobek tells me that Zeporah has disgraced herself. She lives among flock animals and is not worthy of the royal bed chamber of Moses.'*

*Pharoah: 'Surely, Sobek knows that sacrificing the three of them would cause me pain, for they are related to me by blood. The morality of this……'*

*Belle: 'Sobek knows, my Lord. And Sobek also appreciates that the greatness of a gift is measured by how much it pains the giver. And Sobek wants their deaths to be your most highly treasured gifts. And what greater moral duty can my Pharoah have than to obey his Gods? And what greater moral duty can there be than for Pharoah to ensure harmony in his kingdom? And does not a kingdom's harmony require the happiness of its sovereign? And what greater happiness does my Pharoah know than the times he consorts with Baaleezebelle, his favorite harem whore? What moral duty could possibly be greater than my Pharoah's happiness? And does not my Pharoah love the tastes of my delicious peach? Does not my Lord wish to have my peach always ready and eager to please him? And does my Pharoah not know how my lips, my tongue, and my peach always yearn to please him, more than any other; even Moses? What could be a higher moral calling than for my Pharoah to please the gods of the woman whom the gods have sent to please him?*

*'After saying those words to Pharoah, I touched my tongue to his ear, while pressing my vagina and my hand hard against his penis; and I whispered: 'Sobek and Sopdet promise you that the gifts of pleasure you will gain from my favors will far exceed the pain of the gift you give to Sobek.*

'And upon hearing those words and feeling my vagina pressing hard against his penis and after I coaxed forth his semen stream, Pharoah ordered his adjutant to inscribe the names of Zeporah and her two sons onto the parchment rolls of those who were to be sacrificed to Sobek.'

'You are very conniving, my sister soul,' grinned Ms. Lust. 'You have no qualms about dispatching your opposition through guile; and no hesitance over using your seductive charms to realize your wishes.'

'No, of course I don't,' replied Marty, in the persona of Baaleezebelle. 'And, now that I've had them murdered, what difference does it make how I got my way? The pleasure of winning Moses was worth all of it. It was more than feeling his penis securely arrested within my vagina; more than knowing the rapture of his tongue strokes over my clitoris. Oh yes! Much more than those pleasures! It was also the pleasure of observing the shock on the face of my adversary. She had no inkling of her fate until Pharoah's soldiers took her away on the very moment it happened.

'I remember that moment and the looks on their faces. They had no inkling of the fate that was about to befall them. Pharoah had the guards take Zeporah and her two children and bind together their hands and feet so they could not swim away. Their faces were shocked. The guards had no tolerance for her pretense of royalty. The soldiers knew she no longer had credibility. Her horror was palpable. She became white as a sheet. As I witnessed the blood drain from her face, I felt the warm glow of triumph in my breast. My persuasions and incorrigible, shameless vagina held high cards over her morality. Pharoah had honored my god's wishes. Their names had been marked onto the papyrus scroll. They were destined to rendezvous with Sobek.

'As the procession of gift bearers began laying gold, silver, and precious jewels before my throne altar, honoring my pornography *and my gift of fertility to Egypt, Moses, First Prince of Egypt, and I, watched his family being taken away; placed upon the sacrificial barge, then to be taken away from the Nile's shore and thrown to the waiting crocodiles. The truth was finally revealed to me. Moses was a man who was true to his heart; and to me. He was sweeping the Kamatz from his life. Pharoah must have told him of the wishes of Sopdet and Sobek. And Moses had not protested.*

*'My delicious, penis adoring, loving vagina had swallowed morality. Zeporah and her children had no response to the power of my promiscuous sex appeal. They were doomed. Allowing them to be fed to the crocodiles was how Moses untroubled my mind; freed it from any thoughts of them. Moses kept his promise to me. He wanted my love and my vagina; and he would have what pleased him. I can still see the terrified looks in their eyes. I remember how those horrified eyes pleaded with Moses's eyes to reconsider his acquiescence to their deaths. And I remember how his dispassionate eyes looked at them. His eyes registered no regret; no feelings whatsoever. Moses only had eyes for me, from that moment onward.*

*'Suddenly I had this wickedly macabre inspiration. I asked myself: 'Why should another woman's plight spoil my triumph?' Of course, it should not! I decided I should trivialize his wife's importance and her plight. I would signify to Moses that, like him, I correctly assessed that their lives were meaningless. After all, had they not just been relegated to the lowly status of human kamatz? I decided then and there to jape her degradation. Yes! I would mock her loss of status as his wife and mother of their children, for both she and her two sons were soon to have no existence. As the last vision she would see, before she drew her last breath, my insatiable, whoring vagina swallowing up her husband's penis; devouring its plunge to my cervix's depth, while the crocodiles, with their spectacular plunging rolls, consigned her fate to Sobek, the Nile god.*

*'I arranged my pillows to present myself in the Maiden position.*

*brutally ravage me, as if I were his innocent, virginal bride. Seeing my 'come, fornicate with me' gesture from her funeral barge surely sent irony's dagger into Zeporah's heart. And, surely, my smile as my mons pubis rose to welcome Moses' penis to my inner channel's lips caused her spirit to die its agonizing death; even before her body met its death from the crocodiles. Perhaps, by my gesture, she glimpsed her husband's future bliss as my devoted, ardent lover? Perhaps she would feel some measure of happiness for him? I wondered about her dying thoughts; but only for a moment.*

*'I will never know her last thoughts. I only heard her pleas and screams for mercy while Moses' eyes returned their gaze to me. His eyes devoured me. They drank in endless volumes of lust for me. He kissed my lapis tinted taupe eyelids; then peered into my eyes with a look of awe and wonder. His eyes communicated his thoughts. They told me how much he adored me while I earlier performed fellatio with the gigantic penis of a Nubian; how he empathized with my pleasure while I went about relieving the Nubian of his semen; how he became one with me as I licked the entire length of the tremendous shaft and kissed its head before I sucked and stroked it to incredible hardness. And his eyes captured the moment when I threw my head back in joyous exaltation while the Nubian ejaculated into my deliciously sinful mouth; and how he beheld my whoring in breathless adoration, smiling his approval as my crimson lips plied the Nubian shaft, relieving it of all vestiges of its semen.*

*'And I then smiled my sincerest love to Moses, for I knew from his eyes that he completely accepted me as the whore I am. In that moment we connected in the most profound way. Neither of us spoke a word but we knew that we had become as one, fully accepting the character and morals of the other. He would go on to give laws to his people and forge a nation. I would give full rein to my nymphomania without introspection, reconsideration, or guilt; and he would not only accept my immoral character, he would adore it. I now*

could prevent my butterfly morals from taking Moses from Zeporah. I signaled the court musicians to play a bridal tune on their flutes and harps. As the melodious notes from my accompaniment reached her doomed ears, I heard the distinct voice of Moses' wife. She screamed her hopeless plea openly:

"No! and No!" and "Oh Pharoah, beloved uncle, please make them stop. Please spare us! Please spare our lives! We beg you. Please. Please. Sob. Sob. Wail. Noooo!"

'Her pitiful wailings did not dissuade me from my intended conquest. They only stimulated me to be the most irresistible seductress my assembled audience had ever seen. As I became anxiously wet, In anticipation of my divine moment of consummation, I experienced a salutary effect; much like what a predator cat must sense when it knows its prey is cornered and helpless.

'I said to Moses: "Come to me, Moses. Behold your future wife. Make love with me."

'The crowd roared and cheered. They intuited that a consummation was about to take place which would change the course of history. And they wished to engage their spirts with mine and Moses;' and become a part of it. The music; my victim's screams; the rousing chants of the approving gathered crowd, were all giving me permission to devour Zeporah's life and make her husband mine.

'But of course, it would be left to the crocodiles to devour the flesh of Zeporah and her brood. I was only intent upon devouring her husband's heart and soul; and his divine penis. It was time to perform my seduction. I smiled warmly to Moses; spread my legs widely open for him; and motioned him with both my arms and hands to come lie with me. As I clearly signaled this intention to consummate my triumph, I heard Zeporah's piercing scream:

"NOOOO!"

'It came forcefully from the very depths of her lungs; discordant and futile, as if by her screaming she might somehow give Moses *pause and reflect; as if by the mere force of her will she could exert some power over his decision to lie with me.*

*'But her efforts failed. I merely widened my smile and formed a kiss with my lips, signaling him that it was time for him to leave his past and enter his future. He responded to my invitation and came forward, ignoring her deafening, horrified screams.*

*'His lips first touched my vagina's outer lips. He kissed them, reverently, as if he were about to worship all that is holy. And then his lips and tongue plied my inner lips, vibrating furiously, hungrily, causing my wetness to pour forth. And then he probed me deeply with his tongue. I felt his yearning searching; exploring me to discover my clitoris and to connect his soul with my own. It was a divine moment for both of us. I knew he sought to affirm my glorious sinfulness, as if to commune with me in my most intimate place of love; as if he sought to discover holiness in his own soul by acknowledging that I had coaxed many semen flows from many penises in this very passage where he sought to discover his own divine nirvana. I knew he was seeking to learn the true nature of his god within me, in union with my clitoris. He did not hurry himself on this mission. I was aware of his deliberate and thoughtful manner. As he was exploring my scented tastes and savoring my moisture, I came to understand that, for Moses, this was a more meaningful journey than any of his forays into foreign territories to do battle, and more than any of his excursions along the lengths of the Nile. This journey into the depths of my passions was his journey for his lifetime. He was uniting with his destiney.*

*'My mind now became connected with his mind. I could read his thoughts:*

*"Why must I not resist nor reject the forces that compel me to be here, with her, doing this, with her; pleasuring her this way; abandoning all pretenses that I can exist without her? Why? Why must I become beholden to her; this whore; this remarkable, splendid whore?*

"And as I taste her delicious pheromones and partake of her receptiveness, why do I welcome this burning sensation within my very soul? This searing lust I feel for her grows ever stronger within me. Ah, I feel myself being torn away from all I ever knew or believed. As my tongue now strokes loving touches along her clitoris, my mind tumbles ever deeper into an abyss that is a hundred times deeper than the heights commanded by the gods. I roll and revel in this whore's immoral debauchery, which welcomes and beholds me and accepts me as a pitiful mortal man with deeply mortal needs.

"I beheld her face when her partners ejaculated into her mouth. It became enlightened. It waxed joyfully effusive with delight at her conquest. And she did this so earnestly and enthusiastically, penis after penis; as if this were her very calling in life. I suppose it must be! Her immorality is as carefree as a butterfly's! Yes, as a butterfly that seeks to savor every flower; and suck its nectar from it; and take the life essence from every man she entertains. She is splendid and so accomplished in her craft! Her tongue is like an irresistible proboscis which pierces the very heart and guts of a man; and joyfully sucks away and devours whatever remnant moral fiber this man might have within me.

"Oh, and I do so much I welcome her doing this! Yes! To me! With me! I want this! I want her sinfulness to steal my very soul away from me. I want it to consume me! I wish to embrace it and love it and revel in it, for all eternity. I hear Zeporah's wailings and her screams. But I feel only numbness toward her. She is destined for the Nile while Baaleezebelle is destined or eternal life, her soul joined to mine. Zeporah's pleadings for her life and the lives of our sons only ring like lifeless stones in my ears. My mind refuses to hear her. It blocks her sounds away; shields my thoughts from any inklings of morality.

"My thoughts only chase my lusts deeper into the abyss that is Baaleezebelle's delicious sinfulness; and it is a shameless, wanton *sinfulness; and I do, so much, adore it, for it is the essence of her. And I know I have taken a fork in the road which I cannot and will not turn back from; nor ever turn away from; for I love her; only her; and I must have her.*

*"My loins swell from the building raging torrent I feel. I must conjugate this union with my eternal whore; and soon. I cannot bear to withhold myself from her. Denying her my semen would be to betray my soul and my trust in her love. Will this deed of consummation cause my soul to forever plunge ever deeper and more mindlessly into her endless abyss of immorality? Can I cope with what I will become? No; I cannot ask myself that question! My fate is cast! My loins tell me true. I must go where I must go. I cannot turn back! It's impossible to even think it! I cannot tear myself away from her. My soul has become one with hers! And I know love!*

*"But haven't I cast upon myself a dilemma which I shall never be able to reconcile? I will create on Earth a noble people who only worship one god, as Akhenaten envisioned. As his dutiful son and purposeful murderer, I will carry on his legacy for humanity and history. And the people I shall lead out of Egypt must never learn of this conflict which rages like a wild fire within me; that I, their leader, can never, myself, in truth worship their one god. My one true god shall always be the sacred whoring vagina of Baaleezebelle. My essence and the very fabric of my being will always be devoted to her; only to her. The people must never be told my most sacred secret truth. And in the laws which I shall create for them, they shall be forbidden to indulge in adultery, as I am doing now. May my one God understand that I am a mere mortal man. And if he exists, may he forgive my sin; and this woman; this sinful woman, whom I cannot deny, nor from her can I ever bear to be parted."*

*'Miss Lust, my clitoris could no longer hold back the joys it felt from Moses's tongue in those formative moments. Moses sought to taste the juices of my flavorful peach; and he would have them. He*

*brought forth my first orgasm into his mouth; and he savored and drank my loving flows. Then, he reclined and joined his body to mine. He took me into his arms and kissed me. And as his penis head first touched the outer lips of my holy of holies, I felt completed as an uninhibited, shameless, and wanton woman. I moaned, not in a whisper, but boldly and loudly:*

*"Mmmmm. Yes Moses. Yes, darling. Yes, my love. Ohhhh yessss! That's it! Fuck me. Ohhhh. Yessss. So good! You feel wonderful inside me. You belong inside me. Ahhh. Yessss! Mmmmmm. Mmmmmm. I love this. Mmmmmm. I love you, my prince. Come inside me. I want you to. Yes, come. See? I'm smiling. I'm so happy. Mmmmmm. Kiss me. Ah, that's it. So good! Hold me close. Come. Release inside me. I want you to come."*

*'In that moment, I lived the most delicious, exhilarating experience in all my lives. Moses' penis didn't lie. It was harder than a rod of steel. It was forceful, proud, strong; determined to have me; and eager to please me. It couldn't lie. It knew the truth. It loved me; only me. And it wanted me and who I was. As our lips met and our tongues touched, my pelvis responded enthusiastically while his penis deepened its seeking thrusts. Moses' love for me was complete.*

*'I did feel a twinge of sorrow for his family's fate; but Ra had told me they were not to be my concern; that, like all of us, their spirit souls would reincarnate into new lives. I have always believed Ra. He has wisdom that has lived for billions of years. I knew my feelings for those I displaced from Moses' life would be mere transitory feelings. As I embraced Moses and led him down onto my bed to have his penis plunge my deepest depths, I assured myself that I was acting in concordance with my gods, as an obedient, virtuously religious, and glorious woman.*

*'And I then had my prophetic revelation, that my pornographic performances were having a salutary and cleansing effect upon the gathered crowd. I intuited that my pornography and my seduction of*

*Moses were in no way immoral; not by my gods or the compass which set my soul's course. I was a catalyst for change and progress! I perceived that my soul would reincarnate and journey forward through time; and in all my future lives I would champion pornography and seductive whoring as a vital, necessary ingredient which enables change and human progress. I, in that moment, became a force for divine human goodness and glory. And I was pleased with myself.*

*'I believe Moses, not saying a word, agreed with my inner assessment of myself and my soul's divine purpose; and, in that moment, accepted me, completely and without any reservation, as his eternal soul mate. After he turned away from his family and joined me on my bridal altar, he kissed me. He then withdrew his penis from my vagina; to first worship my whoring ribaldry with his mouth. He then, slowly, and sensuously performed the most enraptured cunnilingus that I have ever experienced.*

*'That's when I realized that Moses was adopting the faith and practices of us Hebrews. I had often observed him when he served as a lay helper to Egypt's priests. He worked among the altar keepers. He assisted while, upon the huge white alabaster altar slab, the priests sacrificed the cattle, sheep, goats, and birds to their various gods. Moses assisted as the priests disemboweled their sacrificial animals and decapitated them. Then, he was among the helpers who assiduously cleaned the altar for the next sacrificial ceremony. I saw how he toiled to scrub clean all traces of blood from the slab and its drain gutters. Moses was preparing me! Cleaning me to become holy for his worship! He intended to clean my vagina in an analogous way to how he cleaned Egypt's holy altar! Only I was not a lifeless slab of alabaster; nor was I an ordinary Egyptian woman. Moses knew Hebrew men used oral sex to prepare their women for conjugation.*

*'Moses was honoring me! He wished to tell me by his actions that he wished to adopt Hebrew ways. He wished to clean my vagina as he had cleaned the sacrificial altars. I was being made holy for*

his ultimate sacrifice! After cleaning me of all vestiges of semen from the bulls and my other lovers, Moses would have me ready for copulation. I would be again in my purest state, like a cleansed altar! After I had been thoroughly cleansed and made ready for copulation, Moses would enter my vagina with his penis. Then, to sanctify our conjugation, our joining together in worship, our uniting of our souls, Moses would ejaculate inside me and fill me with his semen. And that ejaculation would be his sacred offering to me, his new god, into my holy of holies! An evisceration of sorts would take place. It would not be the gutting of an animal's entrails; but a sacrifice even more special. It would be the giving up of his spirit soul through his ejaculated semen stream into me; joining his soul to mine. Spilling his life essence into me, we would become as one soul; soulmates forever. Moses had not yet been circumcised as other Hebrew men were. I knew that.

'But he was about to take the first major step in his conversion journey. I intuited that, after he led the Hebrews out of Egypt, Moses would be circumcised with an obsidian blade in his bris ceremony, performed by a skilled Mok. After a couple days, he would heal. And then, with his circumcised penis, our sex would be the most pleasurable imaginable! And he was doing all of this for me! While he performed his divine oral sex tribute to my whoring and pornography, I suddenly received this sensation of euphoric bliss. It was confirmation of my victorious seduction.

'It was the spirits' approval; nay, it was their championing me; my whoring; my pornography! It sweep over me like the enduring, unstoppable, onrushing flood from the Nile. I, and my insatiable wantonness were never to be denied. Humanity needs the cleansing change that pornography contributes to its advancing civilization. I was confident in my vision. Pornography was destined to become a permanent fixture of the human experience; not to be shunned or rejected; but to be welcomed and embraced by a rejoicing humankind, like the salutary flood waters of the Nile! In a profoundly real sense, Moses was preparing my vagina for worship by his penis. I was soon to become Moses' god on Earth!

'While my clitoris basked in the loving strokes of Moses' tongue, I turned my eyes to the Nile. I watched dispassionately while one large reptile gripped Zeporah's head in its mighty jaws and another clamped its jaws about her torso. As if performing a ballet, the reptiles rolled in opposite directions. In my sublime state of cunnilingus, my relaxed, pleasure mind had the most demoniacal and amused thought. Had the crocodiles decided to play their part in my pleasuring? It appeared so! They were about to entertain me!

'Their time perfected rolling maneuver ripped Zeporah's head away from her body. A huge croc's head emerged from below the surface. It's jaws rose high in the afternoon sun, holding Zeporah's head firmly in place in its mighty jaws. As the croc looked at me, as if to gain my appreciation for its might and control, its frightful jaws closed down upon Zeporah's head. I heard the cracking of Zeporah's skull into perhaps a dozen fragments before it disappeared down the gullet of the insatiable green beast. Her head had offered no more resistance than the shell of a bird's egg. Her head was mere child's play for the croc. I then heard Zeporah's sons scream their terrified, futile, piercing screams while they were torn from limb to limb, and devoured by the crocodiles. The boys futilely fought their fate while the crocodiles casually ripped their limbs from their bodies. Their horrified, water choked, desperate cries pleasured my ears. I steeled myself from their horror. I imagined the two boys were not really human beings; but mere Kamatz crumbs; snacks for the crocs. Their lives were not my concern. They were useless to me and of no further use to Moses. They were used up parts of his past life; and now, I comforted myself, they were simply being swept out of my life.

'My amygdala gland began pulsing out joyous hormone secretion spurts; one after the other. My spirits soared to higher and higher heights as the crocodiles rolled and dragged their victims deeper and deeper into the Nile's abyss. My own reptilian gland joined in league with the crocodiles.' I was much like them, then; mentally joined to them; championing them and in league with them; hearing their jaws crunching skulls and bones; feeling the passion of their feeding lust in my loins and loving the finality of it. My amygdala gland became one with their glands. I felt the wildly stimulative sensation. Murder! Yes. Sweet murder! It pleased me. I knew then that my capacity for evil was boundless and eternal. I smiled to my crocodile friends and wished them enjoyment of their magnificent orgy of human carnage and tastes of my rivals' flesh.

'It was an ethereal moment. I had become one of them! Reptilian with Butterfly Morals! Casual destroyer of all things moral! And my reptile friends were worshipping me! Their uncaring human dismemberments and death rolls were glorious tributes to my divinely rapacious whoring. The crocodiles were no longer merely devouring human flesh. They were honoring me; and paying homage to my newly acclaimed status: Supreme whore of all Egypt! And now, wife of First Prince Moses! The crocodiles and I had cleansed Moses of his past life; put it to rest; consigned it to eternity. Oh, I suspected the chroniclers of these events would sugar coat them for future generations; but I didn't care. Moses and I were opening our new pathway; freeing ourselves and our consciences to enjoy our newfound conjugal love. My attentions next turned to his divine, princely penis.

'After my exhilarating, glorious, orgasm from Moses' cunnilingus, I took his penis into my hand and lovingly guided it, once again, into my love channel. As I felt Moses's penis plunging ever deeper into my vaginal depths, I heard the crowds cheering my performance and shouting their hurrahs. With the First Prince of Egypt entwined in my arms, I reached another explosive climax. And then, while his penis was inside me, pleasuring me, I moaned aloud:

"Mmmmm. Mmmmm. Yes! Yes! Fuck me, Moses. Yes! Yes, my love! Ohhh! You feel so good inside me! Fuck me. Oh yes; fuck me beautifully. That's it! So wonderful. So beautiful! Please, come for me. Yes, I want you to. Ohhh. My love. Ohhhh. That's it! I can feel you coming now. Ohhhh. So warm. So beautiful! Your hot cum feels so wonderful. Mmmmm. Keep coming. Hold me close, Moses. I am your life, now. Give me all your semen. Yes, Moses. I want all of you inside me, my love. Mmmmm. Yes. Yes. Keep coming. Keep coming into me. Yes, that's it. Mmmmmm. My dearest, sweetest love. I love you."

'As Moses released his semen into me, I drew my deepest breath. My life was being renewed. I had become Egypt! We were together as one, experiencing the sacred highlight moment of the fertility ritual, as one being, joined in our copulation. In that breathtaking, wondrous, climactic moment, I knew Moses and I were joined in our love and our love of humanity, for all eternity.

'While I then continued fornicating with Moses in every position imaginable; and as he shamelessly pleasured me before our adoring crowd, I glimpsed my future lives as a profligately immoral porn star. I realized that the crowds loved my ribaldry; that they adored my intimate sensuality as well as my boldly uninhibited, calloused displacement of his wife. The crocodiles, somehow, were also aware of this transference of power that was taking place. They had gladly played their part in my pagan fertility rite. My amygdala had resonated with theirs while they feasted on my rivals. I silently cheered for those magnificent Nile beasts. They were my allied change agents; enablers of my glorious, unapologetic, wanton whoring; enabling the mind of Moses to wash away his old life and become a more fertile mind, much as the Nile made Egypt's lands become more fertile.

'I then guided Moses' magnificent head to my thighs. I cradled it there, gently rocking it from side to side while blocking all sounds from reaching his ears. Preventing him from hearing his family's frantic death screams empowered me. But perversely, the screams helped me. They stimulated me to release multiple orgasms. I became enraptured! I was the arbiter of life and death! I enjoyed those thrilling moments; captured them in my mind and remembered them forever. While I nestled Moses' face against my mons pubis, those cries and wailing stimulated me to heights I had never reached before. I had the most glorious orgasms I have ever had. And I, alone, had Moses. I had his tongue, his penis, and his soul. And every part of him adored me. Yes! Such wonders I knew! Even his idealistic soul loved my immoral soul. It loved everything about me; obsessively loved my immoral whoring ways; my lovemaking; my face, eyes, and body; my tastes; my juices; all of me. Moses was my lover now, and forever. Mine! I thrust my mons pubis hard against his mouth while holding his beautiful head in my hands; pulling his face and his glorious mouth and tongue ever more tightly into my vagina.

'Then, with his neck bent low, so that his tongue could reach its fullest extent over my clitoris, I released a trickle flood of fresh orgasmic fluids. Those fluids coursed over Moses's tongue as the Nile was flooding over the remnant body parts of Zeporah and her sons. My orgasm sent joyous trembles through my entire body. I became delirious with joy. My flow crescendo burst containment. I gushed and pulsed wildly; then flowed freely. I shouted:

"Oh Moses! Moses, my love, I'm coming. He... He... He.! How beautiful! Ooooh. I love you, my prince." I took a deep breath "Ahhh! So, goood! I feel soooo wonderful! I love making love with you. Mmmmmm."

'The crowd cheered. They shouted their hurrah's and whistled and clapped. Many surged forwards, trying to reach my dais; tossing flowers and gold and silver coins to me, and trying desperately to touch me and kiss my body anywhere they could. But Pharoah's soldiers held them back. Their enthusiasm caused me to think about the effect my pornography was having on them.

'An inspiring insight revealed itself. The crowd gave no thought or care to Zeporah or her boys. They were forward looking. They only cared about me and my pleasures. Suddenly, I understood why that was. They identified with me as a fallen woman; a profligate, shameless, immoral sinner. Yet, they saw that Moses loved me. He chose me; not Zeporah. And he was entwined in my arms and legs, loving me; worshipping me. Me! Me; the casual, shameless, divinely sinful whore; the porn star who coaxed semen from the Apis bulls; the living representative of Sopdet, their supreme arbiter of life and death.

'A profound truth struck me. In the depths of their souls everyone assembled to watch my pornography knew that they, too, were imperfect humans. They, too, sinned. They lied, cheated, stole, fornicated with partners outside their marriages; and even, in some cases, murdered others. And here they all were, gathered together to witness an immoral woman performing salacious pornography for their pleasured viewing. By my copulations and fellatios, I was letting them know that I accepted their immorality; and that I, like them, was also immoral; completely shamelessly immoral. And this multitude of sinners wished to give thanks to me for acknowledging by my performance, the simple truth that their immorality was acceptable because we are all human. They saw me as their liberator, their savior from guilt and punishment for their sins. And in their gratitude, they sought to give me offerings and they wished to worship me. They sought to make me their living god!

'That's when I had my divine revelation: Pornography was a kind of psychological balm for the masses. It gave people an inner strength to accept themselves as imperfect beings and, regardless, to love each other. I saw humanity's future then. I knew the demand for prostitution and pornography would only increase from that moment until the end of time, because it accepted the human condition and cleansed human souls of guilt. This need to accept and go forward with life was why Jen's endeavor, five thousand years in *the future, would be so wildly successful. Her Inferno Clubs with her carefully chosen jurisdictions and her underaged girls would make her already fabulous wealth even greater. I, a Pagan whore, understood what Jen understood. People love their immoral women and their porn stars. That love is why many will purchase all nine hundred films of their favorite porn star. It's why many will join a porn star's premium service and pay a fortune to sleep with her. And why many will not hesitate to shell out a thousand dollars for her autograph on a glossy photo of her, naked or performing with a penis. There is no art form which better captures human joy than a woman experiencing an orgasm. And people pay to experience that intimate artistry.*

*'In that moment I foresaw all my future lives. I felt joyful exhilaration. But my thoughts returned to the present. I knew Moses and I were not finished. I continued to spasm while Moses' tongue ravished me. I moaned with pleasure, savoring my triumph long after the crocodiles had completely gorged their bellies.*

*'After the feeding frenzy had finally ended, a tranquil peace descended over me and the Nile. And Moses was taking his time, savoring his new wife's favors. He continued plying my clitoris with his fully extended tongue. I shuddered repeatedly from my ecstasy and moaned softly:*

*"Mmmmmm. Moses, you're so good to me."*

*'I had become almost too sensitized to continue with our otherworldly pleasure fest. But I knew Moses loved the pleasures he was intently lavishing upon me; so, I did not pull away. Besides, I wanted him to continue; imprinting my tastes upon his senses and his mind; making my intimacy an integral part of him. I repeatedly said:*

*"Oh Baby, my dear sweet love," while I lived the most sublime pleasuring I'd ever known in my entire life.*

*'Intimacy flowed from Moses' soul and amygdala through his tongue; seeking me, yearning for my soul to bind with his, and*

*connecting our intimacy through my clitoris and my soul. As Moses' tongue communicated his soul's undying love and devotion, my clitoris swelled to bask in the tender, loving offerings from its new, eternal pleasure slave. From his enraptured tongue, my clitoris transported his soul to my amygdala. My own soul embraced his with open arms. I was immensely proud of him. He knew what he had to have. And he had demonstrated manly courage to take what he needed; me. Nothing; no one could deter him from reshaping his life and humanity's destiny.*

*'No mortal woman could ever separate his love from me; not after that day. Our spirit souls were finally home and free to love; free of all things and people who had gone before us. I gorged my insatiable lust. I defined morality on my own terms. From this life onward, I viewed morality as a social construct to be understood and used in my dealings with others; but not as a sensible guide for my own actions. I was pleased with myself; satisfied with all I had done that day. Separating Moses from his family was decisive, quick, and final. It was Ra's way. And the best way.*

*'Sun God Ra saw this joining of our two souls and beamed down his countenance upon us. A beautiful male Monarch butterfly fluttered above us, as if to tell us that what we had done was blessed by the Great Spirit of All Living Things. Blessed because we had heard the call of nature and joined humanity's morality with the butterflies' morality; and in so doing, we moved humanity forward.*

*'This divine moment opened the heavens for me. I understood that heaven was within me. It is not some mythical, abstract place. I understood that all the thinkers, prophets, and scientists who would follow us in years to come, had the wrong concept of eternity. Eternity is not some mathematical construct created by a genius physicist. No, it isn't. I, alone, define eternity. Eternity is within me. Eternity is the orifice within my cervix; that passageway through which life's first seeds are sent; and from which life enters the world. Eternity*

and heaven is this never-ending cycle of copulation and reproduction. This cycle, this heaven, has sanctified my triumphant whoring.

'And, that same divine moment made me realize that there is no such being as God. There is only life. Life is the eternal being. Human life must be our God; and we must celebrate life and the creation process of life. Creation arises from and replaces death; and creation is to be celebrated and worshipped. The rising of the sun; the flooding of the Nile; and my fertility copulation rites are all pleasurable happenings which presage new life; and all are beautiful to behold. My pornography glorifies artistry's pinnacle glory-praise of human copulation. Thus, it is a vital artistic form of creation worship. It thus becomes my duty to perform my artistry in this life and in all my future lives; and to constantly perfect and better it. And if, through my unapologetic whoring, I, a glorious, unrepentant, immoral porn star should displace a traditional family, I must not concern myself, for I am merely a human woman with human desires. And my desires are rooted in the natural order process of human life.

'Zeporah, the wife of Moses, became my victim in that life. She was only one of my many victims in my past and future lives. Before my spirit soul became incarnate in the flesh of Sara, Bathsheba, Salome, Cleopatra, or Isabella; before my seductions of my first Pharoah and his princes, or of Darren, Marshawn, George and Bertie, Dominick, and so many others, my human yearning to fornicate became manifest within me. I understood that I, a human woman, was not like the other animals. I understood that I did not need to come into 'heat' to feel the urge to fornicate. That understanding; that realization that I could seek pleasure through fornication without becoming pregnant and without consigning myself to a lifetime of child rearing was my enlightenment. It was my bite of the apple from the forbidden biblical Tree of Knowledge. Realizing this; that I was naturally given the power to choose my way in life, my purpose *as a catalyst for humanity's progress became clear. I felt a sudden burst of warmth caress me. It was Sun God, Ra, showering me with his blessings; assuring me; confirming that urges and my conquest of Moses and destruction of Zeporah was holy, natural, and right; that I personified natural destruction and creation; that I made the way clear for the creation of new life and new ideas. Torah scrolls neglect to mention my divine intimacy with Moses; or my creative destruction of Zeporah. So be it. But without performing those gloriously, immoral, pornographic deeds, which I performed over that sacred Egyptian fortnight, I believe the Torah would have never been written.*

*'I soon forgot Zeporah and her children. My continuous orgasm had that salutary effect. Moses and I were finally free to love and to be in love; and to pursue our passions above all worldly cares. We became free spirited lovers weeks before leaving Egypt. Our famous exodus came later. Whenever I made love with Moses, everything about our love making was natural and uninhibited. It was as if Zeporah and her sons had never existed.*

*'And in a religious and historical context, they may as well have never existed. They were merely obstacles that blocked Moses' path to destiny. I, and my insatiably immoral vagina, succeeded as nature preordained. Vagina and I, thanks to our incorrigible wantonness, brushed Moses' detractors away from his enlightened path; whisked them away like so many pesky Kamatz crumbs; vanquished them from our lives. I felt good, wholesome, and justified to be rid of them. I loved my own sexuality. I knew Vag and I did a beautiful thing. I radiated warmth and confidence in the certain rightness of my whoring. Thereafter, whenever I tenderly held Moses between my arms and legs, shamelessly making love with him, I knew I was doing humanity's greatest work.*

*'As my orgasm flowed on that transformative day, I knew Moses would again soon mount me. I intuited that I would soon feel his*

*body on top of mine, pressed hard against me. Certainly, I would soon feel his marvelous penis swelling up within me; then retracting ever so slightly before it pulsed and thrusted forward, shooting more massive semen streams through my cervical opening. Moses was a strong, handsome, and passionate, romantic man. He loved lovemaking. I knew he would often fill me with his essence. I also knew my Acacia paste would keep me safe from unwanted pregnancy. I wanted to enjoy the pleasures of our endless love making; but not bear and rear a clutch of his children; at least not yet. Josuah would have to wait until after Mount Sinai; until long after I had my fill of pleasures. After all, in all my lives, I have always been first, a consummate, shameless, and unapologetic whore.*

*'I warmed to the thought that, after he ejaculated into my vagina that first time, Moses would long lie by my side. He would hold me close to him and caress me; grateful to me for his new life. He would tenderly kiss my lips, stare longingly into my eyes, and behold the wonders of my femininity. I would complete him and become his world. And he would playfully pinch my nipples, kiss them, lick, and tongue-tease them. And I would return his kisses. My lips would join his; my tongue would meet his and play joyfully and lovingly with his tongue inside his mouth, while my fingers tenderly caressed his face and lovingly fondled his penis and testicles. We did all those things. We confirmed to each other that my nympho disease state was our mutual, glorious blessing; and that we would always appreciate my natural sexual cravings. We became ardent lovers that afternoon in the sun. And our lovemaking was good and glorious and wholesome. Our love transcended all considerations of whether my plot to dispatch Zeporah was moral or immoral. Those considerations no longer mattered. She was gone and Moses was mine. My mind became completely guiltless and free to enjoy my orgasms without any feelings of shame or regret.*

'I only heard occasional, lazy splashes from the Nile. Hearing them, I realized the crocodiles were thanking me and amusing my mind in their own shameless way. I adored those unapologetic reptiles. I admired their efficiency; and I smiled a contented smile, thinking of their full bellies. Moses also heard their orderly, unhurried splashes. He kissed me passionately, then. He knew what those languid splashes meant. The crocodiles had filled their bellies with his past. And the crocodiles were departing.

'I will forever remember Moses's eyes when they next looked deeply into mine. I knew I represented new life to him; and that our new lives needed to move on. I've never seen any man's eyes more beholden to me than those eyes. I knew then that Moses wanted to unburden himself from everything that once was, and of all things that came before me and my glorious, insatiable, fuck loving, whoring vagina; so that he could have his freedom to enjoy me and our new life together. I knew then that Moses was my destiny.'

'How did you know that?' Miss Lust sought to understand the mind of her mirror's soul.

'He was Prince of Egypt, Pharoah's son. He could do as he pleased. He could have whatever he wanted. And he wanted me.'

'Why you? Why do you think Moses wanted you for his woman? Why do you think he fell in love with you?

'During my pornographic performances, I noticed how he looked at me; how his eyes kept coming back to me. His eyes revealed him to me. They kept looking into my eyes. That's when I first thought that maybe it wasn't because of my appearance; you know; not because of my voluptuous body and smooth white skin; or my make-up, or the breathtakingly erotic pornographic acts I was performing.

'I could read his mind. It was telling me something else. I saw his eyes noticing how my body oils glistened in the moonlight. I began to see his thoughts. He was starting to believe I had been sent to him from above, from Sopdet the fertility goddess. And I caught his eyes *while they fixated on my lips, and my concavity. He was thinking my lips were his passage to a heavenly, other worldly realm. His mind was already nuzzling my concavity, searching for my outer vaginal lips; seeking to enter me with his tongue.*

*'He could not know, and I have never since told him, that the lips of my mouth had already whispered my wishes for Zeporah's fate into Pharoah's ear; and that I had thusly sealed her death passage into Sobek's underworld. While my eyes flirted with Moses, I had no doubt that Pharoah would consign Zeporah and her sons to the crocodiles.*

*'My intuition was correct about whispering my wishes to Pharoah. Pharoah loved consorting with me. He adored my vagina and the many ways I performed my sexual favors with him. He often told me that my vagina delighted him more than any others.' He loved exploring it with his tongue. He knew I would delight him with my appreciations of his favor. He believed his favorite whore should be accommodated.*

*'So, you see, when Moses first joined his lips to mine, he could only hope in the possibility that he could somehow passage from the dullness of his present life into my world of erotic enchantment. He didn't know that I had already arranged Zeporah's death; that I had already made his passage into my world of never ending, erotic romance possible.*

*'I knew Moses wanted me. A woman knows these things. Without him saying it, I knew what Moses wanted. He wanted freedom and he wanted me. He wanted a life with me. I knew I would be his delicious life-giving fruit, already made attainable by my promised inducements to Pharoah. And I knew Moses needed me, his glorious porn star whore. I knew he needed Zeporah to leave his life and depart with Sobek.*

*'So, I made it possible for Moses to change the world. I gave that gift of change to him. My gift was myself. And he appreciated my*

*gift. And when we embraced and his lips finally joined with mine, his penis entered me, completing my gift, while Sobek, God of Death, took Zeporah away from us, forever. Moses and I shared that beautiful moment. While we made our first passionate, intimate love; while his mouth and tongue lavished their desires upon and into my vagina, our enhanced erotic pleasures were enhanced by our beautiful shared vision. My juices began flooding his mouth as the Nile began flooding Egypt. And our ears heard what our eyes could not see: Zeporah's limbs being torn away from her torso and devoured by the crocodiles. We chortled our belly laughs, amused at her misfortune. Our lips met again; this time with an intensity of our passion and blood lust, as my hands guided his penis head to its first touches of my inner vaginal lips. Slowly, steadily, and with sincere determination to please me as he had never pleased any woman before me, Moses' penis penetrated me; then gradually, lovingly, plunged deeper into me for that first breathtaking time of our many, countless times. I, Baaleezebelle, most consummately immoral, shamelessly incorrigible whore in all of Egypt had taken Crown Prince Moses as my lover. As I felt his penis plunge and explore the deepest recesses of my vagina; and as I felt his shaft coursing lovingly over my clitoris; sensitive to my erotic mood and desire, I knew from that moment onward, that Moses loved only me; and that Zeporah could never interfere with our love.*

*'And, she could never distract Moses from his calling or his great work. After that day and for many weeks afterward, whenever I performed fellatio with Moses, I silently thanked Sopdet, my Goddess of brilliance and fertility, and Ra, my God of warmth and life; and I thanked my God, Sobek, for his unceasing devotion to cleanse the world of what once had been. I especially thanked my Gods for my inviting lips; how their coquettish, beguiling smiles first beckoned Moses to approach me. I thanked my Gods that Moses' penis adored the sensuous ways my experienced lips lavished their loving fellatio*

strokes over his yearning penis. And I thanked them for placing into my beguiling, promising lips those seductive words they whispered into Pharoah's ear; those convincing entreaties which convinced him to consign Zeporah and her two brats to the papyrus role of those marked for death.

'And I especially thanked my Gods for sending me my harem mother who taught me how to use my lips and tongue to pleasure a man's penis and his testicles. And I thanked Sopdet for my full, firm breasts and my cherry nipple buds which made men lust after me and that I was not breast fallen like Zeporah. I thanked her for the soft, slippery wetness of my vagina; and that I was not dry, like Zeporah's sandy portal. And I thanked Sopdet that I was born a superior Egyptian, with my smooth, lily white, creamy skin; and that I was not born an inferior woman, like Zeporah, of Egypt's subservient Midian vassal state, with her coarse, sun damaged skin.

'And I thanked Sopdet for making me an unabashedly, shamelessly promiscuous femme fatale, desired by men and skilled in the harem arts of seduction; and especially for endowing me with my insatiable yearning to wantonly copulate and perform my delicious, inspiring pornography. And I thanked both my Gods for opening Moses' eyes to me; for bringing Moses to me; for connecting my lips to his lips; and, through our married lips, also marrying our souls together. You see, Miss Lust, whenever Moses and I kissed, we shared our divine mental telepathy. It was beautiful. And in those moments, my heart could feel his heart.'

'Feel his heart?'

'Yes. I could feel Moses' heart come join with my heart, wrap its arms around my heart; and then kiss my heart. His heart adored mine. It embraced mine. It loved mine completely and unconditionally. And it loved me because I loved myself; and because I felt no guilt about who I was; and no inhibition about performing my pornography. He loved all of me, for the unapologetic whore that is the true me. My heart understood what was happening. It beat more rapidly and more warmly. It seemed as if my heart was singing joyfully because it knew Moses loved me. It knew he loved me for who and what I was. Even though I was, have been, and always will be a sex addicted nymphomaniac, Moses understood that about me. And he loved me! My heart knew he wanted me to be his woman and to be with him, always. It just knew. Especially during those times while I was performing porn with two other men, my heart was certain that Moses loved me, all of me; everything about me, especially my incurable addiction. Moses believed my addiction was beautiful. He adored it. He loved me for expressing it in my pornography. Whenever I think about his unrequited devotion to me, this warm flood comes over me. And it never leaves me. During the many travails of our future journey through the desert, my feeling of being loved was always there. It was my constant source of faith. I have never been happier in all my lives.

'That's when I realized that a man can love a woman who is a completely unrepentant, shameless whore, who joyfully performs pornography and who loves performing her pornography because he understands that woman is completely okay with herself. He knows she is happy with herself and who she is; confident; secure in her quest for endless pleasure and sexual variety in the men she enjoys; and in the many experiences she has with them. She is free of any inhibiting neurosis; free from second guessing who she is or what she wants from life; unafraid to display her sexuality to the world, and most of all, to herself. That woman loves herself. And that woman was me. Moses saw that in me. His heart and soul saw that in me. And I am exactly what he wanted. I was the woman he wanted because he saw that I loved myself.'

'You loved yourself?'

'Yes. Totally. And Moses saw that I loved being a whore; that I had no illusions about who or what I was; and that I loved myself for being what I was. Like, I was totally into my whoring. I loved all the sex I had with all my different partners and I loved all the fellatio I performed; totally loved doing all of it; total enjoyed it and immersed myself in it. Moses needed a woman who was completely happy with whom she was. I saw that he loved me because he saw I loved me. He joined me in my love of me. He saw, through my eyes, that I would love him back, unconditionally, for loving me in this way.'

'And he was okay with you performing porn with your partners?'

'More than totally okay. You need to remember, Miss Lust, this was thousands of years before the Pilgrims first set foot in America. In ancient Egypt, whoring and pornography were glorious, highly respected, and honored professions. Moses adored me while I performed porn. Moses appreciated pornography. He loved the creative aspects of it. He understood it correctly, as the divine art form that it is. He loved the liberating inspiration it gave him. And he loved its expressive, intimate beauty. He loved watching me perform my porn. He never missed a single performance. He practically worshipped me and my performances.'

'Yet, he wanted no one to distract him from his lovemaking with you?'

'Oh yes, I remember. No others; absolutely no one else! He would get very possessive, especially after we became married; while Zeporah's body was being torn asunder during the Death ceremony of Sobek. I know that sounds contradictory to his adoration of my pornography, but Moses was a very complicated man. There was his duality.'

'Duality?'

'Well, yes. In his personal life, he often told me that I and my vagina were his true God; the only thing that he could worship and believe in. I heard him tell me thousands of tines that he loved me and worshipped me and my vagina.'

'He worshipped your pussy?'

'Yes. He told me that he did. He obsessed over it. He whispered to it how beautiful it was and how lovely it was and how much he adored it, every time he performed cunnilingus with me; and he did that practically every day, sometimes two or three times daily, except when I was mensurating.'

'Every day?'

'Yes. He was a man's man. Unafraid. Determined to please me. He wouldn't stop this obsession.'

'Even after you had walked miles in the desert?'

'Yes. Even then. Nothing held him back. It didn't matter if I was sweaty, salty, smelly. He just wanted that close intimacy. Just went right past everything to get inside me and please me. Many times, I never bothered to freshen up.'

'I wonder what drove his obsession?'

'We talked about it a few times. He said he believed the true pathway to eternity was through the small orifice in my cervix. He often had me spread myself open in the sunlight so he could look at it.'

'The donut hole?'

'Yes. We didn't have donuts in the Sinai. But he thought that tiny hole was the true pathway into eternity. I think he was conceptually onto something. He often told me that life is eternal. And that passageway through the cervix is the only path humanity can take to perpetuate life. I think that's why he was so enamored with my Vag; why he worshipped it; why he called it his true God. His God; but everyone else was supposed to believe in the God he created for them.'

'Using the stone tablets for his prop?'

'Right. For them; but not for him. He worshipped between my legs. That was his duality. He even wrote love poems to my vagina and psalms about it which referred to God, when he was actually smitten by my Vag.'

'But how do you explain Mount Sinai and the Ten Commandments? What was the need for all that? Was he schizophrenic?'

'No, not schizophrenic. I said he had a duality. He was mindful and purposeful. He wanted all the other people to believe in this artificial God he created. He used his Ten Commandment Tablets as his prop for that; his sales pitch. He wanted everyone to believe in that God and that God's commandments about adultery and coveting, so he could keep me and my Vag all to himself.'

'Carnal obsession. All about the Vag?'

'Yes, absolutely. He knew my nympho tendencies would never go away. He was smitten by me because he believed that I was a divine instrument of nature, a creation nymph of the Great Spirit who instigated human change. He thought I was sent by the spirits to do their work among humankind.

'But he also knew the other men also adored my pornography. They had seen my performances at the fertility rites. He knew how they lusted after me. So, Moses needed to create a way to keep me and those men separated. His God and the second set of stone tablets with their new commandments about adultery and coveting gave him the authority he needed to keep me all to himself.'

'Duality and duplicitous behavior. Obsessive, manipulative, and contradictory.'

'Yes. Very. And his contradictory behavior was unfortunate for the sons of Aaron. He became furious and they paid a terrible price for having me.

'But Moses never blamed me for that. He loved me unconditionally. I think he loved me especially because I was nympho porn star. Unfortunately, he wanted me all to himself. As time went on, he became very possessive. When we were being intimate, he shut out the entire world. He had this uncanny ability to concentrate and focus. When his limbic mind got like that, I became his entire world. He made me uncomfortable with his possessiveness because the *whole purpose of the fortnight of Pagan fertility rites was for all of us to love one another; to freely fornicate with each other; immerse ourselves in our joys and sexual pleasures, and to create new lives.*

*'But Moses wanted the Tribe to depart from our natural ways and our time-honored custom of communal lovemaking. His possessiveness was the strangest aspect of his behavior. He became obsessed over me because of my whoring. He adored my whoring. It made him see me as his Goddess. He became a slave to my vagina and my whoring. He always spoke adoringly, softly, and sweetly towards me; like I was his love child. He could bark out commands and instructions to all the others; but never did he raise his voice to me. He called me by the most endearing terms, such as: Sweetness; baby face; sweet cakes; love of my life; my everything; my eternal love; and my passion. And, now that he had me; and after professing to love me forever and without any reservation whatsoever for being the whore and porn star that I was, he wanted me, from then onward, to only have relations with him. He wanted all the others, men, and women, to stay away from me. He wanted me all to himself.'*

*'So, the foundation of the three major western religions was based on one man's possessiveness, lust, and domineering tendencies?'*

*'Yes, I think that's true. Consider that all three religions will kill those who oppose their belief system; and all three seek to expand their market share by proselytizing and forced conversions.'*

*'Christians and Muslims do that. But Jews don't.'*

*'Oh yes, they do. Think interfaith marriages. Think adoptions. Queen Isabella just dealt the Jews a huge setback with her Inquisition. They have the smallest market share of religious believers, currently. The other religions are afraid of the Jews because of all three illogical beliefs; Judaism is the least illogical.'*

*'And you, I mean we, don't believe in any of them?'*

*'No. We'd need to be believers to join. It's natural for a crowd to want joiners. It's the group insanity effect.'*

'But since we don't believe, we don't join.'

'Right, Miss Lust. We don't; so, we don't. Ra told me I needed to think things through logically and understand them'

'Okay. Can you remember Ra's other words of wisdom for you?'

'Yes. Ra told me that in all my future lives, I need to consider myself as the goddess of the natural order of things. I am not to be dissuaded by the teachings and preachings of proponents of imaginary Gods. I am to promote and advocate for atheism and the tearing down of established social orders. I am to actively seek out those who are stressed with life's burdens and co-opt them to my natural, promiscuous ways. I am to use my charms and my talents for whoring and performing pornography to tear asunder the fabric of ordered societies. I am to intentionally target and destroy marital and familial bonds; separate husbands from wives; trample traditional values and thoughts; upend established orders. I am the original communist, long before Marx and Engles. And I am to be unashamed and proud of all those immoral things that I am to do in all my future lives; proud of my whoring; proud of my pornography. Ra said that new lives and new beginnings can only come from change; and that I am to be a destroyer; a change agent. And that all change, especially change caused by immorality, moves humanity forward. And change is desired and good.'

## THE 'V' COMMANDMENTS

Right. And you believed Ra. So, later, when you were with Moses and Moses first went up on Mount Sinai and left you down below, you reverted to your old ways; the ways Ra prescribed for you, didn't you?'

'Yes, of course I did. I was, again, a societal change agent. I was happily fornicating with ten different men; all of them taking turns with me. I couldn't help myself. My love of whoring and orgies had *never left me. My nymphomania had always been there, right below the surface of my everyday life. And when Moses went up Mount Sinai and left me alone without him, my nymphomania simply overwhelmed me. The other men had seen me at Pharoah's fertility ceremony. They knew how promiscuous I was. Their eyes caught mine. They didn't need to say a word. I knew how badly they wanted me. And, I couldn't decline to accommodate them. I wanted to hold and kiss their penises. I wanted to copulate with all of them. We all knew Moses would be gone for several days. And the men knew, as well as I did, that I loved having a variety of lovers. I simply had these urges to copulate with other men. So, one by one, I opened my arms and legs to welcome them. And, once I started having intercourse with the other men, I simply could not stop. I was putting on a glorious pornographic display. This went on for several days. I thoroughly loved what I was doing. Several other women joined our orgy fest. And none of us wanted to stop.'*

*'Right. And when Moses saw you with your legs widely spread on his sacrificial altar, beside the Golden Calf, openly defying his wishes, and freely fornicating with several other men, he went insane with lust over you, didn't he?'*

*'Oh yes. He certainly did. Understand that, by then, I had become more than his lover. I had also become somewhat like a mother to him; and he had become like my infant son. As our lovemaking evolved, Moses became more and more infatuated with my breasts. He loved to kiss, tongue tease, bite softly, and suckle my nipples. Our frequent times of nipple play made me feel like, in an emotional sense, I had become his mother. And I, as Madonna to Moses, loved the stimulations of his nipple play.*

*'But Moses had this guilt complex. I think he originated Jewish guilt. Whenever he reflected on the shameful way that he abandoned his family, and felt guilty about allowing the crocodiles to devour his wife and sons, I comforted him. I assured him that it was the will*

of Sobek, the God of the Nile crocodiles. I told him it was their fate; that they were to become part of the cleansing and renewal in the fertility ritual; and that they had honored the great Nile God by sacrificing their bodies to the renewal of the people's fertility. And that he, Moses, by honoring my pornographic performances; choosing me over his family; and by sacrificing his family to honor Sobek, the crocodile God, he had also been reborn.

'I then shoved my nipple into his mouth and caressed him. I reassured him that he did the right thing; that humanity had greater expectations of him, and that his family had gotten in his way, obstructing his great potential; blocking humanity's progress. And that he had me now. And that I truly understood this need he had to advance humanity. And that I was supportive of his great goal. And that I was much, much better for him in every way; emotionally, sexually, and spiritually than Zeporah, who came before me. I assured him that I and my vagina were his new family; and that I would be his loving, faithful wife. I told him he needed to always trust his limbic mind's natural desires and never resist them; for that was the will of this new God he was so excited about.

'Then, I inserted his penis into my welcoming vagina. I hugged him tightly and kissed him while we fornicated; all the while praising him for making the better, more noble choice for himself and for all humanity. I cooed sweet encouragements in his ear and purred like a satisfied kitten while he fucked me; complimenting him for putting the needs of humanity above the selfish needs of himself and just one family. By frequently copulating with him and praising him in this way, I cleansed him of all his feelings of guilt. He became convinced that my immoral whoring was his true companion on his pathway to human redemption. He became consumed by my nympho whore lust and my eager to please vagina.

'So, by the time The Tribe had arrived at Mount Sinai, Moses' love for me and his need for my constant reassuring comfort had *become all consuming. He loved me more than he had ever loved anything or anyone before. I had already become his Madonna.*

*'But my own compulsions to engage in unbridled nymphomania had not changed. Of course, I lied to Moses about being his faithful wife. I never intended to be faithful to him. I was a whore, forever committed to my whoring. As a whore, I continued to lust after many of the men and some of the women who traveled with us on our journey through the desert. As I walked alongside several of the others, my nymphomania cravings surged in my blood. I vividly remembered my pornographic performances and how I had greatly pleased Pharoah and the crowds. As we trekked along, I was finding it harder and harder not to act on my cravings. My breasts ached to fornicate with many of the others. It became impossible for me to reconcile myself to a monogamous life with Moses. I didn't want that. I was an unapologetic sex addict, forced to live through this intolerable forced withdrawal from my essential need for variety.*

*'When Moses decided to climb to the top of Mount Sinai to create his stone tablets, I felt incredibly lonely. My promiscuous impulses simply overwhelmed me. I knew I had to do something. I had to seek out intimacy with new partners. I knew that was my opportune time to act.*

*'I urged the gathered tribe to relive our old, glorious days of orgy sex; to honor ourselves, our fertility practices, and our real human needs to fornicate and surrender ourselves to our limbic desires. I placed myself high up upon our tribal altar and spread my legs widely to welcome all who wished to celebrate our respite from the confining lifestyle that Moses had imposed upon us. Many men responded to my advances. I succeeded spectacularly. Their limbic minds controlled them. One after the other, they came to me and offered their penises to me. Soon, I was fornicating and performing fellatio with several of the handsomest young men in our tribe. I was finally free of Moses; finally free of his oppressive, misogynistic rules.*

Men were adoring me; their semen was flowing freely into my mouth and vagina; and I was loving myself again. I felt uninhibited; elated while joyously performing my porn. I was being glorified, again.

'But then Moses came down from the mountain. When he saw me cavorting with so many others, and thoroughly loving my pleasures, he simply lost his mind. Seeing penis after penis entering my mouth and my vagina caused him to experience a monumental upset. Poor Moses. He had such a fragile psyche. He was so rigid!

'In retrospect, Moses was a hopeless narcissist. And, like a lot of men, he believed he had some kind of natural right to own me and control what I decided to do with my own body. When he witnessed semen shooting from penises onto my adoring tongue, and others penises ejaculating semen into and onto my vagina, he first trembled and cried.

'I urged him to relax and not be repulsed by what was only natural. I invited him to join us. Mine was an honest, heartfelt invitation. I wanted him to share in the joy I felt while my nymphomania was being assuaged. I wanted Moses to come to me and fuck me; share intimacy with me, while I was in the throes of my elation. I thought he would benefit from sharing my divine experience with me; hopefully lose his inhibition and relax.

'But Moses did not answer me. Instead, he lamented that his whole world had been upended; and that all of us had betrayed him. Then, he went berserk. He screamed at the other men to get away from me. He threatened to kill any man who so much as touched me. He became like a mad man in an infuriated rage state.'

'Right. And that's when he decided he needed to change the tribe's worship practices so he could have you all to himself. That's when he smashed the stone tablets of laws he had created. That's when he ordered that the Tribe must follow a new religion: His religion. And that's when he killed everyone who wanted to keep the old ways of communal love. During this genocidal purging, Moses destroyed all who opposed his will. He ordered those who did not want to follow him to stand aside. Then he and his loyalists murdered those dissenters. I felt badly for the men he murdered. And I felt badly for me, too. So many lovely penises, wasted. And wasted for what? This new idea of God and these new laws he claimed were given him by this God! I thought he had gone mad.

'But he didn't stop with the murders. He doubled down. He then commanded his loyal followers to adopt a new set of laws: his new set of laws that this God was giving him. He went back up to the top of the mountain where he carved a new set of laws with two additional laws onto his second set of stone tablets. Those new laws included the adultery commandment and the commandments against coveting another man's wife or his ox or his ass, or anything that is your neighbor's.

'If you think of those new laws as the 'V,' or 'Vagina' commandments, and consider the historical context during which Moses gave those laws to the people, and the reason why he gave them when he did, you can appreciate the tremendous power and control Moses exerted over the early Hebrew tribes. After Moses gave his new set of laws to his formative Tribes of Israel, he claimed you as his wife and sole property; and he declared you off limits to all other men. He already had one commandment forbidding coveting in his first set of commandments. He felt he had to make another man's wife more explicitly off limits, especially you; hence the second set of tablets. He threatened the other males with death if they consorted with you. And in his effort to reclaim all your affections to him and him alone, he made intensely passionate love with you for days and weeks afterwards. He kissed you everywhere; and ardently performed cunnilingus daily; and he professed his undying devotion to you, his glorious, eternal whore. He swore that he loved you with every fiber of his flesh and every bone in his body. Remember?'

'Yes, how could I forget? He was obsessed with me. I was his love object. He couldn't get enough of me!'

'Right. And also remember, in those formative years going against the will of Moses was punishable by death. He had already murdered an Egyptian overseer, his wife, and kids, and half the tribe at the foot of Mount Sinai. He was, essentially, a ruthless, possessive dictator; and his edicts needed to be obeyed. But as much as he opposed slavery, he became a love slave to you, Marty, in the personage of Baaleezebelle. He changed the world's perception of women because of you, Marty.'

'But I never wanted him to change the world's perception of women, or of me. I didn't want that. I wanted to remain a whore. I loved performing my pornography. I loved having sex with many different men. It's just so much more fulfilling than a monogamous relationship. I don't know why Moses couldn't accept me for the way I naturally was.'

'I know you don't understand why. It's hard to understand narcissism. But what a woman wanted didn't matter to history's greatest control freak. And Moses had the physical strength to demand that he got his way. He was an uncompromising bully. So, in his newly ordered world, in a real sense, he made a woman's honor a sacred thing. He reset the world's morality and placed it upon a new historical track. And he invented a new religion and an artificial, imaginary God, all so he could have you and your fabulous vagina all to himself. Obsession will do that to a man. He loved you and your delicious cunt to the limits of his obsession. Think about what he did, just so he could possess you and your vagina. He killed half the people in his tribe so that he alone could possess you! Think how profound that was! Your love story with Moses is the greatest, most profound love story in the history of the world. Remember?'

'Oh yes. I will never forget Moses. He was the most passionate of all my lovers, ever; everyone whom I can recall throughout human *history. He loved touching me; oiling and massaging my breasts and my derriere; obsessively kissing my nipples and my vagina. I was his sole addiction, not his imaginary god. I believe he knew he had short changed me, by denying others from having me. He also knew I missed my old lifestyle with my multiple lovers; so, he tried so very hard to please me and compensate for what he had denied me. He even took special herbs to make his penis swell larger. I appreciated that considerate aspect of Moses. It did console me some. Bigger is better.*

*'We made ardent love every single day; oftentimes two or three times a day. He told me I inspired him. And I know that was true. I was his source of strength. We both loved our lovemaking. Every time we made love; we were like children discovering the ultimate joys of life for the first time. It was our joy; our beautiful bliss. We had this incredibly intense lust passion for each other, like the spirit souls of Poon and Tang, those two butterfly lovers. Yes, I will always remember my life with Moses. We were like those two mating butterflies, tumbling through the air; unaware and unaffected by anyone or anything in the world around us. It was our endless honeymoon, like we could never make love often enough. He called me his soul mate. He treated me a lot like Bob does, with all his kisses and touchings. Mmmmm. And those delightful hours of cunnilingus. How could I ever not remember that? It was a truly wonderful time.'*

*'But like many marriages, it had its rough patch, didn't it?'*

*'Yes, Miss Lust. You would remember that incident, wouldn't you? I think you are referring to my affair with Nadav and Avihu, Aaron's sons. Well, I simply couldn't help myself. My limbic nymphomania never left me, no matter how many times Moses had me. I always craved more. You see, those boys began coming into our tent while Moses was away with the tribal leaders and the judges, meeting with them, planning our journey, discussing the tribe's problems.*

*'I remember how our liaison began. I was alone in our tent when Nadav and Avihu entered:*

"Moses is not here," I said. "He is in the meeting tent with your father, his brother, Aaron. They are discussing tribal matters with the heads of al twelve tribes. They will be there all afternoon. Moses will not return here until sundown."

"We have not come here looking for our uncle, Moses," said Nadav. "We have come here to talk with you. What should we call you? Aunt Baaleezebelle?"

"No. Don't be ridiculous," I said. "I am one and two years younger than the two of you. Call me Belle. What is it that you want?"

"We want to meet God. We know Moses keeps him here, in his secret curtained off place called the Holy of Holies. Can we meet him? Can you let us go into the Holy of Holies so we can see God for ourselves? Moses always tells everyone that God told him we should do this and God told him we must do that. But none of us have ever seen God. Only Moses sees God. We'd like to see God, too. Can you show us to him?"

"I can let you into the Holy of Holies. Moses keeps the Ark of the Covenant in there. Come here, with me. I'll show you the Ark. You can look inside it and see for yourself." I then took Nadav and Avihu into the Holy of Holies and showed them the Ark. I took the cover off the Ark and they looked inside."

"Where's God," asked Avihu. "All I see are some parchment scrolls."

"That's right," I said. Those scrolls are the words that Moses and the scribes are fashioning into the Torah, which he will give to the tribes. Those words are God."

"But if God is a person who Moses talks to; then where is the God of Moses?" Nadev was perplexed.

"God is inside the head of Moses," I said. "He imagines that he talks with this imaginary person whom he calls God."

"But he also said God spoke to him from a burning bush; so, that could not have been form inside his head," spoke Avihu. "Tell us,

'In answer to Avihu's question, I told the two sons of Aaron to stand before me. I then dropped my robe and appeared naked before them. "Take off your clothes," I commanded them. And they did as I commanded them. "Now here," I said, taking the hand of Avihu and placing it upon my vagina. "Here is the burning bush Moses speaks of. My vagina becomes excited and hot within me, like a burning fire, when I feel stimulated; and when I desire to copulate with a male's penis."

'I moved my body closely before the two of them. "You are breathtakingly beautiful," said Avihu, as he placed his hand upon my breast.'

"Do you find me desirable?" I asked the two of them, while I smiled to them and placed their hands upon my breasts. I then stepped even closer to them and kissed them both upon their mouths while their fingers naturally explored my breasts and teased my nipples with their gentle pinches. Then, both Nadev and Avihu began sucking my nipples with their mouths.

'I gently rubbed my fingers over their arms and necks to stimulate them. Then, after they became comfortable with my touchings, I embraced them both, one after the other, so they could feel the heat of my body against them. By our closeness, I could tell they both wanted me. I then took each of their penises in my hands and gently stroked them to hardness. Then, standing closer still, with my body pressed closely to theirs, I took their penises; first Avihu's penis, then Nadev's penis; and I inserted the very tips of their penises; first Avihu's penis, then Nadev's penis, into the outer lips of my vagina; and I whispered seductively while I asked them: "Can you feel how wet I am? Can you feel the heat that comes from inside me? Would you like to stay with me a while?" I softly purred these questions to them while I kissed their mouths and gently massaged their testicle sacs. I then asked them: "Would you like to discover how wonderful it feels to be inside me? Would you like to discover the true God of Moses? Would you like to worship in the same holy of holies where

'I didn't wait for them to answer. I kissed them longer and more longingly, flicking my tongue against their tongues, while I continued stroking their penises. I then said to them in my most confidential and lovingly sincere voice: "If you will promise me that you will keep our worship services our special secret, I will acquaint you with the wonders that Moses worships. Would you like to know me as Moses knows me?" Both boys nodded their heads and told me: "Yes."

"Then, come with me; come to my bed; and lie down with me," I whispered with my most sinfully seductive voice. "Moses will be gone all afternoon. While he is away, discussing things with the tribal elders, making plans for the twelve tribes and giving orders for the days ahead, I'd like you to know the true God of Moses. Would you like to be with the God that lives inside his burning bush? While Moses is away, let's play God together. You'll pleas my god and I'll please your gods. And together, we'll become God. Let's please our true gods with our mouths and tongues and my vagina and your penises while we are here together, all afternoon. Let my bed become our holy place while Moses and the tribal leaders are at their meeting place."

'It was Nadev who spoke first: "Belle, are you saying to us that you will share your favors with the two of us? Are you saying that we can know the true God of Moses in the same ways that Moses knows you? We know how beautiful you are. We remember your spectacular pornographic performances during the ceremonies for the Fertility of the Nile. Are you saying you wish to copulate with us; perform fellatio and cunnilingus with us, as you did during the Nile ceremonies?"

"Yes, my darlings Nadev and Avihu," 'I said in my most enthusiastically assuring voice,' "That is exactly what I am saying."

'Avihu seemed afraid and cautious. In his timid, fearful voice he sought my assurances:

"But Belle, Moses has told us the commandment about adultery. He said if we disobey that commandment, we then disobey God and *we will be punished. You are his wife. Are you not afraid of God's punishment for committing adultery?"*

*'I then pressed my loins close against Avihu's thigh while I kissed his mouth and stroked his penis. I chortled to him in a playful way:*

*"Avihu, Moses may believe those things he tells you. They serve him well because he knows that you fear him and that you believe the things he says his God commands of you. But, be assured, my dear sweet Avihu, the God that Moses worships is not my God."*

*"But who then is your God, Belle? Where is he? Why have I not heard of him? Could you show him to me?" 'The questioning words of this uninitiated virgin boy made me chortle more boldly and convincingly:*

*"Avihu, my sweet, innocent child. Can you not understand the wonder that you are? Do you not know; are you unaware of how magnificent you are? Do you not sense how deeply I long for you; to have you enter me; to know your penis inside me? Avihu, my dearest, sweetest boy, I am holding my true God in my hand and I am stroking it. I love to suck it in my mouth. I love to mouth your testicles while I stroke it. I love to feel its semen shooting onto my tongue while I am licking and sucking it. I love the taste if its semen. I love the majesty of all of it. I am beholden to the wonders of it. I love being with it and doing all sorts of pleasurable things with it. And I feel no shame or inhibition while I am with it and doing all those wonderful things with it. I must know it completely; and I must feel it thrusting inside me.*

*"Avihu, understand what I am telling you: Your penis is my only true God. And I wish to worship it, today and often. Now, let us not talk any longer. We have hours until sunset. Let us not waste our precious time together. Come, both of you. Come and lie down with me. And allow me to worship my Gods while Moses is away talking about his."*

'I then took them to my bed and completed my seductions by acquainting their penises with my insatiable penis lusting, slippery, ever welcoming vagina and my loving, passion filled thrusts. And there was such a wonderful sweetness in our love making! I adored those boys. Their penises were my dreams come true. I loved them.

'And that was how my love affair with my nephews, the sons of Aaron, began. You cannot blame me, Miss Lust, for stealing their virginity. They were so strong and handsome! And they had such marvelous, hard penises! And such wonderful stamina! We made love for hours! What was I to do? Turn away from the temptation of their young bodies? Deny my own true essence as a woman? As a creature of nature and a nympho whore? What sort of nymph would I be if I held myself back? Could I then live with myself, knowing I had denied myself such glorious pleasures? I can't imagine how I could have done that. I could not be unnatural to my natural self, could I? Of course not! That first time Nadav and Avihu exposed themselves to me, I simply could not resist them. Their penises were so beautiful! Oh! Magnificent! So large! Gasp! and hard! Yum! And so eager to enter me! Mmmmmmm! Yummmm! My nymphomania simply overwhelmed me, Miss Lust. I simply had to suck their penises and welcome them to my insatiable vagina.

'I performed fellatio and fornications with them for hours that afternoon. And practically every day thereafter! I did so many incredible things with them! Mmmmm! Wonderful! It was all so beautiful! Intimacy with two virgin boys for their very first time! Mmmmmm! How delightful! I was soooo in the mood to fuck them! Their eyes were filled with wonderment. They adored me. We joyfully explored many positions! Yesssss! Mmmmmm! So wonderful!

'I'm sure I shocked their virgin sensibilities with my ribaldry and how uninhibited I was and how shamelessly and wantonly I craved experiencing all manner of sexual pleasures with the two of them. They fell deeply into unbridled love and passion lust with me and my vagina. I wanted them to know the same pleasures that Moses knew. They hungered for the pleasures of my mouth and my vagina, every chance they had to be with me, from that day onward. We couldn't get enough of each other! Mmmmmm! It was soooo wonderful! Tee he! Just thinking about it makes me giggle like a school girl.

'It was much like my love making in my present life with Donny and Billy, the twins I met while in WEX school. Like I did with Donny and Billy, I often copulated with Nadav and Avihu for hour after hour! Like those two twins, Aaron's sons also had penises that could ejaculate repeatedly! Yes! They could! First, Nadav would come inside me; then Avihu. Then, I would suck both of them hard again and they would again come inside me; and then we repeated this a third time! Their young, teenaged penises seemed unlimited in the volumes of semen they could stream over my clitoris! Yummmm! So lovely!

'I loved intercourse with them; just totally loved it. It was so wholesome and joyful. Like when I often did with twins Donny and Billy, we three also experimented with many different positions. We became lovers. I could not help myself! I loved kissing their mouths with my mouth and exploring their mouths with my tongue. And I loved their touches all over my body and feeling their penises inside me! I loved sucking them and feeling their penises become firm in my mouth. Having their young, hard penises pressed against my swollen clitoris while I orgasmed electrified my libido! Mmmmmm! So sweet! I remember all of our times together so well. Those boys were so virile and strong! I couldn't fuck them often enough! I became addicted to young male penises in my Egyptian life; and I have been ever since! My nephews were such beautiful boys. So sweet! And, they loved, just totally loved, pleasing me! Mmmmmm! I wish we could have gone on like that forever! It felt so wonderful to fuck for hours like that and have orgasm after orgasm, like I did! It was soooo wonderful! We had such wonderful times together. Mmmmmm.'

'But Moses found out.'

'Yes, sadly, he did. We became careless and we got caught. It was so unfortunate. He discovered us in the act of lovemaking. I don't know how he found out, but he did. He surprised us. He came into the tent while we were naked; and he observed us in the midst of our fornications; while I was performing fellatio on Nadav's gorgeous penis, and while Avihu was ejaculating into my vagina. Moses took it badly, as if my vagina, his true God, was being defiled. He became enraged. And when Moses got that way, he became very strong. He fell upon Nadav and Avihu and slit both their throats, murdering them. I felt terrible, watching him murder them. Not only was he taking their lives away, he was also taking away my greatest source of pleasure in that miserable desert!

'He wrapped their bodies in their garments and ordered tribesmen to drag them away from the tent in their garments. The men were ordered not to touch their bodies because they had sinned and were unclean. Moses followed the men and ordered their bodies, with their garments on, to be thrown into the communal camp fire and burned until their bodies became unrecognizable. Moses said they had defiled God's commandments and their punishment was just.'

'How did you feel about Moses after that?'

'Well, I always knew he was strong; strong willed, and dictatorial. I knew what I and the boys were doing was wrong by the new standards Moses had set for us; but I thought their punishment was too harsh. I knew the commandments were really Moses's commandments because I knew this God he always referred to was a fiction of his own mind. So, I felt kind of weird; like all of us in the tribe were following the dictates of a madman.

'But part of me also realized that Moses had honored me; and he had greatly honored the majesty and sanctity of my vagina, by murdering those boys. He told the people that I remained his true and good woman; that I was pure of heart and, although I had committed adultery, like those boys had, I must not be punished for my wrongdoing. He said that a woman who commits adultery must always be seen as innocent because of her sex. She must be seen the same way a butterfly or a flower is seen. The butterfly must be free to pollinate the wildflowers. And the flower must be bright and delightful of fragrance in order to attract bees to itself; for the flower must be this way in order to propagate life; and that propagation of life is good.

'So, like butterflies and flowers must not be punished for what is their true nature, likewise, a woman must also not be punished for what is also natural to her true nature. But men must be different. Men must be the stronger sex. Each and every man must strictly heed the Ten Commandments of Moses; all ten; each and every commandment. Moses insisted that discipline among men is vital to the well being of the Tribe; but as to discipline applied to women who fornicate and commit adultery? Not so much. So, while the boys were killed, I was spared.'

'So, nothing changed between you and Moses after he learned you were an adulteress?'

'Oh no, there was a change. He punished me; but it was in a way that brought us closer together.'

'What way?'

'He built a penalty box out of sticks. It was a contraption that held my legs apart while I presented myself in the doggie position. I was made to be submissive while Moses slapped my tushie and entered my vagina from behind.'

'But surely, when you did porn and with Moses before, you were slapped on your tushie?'

'Well, yes. Those slaps were expected and very stimulating; exciting. They made my libido soar. I loved those slaps. But these were punishment slaps. They were very hard slaps. They made my eyes water with tears. They hurt. But then, after he had entered me and had thrusted deeply into me, I got the sense that Moses needed me in this way. I intuited that he needed me to be his 'Bad Girl" this way so he could justify his dominance over me. I realized he needed me to be his whore so he could feel like a man in control of his woman. And a funny thing happened in my mind after he slapped me. I realized that I needed him to do this to me so he could demonstrate his need to punish me out of his love for me. And that's when I knew we had entered a whole new dimension of our love. And in a twisted thinking kind of way, I was actually dominating him; making him need me to prove his manhood. It's a little complicated; but having our animal sex that way brought us much closer together. Our love was suddenly much deeper and more committed and understanding and our acceptance of each other's needs was much stronger and more trusting than what we had before.'

'How did you feel about that?'

'Blessed. Fortunate to be alive. And Moses made me feel good and wholesome about myself when he explained things the way he did. I also felt profoundly desired and loved; kind of like I and my vagina were holy and special. I think every woman feels deeply loved when she knows her man has murdered for her; and when he punishes her for straying from him. She knows he needs her and the need is real and strong. She knows she means everything to im. I suppose that is the way to describe how I felt. After he murdered those boys, and after we did our bondage and masochism sex with dominance and passion thing, Moses loved me with a fever-lust unlike anything I have ever experienced in all my lives. He was insanely possessed with lust over me. We made love with such passions I sometimes thought we would both die of exhaustion.

'And I loved feeling his penis inside me more than I ever had before! We had fabulous sex! Afterwards, when it was over and he had finished, he helped me out of my knee spreader. He then lied, exhausted, next to me. For the longest time he held my head against his, my face and eyes looking into his. Finally, he said:

'You know me.'

'By his words I knew he meant that he knew I had to be the way I was so that he could be the way he was; that he needed me to be his whore, so that he could justify in himself his dominance of me. And I was okay with that.'

'I smiled. I kissed his lips. It was my honest way of letting him know that I knew he was a complicated man who needed to be the way he was. And I said: 'Yes.'

'Our intimacy became sweeter and more endearing after we used that knee spreader. Moses would lie with me and stare at my vagina for the longest times; and then he would kiss it and tell me how beautiful I was and how much he loved making love with me. I knew we had achieved true intimacy and true love. It was a beautiful time in my life. I knew I meant the world to Moses. I knew he needed me in his life more than he ever needed me before. And I loved and appreciated him as my protector husband and as my lover man more than ever before.'

'And there were no more episodes? You had no more interlopers?'

'Well, yes; Of course, I had many more interlopers but no more murder episodes. Moses never killed any of my other lovers. Moses came to understand that, while he had taken the whore out of the harem, he could never take the whore out of the whore. You see, my nymphomania is completely natural. I was unable to resist temptation.

'I explained this in great detail to Moses; that, while I was a natural nympho, I nevertheless truly did love him. Eventually, we came to a tacit understanding. When he was away from our tent for any extended period of time, he needed to expect and accept that I would be visited by my different lovers. And, from time to time, Moses would have sadomasochistic sex with me, letting me know how much he needed me and loved me. And I was totally fine with our new arrangement. You see, as I explained to Moses, I needed to be accepted in society as a respected woman; a woman who was married, but also as a total woman, a woman who loves fucking.'

'Oh, so you were the first self-declared MILF (Married, I Love Fucking) woman!'

'Well yes, I suppose I was! My situation was well understood and quietly accepted. After a while, the entire tribe became accustomed to my status as the wife of Moses as well as a discrete, but uninhibited whore who had liaisons with twelve additional lovers. Everyone understood the arrangement. It was very similar to the arrangement I have in my present life with Bob. Bob knows, like Moses knew, that I must have my dalliances; and Bob accepts that about me. He, like Moses, is quietly pleased to be partnered with a sexually liberated woman.'

'But Bob doesn't do sadistic sex with you, does he?'

'Ha! No, not exactly. He does what I would call BDSM light. He sometimes pinches and bites my nipples and does love slaps on my tush while we make love and I tell him about my trysts with other men and my porn partners. He stimulates me just enough to excite and arouse me and get me totally into the mood to make love with him. I think our relationship is pretty much like the relationship my mother, Susan, had with Marvin.'

'But in your life with Moses, you more or less wore you MILF designation as a badge of honor? Am I getting this?'

'Yes, being MILF is nothing to feel ashamed about. It's simply declaring that you are a total, sexually complete, woman; that you, not your husband, control your body; that you decide with whom and when and where you wish to have sex. It also tells the world that you have confidence in your relationship with your married spouse and you know he's not going to go 'Mischka' over you fulfilling a very *natural need. It notices the world that your marriage is a mature, guilt free relationship.*

*'I think the MILF designation should be worn proudly by every woman who wishes to add variety to her married life. Flowers are visited by different bees and butterflies. And butterflies visit different flowers. Why should our morality be different from Butterfly Morality? Natural immorality is honest and wholesome. It shouldn't be dictated to, or bottled up. That only breeds frustration, which leads to uncivilized outcomes.*

*'Moses is the cause of all of humanity's problems. If he hadn't been so headstrong and possessive, he would not have gone up Mount Sinai that second time. He would not have added the commandments about adultery and coveting another man's wife. When he made those inserts into the tribal laws, he basically pitted his 'One God Fits All' rules for human behavior against nature's rules. Nature made human women different from other female animals. Nature made us naturally promiscuous. We know sex is beautiful. The other animals do not have that knowledge. Nature made us different this way because nature instinctively knows that humanity is destined to populate the entire universe. Nature wants women to experience pleasure; and lots of it! Nature wants us to be naturally polyamorous; and to breed freely; and to populate the universe. Control freak Moses, wanted his woman to be exclusively his; like his ready handy personal sex toy. That stymies nature. That prevents a woman from copulating with a man she craves and it limits human diversity. Moses' selfishness is the root cause of all the wars and strife humanity has suffered, ever since he went up Mount Sinai that second time.*

*'Women must be allowed their natural sexual freedom. After all, what's so terrible about a woman having sexual variety in her life, if it makes her feel more like a woman? What's the harm if*

everyone accepts that she's a very loving person who wishes to give more of herself to society? We women need to rid ourselves of Moses' straightjacket. I believe the more women who declare themselves to be MILF's, the happier and more well-balanced society will become. Don't you agree, Miss Lust?'

'Oh, absolutely I agree, Marty! So, after Moses acquiesced to your MILF status, did things go more smoothly for you?'

'Oh yes! The tribe, Moses, and I settled into a beautiful rhythm. We broke camp; traveled; foraged; pitched tents; prayed; ate; made love; slept; woke; Moses made his forays to explore the terrain ahead and discuss tribal matters with the leaders of the twelve tribes, while I discretely entertained several of my lovers. Then, we broke camp; and we repeated this routine for, literally, years; on and on we wandered through the desert. I can remember how Moses would lead the tribe for about three to five miles every few days or so, so the animals would have fresh grazing. Then, after we pitched our tents, he gathered the leaders of the twelve tribes and the scribes. That's when they wrote down the tribes' oral homilies and created the Torah.

'And while they did that, I made love with my lovers in our tent. Everything was harmonious. In a weird sort of way, I believe my lovemaking was the cohesive glue that held the twelve family tribes together. I was our tribal tie back to Hathor, the Egyptian female cow God, the source of joy and fertility, and the god who calls us to love life; which, of course, includes loving sexual freedom. In a real sense, what I offered the tribal males was the opposite of what Moses and his imaginary God offered them.

'They remembered seeing my pornographic performances. They remembered seeing me perform my fellatios and my copulations with the Apis bulls. They remembered seeing the semen from the bulls stream into my mouth and my vagina. And they remembered how joyful they felt when they also experienced my fellatios and my copulations. They believed that I had received divine life from the

Apis bulls and that I was their true Goddess, placed here on Earth to show them the pathway to eternal life. They believed my mouth and vagina were the true pathways to eternal life and happiness. And they knew what I offered them was real and tangible. And they loved and adored me for sharing my holiness, and my love of life and sex, with them. I and my insatiable libido were the real, earthly ties that bound our early Hebrew tribes together. I think Moses secretly appreciated my natural nympho character trait. He knew what I was doing. And he knew that I and my partners were indulging him and his fantastical homily versions of his life's experiences. I know he loved me more because of my permissive and promiscuous nature. I always gave freely of my love; always shared myself with the others. In this very constructive way, I complemented Moses. And he loved me for who I was.

'Moses was very domineering; always barking out orders and commands. He always insisted on blind obedience. He was a man on a mission. He was whipping the tribe into shape so they could conquer all the lands west of the Jordan River. Moses was smart. He made peace with my nympho proclivities. He knew I was helping him keep the tribes united. The two of us had our mutual understanding; our silent camaraderie of purpose. Moses accepted me, as I was, as his lover; much like Bob accepts me now, in this life.

'All our moving and camping, taking down our tents and pitching them up again, packing up or belongings, and unpacking them sometimes got confusing. And there came a time when I somehow forgot about my birth control. Thanks to that slip up, Moses and I had a child. We named him Joshua. I think he was Moses's child; but I wasn't sure. He could have been sired by one of my other lovers. But Joshua had many of Moses's Egyptian features; and he grew to become a very strong young man; a true warrior, like Moses. I was thrilled with my son; very glad I conceived him; and very proud of him.

'Later, when Moses and I became older and infirm, we pitched our tent for the last time on the hills overlooking the Jordan River. Moses told the Tribe to leave us behind. We sat there watching the Tribe going away from us; leaving us behind, as they departed for the Jordan River. Moses held me in his arms and held my hand. Together, we cried as we watched Joshua lead the twelve tribes across the Jordan. We had become too feeble to follow the people across the Jordan. We knew the end of our lives was near.

'We watched the twelve tribes fan out over all the promised land, devouring all the native Bedouin peoples' lands that lay before them. The Hebrew Tribes were like so many caterpillars, devouring the land between the Jordan and the Mediterranean Sea, like the land had become their milkweed leaves; ripe to be devoured by the twelve tribes of advancing caterpillars. After the tribes had split up, some of them going north into Galilee; some others going south into Judea and Sumaria, Moses and I simply held each other in our arms. We knew our time had come. We kissed one final time. Like Poon and Tang sat in a tree overlooking their caterpillar offspring while those offspring devoured milkweed leaves, we watched our spiritual off-spring, the tribes of Israel, growing and flourishing; devouring the crescent lands and turning them fertile. Then, like Poon and Tang died, Moses and I also died.'

'You have extremely good recall, Marty. You lived during the time when Moses decided that male misogyny, led by, ordered by, and prescribed by him and his laws would dominate all tribal reli-gious thoughts and ways. To possess you, he needed to destroy the natural ways of communal love and prostitution worship. That's why he had the followers of Apis Bull worship, or communal Baal worship, put to death that day he came down from Mount Sinai, after he carved his laws into stone. And that's why he murdered his brother's sons.

'You lived during the time when Moses perpetrated his great

moment when Moses invented God. From that beginning, the tribes' oral homilies became codified into the Torah. Remember: Moses was a power crazed man who treated his children and his first wife horribly. He forsake them to be with you. And he consigned them to the crocodiles of the Nile. At his core, Moses believed women were unimportant and inferior to men; except for sex and breeding. But in their sexual role, Moses held women in awe because of women's natural ability to create life, which men cannot do by themselves. And he became obsessed with you, Marty. He was a mortal man with passions. And you were the object of his passions.'

'Yes, Miss Lust. We had many discussions about God. I explained to Moses that I was not like the others of the Tribe. I could not accept his concept of a vicarious, abstract God. For me, God had to be something real and tangible. He needed to accept me for the whore that I was. God, for me, was the male penis. And, like the shameless, incorrigible whore that I was, I always had many Gods. And, I loved all my Gods.'

'And he came to accept that about you?'

'Oh yes. He was more into power and dominance and tribal governance. Moses forbade women from having any voice in tribal governance. Women were a threat to his power; especially women who engaged in fornication rites. He understood how our feminine limbic powers caused men to obsess over us and placed them under our spells of lusts. Moses feared women's limbic powers over the minds of men.

'He knew that men could not surrender to women's limbic powers if the tribe was to survive. He needed to create a male hierarchical society. That's why he invented God. That's why he had my vagina worshippers murdered. I could not be allowed to lead the tribe away from him. I could not return the tribe to its old ways.

'And, he believed that he alone, would be entitled to have relations with me after that. Moses foresaw that communal intimacy of creating a male hierarchical worshipping order founded upon an artificial abstract God. I was way ahead of my time; way ahead of Marx and Engles and Cloward-Priven materialistic communism. My vagina represented the true origin of communism, essentially a communal, materialistic world that has no need for the God envisioned by Moses. Moses was an anticommunist.'

'Well, he certainly was a control freak.'

'Yes; he swept away historic communal intimacy and tribal sharing of my vagina. He crushed that earliest form of communism. His concept of God and religion has suppressed progressive communism for the last six thousand years. Pornography is a modern-day form of communism; and it is also secret form of worship for many. It has yet to become formalized into a religion and granted tax exempt status; but that will come in the future. After all, the constitution guarantees freedom of religion! Thanks to ever more sensational modern pornography and improving promotional efforts, communism, based upon intimacy sharing as a form of deity worship, is making a heathy comeback. I'm glad that many consider my artistry to be progressive with socially redeeming qualities. But I have often wondered, since I made love with Aaron's sons and changed their belief about God away from the beliefs of Moses and their father, Aaron, does that make me a bad girl?'

'No, Marty. You are not a bad girl; not in the eyes of a true anti-religionist communist. You were simply rebelling against the unnatural, unrealistic constraints that Moses had imposed upon the early Hebrew tribe. No; you were simply being a wonderful, ecumenical girl; openly sharing your intimate limbic self and the wonders of your lovemaking. You were doing a truly good, unselfish, thing. Moses was the narcissistic control freak; obsessed with his selfish, flawed thinking. He tried to control you because he feared your natural power. You've never been a bad girl, Marty. You've always been a very welcoming, loving, and good girl.

'You are a wonderful girl, Marty; a goddess. You are the living embodiment of prostitution worship, returned to humanity; returned to set us free from the insanity of religion. Look at all religions as a Moses led detour away from natural Pagan worship practices. But despite the religionists efforts to suppress them, the old humanistic ways are returning; naturally and in the form of pornography. You, as the glorious porn star you are, are setting humanity free to again worship naturally, as you did with the Apis bulls and your many partners during the Egyptian fertility rites. And you are blessing all humankind with your limitless promiscuity and fertility. You are wonderful, Marty! You are adored, Marty! You have been sent to humanity by the Great Spirit! You have BUTTERFLY MORALS; the morals of the Great Spirit and the morals of a free woman.

'You do not have religion-based morals. That's why you love sex so much. BUTTERFLY MORALS explains why you experience your overwhelming urges to fornicate. It's your freedom-based lust urge; and it's natural, wonderful, and healthy. BUTTERFLY MORALS explains why you dream about intimacy with hundreds of men. It's because of your natural instinct to make love. BUTTERFLY MORALS explains why you have no concern for feelings of women whose husbands you seduce, or what becomes of them, and why you have no cares about religious or secular laws. You cannot and you should not have those concerns. You are a free spirit; free as a butterfly. And you must live by your higher, natural, law.'

'I understand. But my experience with Moses leaves me confused. I do not understand. Why did he choose me? Of all the girls who participated in the fertility rites with the Apis bulls, why me?'

'I can answer that. I remember the moment well. The other harem girls were performing sex acts with the bulls because they were expected to. They had no choice. But you were different. Your name was Baaleezebelle. You were the most acclaimed prostitute of the ancient sex cult of penis Baal worshippers. As the harem's cult leader, you proclaimed that the male penis was your only true God; and that you were committed to pleasing it and worshipping it. And you were wildly enthused about the opportunity Pharoah gave you to display your promiscuity and perform your sex acts with the Apis bulls.

'And you beamed with pride when you displayed your semen pool. You personified fertility. Your convinced Pharoah and his princes that your semen flowing vagina was the mirror image of the life-giving floods of the Nile. In those moments of your revelry, you became the Nile. You became the human form of the Nile. You became humanity's source of life: Goddess, creator, and giver of new life. And the receiver of old life. You were adorable with your innocence and your openness; your conviction in the rightness of your glorious, uninhibited whoring. You like the Nile, could not be concerned with the lives you were drowning away.

'I can still recall the gleam in Moses's eye while he first beheld you. In his mind, you became holy; your vagina became the sacred vessel of his life; the object of his worship. In those moments of your sacred fornications, you captivated his limbic mind. I could read his mind. You had captured his soul. He wanted desperately for you to sit your vagina upon his face so he could perform cunnilingus while you orgasmed until your own face broke out in joyful radiance. He felt an overwhelming compulsion to kiss the mouth that had received the semen of the bulls and dozens of male partners. He lusted to join his mouth and tongue with your glorious promiscuous holiness. He needed to honor your profligate mouth and your wonderous, wanton vagina and make them his own.

'That was the instant he decided you would become his true God; and he would create his abstract God for everyone else. That was the very instant when he made up his mind to change his entire life to accommodate you and your ways. After that fortnight of fertility rites, he decided he would announce that he no longer wished *to be married to his wife; and would order that his wife and children be committed as his sacrificial offerings to renew the fertility of the eternal Nile. And after announcing that, he would also announce that he would take you as his new wife. In that moment, your vagina became his world and his life's mission to adore and to please.'*

*'He did that, didn't he? He consigned his wife and children to the crocodiles. He discarded them, like old possessions, and declared that I, Baaleezebelle, was his new wife. Was I that desirable?'*

*'Yes, Marty, you adorable whore, you most certainly were. Surely you remember that glorious time. He was a prince of Egypt. He was the favored son of Pharoah. He had great, unquestioned powers. He could do anything he wanted. And he wanted to make the way open to have you as his wife.'*

*'So, it was out with the old and in with the new? Just like that? Is that how you remember it, too?'*

*'Not quite. First there were details to tidy up. You see, Marty, this was a time when Egypt was wracked with conflicting ideas about their gods and how to worship them. The Pharoah was Akhenaten. His wife was his sister, Nefertiti, Akhenaten was a little wonky. He got it into his head that, instead of having three thousand pagan gods to worship, the Egyptians should only have one god, Aten. Aten was much like the traditional god Ra, the Sun God, only Aten was all encompassing of all the other thousands of gods as well. Aten did more than just warm the Earth, like Ra did. Aten healed the sick, caused fertility, guaranteed life after death, found lost possessions, guaranteed safe travels, victory in battles; everything. By replacing thousands of gods with one god, and by cutting off funding for the priests and their temples, Akhenaten consolidated his power but alienated hundreds of priests who cared for and presided over the worship tithes and rites of the numerous other gods. Akhenaten's oldest and most favorite son, prince Moses, went along with his father's one god idea. Moses, like Akhenaten, loved power.*

'Akhenaten knew trouble was brewing with the priests. He was old. He sought to preserve his kingdom and to shield his sister from the coming uprising. He summoned Moses:

"Moses, my son, I wish to leave this Earthly place and go away to find my peace with my God. I leave it to you to carry on my belief and my vision."

"How, Father? What would you have me do?" Moses was willing but knew not the way to take up the mantle of monotheism.

"My sister, Nefretiti, will approach you. She wishes to maintain tranquility in the kingdom. I know her. I know her ways. She is beholden only to herself. She will conspire with you to murder me. And murder me, you must. Do not equivocate. I am ready, and I prefer to die suddenly. A long death does not befriend the dying. After you murder me, you must then leave Egypt; take your family and the Hebrews with you. Make yourself a new kingdom; a new people who believe in only one god."

"Why the Hebrews, Father?"

"They are impossible. They bind only to each other. They refuse to assimilate into our culture and our ways. Nefretiti cannot rule them. Better that you take them."

"I will obey you, Father; but Zeporah and my sons cannot come with me."

"No?"

"No, Father. They are of Midianite blood; neither Egyptian, nor Hebrew. And Zeporah is an idol worshipper. Success of our vision requires that I leave her with Nefretiti."

"She would not be good to her, Moses. Nefretiti knows she would be queen should you decide to return and claim the throne of Egypt. And what should you do for a woman?"

"Then, I will leave it to you to decide what to do with Zeporah. We have some time. Nefretiti has not yet approached me. And for a woman, I would like to take Baaleezebelle with me."

"The most beautiful whore in my harem?"

"Yes, Father. In the afterlife, you will not long have need for her."

"True. Than it shall be so. I have noticed how Baaleezebelle favors you. Events should accommodate your wishes. I will do my part, my son."

'So, Nefertiti, loving power, and being much more dedicated to self-preservation than her brother, and wishing to void conflict with the priests, conspired to have Akhenaten, her husband, murdered; thus, making herself Pharoah of Egypt. And here's the clincher part of the story: The assassin Nefertiti chose to put the knife into Akhenaten was none other than their son, Moses.'

'Moses? Just like Akhenaten prophesized?'

'Yes, Moses. Remember, like it was practiced in Ur by Terah and Abram and Sara; incest was also practiced in Egypt. Incest was the tribal way of perpetuating tribal power and control by the male hierarchy. Terah did Sara, his daughter. Abram did Sara, his sister. Akhenaten also did his siter, Nefretiti. And Queen Nefretiti did her son, Moses. Nefretiti wanted peace and tranquility in the Kingdom. She wanted to make peace with the priests. Akhenaten wanted his one god concept and social uproar. He wanted to diminish the power of the priests, as did Moses. So, Nefretiti, seeing that power would ultimately reside with the priests, put one loser, her son, Moses, on her other loser, her husband and brother, Akhenaten.

She restored Egypt's traditional multi thousands of pagan gods worship practices and solidified her power with the priests. And, as you know, Marty, Nefertiti, like Moses, also loved consorting with your vagina.'

'Yes. I remember. Nefertiti often called me from the harem to perform cunnilingus with me. We loved each other. We had wonderful girl-girl sex.'

'Yes, you did. And when Moses wanted to pursue his father's one god concept the decision was made, by Nefertiti, that Moses, her oldest son, needed to leave Egypt and take his followers with him; his followers being the Hebrew slaves and worshippers of you, their favorite prostitute, the Hebrew Baaleezebelle, and your fabulous pornographic performances. Clever Nefertiti avoided conflict in her kingdom by giving Moses and his followers a great portion of Egypt's wealth. She gave her eldest son a good start when she sent him away.'

'But wait, Miss Lust! I saw a movie where the Pharoah during the time of Moses was Pharoah Ramses. And the Torah Exodus story tells of Moses murdering an overseer of Hebrew slaves; and God's curse on Egypt with the death of first-born males! And there were plagues of locusts and frogs; and sticks that became snakes; and the Nile turning to blood; and Pharoah's charioteers chasing Moses into the Red Sea and drowning, while the Hebrews escaped. Are you saying none of those things happened?'

'Of course not. None of those things ever happened. Those were just homilies spun by bearded tribal leaders to create monotheism; and to use their 'One God Fits All' concept to control women. Use your common sense. Moses had nothing to gain by killing an overseer; but he had everything to gain by killing Akhenaten. Wake up, Marty. Smell the coffee! Sticks do not become snakes. Locusts and frogs routinely infested Egypt; but those were eaten as bountiful food delicacies, given up by the gods. And the Red Sea's parting was just a fairy tale to explain the Hebrews' separation from the Egyptians. The death of first-born males was the Exodus cover story homily that explained away the fact that Nefertiti wanted peace in her kingdom, which she got by parting ways with her oldest son, Moses; sending him away with half the wealth of Egypt and her best wishes, like the good mother she was.

'Nefretiti was an imminently practical ruler, unlike her ideologically challenged husband, Akhenaten. She recognized that Moses now preferred sex with you to sex with her. Her second son, Tutankhaten, was a young ten-year-old. She first performed fellatio with him when he was eight, after experiencing his first erections. Now he was ten and able to ejaculate. His penis stayed erect for over an hour at a time; and it pleased her greatly. And the boy was far more pliable than Moses. He obeyed his mommy's commands. And Nefertiti, as Little Boy King Tut's regent, then restored Egypt's natural, traditional multi-god, Pagan worship practices. Prostitution worship and communal fornication rituals, including the sacred fertility rites with the Apis bulls, were continued. The priests' powers were restored. They made peace with Nefretiti, their new Pharoah. And the people were greatly relieved that their conflict over what gods they were expected to believe was resolved.

'Nefretiti released all her Hebrew slaves to Moses. She never cared for them anyway because they cleaved to their Hebrew ways and language, which Nefretiti didn't understand; and they were obstinate people who refused to speak Farsi.'

'But without their slaves, who would build the pyramids?'

'The Hebrews never did pyramid work. They were generally too slightly built for that sort of work. They did crafts and palace work; the making of pottery and decorative painting; the cooking, cleaning, errand chores, chamber pot duties, entertainment and magic, those sorts of work. The larger boned Egyptians and slaves from the regions of Babylonia and Africa did the manual labor of pyramid building. Ah, I see we have digressed.

'But yes, Marty, getting back to Zeporah and how you, as Belle, got rid of her: It really was just like that! Quick! Fatal! Final! Gone forever! No coming back to bother you and your fabulous whoring. No complications; no family court; no waiting period; no child support orders; no court dates. Just your clever deception-divergence scheme with Pharoah Akhenaten to facilitate her murder. You executed your plan brilliantly.

'This was humanity's more primal time; a time of agricultural worship and symbolism and superstition. And a time of heated Pagan passions when the limbic mind, expectedly, often governed human behavior. And that behavior, born of emotional lust, was accepted and revered; accompanied by hallucinogenic drugs and ordained by the gods. Emotions, that madness of crowds which Nietzsche described, often played out in the public arena's broad daylight. And the salacious behavior of a sensational porn star seducing her man while the spellbound crowd of blood thirsty pagans cheered her on was applauded and revered as normal, even deified, behavior. Barbarity was exalted!

'Moses was smitten by you. He craved you. He made no effort to conceal his lust for you. Seeing his wife and sons consigned to be shredded and eaten by the crocodiles concerned him, not in the least. His limbic pagan mind had already discovered his truest God. He knew he had found his god between your perfectly sculpted legs. His mind was fixated upon your delicious, delectable, irresistibly slippery smooth, heavenly vagina. Nothing was more compelling. Zephorah had no chance. The crowd clapped at seeing her demise, while they cheered your fornications.

'I watched Moses carefully that day. His eyes fixated on you while you consorted with the other princes. He saw the joy in your eyes, your smile, and mirthful laughs while you performed your breathtaking porn; and he read the honest happiness in your face. He saw how much you loved copulating; how facile you were with the many penises that pleasured you. I observed his quickened breath, his slackened jaw. His heart throbbed for you. He was agog with the spectacle of a woman in the throes of unashamedly pleasuring herself. I read unbridled passion wildness glowing in his eyes. His mind became transparent to me. I could read his thoughts. He was thinking:

'Mmmmm. Mmmmm. I want her. I crave her. I adore her. I must have her. I so badly want to taste her vagina with my mouth and tongue; and I must fuck her. She is the grandest, most spectacular, most glorious, most sensuous, most inviting, most uninhibited whore in all of Egypt. I must adore her. I must worship her. And I must love her!'

'He wanted to capture your joy of lovemaking for himself. He was smitten. He wanted you. More than anything or anyone else in the world, he wanted you, Marty. He wanted to make you, his world. He decided, in that moment, that he would give up his claim to the throne of Egypt for you. He decided he would murder his father, Akhenaten, the Pharoah of Egypt, and leave Nefertiti, his mother, Queen of Egypt, and all his princely comforts and all his concubines and his wife and children, for you. He needed you that badly. He appreciated your overpowering sexuality and he decided, no matter the cost, that you were priceless; and he had to have you.

'I saw his chest heave with lust for you. I saw how he adored every thrust; every twist; every gyration of your pelvis while you fornicated; how you immersed yourself in your quest to feel the pleasures of your partners' penises in your vagina; your every orgasm scream of:

'Yes! Ohhhh! Yes! Mmmmmm! And: Oh my God! Yes. Oh Yes, yes, yes! Fuck!'

'And I saw how he became spellbound as he watched your vagina's purposeful canting, exerting its irresistible downward pressures upon the tops of your partners' penis shafts; stimulating them to ecstasy; and causing them to erupt with their offerings of semen into you; and how those semen offerings spilled so freely from your vagina; and how radiant your face became with the divine holiness of your coital accomplishments. You were becoming his god during those memorable moments.

'And your vagina was becoming his holy place. He wanted to kiss it and immerse his tongue in it; and profess his adoration of it, to you. He knew in those moments that he needed to dedicate his life to worshipping you; and that his life's true purpose was to enhance *your pleasures. He desperately desired to copulate with you. He would have rather died than not have you. In that seminal moment he decided that you were more important to him than everything and everyone else in the entire world. His ardor for you; his carnal lust was that strong. You became his one true love and his only true god. In those moments, he decided he needed to abandon his wife and sons to the Nile crocodiles, for you; and for your freedom of mind from any sense of guilt or challenge from Zeporah.*

*'Moses instinctively knew that you were the key to unlocking his boundless creativity and his new life. And that, with you by his side, he would change the world. You became his divine calling. He adored you. From those moments when he observed your righteous fornications at the fertility rites, he became obsessed with you. That obsession became even stronger, so much so that he later murdered half the Hebrew people; so that, he Moses, lawgiver, and leader of all the tribes, could solely possess you.'*

*'I understand the lust effect, Miss Lust. But that was my soul's first display of my pornography. When you telescope from six thousand years ago to the present, some modern-day viewers of pornography have a very different reaction. They see porn as the subjugation and brutalization of women. Scenes where I'm doing threesomes or orgies; or when my partner is choking me or slapping me or putting his foot on my head or neck while he penetrates me are viewed as rape scenes.'*

*'I know; but you cannot control how people perceive your porn, Marty. What's important is how you perceive it, while you are performing it.'*

*'Well, my partners sometimes do those things for effect; to stimulate me and the viewer. I can always tell them to stop if I feel they are getting abusive.'*

*'But you have never told any partner to stop, have you?'*

*'No.'*

'Why not?'

'I have never felt anyone getting abusive. All I've ever felt was stimulation. Besides, I loved where I was.'

'And where was that?'

'On stage with my best friends.'

'And who are your best friends, Marty?'

'The penises.'

'Wow. Profound. Well, I think porn also can have an indirect effect upon people who bear the consequences of it. I'm thinking back to what I noticed about Pharoah.'

'So, we're back to Egypt and my seduction of Moses?'

'Yes. While it was becoming obvious to everyone that you had captivated Moses, I paid close attention to Pharoah and his reaction to what was happening. I observed Pharoah's eyes. His eyes were eagerly drinking in your pornography. They thirsted with lust for you. But he also understood that you were stealing Moses from Zeporah. His eyes noted the pleas with which the eyes of his niece, his brother's daughter, and wife of Moses, were begging him to spare her life and the lives of her children.

'But he was also a discerning Pharoah. He understood the necessity for renewal. He knew it was not possible to keep the old as well as the new. That would contradict the essence of the fertility ceremonies. He noted that the people heartily approved of your fornications and your divine pornography. He heard them clapping and shouting their raving approval of your pornography and your seduction of his son. And, for the sake of his own and Nefretiti's power, he wished to do nothing to diminish the peoples' belief in you or their acceptance of you and your ravishing pornography.

'He was a far-seeing man. He appreciated that creativity arises from destruction. Like the Nile floods sweep away old detritus from the fields of Egypt and bring new fertility and new crops and new life to his people; so, too, does destruction and renewal of the human kind. He appreciated that your splendid whoring was the catalyst which would renew and reinvigorate the creative genius of his son, Moses. He understood and accepted that, by consigning Moses's wife and children to the crocodiles, Moses would be free to create his great work. He did not realize at that time that this great work would be the Torah; or that Moses, with the help of his writers, would create a new nation and a historic, irrevocable breach with Egypt; or that this new nation would move humanity forward. But he was aware that his wife, Nefertiti, would use Moses to murder him.

'I only saw a Pharoah who recognized that the assembled masses loved you and your pornographic performances. He recognized you as the equivalent of a modern-day box-office sensation; a best actress for the Academy Award. I also saw a man who deeply loved his son. I saw Pharoah's eyes turn away from the pleas of his niece and lay their loving gaze upon you, Marty; knowing that you were his son's future. I saw his eyes give their continence and blessing to you and their praises and adoration to your magnificent whoring. In a sense of preordination, Pharoah became history's first aficionado of your spectacular pornography. He appreciated the immense importance of what you were doing. He understood how your passion for human intimacy would spark Moses, his son, to achieve an even greater greatness than he, as Pharoah, had achieved.

'In his fatherly way, Pharoah blessed you, Marty. He instinctively understood that human intimacy was humankind's only true God. And he wished that great blessing, which only you could deliver, be bestowed upon his son.

'Pharoah knew exactly what he was doing. He knew, by turning away from his niece, he was giving his assent to the endless pleasuring's of your clitoris by the tongue and penis of his son, Moses. He knew he was sanctifying your glorious, insatiable vagina and all its shameless, craven wantonness. By effectively giving Moses to you, he *gave his greatest blessing to you. And, I believe, vicariously, Pharoah also, wholeheartedly, loved you.'*

*'Thank you for that explanation, Miss Lust. I guess I can understand Moses's obsession. I also suppose Pharoah experienced a bit of voyeurism about me. Many of my Premium members feel that way, too. But I don't understand why Moses needed to be so domineering over the people? Why did he feel the need to bully everyone? And why, once he had me, did he treat me special and different from all others in the Tribe? Why did he isolate me? Why did he keep me hidden away? And why did he never once mention our love in the Torah? Did he want people to believe he was a sexless eunuch?'*

*'Marty, you need to understand. Moses was history's ultimate alpha male. He craved power. His personality was that of an iron fisted dictator; a precursor to the personalities of Mussolini, Hitler, Tojo, Lenin, Stalin, Mao, and Genge's Kahn; all killers to attain power. He was an extraordinary man; and ultimately, he was all about getting the best of everything for himself. He set the example for every male in the tribe and all the tribe's males ever since. He saw himself as the authoritarian law giver to the Hebrew tribes.*

*'He could not let the people know that he had a limbic component to his mind; or that it overwhelmed and consumed him with passion lust. He could show them no weakness. He could not reveal his passion lust for you. That meant not discussing his love for you. That meant keeping you hidden away from the others; not allowing you to flaunt your sexuality. That meant focusing on his legacy; creating the Torah. He was very driven; consumed with his authority and his laws; and he was deviously clever.*

*'Moses understood the keys to power, which were posited by Machiavelli, seven thousand years before Machiavelli even wrote his book, 'The Prince.' Moses knew that, to have you all to himself, he needed to change the tribal laws, or else he would face fierce*

resistance. He needed to make the tribe accept that they could no longer have fertility rites. No more communal orgies!

'He needed to convince his followers that there was a new, artificial, imaginary God; and that this new God was giving them laws that they needed to obey. Among these laws was the commandment forbidding adultery and the commandments about not coveting what someone else had, especially another person's spouse. Once Moses murdered those who objected to his new laws, during the Golden Calf fertility rites, he was free to have you exclusively to himself.'

'He wanted me that much?'

'Yes, Marty. He was obsessed with your wanton immorality; your joy of lovemaking. He wanted all of you, all for himself, always. He was not about sharing you. He wanted to eradicate the old Egyptian ways; eliminate the fertility rituals; put a stop to communal lovemaking.'

'So, the giving of the Ten Commandments was because of his lust for me?'

'Yes, absolutely! His religious rebellion was necessary to change the Egyptian culture's belief structure; drive it out from the ways of the Hebrew tribe. He forced change upon the people; killed all dissenters. Moses was pure Machiavellian. I think Machiavelli must have studied Moses. The way Moses led and governed was the early blueprint for Machiavelli's thinking. The way Moses split the people away from their past culture was classic Machiavellian. Sudden. --- Forceful. --- Murder. --- Seize power. --- Change by edict. No more fertility rites! No more group orgies! Only possession of one woman by one man. Only sole possession of nympho Baaleezebelle, and her fabulous, insatiable vagina, by Moses, the lawgiver! The Ten Commandments were the result of one man's romantic obsession with the world's most ribald whore.

'Moses used the Torah homilies symbolically, not as actual fact. He omitted many things, not to cause harm; but to focus the *people on his spiritual messaging. There was no exact counting of forty years in the desert. Forty years was only to help Torah readers realize the Hebrews endured a prolonged spiritual abyss. His climbs up Mount Sinai were symbolic of humanity's natural quest for spiritual enlightenment. And he tried twice because he failed to achieve enlightenment the first time. The Golden calf was symbolic of materialism and communal love by shared intimacy. He needed to overcome materialism. He needed to squash communal intimacy and institute monogamy so he could have you, all to himself. He needed to climb Mount Sinai that second time. He had to make the tribe believe they had something stronger than communal intimacy.'*

*'What? What could possibly be stronger?'*

*'Spirituality.'*

*'But why not mention our love? We had such a beautiful, intimate love!'*

*'He intended to make the people believe in themselves; make them believe they only needed spirituality. He needed to make them believe that, even though they were stumbling around in the desert, trying to find themselves, they were God's chosen people. He needed to make them believe that their belief in themselves as a tribe was all they needed; that they didn't need anyone else; that they could count on themselves to survive, thrive; conquer other cultures and nations when it was necessary to do so. He essentially brainwashed them to think of themselves as different and apart, and better than all other tribes and nations.*

*'He convinced them that they could do no wrong; that God always had their back. Headstrong or stiff necked are terms that describe the mindset which Moses sought to instill in his people. He wanted them to believe they were beholden to no one; dependent upon no one; resilient to all stresses and adversity; exacting in word and deed; and confident in the rightness of God's decision to make them his chosen people. And that mindset has stuck with*

them through the ages. He made that belief system so strong that the Israelites became willing to kill and destroy all who opposed them.

'Moses was not about love between a man and a woman. He was about love of the idea of one god. Oh, he loved you, all right; but if he had his writers weave his obsessive love for you into their Torah text, it would have changed the Torah's sacred spiritual text into a romance novel. And Moses didn't have the time or inclination to write romance novels. He was intent on creating the Israelite peoples' belief system.'

'But what did 'He' want? What did 'He' really want for himself?'

'Oh, You! Definitely you! He wanted you, Marty; you and your sensational, nympho crazed vagina. You were his rapture. He loved you with all the obsessive powers of his limbic lust.'

'But he didn't need to murder all those people to have me! He knew I loved him! He had conquered my feelings! I knew he was devoted to me when he had his wife and kids murdered. He knew I was committed to him. He already knew he had me!'

'Yes, but he did not want to share you. He feared losing you. Many obsessive-compulsive narcissists are paranoid about threats to their power. You, if set free to copulate freely and wantonly, communally, would be a threat to his power. You were his woman, whom he needed to control.

'He became as possessive as a male salmonoid, chasing away other male salmonoids from his clutch of eggs. You carried a precious clutch of eggs in your womb, Marty. He wanted to be the only male to fertilize your eggs; and for that, he needed to keep all other males away from you. He instinctively knew that your vagina was where his concept of 'One God Fits All' clashed with natural reality, and lost. He could not risk that. He needed to contain and control you. He remembered how wanton and profligate you were during the fertility rites; how you joyfully milked the semen streams from the Apis bulls; how you gleefully consorted *with the other princes; how much you relished your whoring. He understood your nymphomania.*

*'He saw how the other princes and Pharoah himself adored your whoring; how they raved and applauded you when your vagina and your mouth coaxed away the semen streams from the Apis bulls; and how you fornicated with uninhibited pride, with multiple partners; and how you squealed with delight while your partners licked your clitoris while performing cunnilingus; and how you smiled with your beguiling smiles while you, proudly and wantonly, often held open your vagina to display your overflowing semen pools from the hundred partners you had drained of semen over that fortnight of fertility rites. He saw how you smiled your beguiling smiles as you welcomed each new partner with your wanton kisses; how your mirthful, teasing lips seemed to proclaim:*

*'Yes, I am a whore. I am the most highly prized whore in Pharoah's harem. And my flesh is soft and inviting. And my skin is lily white. And I am the most sensuous whore in all of Egypt. See my mirthful smiles while I fornicate? Hear my delightful squeals when I am fondled and touched? Would you like to touch my warm welcoming breasts? My tongue has received and savored many ejaculations. Come, meet your tongue to mine. Taste my mouth. My vagina has milked semen from the Apis bulls and from many lovers. Come, couple your mouth to it. Would you like to discover my clitoris with your tongue? Would you like to pleasure me? Taste my sex? Discover my immorality? That's what you want, isn't it?*

*'Yes, as you can plainly see, I have no morals. But you love that about me, don't you? You want more of me, don't you? By the ways my kisses and tongue play with your mouth and tongue, can you imagine how badly I need to feel your hot cum spurting over my clitoris? By my kisses, can you tell how badly I want to suck your penis and how much I'd love to fuck you? By my kisses, can you imagine the joys we will share while we fuck? Mmmmmm, can you imagine*

*how wonderful your penis will feel when it's inside my vagina? Mmmmm. Mmmmmm. You do want to fuck me, don't you?*

*'Can you imagine how slippery wet and warm my vagina is? Can you imagine how wonderful your penis will feel when it is immersed inside me? Can you imagine how impossible it will be for you to ever forget how wonderful my vagina feels to you while you held your penis inside me? Can you tell how badly my vagina needs your penis inside her?*

*'Have you seen how much I love displaying my vagina after a penis has ejaculated inside me? Haven't you noticed what a prideful whore I am while I'm flaunting my semen filled vagina for all the world to see? And demonstrating that I shamelessly did what I love doing? Wouldn't you love to have your penis come inside me? Mmmmm. Admit it! Sure, you would! Can you imagine how wonderful you will feel while you ejaculate inside me? You want to make love with me, don't you? Sure, you do. So, put your cares aside and come to me. Come to me, now. I want you.'*

*'And Moses saw how you smiled with joy and adoration as you beheld each partner's penis and welcomed it with your tongue and your lips; and how you slathered it with your sucking and prepared it for the divine moment when you guided it to touch your outer vaginal lips, and then welcomed it with your thrusting hips as you guided it deep inside you.*

*'He realized you were the world's consummate whore; prideful and glorious in your whoring. He recognized that the other men and the princes also saw that quality in you. And he felt his skin flush hot with jealousy. He wanted to possess you. And he witnessed the way men jostled for the honor of perfuming cunnilingus with you while you joyfully stroked and sucked other men's penises; and he noted how much you enjoyed those attentions lavished upon you and how delighted you were in having your vagina pleasured by men's tongues. And he saw how you shamelessly took each of those*

hundred men from their wives and babies, cleaving their love and adoration to you; thus, consigning their babies to their death rendezvous with the Nile crocodiles and their wives to lives of slavery.

'Moses noted how Pharoah and the other princes revered you; how they seated you upon your pillowed throne chair, high above their sacrifices. He noted how regally you sat there, with your leg casually splayed over an arm of the chair; semen flowing freely from your vagina; while each of your hundred consorts placed before you their offerings of gold and jewels; paying homage to your splendid whoring, while their wives consigned their babies to the guards for delivery to the crocodiles. In those moments, Moses realized the people revered you as their Goddess.

'And Moses treasured the way you knowingly smiled and mouthed your kisses to him after you watched the guards march his wife and children to the barge. He knew then, as he came to you, that you appreciated that he had them delivered to the crocodiles in order to make the pathway clear for you to become his wife; that you approved of their impending deaths. In those moments you attained the pinnacle of your glory; and you became idolized by all who were present; and you became the true God of Moses.

'You could not and did not concern yourself with the lives of others. Their lives were beneath you. You were wholly committed to immersing yourself in your immoral wantonness. You were shameless, undeterred passion-lust, personified. Moses knew, in those unforgettable moments, that you, alone, were the most splendid, most desirable whore in all of Egypt. He knew that it was in your nature to willfully, wantonly promote your profligate sin-lust cravings to other men; flood their limbic minds with lust for you, like it was in the nature of the mighty Nile to flood its new, life-giving waters over the lands of Egypt.

'But there was a great irony about Moses. His cravings for you arose from the old Egyptian ways of communal worship and fertility rites; but he wanted a way of life that gave him sole possession of you. Moses could not stand the thought of sharing you. In those moments when he resolved his contradiction, you became more precious to him than all the jewels and gold in Egypt. He would willingly have traded the world for exclusive intimacy with you and your fabulous vagina. He couldn't risk that you, likely, would naturally want to copulate with others; that you might leave him to whore, or even, possibly, return to Egypt where new Pharoah Nefretiti might open her arms to welcome you back as the most desirable whore in her harem.

'So, yes Marty, you conquered Moses. That came natural to you. He was, after all, a mere mortal man. And no man can resist you. You have the spirit of conquest residing within you from the spirt DNA of the Anunnaki. No man has ever resisted you; not even Moses. The Great Spirit put you on Earth to propagate human love and connectivity through your Butterfly Morals. But Moses could not risk that you might flutter on to become intimate with others. He had to possess you.

'But you do love to flutter. You were history's first porn star; with the natural and resurrecting soul of a nympho whore. Fluttering; having amorous affairs with multiple partners is natural for you. You are completely comfortable with it. So, do not resent Moses for being possessive with you. He was merely at the beginning stage of his gilgul, his soul's eternal passage towards enlightenment.

'Look how far humanity has come! You have Bob now; and all your many lovers. Bob is possibly a recent reincarnation of the soul that once traveled with Moses. The two men actually have a great deal in common. They both adore and love you because they recognize that you are passionate about moving humanity forward through your practice of intimate artistry. Where others take offence, they both see intimate beauty in your pornography. They both see you as a human butterfly with Butterfly Morals. And they *both adore you for who and what you are. And both men believe in you and love you.*

*'Just look how wonderfully Bob treats you. Look how completely comfortable he is with your whoring. He loves you; and he loves knowing he can accommodate you, so you can freely enjoy your cravings for intimacy. And you do love having your freedom to enjoy your casual intimacies with many lovers; with Carl, Marshawn, Josh, Fred, Ed, Travis, Dom, and Charles, your European Prince, to name a few. So, here we are in present day. You now understand that it is natural and good for your mental health; and progressive for humanity for you to continue making love and creating more of your spectacular porn films. And you also know it is good for your mental health and self-esteem to commit your murders, as David explained to you.*

*'Can you now accept those truths about yourself?'*

*'Yes, Miss Lust, I suppose I can. I must. I am who and what I am; and I cannot change myself.'*

*'Good. And you should not fret about changing into someone you are not. Nietzche said that it is rare for one individual to go insane; but it is common for a crowd of humans to be insane. You are unique; alone and apart. It is those who believe in their religions who are insane. Religion; that belief in an imaginary, fictitious, manmade God, is the practice of group insanity, sanctioned by tax exempt status. It causes more wars, genocides, and loss of life than it causes peace. It's never viewed objectively by its practitioners because they all view their beliefs from the perspective of their respective echo chambers. That echo chamber is all their minds know. It's a comfortable place for their minds to be. And they see no reason to leave that comfortable place because the harm they inflict are harms upon others; not themselves. Only when their world view is shattered do they reflect upon whether their beliefs were rooted in reason.*

*'The German population from the advent of the Nazis until losing World War Two was fervently invested in the state-based*

religion of Nazism. Religious cults and idol worship practices have risen up and later disappeared throughout human history. Why will today's religions be any different? When upheaval shakes these religions and the people discover that their gods made no difference to their outcomes, the people will seek a new form of group insanity to latch onto. So, you see, you are much less likely to be disappointed if you believe in yourself. It's an internal thing. You must believe in yourself. You can do it.

'Just because the world has gone mad with its religions and its hatreds and its wars, does not mean you need to join them. Stay free. Embrace and practice your free-spirited love. Restore humankind's adoration of whoredom to its venerated pre-religious status. Restore humanity's adoration of pornography to be the guiding light that shows us the way to greater freedom, greater human love, and progressive change. Show the world, through your beautiful pornography, that human intimacy is a glorious and wonderful thing.'

'I will, Miss Lust. Oh yes! I certainly will! I love my life and I have no shame or regrets about creating my glorious porn. I feel rapture while I'm on stage, performing my intimate artistry. I have to be the girl that I am. I have to be able to do whatever I want to do; and to be able to do it with whomever I want to do it with. That's just who I am. And I love what I do.'

'Good Marty. Always remember, you have become a notorious, world renown porn star with a wonderful life. And your soul will continue having more wonderful lives; forever. Can you appreciate that you and Moses lived during that historic intersection of the limbic and the rational; that you both lived and experienced the ultimate passions of both your minds? He changed the world's way of seeing God. And you are now simply changing the world back to seeing God as human intimacy, once again. And you are succeeding brilliantly! So, can you now let go of your disappointment that Moses didn't write about you?'

'Yes, Miss Lust. I can accept that Moses and I lived our ultimate passions. I recognized him as a uniquely exceptional man, a true Mench and a historic figure. I fell deeply into love with him and loved him with every fiber of my being, even in the marrow of my bones. Ours was the most wonderful, exhilarating, most spiritual love of all my loves. Moses is my sweetest memory from all my past lives. Our great love is history now. I must let it go and keep moving forward. I now understand that it is natural for me, as a modern human woman, to feel free-spirited and unashamed about my intimacies.

'And, now that I have David's protection, I need have no qualms about committing my murders. Intimacy and murder both give me my wonderful sense of empowerment and freedom. I've known for a long time that both my intimacies and my murders are blessed by the spirits. It's my spirit's ways of asserting my power; like dominance and murder were the methods Moses used to assert his power.'

'Good. Then, let me help you rationalize your behavior. Since it is perfectly natural for you to murder; and since your murders are blessed by the spirits, you should have no reason to feel guilty about murdering. Isn't that true?'

'Yes, that's true.'

'And you also know these matters about your hybrid DNA and your proclivity to commit murders and your carnal messaging to the spirit of your dead father must at all times be kept strictly confidential between your own mind and your voices; otherwise, people would find out we are both insane and you'd be institutionalized. Noone would believe you when you tell them you have a special voice that speaks to you from your feelings. I don't want that. And you don't want that. So, you do understand that you must keep these matters secret, just between us, don't you?'

'Yes, Miss Lust. I do understand. And I will.'

'Good, Marty. Then, can you now go forward and continue to murder with a clear conscience; and can you feel good about committing your murders?'

'Yes, my precious feeling voice of Miss Lust, I can. I understand my purpose much better now.'

'And you love to commit your murders, don't you?'

'Oh yes, Miss Lust; very much! I do love to commit murder. I do. I really do. I love doing them!'

'Very good, Marty. Now stop feeling guilty about committing your murders. History absolved Moses of his murders. You will be absolved, too. Your murders are morally right and beautiful. Besides, they give you pleasure. Always remember, just like the Anunnaki and your Pagan whore ancestors committed murders to move humanity forward, so do you. Always keep in mind that what you are doing is good and beautiful.

'Take your thoughts away from me now. Return your mind to the present. Go and enjoy Cannes with Dom. Focus on making love with him and on creating your sensational mouthwatering porn films; and on your Premium Service Members; and on your sweet romantic home times with Bob, until David needs you for another murder. Goodbye.'

Miss Lust vanished from Marty's feelings.


'Why am I doing this interview?' Marty regained control of her thoughts and returned to the present. She whispered to herself:

'Why don't I tell Consuelo how I really feel? Why not blurt out that I want to give up sex work entirely, that I want to stop working with David, and that I want to run off with Bob to a little house in the countryside; and have babies with him; and just love him and enjoy my babies and be happy?

'Why can't I say what I really want out of my life? Oh, yes, I know. How could I forget? It's my nymphomania! It's my DNA and my conditioning. I MUST have sex to fill my empty feeling. And if I went with Bob, I wouldn't have my empty, craving feelings and I wouldn't need to have as much sex; but I LOVE having sex so much; and with many different partners! It keeps me stimulated. I HAVE to have it. So, my body won't let me do what my heart honestly wants to do.

'I'm trapped. I want to be someone whom I cannot be; but I COULD be that someone if I could only be honest. But, IF I was honest, I'd be giving up everything: all my fame; all my money; my partners; all that fantastic sex. I'd have nothing. I'd still have Bob. But I have Bob anyway. He's my quiet, understanding enabler.

'Maybe I'd be a happier woman if Bob got angry with me and forbade me from making my porn films. But Dom loves my porn films and he wants to help me make more of them for the big screen. That's so exciting! I can't say no to an opportunity like that. I love pleasing Dom. I don't know what it is. Maybe its his money and all that power. And, I absolutely love having sex with him. Mmmmmm. I feel positively wonderful just thinking about it. I love having Dom's penis inside me.

'But maybe if I tried to settle down and have a family with Bob, I wouldn't have Bob at all. He'd know I wasn't being my true self anymore. He'd know I was denying my nymphomania, wouldn't he? Sure, he would. He'd know he didn't have the real me anymore. Then, maybe Barbara would get Bob.

'Gads! That would be horrible! Then what could I do? No porn career, and no Bob! How could I start over? I can't let that happen! That's my worst fear. It terrifies me. I cannot let Consuelo see that I am afraid of anything. That would destroy my image. My head is spinning. Why am I feeling so messed up right now?'

*"Marty, were you saying something, just now?"* Consuelo caught Marty's lip movements.

*"No, I wasn't talking to myself."* Marty denied an obvious truth. *"I just move my lips while I think some thoughts sometimes; that's all, Consuelo."* Marty caught herself.

Barbara's keen power of observation also caught Marty's slip up. She shared it with Big Horse:

*"There seemed to be an awkward moment there, at that weird confusion break during Marty's interview. I believe Consuelo Lovely caught Marty talking to herself,"* commented Barbara to Bob.

*"I thought I noticed you talking to yourself,"* continued Consuelo. *"Your lips were sort of moving like they were saying things. Can I help you with anything? Would you like a glass of water?"* Consuelo asked Marty.

# CHAPTER FIVE

*Blow your own horn. If a horn isn't handy, well, use your imagination. (Rosemary Ness-Bitner, author)*

## EMERGING

*"Oh, sometimes my lips just do that when I have an erotic inspiration, that's all Consuelo. It's nothing. Really, it's nothing. Let's see, where were we? Oh yes, The Cannes casinos were an eye opener for me. I saw how the continentals do business."* Marty returned her mind to the present. She continued speaking for her interview.

*"Subtly, gentlemen from Switzerland, Lichtenstein, Luxembourg, Monaco, Germany, France, Italy, and Greece approached our table. They asked if I would please take their cards and have my service call them. I did that, of course. In the weeks that followed I was receiving offers to accompany several of them to various trade shows and sporting events for a full week's time. My service raised my prices to a whole new level.*

*"I was charging a quarter million dollars for an unrestricted week of my time with them. I didn't quite understand this new game, at first; but soon I was promoting luxury cars, private airplane time shares, luxury hotel time shares, an exclusive world travel club, an exclusive adult resort, exotic customized automobiles, high end performance tires, a luxury yacht manufacturer, and an exclusive world-wide catering service.*

"I was photographed wearing my Premium Line transparent bikinis while getting kisses and respectful touchings to my highly esteemed vagina from many admiring hands. I was kissed and touched while in revealing positions in the back seats of luxury limousines. I was fondled while lying naked, with my mouth and hands on yearning penises, sprawled shamelessly on fold-out beds in private jets; smiling coquettishly while noticing a hand groping my derriere as I walked through the doors of an exclusive resort; provocatively posed while wearing my see-through Premium Line bikinis; welcoming my breasts being hand massaged while lying seductively naked; kissing a gorgeous penis on sumptuous king sized beds on luxury yacht; being groped while wearing my Premium Line see-through negligee; holding onto the open door of a helicopter while smiling, holding my outstretched leg high, and wearing my Premium Line see-through, reveal all, bikini while waving to the camera; and posing suggestively in one of my high end, Premium Line transparent jeweled bikinis beside an Indi 500 race car, with one hand on one of its tires; the other hand waving while I smiled.

"I received huge endorsement fees for those gigs in addition to my weekly rate time. What a revelation! I had often heard the phrase: 'Sex sells.' But it never occurred to me how profoundly true those simple two words were. I had no idea that my porn star's profligate, wanton vagina could deliver sales on the scale that my promotions achieved. I had no inkling that my sponsors would be willing to pay me the millions that they paid me to position their products with photographs and film clips of my famous, penis craving vagina. I was blown away. Before my European tour, I never realized that my immoral, sex crazed vagina could, in and of itself, be commercialized as a priceless marketing asset.

"Soon, my face and figure adorned millions of marketing brochures. I was portrayed in some marketing blurbs as 'Porn Star, Extraordinaire.' In one gig, where I'm cast as 'Woman on Top of the

World,' I leaned over the top of a huge globe of the world with a low-cut halter top exposing my ample cleavage; beaming my brightest smile while blowing a kiss to the world. I was promoting a world-wide exclusive travel club that included beautiful women for escort companionship. Its membership costs a million dollars. Europeans' adoration of ribald, uninhibited, shameless, whoring absolutely blew me away, Consuelo. Their appetite for perverse pleasuring themes with my vagina seems insatiable. The continentals heartily approve of my absence of morals. And they love me.

# CHAPTER SIX

*To unlock a man's thought closet, unzip his pants. Let his penis do the talking. (Rosemary Ness-Bitner, author)*

## DELIVERANCE

*"While at Cannes I met Charles, a middle-aged gentleman, fabulously wealthy heir to over thirty billion Euros, not including his prized art collections. After I agreed to pose for him, his private jet flew me to Paris. He said he'd meet me at Charles de Gaulle airport, but he didn't. Instead, one of his limos picked me up and whisked me to his estate. After he showed me around the grounds, he unlocked the doors to a huge three-story building.*

*"Well, Consuelo, what he had inside that building totally blew me away. There were hundreds of valuable sculptures and art pieces. He had many of the best works of the best artists that ever lived. And, Consuelo, they were all nudes! I was shocked. I would learn later just how much Charles adores the naked female form.*

*"Charles walked me through this huge gallery of his collection of masterpieces. He showed me picture after picture. Charles has perfect recall. He described the background of each picture from his personal knowledge. There were portraits, nature scenes, impressionists, cubists, abstracts, and extremely valuable pieces of rare classic period art. In the back rooms, behind steel doors in humidified rooms, Charles had hoarded away the finest works of Picasso,*

*Rembrandt, Rubens, Manet, Gaugin, Monet, Klimt, DuChant, Modigliani, Matisse, Gerome, Courbet, Ingres, Goya, Velazquez, Durer, Botticelli, Leonardo, Michelangelo; and on and on. It was a seemingly endless, priceless collection. And before each piece there was a velvet viewing bench. Charles asked me if I would be willing to pose for him while he photographed me. I felt honored to be asked; so, of course, I agreed.*

*"I posed in varied exotic lingerie ensembles before Charles' favorite pieces. Before Rubens' 'LEDA and the SWAN,' I first stood between the painting and the viewing bench in a pink chiffon bodice and black lace teddy. Slowly, I smiled and turned my body and varied my poses while Charles clicked his camera's shutter. Deliberately, I puckered my lips in a pout and smiled my most alluring coquettish smile as I removed my bodice and cupped my breasts for Charles and his sexually aroused camera. I became temptation personified. I blew my seductive, come and fuck me kisses to the camera and turned around very slowly, pausing, lifting my breasts, while bending my tush to the camera; all the time, smiling my inviting, please, please come hither and hold me and fuck me smile. I pinched my nipples and lifted them up, as if offering them to be tasted, while I smiled my best teasing smile to Charles.*

*"I could tell that I was getting Charles excited. He clicked his camera's lens faster and faster. I next opened my legs slightly, while turning and bending; seductively rubbing my vagina with my hand while gradually revealing my vagina. Then, I held myself open and offered Charles first a full rear picture view; and then my full-frontal view. I asked Charles whether he liked what he was seeing. He assured me that he very much did. I was now certain that Charles could not be mistaken about my intentions to have sex with him. I then moved my face very close to Charles' camera and smiled my most teasing coquettish smile. Then, licking my lips, I slowly removed my teddy.*

"I then pursed my lips and held my index finger to my mouth. My finger pretended it was a penis. And I pretended to lick it and suck it. As I licked the underside of my finger, suggestively stimulating my finger-penis, I also rubbed my hand over my vagina. Charles alternately pointed his camera at my lips and my vagina, while clicking the shutter rapidly. I sensed that his libido had become fully engaged; and his desires to become intimate with me were driving him crazy with passion lust. I instinctively knew we were getting close to our magic moment. I felt certain that, behind his camera, Charles knew I was inviting him to put the camera down and make love with me. But Charles did nothing. He was not responsive. He became an enigma; a challenge; somehow a man who willfully declined to fuck me. I was not deterred. I knew there had to be something deeper going on in Charles' mind. And I became determined to figure him out.

"I decided to lay upon the viewing bench. I rested one foot upon the floor and raised my other foot to the bench; then tucked my foot beneath my raised leg. I rolled my body slightly toward the Rubens behind me. This pose presented Charles and his camera a highly seductive reveal of my vagina from behind. The camera continued clicking. But Charles did not touch me. I started wondering what it would take to get Charles to touch me, somewhere; anywhere; anything to signal me that he was ready; anything I could respond to. By now I was getting moist just imagining that we would come together soon; but I had no idea what I needed to do to make that happen.

"I thought, perhaps a prop that might elicit the suggestion of a bedroom scene would help Charles. A white satin sheet was conveniently near the viewing bench. I sat upright on the velvet bench, seductively arched my back, held the sheet between my legs; laying my head against its fold, which I held in my hand. I presented myself as a demure, vulnerable kitty who was more than willing and eager to have sex. And, communicating intimate projection thoughts to

*Charles, I kissed the sheet. Charles became wildly excited. His camera clicked wildly, capturing ever conceivable angle of my face and body while I, pretending to be Leda in the picture, gave my best impressions of erotic sensuous love-making with my imaginary swan. Surely, I thought, Charles could imagine himself as the swan. Surely, he wanted to become the swan. Surely, he would soon come to me; take me into his arms, and make love with me. But nothing. Instead, Charles wildly, rapidly, clicked his camera. I decided to move to the next masterpiece and try a different prop scheme; something perhaps more explicit and erotic. I retrieved some items from my carrying bag and prepped myself with a pastel blue, silk nightgown for my next scene.*

*"In a similar seduction manner as I did with the Rubens, I gradually removed my nightgown and ever so slowly and seductively pulled down my white transparent panties before Durer's portrait of Eve. After I became completely naked, I lay upon the viewing bench, my widely spread legs revealing my vagina to the camera. I then held a red apple to my mouth. My eyes flashed totally erotic vibrations to Charles. I was letting him know that I was a very willful sinner. My goal in this sequence was to bring the original sin of Adam and Eve forward to our present day's immoral, debauched world. I was delighted to tease Charles with my fantasy recreation of original sin. I held my vagina invitingly open and even canted my hips in mock thrusts, clearly signaling that I wanted to be fucked; all the while taking sensuous, deliciously sinfully small, teasing bites of the apple between my sin loving, temptress smiles. After a few bites, I licked my upper lip, revealing the underside of my tongue. Surely, I thought, Charles would imagine my tongue plying its favors over his penis. I became highly stimulated while I did these erotically signaling poses. I began feeling this desperate urge to fuck Charles. Meanwhile, my host's camera clicked wildly. Charles captured dozens of close ups of my lips and vagina. But he still stayed away from me and did not*

*touch me. I became more determined than ever to seduce my prince. Somewhere, from the recesses of my limbic mind, I felt something stir. I just knew, in that moment, that I was going to fuck Charles. I had what I would call an anticipatory imagining. In my mind's eye, I could already see my lips stroking Charles' penis during our first of many intimate, loving fellatios. But the next painting, a Picasso, beckoned me to continue my seduction quest.*

*"Before Picasso's "Nude and Green Leaves" Charles had me strike a demonstrative posse with my feet tucked under me, one elbow behind my neck, head flung back with my breasts uplifted and protruding. I stretched back, gradually lifting my breasts higher and higher as the camera's shutter clicked. Charles was framing my body from a distance. From the gallery's lighting panel, Charles caused a bright yellow beam of light to flow over my body. The two of us were working together now. We were creating the effect of a sensual nymph-goddess, awakening from her deep erotic sleep at sunrise. Then, Charles changed the light tones and hues, ever so slowly. My skin responded with sensation feelings. My moods changed as the light moved from yellow to taupe, then to shades of softer and softer violet. I was becoming highly aroused from the effects of the lighting changes. A chameleon-like impulse coursed through my blood and raised the heat of my skin. My nympho urges signaled me. I knew I positively needed to fuck Charles. I wasn't sure what was happening to me. But I suddenly felt vulnerable. Other men had dominated me; but those has always been hands on, physical affairs. Charles didn't do any of that. I was getting to know him through our silent communications. I knew there would be no slapping or choking; no biting; no spreaders or clamps. No, none of those things; no wan balls; no BDSM. But these poses; this mood manipulation with the lighting was actually more effective than any other stimulations I had ever received from any other man. I was going crazy inside. My libido was in overdrive; yet I could do nothing to satisfy myself.*

*I knew this day could not end without experiencing intimacy with him. By now, I desperately wanted to have sex with Charles. I was so anxious for him to start. I wanted his fingers in my vagina, probing me, stimulating me; anything; but please, please, I thought. Charles! Please start! I wanted him so badly! I knew I needed to get a grip. This needed to play out on Charles' timetable.*

*"I whispered 'Oooh, that's very nice, Charles,' as Charles continued snapping the shutter. My passions awakened within me. My skin seemed to know Charles adored seeing my body in the different lights. And then, just as I began to understand just how wildly aroused the lights were making me. The light tones changed again, from light violet to darker violet; and then to a shade of faint pink; and then, slowly, to a darker pink. This darker pink was sending throbbing pulsations down my clitoral tentacles. Now, not just my vagina, but even my legs were feeling this overwhelming urge to fuck. 'AHHH,' I said, more audibly this time. I couldn't hold back my desires. I could no longer mask my feelings of arousal. Then finally, the pink shading blended into red. It was a light red at first, then a deeper passionate red. I felt suddenly electrified, like my vagina had suddenly burst into flames.*

*'Oh, Charles! Oh Charles! What are you doing to me?' "I asked, near breathlessly, in my most teasing promiscuous voice. My nymphomania had become fully awakened. My mouth wanted to join Charles' mouth and begin kissing him wildly. My entire vulva was experiencing this raging fire. I wanted Charles to take me now; push me down on the view bench and ravage me. I wanted to discover his penis so badly; feel it thrusting inside me; loving its penetration and deep plunges; I almost screamed for him to fuck me.*

*"But I held myself together somehow and waited patiently. This was his gig; his way of getting somewhere. I intuited that I needed to go with the flow of things and be a good partner for him. I've had many lovers who liked to take me slowly; but this was beyond*

anything I ever knew before. This was excruciatingly, torturously slow. I was like a minx in heat. I was so ready to fuck. I had this feeling I get sometimes when I'm totally into a lover and his penis. It's this sensation that tells me I could fuck all night long.

"But then, Charles moved closer to me. I knew I'd need to wait even longer. He continued clicking his damned shutter. The thought crossed my mind that he could be a psycho; that what I was doing with him and his camera could somehow be dangerous for me. But I pushed back against that thought. I told myself that he was just being very timid and boyish; that there were some deeply seated needs inside Charles' mind; and that, with my patience and my sincere love, he would reveal those needs to me. And then, we would become true friends and true lifelong lovers.

"Anyway, I decided I needed to continue. I needed to trust Charles and just let myself go. I'm not at all religious, but this was my 'Leave it at the foot of the cross' moment. I decided I needed to play along with this strange game we were playing, no matter how maddening it became. And, above all else, I needed to find it in my heart to love Charles; just love him! Then, closer still, he captured close-up shot after close-up shots of my breasts, taking at least a hundred photos, until his lens was only an inch away from my nipples.

"I intuitively felt a powerful invisible bond forming between myself and Charles. I sensed his eyes thirsting to lick my creamy white skin; his lips wanting to suckle my nipples, and his tongue becoming eager to savor my orgasmic juices. I knew his eyes were doing much more than just seeing me. They were beholding me; taking in the wonder of me; measuring me; feasting upon my flesh, imagining they were watching my facial expressions of pleasure while he was ravaging me with his magnificent, fully erect, very hardened penis. I felt Charles' eyes visually titillating, licking, tongue teasing, sucking, and pinching my nipples. And I imagined Charles's eyes magically sending his soul deeply into my soul and immersing his parched loneliness inside my intimacy; so that he could lose himself forever within me; this totally immoral, incorrigible, promiscuous but loving whore he had decided he could finally trust and love.

"I sensed escapism held Charles in its grip. I asked myself: 'Does he see me as his life-saving oasis? If he does, why doesn't he do something? What's preventing him? Surely, he must know I want him. He must know that I would welcome his advances; that I would offer no resistance; only encouragement. Why doesn't he touch me or kiss me? How can I be any more obvious that I want him to initiate contact with me?'

"There I was, posing live; making alluring gestures with my eyes and facial expressions; signaling that I was imminently kissable, touchable; and welcoming to him. I was a real woman in the flesh; hoping for, eagerly waiting for his approach, posed amidst a dessert plate of lust-beckoning artistic masterpieces; but those were all silent, unresponsive, lifeless painted nudes. Those naked portraits must have, ordinarily, for hour after hour, stirred Charles' lusts and fired his imagination. He must have spent countless private hours imagining that he was making love with those voluptuous females in those paintings. But I sensed that this day, in these erotic lens capturing moments, the nudes in those paintings were no more appealing to him than so many grains of sand. But I was different for him; a whole different experience. I was live. I was real. And Charles wanted me. He wanted the real woman, me; not some imaginary tryst with an imaginary woman in a painting. I instinctively knew he wanted to make love with me. I knew he wanted to immerse his soul in mine. This is something every woman just instinctively knows about the man she is with. I knew I wasn't wrong. A woman somehow knows these things about a man. I was more certain that Charles wanted me than I was about anything, ever in my life. Charles wanted to come out of this shell he was in. He desired to partake of real life.

"Charles' eyes stayed riveted on me. They were fixated, like those of a man possessed of a parched soul that thirsted for love. I could feel his soul struggling mightily to reach mine. I felt his eyes carrying his thoughts; desperate, pleading thoughts. His thoughts crawled to me across the blistering hot sands of something forbidden to him. The hundreds of assembled lifeless nudes in those paintings were awakening and becoming our witnesses. I sensed them watching us. They wanted to see Charles breaking free of his restraint. They yearned to reach out to me and Charles. They yearned to immerse his tortured soul in my soul and join his living body to mine. It was as if they believed they would come alive again, if only the two of us would become intimate. I could almost hear them all crying out to us:

'Make love! Become lovers! Yes! Make love! Do it! It will be beautiful! Just take her in your arms, Charles. She wants you to. Go to her. Hold her. Hug her. Kiss her. Press your hand against her breast. Feel her heart. Place your hand inside her panties and touch her sex. Feel her there. Massage her there. Finger her. Peel down her panties. Kiss her there. Let her know how much you want her. Touch your penis to her outer lips. Feel her hands on your penis. Feel her guiding you inside her. Feel her loving you. And love her, Charles. Love her.'

"It seemed like his soul's survival depended upon him crossing this unseen, punishing divide; and plunging into my welcoming salvation. His entire body betrayed his unmistakably deep longing for intimacy. I felt it. In that moment, I wanted him more than I ever wanted any man.

"I noticed how Charles often puckered and whetted his lips while he stared into my face. His eyes now kissed mine once again; then they darted away to stare at my lips. This time, they lingered on my lips. Charles is a remarkably handsome man. I was becoming frustrated, wishing he would do something; make some kind of move, anything. I asked myself: 'What's wrong? Why is he holding back?

He knows I'm a notorious porn star. He has to know, from seeing my films, that I love making love; that I'm completely uninhibited and shameless about my promiscuity; that nothing would hold me back from making love with him. Logically, I'd be completely agreeable and amenable to having sex with him. He's not stupid. So, What's holding him back?'

"But I didn't challenge him. I remained in control of myself; continuing as his perfect model. I began to study his fingers. They often left his camera to motion sense the air and signal to me the many ways he wanted me to move my body. It seemed his fingers imagined how they would feel while touching my body, everywhere. These thoughtful, deliberations told me that Charles was a perfectionist; and an extraordinarily sensitive, loving man. By the way he savored every second of these preliminary moments, he was allowing me to know him better.

"His finger-hand signals did more than reveal the positions he preferred to see me pose; they helped me realize that Charles was a very sensitive, caring, passionate man. They fired my desires and caused me to feel these raging stirrings in my sex. I felt myself blushing from something much more profound than modesty. There was a rising awareness that we were forming an unbreakable, trusting, relationship bond. Our two hearts were feeling each other's need. Unspoken empathy was guiding us somewhere. Neither of us knew where; but we were coming to know that we could trust our mutual sense. And that we were in this beautiful process of revealing our love to each other.

"My sixth sense assured me that Charles had fallen in love with me. This splendid man, this aristocrat prince with his immense wealth and good looks, culture, and continental refinements, who was just now revealing his sensuality, wanted something more than sex from me. He wanted me to be his friend. And he actually, truly loved me.

"I knew he did. As a woman, I knew. I knew he wanted me to capture him, enshroud him in my immoral world and harvest his soul. There's this certain sense that stays with a woman once a man has established trust with her. It's undeniable and unshakeable. Every promiscuous woman feels it when her man gives off a certain vibe. Men can't hide it from women. Their senses have not evolved that far. They don't even know how to conceal it. Most men understand this and don't even try to conceal it; and those who do try to conceal it, fail. Some people label it 'chemistry.' It is a kind of chemistry; but it is more of a bonding of feelings kind of thing; more like when sodium and chlorine unite to create salt. By themselves, both elements are toxic; but together, they become the key to life itself.

"Love is a bonding like that. It begins slowly. There's this joining of emotions and feelings. It creeps up on lovers, silently, without them even realizing it's happening. But it's presence can't be denied. It comes as trust builds. Then, suddenly, it's just there. While it's happening, a woman knows. She recognizes it before the man does, because she's more sensitive to it; more able to feel the man's vibes. The vibes the male gives off can tell her this could be a wonderful thing; or his vibes might scream to her to run for the hills.

"I caught Charles' vibes. I know men. Charles wanted me; but not just for sex. Charles wanted me for all of me. His emotions were vibrating like a vibrator on high speed. They were unmistakable. And, like a vibrator, they were stimulating me. Every feminine instinct I had told me that Charles was dying to hold me in his arms and kiss me passionately, as a prelude to making love with me, right there on the viewing bench. Love in every form of love and in every position; and with delightfully pleasing cunnilingus; absolutely with uninhibited, loving cunnilingus. I intuited that Charles was dying to cup my mons pubis to his face and ply my clitoris with his adoring tongue. I was surer of my read-on Charles than I've ever been about any man.

"But Charles did nothing to confirm my feelings at that time. Not yet. He wasn't ready. I considered that I was possibly being presumptive; possibly being off on my signal reads; or, possibly he was just incredibly shy. He continued clicking his shutter lens, as if he was trying to deny his signals and stifle his vibes. I did nothing to stop him. I played along. I thought it best to allow Charles to continue in control; allow this mysterious barrier which separated us to dissolve on its own; and in its own time.

"Charles next fussed with his lens focus to capture perfect close-ups. He then clicked off some fifty photos of my left nipple; then another fifty of my right one. While he did this, the light colors continued shifting and changing, I was going out of my mind with passion fevers. I was dying to get up, pull Charles to the floor and mount him, without speaking a word. I think he sensed that.

"But I did no such thing. I knew it was not my place to take control. Not yet. Not this first time. Instead, I waited. I posed. I preened. I tried not to scream out to him to take me and make love with me. I held myself together somehow; restrained my inner trembles of anxious lust, while my passions raged within my breast and loins. I restrained myself; and, at the same time, I promised myself that, before this day was over, Charles and I were going to make love.

"Charles photographed my nipples from every conceivable angle and distance perspective, from the fullness wide angle shots of my left and right breast mounds, to narrow close ups of both my areolas and extremely tightly focused close ups of my nipple buds, taken from just one inch away. The lighting colors continued changing. The effect of that was driving me crazy with a certain kind of erotic lust madness I had never experienced before; and I can't adequately describe it in words. I was on the verge of screaming to Charles:

'All right! Enough of this madness! Just fondle me, if you wish. Kiss me. Finger me. But do something! Please, just DO something! Be a MAN! Touch me! Squeeze my breasts! Suck my nipples. Pinch them. *Come on, do something to me! I don't care how you start fore-play; but please, get on with it. I want you to DO something!'*

"It occurred to me then that Charles might have a breast fetish, or possibly childhood issues relating to difficult nursing experiences with his mother. I didn't feel it was my place to inquire about the reason he took so many photos of my breasts; so, I moved on to the next painting to perform my next pose. I ran my fingers through my hair to stay in touch with my own reality. I looked into Charles' eyes with my most inviting, sexiest, pouting coquettish smile, and my deepest, come hither, 'I long for you,' eyes. I've never given any man so many obvious hints that I wanted him to have sex with me. But Charles did not respond. He only motioned me to the next painting.

"I did similar routines before Titian's orgy pleasuring 'Venus,' Rembrandt's unapologetic, shameless, conspiring 'Bathsheba,' Gaya's 'Nude,' Moreau's 'Scantily veiled Salome, proffering her delicious sexual nirvana in exchange for the head of the Baptist,' and Manet's invitingly, glorious 'Olympia.' The gallery's lighting colors continued changing, heightening my raging lust fires, as if that were even pos-sible, while I sensuously performed each of my artistic reveals before each painting.

"Before each painting I slowly removed my bras, erotically slipped out of my panties; teased the camera with my tongue-reveal-ing lip mouthing's and my suggestive kiss blows; my imagery evok-ing delicate finger licks; my slow, semen drinking finger sucks; my longing, touching teases; my explicit, stimulating fingerings of my vagina; my slow, languid turnings and bendings of my sex craving body as I flirted with the camera while smiling; batting my eyes, erotically touching my body and my vagina; and cupping my breasts; and smiling provocatively while pinching and releasing my nipples; and sitting in all sorts of erotic poses while I held myself open; and displaying my vaginal lips and touching and rubbing myself long-ingly, while Charles photographed and the shutter clicked. With every camera click I imagined Charles' holding me, kissing me; his penis lovingly brushing against my outer lips, stimulating me before entering me, filling me with unimaginable pleasures, as we joined our souls.

"I noticed Charles moving closer and closer to me. Eventually, he was taking pictures of my vagina from only an inch away. I knew he had to be highly aroused. My skin felt the heat from his body. I knew he wanted me. The magnetism between us was unmistakable. My instincts screamed and echoed inside my mind that Charles was madly, deeply in love with me; and that he was barely able to contain his composure. I was certain he was struggling inside some invisible boundary which he was afraid to cross; trapped within his imagined confinement. My mind wanted to break our silent spell and speak to him:

'You are dying to be freed of whatever it is that's holding you back, aren't you? You want me, don't you? You're crazy in love with me. I know you are. I can tell. I know you're reaching hard to find a way to open the subject of making love with me. Why don't you just ask me? I'd love to be your lover. I want you. I want to spend the rest of the afternoon making love with you. Please let's do that. Please open up and talk to me. Why won't you talk to me?' I didn't say a word; but I wondered.

"Charles indicated we should move to the next pose without saying a word about his feelings. We came to Corbet's 'Origin of the World.' There, before the sumptuous mouth-watering, irresistible, pubic haired, riot wild vagina, I performed at my sensuous best. I stripped ever so slowly, blew my heartfelt kisses to Charles, and moved through my poses with very deliberate, prolonged pauses. I sensed that, for some reason I could not yet know, this particular painting held some especially profound significance for Charles.

"By now the contrasting, ever changing, colors of the lighting were making my entire body seethe with wild, barely controllable *animal lust. I was losing all sense of self control, trying to hold my passions in check while continuing my seductive reveals as Charles instructed me. As I exposed more and more of my body Charles came closer and closer to me. Soon his camera was clicking an inch away from my nipples and then, inch by inch, lower and lower, as if the camera had miraculously become the proxy for Charles' mouth.*

*"He continued clicking past my stomach and lower abdomen until he was clicking frame after frame of my vagina. I didn't move. I couldn't see any more than the top of his head and I couldn't make sense of whatever exact image he was trying to capture. Then, he asked me to completely recline on the viewing bench and spread my legs open widely; which, of course, I did. My pose mirrored the woman's pose in Corbet's 'Origin of the World.'*

*"Charles' camera was there, again; much, much closer now, only an inch away from my sex. He clicked the shutter wildly, continuous. He became frenzied, clicking the exact same close-up shot of my vagina about fifty times. This experience was beyond bizarre.*

*'Does he need to capture some imperceptible movement of my body; perhaps capture some quiver motion of my vaginal lips?'*

*I asked myself that. But I wasn't moving, anywhere or in any way. I was certain every picture would turn out to be exactly like the dozens of pictures he had just snapped before.*

*'Is he going crazy? Are my pheromones causing him to lose his sanity over my vagina? Am I also going crazy, along with him? Everything about this rapid camera clicking is crazy. There cannot possibly be any difference from one image of my vagina to the next. Why would any man do this?' I asked myself those questions.*

*"He then asked me to hold myself open with my fingers, which, of course, I did. Now he wanted an even closer, close-up, really a gynecologist's view, with his lens peering for images deeply inside my vagina. I wondered silently, almost laughing to myself:*

'Does he think he can glimpse heaven inside me? Perhaps, for him, he can? I cannot know. Never before has any man been so entranced by the inside of my vagina.'

"My pose was even more provocative than the woman's who posed for Courbet's 'The Origin,' if you can believe that could even be possible. After all, I had my butterfly wings; and my smoothly waxed vagina gleamed from my specially blended oils and the lighting plays. The woman in 'The Origin' unashamedly sported a massively riotous furry muff. When I thought there was no way any photographer could take a closer close-up of a woman's vagina than Charles had taken of my special Gloria Butterfly Girl, Charles changed to a magnification macro lens, made especially for taking extremely close, close ups. While I held open, he brought his camera extremely close, to within a half inch of my vagina. Through my sex, I could feel the coolness of the camera lens as he brought it next to my heat.

"Charles again clicked wildly, photographing every minute detail of my vagina from no further than a half inch away. He attached a special ring light to his camera which produced an extremely strong light for close ups; and then he held the lens so close I could feel the coolness of the lens, now practically touching my vagina; and then he clicked about twenty additional photos. He wanted to capture the innermost channel views into the deepest depths of my sex. But why? Then the clicking suddenly stopped. He put the camera down on the floor. He stared at the vagina in the Corbet painting for awhile, and then he stared at my vagina, as if trying to comprehend the beauty of the feminine vagina or possibly making a comparison between my smoothly waxed vagina and Courbet's portrait of his wildly, bushy lady.

"I thought:

'Is this understandable? Charles is comparing pussies, isn't he? I keep myself cleanly waxed. I pride myself in being hair-free, creamy soft, sweet smelling and inviting with my fragrances of lilac, lily, and gardenias; and I keep myself mouth wateringly delicious to my lovers' tongues' tastes. The woman who modeled for Corbet's Origin openly flaunted her massively tangled mess of pubic hair. That painting gave off the impression that her smells and tastes were completely natural, too. I wondered: was Charles comparing mental images of women's smells? But why the woman in 'Origin'?

'Perhaps Charles has had those same impressions about her, or about some other woman who reminded him of her? Charles could not have known that model who posed for Courbet. That work was created almost two hundred years ago. Perhaps that demonstrably provocative image of her sex intimidates or belittles Charles somehow? Perhaps every woman's vagina intimidates Charles?

'Perhaps he's afraid he can't handle a woman's sexuality? Maybe he observed that I'm always cleanly waxed and glistening in my films; and that my partners always enjoy having oral sex with me. Everyone who has ever seen my films knows my partners love performing cunnilingus with me. Maybe Charles noticed that and fixated on that aspect of my sexuality? Is Charles now trying to reassure himself that I'm not intimidating; that my vagina won't bite him or give him a sexually transmitted disease?'

"I knew my feelings didn't lie. I completely trust them. I knew this man loved me. I knew he wanted me. I was sure of it; but I was not sure about the way he wanted me. I was confused, and I felt I needed to be cautious, lest I might frighten him or cause him to suddenly lose his desires for me.

"But He was inwardly crying out for my help. He desperately wanted me. I knew that. But I also knew I was missing something. There was something he was afraid to tell me. Perhaps it was the reason he took those interior close ups?

"Then Charles returned his eyes to the Corbet and stared some more; and then his gaze returned to stare at my vagina. He began weeping softly. This went on for a good full minute. After he composed himself, he said:

'Marty, you are incredibly beautiful. I am totally in awe of how beautiful you are. I'm so sorry.' And then he cried some more.

"I couldn't understand what was wrong. 'Why are you crying?' I asked, 'Have I failed you somehow?'

'No, it's nothing you've done. You are a total woman; a beautiful, natural woman. It's me. You're only here for a day and I've just begun to appreciate how beautiful you are. You're more beautiful than all these pictures. Being here with you in the flesh I can appreciate that now. I love taking pictures of your body. I could take pictures of you forever. I can't stop taking pictures of you. I can't help myself. I wish you could stay longer.'

'Charles, you said: 'it's me.' What did you mean by, 'it's me?' Why did you say that?'

"I needed to hear him tell me what this was all about. I needed him to tell me the truth. I asked him why I was there and why he was taking all these photos; and, especially why he needed to take all those repetitive close-up shots of my vagina.

"He protested. He said it was way too sensitive and embarrassing to talk about; but I persisted. I told him I'd try to help him if he'd please share what was bothering him. Finally, he took me by my hand over to the far wall, opposite the naked bush of the 'Origin' woman in the Corbet. We sat there, on the floor, beside each other. I was naked, with my back propped against the wall and my legs tucked against me, waiting for him to say something. We both sat staring at the naked bush in the Corbet portrait.

'Did I disappoint you?' He spoke in a barely audible whisper.

'What do you mean?' I asked, 'in what way?'

'When you posed with your hand holding the foot of your raised extended leg, you revealed your sex in such an obvious way; and then when you were on your knees and I was behind you shooting *frames, and you held yourself open, you again revealed yourself; and then again, when your pose was identical to the woman in the Origin, you again held yourself open and I...............'*

*'Oh,' I interrupted, 'do you think I was disappointed because you didn't seek to make love with me?'*

*'Yes, I thought you might have been, were you?'*

*'What, disappointed?'*

*'Yes, were you disappointed in me?'*

*'No, I was not disappointed. I assumed you didn't want to. I just didn't understand why you didn't want to.'*

*'You did? You thought that? Did you want me to?'*

*'Yes, Charles. I very much wanted you to do whatever you wished to do, Charles. I was just surprised, that's all. I've posed many times before; and every other time the photographer or artist simply began kissing me and making love with me. I was just surprised that you didn't show any interest in me, that's all.'*

*'Oh, I was interested all right. I wanted to make love with you.'*

*'Then, why didn't you, Charles? I would not have denied you.'*

*"A long silence followed before he finally spoke. 'My mother beat me very severely when I was a boy,' he began. 'I was in my room. I thought I was alone. A friend had given me a girlie magazine with a fold out centerfold. I was sitting on the edge of my bed staring at the woman's open vagina. I was fascinated by that photo. I was obsessed with it: totally taken by it. I was trying to imagine what it would be like to kiss that woman's vagina and hold her and make love with her. I thought she was remarkably beautiful, just like I think the woman in the Origin and you are also remarkably beautiful. I have those same feelings when I sit before the Origin and, now I have those feelings again; and they are even stronger; much, much stronger being here with you.*

*'I couldn't put the magazine down. I couldn't do that. If I did, I'd be betraying that woman in the photo. I couldn't bring myself to stop*

*looking at her. I loved her even though she was only a photograph. I mean; I don't know how to explain this. But I deeply loved her. I adored her. I was only a boy who would have died for her. I can't explain it. It's how a boy feels about a woman sometimes. That photo of her vagina overwhelmed me. This wonderment came over me and it stayed with me. It wasn't an obsession. It was something deeper and more profound. I felt this smitten wonderment, this devotion to this woman and her beautiful sex.*

*'I don't know how long Mother stood behind me, watching me stare at that woman's vagina. She must have been there ten minutes or longer. I was so engrossed in that photo. I was holding it up to my face, pretending to kiss it, wishing that woman was there, pretending she'd climbed out of the photo and was standing before my face; and then, I actually kissed that fold-out picture, right where her vagina was. I was pretending, imagining, I guess you could say. I prayed that she would come to life and become real. I didn't have any idea Mother watched me the entire time.*

*'Suddenly, without warning, Mother slapped me hard on the side of my head. I was shocked. She continued slapping me with both her hands, back and forth on both sides of my head. Then she pounded me with her fists. She was hurting me; badly. She screamed at me, telling me that the woman in the magazine was dirty; that women who do that sort of thing are dirty and evil; that a woman's vagina is not for me; that women's vaginas are dirty and evil; and that women who use their vaginas for anything other than procreation are very wicked, very bad women. And that she'd punish me severely and I'd go to hell if I ever went to the kind of woman who was like like that woman in the magazine; because those kinds of women were naughty and immoral. And they were the wrong kind of women to get involved with. And that my mind was dirty and ungodly to even have thoughts about that kind of woman.*

'Mother raved on and on about how terrible it was for me to look at that picture. All that time Mother screamed at me I blocked out her screams and thought about how much I desperately loved that woman in the picture. I truly wanted to find that woman in real life, wherever she was, because she was so unlike Mother. I wanted to go to her, be with her, hold her in my arms, and kiss her vagina. I wanted to kiss her vagina every second of every day for the rest of my life. I was that smitten by that picture. I was only a boy then, but that longing feeling has never left me.

'I've had problems with women ever since that day. Mother harped and harped about how I must never think about the kinds of women who are like that woman in that picture; the kinds of women who would allow men to take dirty pictures of their vaginas. I have been made to feel ashamed of myself and dirty, like I'm a bad little boy, whenever I try.........' Charles paused.

'Try, try what?' I asked Charles point blank and stared into his eyes. He didn't answer. I held his hand up to my cheek and looked at his lips. 'Try what, Charles?' My eyes searched his face. 'Tell me, Charles, what do you try to do?'

"I slid my body next to his and pressed my side against his. 'Try what, Charles? Tell me.' My eyes searched deeply into his. I persisted. 'I want to know. If you tell me I'll help you. I honestly want to help you.'

"He started crying again. Obviously, Charles was psychologically tortured. He had a very domineering mother. His issues with his mother and that childhood experience had destroyed his self confidence. His money, his art collection, were both ways for him to avoid confronting his boyhood issues. I was shocked. Charles was worlds away from being a normal, sexually healthy male.

"His eyes told me he was desperate to escape his mental prison. His sorrows reached my inner soul. His mother had psychologically abused him and walled him off from love; isolated him from all women, except her. Empathetic tears rolled down my cheeks:

"I wondered: How could a mother abuse her son this way? Why did she arrest his normal development and confined him to his childhood? Charles desperately needed a confidence boost.

"I put my arm over his shoulder and drew myself closer to him. He needed to be hugged. I hugged him and held my hug."

'Tell me. It's okay.' "I whispered. I kissed his cheek.

"He shook his head: 'I can't. I'm sorry,' his deeply damaged soul choked out his whispered apology.

'Yes, you can, Charles. You really can. It's okay, honest,' I said. I kissed him again on his cheek, this time holding my lips to his cheek. I placed my hand above his knee. 'I need you to tell me, Charles. It means a lot to me, honest. Don't be afraid, Charles. I'm here for you.'

"He sat and stared at Courbet's Origin for the longest time. More tears rolled down his cheeks. His hurt was profoundly deep. His was a damaged soul. And he knew it. Finally, he turned his head and looked into my eyes. 'I have never made love with a woman,' he spoke softly. He tucked his lips into his mouth and looked away from me, embarrassed. When he finally turned back to me, his lips were bloodless white from the clenching pressure:

'I took those close-ups because I dream about you. I spend hours every night fantasizing about making love with you. When Mother moved to the guest cottage, I started watching adult films. About two years ago I saw a film of you for the first time. I watched you making love. I've watched your films ever since. I've become obsessed with you. I love watching your films and seeing you making love with different men. I know Mother told me that women like you are bad. She believes she knows what's best for me; but watching you making love makes me love you more and more, every time I watch you; every film you make. You are beautiful. The things you do with men and their penises are beautiful. I don't care that your films are called pornography. What you do in those films is beautiful and I love watching you. I cannot stop watching you. I'm obsessed over you. Even though I've only met you today, I feel like I've known you for years. Your films have caused me to fall in love with you. I'm certain that I love you. Maybe I'm crazy. I don't know.'

'Charles, do you masturbate while you watch my films? Is the reason you took those close ups, so you could imagine having your penis inside me? Were you imagining that your camera was your penis?'

'Yes, oh my God, yes. You have no idea what being obsessed over you is like. It's intense. It's constant. I can't not think about you. I fall asleep dreaming of you. I dream I'm making love with you. I dream I've buried my face and my tongue in your vagina. I want so much to love you there, and in that way. But I don't think I can. There's this barrier. You're supposed to be bad for me and off limits. A voice in my mind tells me Mother will punish me if I did that.

'Mother said women like you are naughty and immoral and evil and bad for me and that I should never go anywhere with a woman like you, or do anything with a woman like you; that it's wrong to fall in love with a woman like you because a woman like you isn't capable of loving anyone. She said your type makes love with hundreds of men. Is that true? Have you made love with hundreds of men?'

'Yes Charles, that is true.'

'But isn't that immoral?'

'No Charles. It's not immoral. It's not immoral when I make love out of love and feelings for the man whom I'm with. It's beautiful.'

'But Mother said women like you are dirty down there.'

'Charles, you're misled.'

'How? I don't understand.'

'Do you ever kiss your mother's mouth?'

'Yes, when I greet her and when I leave her.'

'Charles, I swear to you; like all good conscientious whores, I am cleaner there, inside my vagina, than your mother's mouth. And my mouth is cleaner than your mother's mouth.'

'Really? Is that true? How can that be true? Your films. I've seen hundreds of your films. Your mouth has performed fellatio with hundreds of penises.'

'Yes, Charles. My mouth and vagina are completely clean. I use very sanitary products and I keep myself scrupulously clean. I even taste and smell fresh in my mouth and my vagina. I'm very proud and conscientious about my cleanliness. I always take extremely good care of myself. I would never lie to you. And I assure you, my tastes are far more inviting than anything you have ever tasted. You'll see when you kiss me.'

'You mean………? In your mouth? Or do you mean…….?'

'Yes,' Marty interrupted, 'I mean when you kiss me everywhere. I want you to kiss me everywhere. I will love having you kissing me everywhere. It's beautiful, Charles.

'Do you like the tastes of cherry pies, Charles?'

'Why yes, why?'

'How about apple pies? How about fresh peaches? How about delicious mint?'

'Why yes. I love all those tastes. Why?"

'Because, Charles, I taste better than all of those tastes. I do. You'll see. You'll discover you'll love all my tastes. I promise. Everywhere you taste me, Charles; in my mouth, and in my vagina. You'll see what I mean. I want your tongue inside me, licking my clitoris. You'll see how beautiful it is; how wonderful we will be together. You'll want to have me often, I promise. I know you want to do those things with me, Charles. And, I want you to do them with me. I want you to taste my difference.'

'Oh. Yes, I do want to. But honestly, I don't know what to think. I'm afraid. But in truth, I can't help how I feel about you, Marty. I *feel like a helpless boy. I love you. I know I love you. I love all the things you do in your films. I think everything you do is beautiful, and good. I feel good while watching you having all the orgasms you have. You're always smiling and chortling with your partners; you love your lovemaking so much. I adore you while you're doing that; while you are enjoying having sex. And I love your orgy films where you are simultaneously thrusting upon a penis while performing multiple fellatios with several partners. I find myself wishing I could be kissing your vagina while you are performing those scenes. You are so full of life; so glorious; so majestic; so adorable. To me, you represent my ultimate dream woman; my bliss; all that I could ever wish for in a woman. I see you as a deity. You are life, Marty. You are the inspiration for life and procreation. You are heaven sent to humanity; the very best of all of us.*

*'Your orgy scenes bring out a certain intensity within me; and I realize how deeply and profoundly I love you. Those scenes make me palpitate with desire for you and they take my breath away. I adore you, Marty. I positively adore you. I can't explain it. Maybe it's because you are everything Mother said I should avoid. But I can't help falling in love with you. I feel this overwhelming happiness for you. It's like your release from all inhibitions becomes my release, too. All my cares leave my mind while I am watching you. I love feeling happiness for you while you are having sex. I know I shouldn't love you like I do, but I can't help myself. It's like you somehow reach inside me and take my soul from me and keep it with you. I am smitten; hopelessly in love. I just totally love you and everything about you.'*

*'Charles, what you are feeling is perfectly okay. It's normal to love a woman the way you love me. You should love me like you do. It's okay. It's really okay. I want to love you, too.'*

*"I reached my hands to Charles' head and held his face, bringing it close to mine. His eyes flowed tears. His confession of love was as*

honest as any woman ever heard from any man. I knew he loved me. For the first time I saw stirrings of healthy sexual life in his eyes. Then, I kissed him for the first time. My kiss was soft and loving. This was a sensitive time for him. I didn't pull away. I knew it was important for him to have me close and know that I was there, as long as he wanted me close. I held my soft kiss on his lips, hoping he'd respond.

"I moved my hand higher on his leg, closer to his penis. When he responded with a stronger, open-mouthed kiss, I opened my mouth as well. When our tongues touched, I felt a sudden surge of electricity flowing steadily and continuously from my limbic zone into my blood and spine; and reaching into my sex. I felt the heat and slipperiness of my sex urging me to reach out to Charles, take his penis inside me and love him; totally love him with wild abandon. I French kissed him with a deep soul-searching kiss, my tongue entwined in his.

"I felt true love for Charles. It was finally happening for us. It was that deeply connected sort of love that enters my soul when I know my partner is being completely honest. I knew in that instant that I needed to help Charles out of the cocoon his mother had wrapped him in. I knew by helping him, I would help myself, too. I would be opening a door for both of us to our beautiful, wonderful love. In that moment, I knew Charles and I would become lovers. Our love would flutter above all his inhibitions and chase them away. It would be special, beautiful, trusting, innocent love. I felt it happening.

"My intuition told me I first needed to be Charles' trusted friend. We played with each other's tongues like we were two teenagers, discovering kissing for the first time. After our prolonged kissing, I placed my hand upon his penis. He was very hard. He didn't flinch or pull away. He was beginning to relax with me. So, I took both my hands, smiled a mischievous smile at him and tickled his ribs. He started, squirmed, and laughed a spontaneous, squeaky laugh.

*Our connection breakthrough had finally happened. We had that honest, together moment, that true friends share. Suddenly, we were playmates. His tensions evaporated. Charles was enjoying himself; and me!"*

*'Charles, Your mother is partially right,' I said. My hand found his fully erect penis through his trousers. His body was ready. 'I AM a very naughty girl; and I AM totally immoral. I'm a VERY immoral whore; but, Charles, I am NOT an evil person and I am NOT bad for you. And, I am NOT dirty down there. I keep myself very clean. I wash and douche there and I use a bidet. I am cleaner there than any woman's mouth.'*

*'But all those penises that have been inside you? Don't they leave something in you?*

*'No Charles, they don't. After they ejaculate, I clean myself thoroughly. There's no trace inside me. There's nothing left in me that shows they were ever there. Look at it this way: Imagine a flower. Many bees come to the flower and drink the flower's nectar. The bees love the flower. They love its nectar. They visit the flower often. The flower stays fresh and ready for its next bee. It does not hurt the bees. It loves the bees. And the bees love the flower.*

*'So, think of my vagina as a flower and think of the penises as bees. They come inside me and make love with me; and I make love with them. There's nothing dirty or wrong about it. I don't hurt the penises. I love the penises.'*

*'But how can you love a man when so many other men have already made love with you?*

*'Charles, try to understand. When you are with me, no other man will be with me. When a bee is inside a flower, no other bee is in there at the same time. The flower only loves the bee that is inside it. I'm the same way. When you are kissing me there; or when your penis is inside me, you are the only one I love. My mind shuts out all the others who have kissed me there and all the other penises that*

*have been inside me. You are the only one I care about. You are the only one I love.'*

*'Your mind can do that?'*

*'Yes. It does do that. It becomes completely focused on you; only you. And I adore you and love you. And for that time, you are with me, you are the only person in the world who matters to me. I totally love only you; and I give myself completely to only you. I have a good heart and I'm a good friend. I will be GOOD for you. I promise. You will love me as your friend, Charles. I'd like to prove that to you. Do you know what we need to do?' I asked him.*

*"He shook his head while looking deeply into my eyes. I think he knew what we needed to do. Maybe he hoped I'd say what I was about to say."*

*'We need to make love, Charles. We must. You need to discover what it feels like to love a woman, for real. Trust me about this, Charles, there's a world of difference between masturbation and having intimate, loving sex with a real, live, caring woman who deeply loves you. You'll see. We need to go to your chateau next door, to your bedroom. We need to chase Mommy away from there, forever. I very much want to make love with you, Charles. And I want to keep your mother locked outside while we make love. She doesn't belong in your bedroom; and, she doesn't need to know what we're doing, Charles. Can we do that?'*

*"He nodded his agreement with my suggestion. His chateau was eighteenth century palatial, appointed with tapestries and renaissance furniture, seven fireplaces twenty bedrooms; you know, spaciously opposite from a Manhattan walk-up apartment. When Charles opened the door to his bedroom I was stunned. There were about thirty framed ten inch by fourteen-inch-colored photos of me in various staged of undress or naked, and photos of me having intercourse and giving felatio, and photos of me participating in three different orgies.*

"I turned and looked at him. My questions were in my eyes:

'I told you. I have all your films, every one,' he said, apologizing for his voyeurism. 'I've longed for this moment, to have you here with me. I've watched you for two years now. I love watching you having sex.

'While I'm watching you making love, something happens inside me. It's this overpowering feeling. It wells up from deep inside me and it just sort of overwhelms me and consumes me. I don't understand what is happening to me. I feel this adoration; like you are my Goddess and you are divinely inspired to do what you are doing. And it's so beautiful; and I wish I could be there with you; being part of what you are doing.

'But then this thought comes onto my mind. I wonder how can it be possible that you have kissed and licked so many hundreds of penises; and that you have mouthed so many men's balls and rolled their testicles in your mouth? I wonder how can it be possible for you to do that?'

Marty placed her hand on Charles' hand. Her eyes smiled into his eyes.

'Oh Charles, that's easily explained. I have a masseuse. She keeps my neck and shoulders completely relaxed. Performing fellatio never taxes me. My neck muscles are highly trained. It's second nature for me.'

'No Marty,' Charles frowned. His eyes were puzzled. 'What I meant was: How do you deal with what you do, psychologically? I mean, Mother says women like you are evil; you are creatures of Satan or even Saten himself because what you do is so immoral and so much against what I was taught in my religion; so antithetical to what the bible says about morality. You've heard of Sodom and Gomorrah. Well, aren't you worried that you may be condemning your soul to hell? I mean, haven't you ever given yourself paused and asked yourself whether you might be offending God?'

'How do I deal with it psychologically? Oh Charles, that's easy. I love it. I thoroughly love performing fellatio. I love male penises. I love kissing them and licking them and sucking them and bringing them to ejaculation in my mouth. It's all a joy for me. I always look forward to every fellatio scene. I guess I'm just a whore who loves her work. Try thinking of me this way: I'm a female model, just like every other female model, except I model with penises in my mouth and vagina. It's not complicated. It's not something to get judgmental about. I enjoy what I do. It makes me feel liberated and free. I'm happy, Charles. And I am not Satan. And my soul is not going to hell, because there is no such place in the first place. That's just religious clap trap, Charles. There is no heaven. And there is no hell. There is only humanity, Charles. And making intimate love and connecting with others during lovemaking is beautiful and natural. And making love moves humanity forward.'

'But don't you think the world needs its religions?'

'No, Charles. I don't. What do we need religions for? Did God invent the car, the airplane, or the telephone?'

'Well, no. Men invented those things. But we need religion to hold families together, don't we?'

'I don't know about that, Charles. Religions are the causes of strife and wars. How do those things hold families together? Do religions prevent divorces? I don't know about that, either. But consider this, Charles: Before religions, before six thousand years ago, I do not believe there were many formal marriages. I believe people lived in tribes, much like modern day monkeys and gorillas. And there were no divorces. I think the entire tribe took part in child rearing, like monkeys and gorillas do today. And, I think children grew up without hearing their parents bickering over who gets visitation rights and who gets the house and the cars and the stock portfolio. So, how, exactly, is marriage so wonderful, anyway? And wouldn't we all hold together in a more civilized way if we just lived as groups

under secular laws without the adultery and coveting commandments? Why not try parallel experiments? Why not let some people
live with religion and marriage and other people live in groups without marriage and without religion? Why not see how things work
out and let people choose?'

'You sound like you believe in communism. Do you?'

'Maybe. I don't know. But I know I don't believe in God or religion. Religion shuts down thinking and holds humanity back. I'll
never understand why people choose to believe men who wear fancy
robes and spew fantastical homilies that try to relate our lives to
unrelated things and fairy tales that proclaim their ways are the
right ways and everyone else's ways are inferior ways; and their people are included and others are excluded. There have been genocides
because of those distorted ideologies. Just look at what the Catholic
Church did to the American Indians. I mean, consider these last
over five hundred years of genocide and subjugation. What right
did the Church have to crush those human peoples and their way of
life? How can you justify the thievery and the killing; the abject poverty? While the Church and its leaders roll in gold! It's inhumanity
to other humans. To me, that's what religion represents.'

'I had no idea you were sympathetic to the Indians, Marty.'

'I'm not. They mean nothing to me. I even have a personal issue
with a particular Indian woman; but I don't want to talk about
that. In truth, Charles, I don't give a damn about the Indians. I'm
a whore; a porn star. My energies are focused elsewhere. I just don't
care for the hypocrisy of religion, that's all.'

'I think I understand your thinking. But don't you ever feel a
sense of guilt over what you are doing?'

'Like doing what?'

'Well, to other people; like those films you did with that black
man with the huge penis; Marshawn is his name. I read those stories
about the two of you; about how his wife, Allayah, swore you were

evil; a creation of the Devil; a living Satan. She was very upset. She claimed you destroyed her marriage and her family.'

'Yes, I know she said those things. I did destroy her marriage. She was telling the truth. What about it?'

'Well, after I read those articles about how you broke up her marriage, I went back to the films of the two of you. I saw how you worked your fingers over his penis shaft; how you twisted your hands over it and how you finger pressured the top of it while you stroked it. You showed you know all the ways to sensitize a man's penis and make a man powerless to resist you, don't you?'

'Yes, Charles. Of course I do. You wouldn't have any interest in a woman who didn't understand those things, would you?'

'No, I guess I wouldn't.'

'And while you watched that scene, you imagined I was doing that same thing with your penis, didn't you?'

'Yes. I did. And I wished so much that it was my penis you were stimulating; and not his.'

'We'll do that, Charles; and many other things. You'll see.'

"But Charles was not quite ready. He wanted to talk some more."

'I saw how you licked Marshawn's penis shaft from scrotum to tip; how much you seemed to love doing that. And I watched intently the scenes where his penis tip lay upon your open-mouthed tongue and you gave his penis tip your barely perceptible tongue coaxing while it spurted voluminous volumes of semen onto your tongue. You chortled and smiled; your eyes were communicating how delighted and pleased you were that Marshawn was ejaculating into your mouth. That pleased you, didn't it? You loved what was happening when he came into your mouth, didn't you?'

'Yes, Charles. I loved it very much. I loved it immensely. I love all my male penises, Charles. I love pleasing them. It's not work for me. I love doing those things and many other things with my male penises.'

'But while you were performing those scenes with Marshawn, you surely had to know you were stealing him from his wife.'

'Yes, of course I knew I was doing that. I believed I was driving her crazy with jealousy. That made the scene that much more exciting for me. I totally loved everything I was doing; and I totally loved that I was also destroying her marriage. Soooo? What's your point, Charles?'

'Well, I just wonder about what things were going through your mind while you were performing those fellatios? Didn't you feel any guilt about taking him from his wife?'

'Oh that! No, Charles. Of course not! I never feel guilty about taking any man from his wife. That never even enters my mind; never! When I know my partner has a wife who is watching our lovemaking, it just makes my orgasms sweeter, that's all. I knew what I was doing with Marshawn. And I felt elated and joyous about it.'

'But a family was destroyed. How can you not feel guilty about your role in causing that to happen?'

'Because, Charles, I do not believe in the concept of the family unit with the man in charge. I believe it takes a community or a village to properly raise children; to expose them to all sorts of stimuli and all sorts of different ways of thinking. I also reject the concept of religion. I think religion is group insanity. And guilt is a ridiculous religion invented concept; and I simply choose to not believe in the concept of guilt when it comes to intimate relationships. Of course I do not believe it is okay to lie, cheat, steal, or murder. But I do not believe in religion, Charles. I do not believe in any religion's teachings. Religion is a nonsensical rabbit hole that much of humanity has dived into. I think religion, per se, is a mistake. Humanity has been lost in this religious rabbit hole for about six thousand years. And I am trying, through my explicit erotic intimate artistry, to pull humanity back out of that rabbit hole.

'You see, Charles, religion no longer governs us like it did six thousand years ago. We have secular laws now. And, under secular laws, when two consenting adults decide they wish to have sex or make a porn film, they can do that. It's perfectly legal. Immorality is just as legal as morality, understand?'

'Yes. I understand that legality part. But didn't you feel anything for Allayah, his wife? Didn't you feel any sympathy for her situation? After all, you were destroying her way of life.'

'No, Charles, I did not feel sympathy for her. Her religion was the cause of her misery, not me. Her religion placed her, and she allowed it to place her, in her ridiculous, untenable position. My erotica, those explicit scenes everyone raved about, freed Marshawn from his religion. Indirectly, by pulling Marshawn out of the religious rabbit hole, I pulled Allayah out of her rabbit hole, too. I helped them both understand the power and the beauty of human intimacy. While I performed those scenes with Marshawn, I felt glorious. I knew I was liberating him; and her. I felt only joy for unburdening the two of them from what had been; their ridiculous religious nightmare.

'Charles. I believe that my explicit erotica, my pornography, is far more humanistic and enlightening and loving than any religion. I believe that religions are far beneath what I do. My pornography inspires people to love and to live; and enjoy life and one another. Religion inspires people to live in fear and in awe of life after death. It's like voodoo to me. I makes no sense. My messaging is to love and make love and embrace life. Religions message death and spew vitriol about those who are not of the same mind set. Religion trains its followers to embrace death. That's ridiculous. We humans should embrace life, not death. Does that help you?'

'Yes. Is that why I am so fascinated by your films? Is it because they are works of art? Do you believe you are creating artistic work while you are performing in your porn films?'

'Oh, yes, Charles. I do. I truly do. That's why I put my heart and soul into every scene in every film. I do believe I am creating the most beautiful art in the world. I believe pornography is the most glorious *genre of all artistic expression genres. And I believe it delivers the message of love and human acceptance and understanding. I believe pornography is vital to the human condition. It relieves our stresses; opens our eyes and expands our minds. I believe pornography opens us up to new ways of seeing ourselves and others. My films sell so well because, more and more, people see them as life appreciating; and they love how the films help them see life and human intimacy as wonderful and beautiful. They expand and enlighten us in so many ways. They reduce our inhibitions and open us to be accepting of others. Never think that my work is the work of the Devil, Charles. It's humanistic. It's meant to be enlightening and beautiful.'*

*'I see. I love art. And I feel like I'm watching the most beautiful art ever created in the history of the world, every time I watch you perform. I love watching you. I can't help myself. You're so beautiful. Your love making is so erotic and so beautiful. I........'*

*"I cut him off: 'Charles, why, with all your money, didn't you just call my private service? I would have come to you. We could have made love years ago. I would have been very pleased to become your lover. Why did you feel the need to do this elaborate ruse? Why the photo shoot in your gallery of nudes? Why your private museum's hundreds of statues of female nudes? Why....'*

*"He cut me off: 'It's MOTHER,' "he bellowed. His face and eyes searched the ceiling." 'She has tormented me, all my life. She doesn't want to share me with any other woman.'*

*'You mean she......? NO, don't tell me! YOU and your MOTHER......???'*

*'Oh, no Marty, it's not incest. We don't do that.'*

*'Charles, it's okay. I'm not judgmental. In many societies, it's perfectly normal. But if she was using sex to control you....'*

*'No Marty. I told you. It was nothing like that. I never did it with Mother. It's not about incest; not at all. It's her mindset. It's her need to control me; just her mind control over her dutiful son. She doesn't*

hit me anymore. She's too badly crippled by arthritis now; but she's still alive. She lives alone in the guest cottage at the far end of the estate. She prefers living there because everything is on one floor. She has her two servants and her two Yorkie dogs; and her movies and chocolates. But she's here on the grounds, close to me. And she constantly watches my chateau from her window. I'm certain she knows you're here with me. You'll see. That phone will ring any minute.' He pointed to a black land line phone on his nightstand."

"I immediately opened my purse and found my handy five-inch hair cutting shears. I went to the phone by his bedside and cut the cord to it."

'Charles,' I said, as I wrapped my arms around his neck and kissed him: 'We've just cut your cord to Mommy. You now have freedom from the morality police.' I held his hand against my breast. 'I'm here, Charles, and I want you. I want you to make love with me. I want you to fuck me. I want you to perform cunnilingus with me. You are going to fuck me and you are going to perform cunnilingus with me. You are going to discover that my shameless immorality is wonderful. It's all in my attitude. My attitude is the most desirable thing about me.

'I want you to discover for yourself why I'm the world's top adult film star. I want you to learn for yourself the honest passion lust my vagina feels for your penis, this very minute. I want you to know me and make love with me as your very own, incorrigible immoral, porn star whore, who totally and completely accepts you, loves and adores you. I want to totally love you in every way your imagination wants to make love; and I want you to love me for being the immoral whore that I love being.

'When we make love, Charles, I want you to ask yourself how can it be that exchanging seminal fluids during love making would be any less an act of love than making breakfast for someone, or going hiking or horseback riding with someone, or seeing a show with someone? I want you to think about the role of intimacy in love and loving relationships. Ask yourself: How intimacy can be any less a form of love than sitting in a church pew with someone? Ask yourself: Can the confidences that arise from an intimate relationship with someone be anything less than honest love? Charles, you're about to discover how beautiful and enduring and precious our immoral love will be. I promise you, Charles, after we make love, your mother will never bother you again.'

'You think it's that simple?' he asked.

'Oh, yes, Charles,' I whispered as I opened his opened his trousers and dropped them to the floor. I held his balls in my hands and fondled them; and just as I slipped my eager lips onto the head of his stiffened penis, I said, 'Love is this simple, Charles, and it's incredibly beautiful.'

"That's how I rescued Charles from his mental torment, Consuelo. There's a Latin phrase: 'Simul Justis et Peccator,' which means all of us have within ourselves the qualities of both saintly goodness and sinner. By using my immoral sinfulness to save Charles from his personal hell, I performed a saintly duty. I released Charles' sexuality. Hopefully, some future day the Church will recognize the goodness we porn stars bring to human kind, by accepting and promoting The Modern Morality Standard. My fondest wish is to be canonized as "Marty, Patron Saint of Immorality." Perhaps future generations will see a statue of me, naked with penises in my mouth, vagina, and hands, positioned prominently in Saint Peter's Square. Standards of morality are constantly shifting. A return to pagan worship of nature and beauty is gaining popularity. I am sincerely hopeful that my liberating good works will, someday, be acknowledged.

"Charles and I made beautiful sweet love that afternoon. He had a fabulous orgasm. He repeatedly ejaculated inside me. I'll always remember how ecstatic I was when his first hot cum flooded into me. And his eyes! Charles' eyes danced with joy and the fires of life. He knew happiness and love. It was beautiful to experience his release into me. I felt him surrender his soul into mine. It was a divine moment.

"Charles' love is real. I can tell whether a man loves me by the ways he makes love with me. Men who think of me as an immoral porn star, and who want to experience me to find out what sex with me feels like for them; well, those men make love a certain way. They're detached from my feelings. It's impossible for them to disguise their purpose. They simply want to 'get off inside me.' They'll remember me as something they conquered. They'll brag about doing me to their friends.

"But those men who love me, for me, as their friend and confident in a special valued relationship, are different. They make love with me in a completely different way. It's not about the positions or techniques they use. It's the feelings they impart to me and the feelings they allow me to impart to them. Their goal in love making is to please me, to make me happy and have an enjoyable experience. It's different. Our love becomes genuine. Wonderful feelings flow between us. It's a truth we feel. It can't be faked. That feeling separates my long-term lovers from other men. It's not about the gifts a man gives me or the words he says to me. It's about how I feel while we make love.

"When Charles and I made love our first time I knew it would be enduring love. I knew he loved me, for me. He loved something within me. It was deeper than my immorality, my notoriety, and my films. We discovered romantic love. Charles became a true love. He understands that an adult film actress needs romantic love every bit as much, and probably more, than other women need love. He appreciates my livelihood is making love. And he appreciates that there are different kinds of love. He and I have the best kind of love, Consuelo. We love each other for who the other is. Charles knows how important our love is to me. I now see adoring love in Charles' eyes. Whenever we're together, it's there; and I feel its constant presence in our love making. We have something beautiful, Consuelo.

"After our first time I whispered to Charles how immensely proud he made me. I welcomed his conversion to the Modern Morality Standard. We've since become wonderful lovers. We have our special bond because I helped him shed his guilt cocoon and discover freedom.

"I missed my flight home, of course. My Premium Service had to shuffle my appointments. But by making love with Charles for three more days, I gained something much greater than a new premium member. I gained a lifelong friend and lover who loves me exactly as I am. My friends and lovers give my life meaning, Consuelo. I do everything I can for them.

"Charles and I see each other about once every two months. He's very intent on pleasing and loving me. He loves placing me naked on his lap with my back to him, his penis inside my vagina, while he kisses my neck and back and fondles my breasts. We get big together, if you know what I mean: His penis swells inside me and my clit grows two or three times her size, with her tentacles making pulsing love vibrations all the way into my upper thighs.

"We slowly work up to our first orgasms this way before we begin our extended kissing, foreplay, and lovemaking weekend. We go to social events and fine dining together, too. Charles is proud to have me on his arm. I'm no longer the only woman in his life, but I am his favorite. He now enjoys several European porn stars as well as me. He plans to have one of his other girlfriends visit us for a threesome. Still, about once every eight weeks or so, Charles likes being alone with me in his bedroom. We watch my films, compare our feelings about my different scenes and make our own passionate love. We have a beautiful erotic romance.

# CHAPTER SEVEN

*Realize your potential. You have no limits. Avoid ruts. Butterflies avoid ruts. Be a butterfly. Flutter from flower to flower. Let yourself be happy. Flutter! (Rosemary Ness-Bitner, author)*

## IMMORAL BUTTERFLY

*"And Consuelo, here's the remarkable thing about intimacy. Intimacy begets more intimacy. When people love each other, inhibition falls away and romance gets more romantic. I personally view cunnilingus as the ultimate declaration of trust and love. When your man is all in for you, he'll show his ardor by trying his best to pleasure you. The vagina kiss is a cairn, a signpost, on the trail of intimacy. I know when my man wants to go down on me, he's intent on proving that his love for me is real and enduring. I love the man who passes that cairn on his way to my heart.*

*"My sweet Charles loves kissing my vagina now. He eagerly and beautifully kisses me. He is adorable. I love the intimate pleasures his tongue gives me. He performs oral sex freely, lovingly and with heartfelt passion; and he loves performing cunnilingus often. He has years of catching up to do, but he's quickly making up lost time. I'm immensely proud of him. He's fantastically wonderful at giving orgasm pleasures to women because he's one of few men who have made the effort to fully understand the female clitoris. Its anatomy and sensitivities are now Charles' obsessive preoccupation.*

"He studies how the female clitoris responds to different stimulus methods, and the many ways a partner's tongue can please it. He's learned to perform cunnilingus to different musical themes, from Little Richard's 'Tutti Frutti' to Chopin's 'Polonaise in A flat major, op53,' and Chopin's preludes! Oh, Consuelo, it's impossible to express how much I love Charles' initial flicking tongue touches to my clit during those teasing Chopin preludes. And, Tchaikovsky! Oh, how I do so much love to orgasm to 'Swan Lake,' and then there's that fabulous '1812 Overture' where Charles keeps bumping my Gloria clitoris, swelling her up to three times her size while I explode time after time as Charles' tongue coaxes me back up to full recharge and then sets me off exploding again; and my mind is screaming: 'YES! YES! YES,' while those canons are blasting 'boom. Crack! boom Crack!... boom Crack! On and on. Giving me endlessly pulsing orgasms.' I spurt and relax; build up again, and spurt all over again for the full fifteen minutes of that overture. Charles leaves me breathless and exhausted from pleasure.

"Charles knows how much I love Puccini's Madam Butterfly. On every one of my visits, he treats me to cunnilingus while we listen to that opera. As I listen to the words of 'Un bei di Verdremo. One day we'll see,' I experience this erotic, spiritual transformation. My clitoris swells with my hopes for my future as an adult film actress. It's like my entire body enters this prayer state where I am so grateful to be a porn star and my body is praying that I can continue performing porn forever.

'I feel complete absolution and vindication for all the licentious sinning I've ever done since I left high school. I feel a deeply spiritual understanding sweep over me. Spiritual forgiveness happens. I attain my absolution. The marriages I destroyed were not my fault. Mother left me to fend for myself. She showed me prostitution's rewards. She showed me the way forward. I can forgive myself and love myself and feel wonderful for who I am and what I do. I feel beautiful and serene.

"As Puccini's opera moves toward its crescendo, I approach my climax. I imagine performing spiritual goodness. I imagine dragging a ridiculous marriage that should have never happened into a bottomless, iniquitous, shamelessly immoral mud wallow. There, I cavort in carefree bliss with the husband. I seduce him. I convert him into becoming my adoring, loving partner. We then perform all sorts of debauched acts. The husband tells me he wants to be free of her and only be with me. While he watches me, I hold the wife's obstinate head under the mud, immobilizing and suffocating her face by squeezing it firmly inside my lust- possessed thighs. I hold her head down while keeping her mouth forcibly cupped to my vagina. She struggles helplessly. She says she can't breathe. I won't let her. I no longer need her. Her only purpose was to please me, submit, accept my control, and ultimately die.

"I fantasize I'm in these dual ecstasy throes of seduction and murder. My libido intensifies. My orgasm will happen soon. I know it will. I can feel my clitoris throbbing. I am anxious to explode; but I hold off and wait. My task is unfinished. I hold my wedding ring neckless of my previously seduced husbands. They become one, their memories flood back as all my lovers become my one composite lover. Their vanquished wives' spirits become my one composite victim. Her name is Morality.

'My spirit soul soars to the heavens as I condemn Morality to purgatory. She dared to resist me! I make her perform penance. I chose Irony of Ironies for her punishment. I doom her to pleasure me, force her to love my wickedness; and enjoy herself against her will, while I shamelessly cavort with her husband. I flaunt my domination over her. I feel no guilt; only glory.

"I make her first join her mouth to my vulva. Her tongue must give rapture to my clitoris. She must indulge me and give me pleasure. She must prepare me and hasten the way for my orgasm. As my libido charges with the fullness of my explosive lust, I hold Morality's *head tightly between my thighs. I know I am suffocating her. She is drowning in my iniquity. I feel her desperate struggle within my loins. I feel indescribable pleasure knowing I am drowning her in my wantonness.*

*"My sex pushes firmly against her mouth. I demand that her tongue extend over my clitoris and slake every impulse of my insatiable lust. I receive her final desperate pleasure licks. Then, as Morality's life expires, I release her from my thighs. She slides lifelessly, beneath the mud and into my eternal spiritual abyss.*

*"Then, Charles' magnificent penis replaces her dying helpless tongue. My clitoris feels his loving, throbbing organ. It is splendid, hard, shameless, and free of the oedipal inhibitions that once restrained him. By loving me and thrusting into me in his wildly passionate and abandoned way, I know Charles is mentally killing his mother. We're killing her influence, together. And, I feel wonderful about that for him; and for me. My Immorality feels more magnificent and wonderful than ever. As Charles gains his rhythm inside me, as my mouth receives his mouth breaths of passionate lust, my soul tells me all is well. All is beautiful.*

*"Now, my sensually exquisite feet locate Morality's shoulders. They push her ever downward. She is beneath us. As the lust-tingling tips of my widespread whoring legs summon my power, I imagine them dealing Morality her final downward push. She descends; into the bottomless abyss of my sin wallow. She spirals down, through my shameless murky debauchery; and she disappears forever into the endless void of bereft souls. She is lost, waiting haplessly for her mortal fate in the dark, terrifying void of my unapologetic whoring. She knows I, the whore, the porn star, have become the arbiter of her future. She's at the whims of my sexual lust.*

*"The mental jackals of her new reality discover her lying there naked and exposed. It's a dark, unprotected world. The jackals have no mercy. They mock her first; then they attack her without mercy;*

*tearing away her morality flesh. Her moral lifestyle offers her no protection. The jackals play homage to me, the whore, the porn star. They honor and praise me for my most recent morality killing. Morality discovers everything that she ever believed was a mistaken belief. She was lied to. The jackals then devour her virtuousness and her lifestyle.*

*"She discovers that her husband will not protect her. He is with me now. He is my newest lover. I tell him to ignore her pleas. He closes his ears and his mind to her cries. He kisses me. He obeys me. I don't care what happens to her. I seal off my mind to her plight. I have no feelings for her. I rejoice in her demise. I do not feel evil. I have destroyed her. She is Morality, my mortal enemy. My spirit soars. I know I converted another soul to the Modern Morality Standard.*

*"My intensity builds. I prepare to orgasm. I escape the world's confining realities. I become a dazzling enchantress. I become a butterfly, fluttering above life's cares. Morality's life lies below me, in tatters, a shredded cocoon, submerged in unforgiving mud. Her husband escapes with me. We flutter together, above the bottomless mud pit; our sex organs are joined; we're feeling our blissful love. Then, I climax. I explode wildly.*

*"While I gush, I thank the spirits for my lust drive and my abilities to help this husband achieve his salvation. My passions soar heavenward. I imagine the dejected, defeated feelings of Morality, while she chokes and drowns under the mud of my relentless, iniquitous whoring. I know she will never bother us again.*

*"I lift my newest lover far above his mud drenched cocoon. My arms and legs engulf him. Naked, we rise heavenward. He embraces me in his arms and kisses my mouth; then my forehead and eyes, my neck, my creamy white shoulders. Lower now he kisses my chest and breasts. He sucks my nipples and plays his tongue over them. I experience titillations and shivers. Lust courses through my body. It's time! My orgasm explodes again. My unfettered passion lust throbs*

in my wildness. I am glorious. I am an unrepentant whore. I am a proudly immoral porn star.

"With me, Charles attained his boyhood dream. He kissed the forbidden vagina of his dream girl. While his tongue loved my clitoris, his mind imagined he performed cunnilingus with the 'Origin' by Corbet, as well as with me. Now, we enjoy frequent cunnilingus. The erotic film actress he once idolized became a real woman. She entered his life, and loved him. With every stroke of his tongue along the sides of my clitoris and with every one of his gentle tongue taps, Charles imagines performing intimate scenes with me in my films. I encourage him to let his imagination play this way. I've helped him shatter his inhibitions this way. I've become his true friend. Our friendship is solid and healthy; open and honest. And we love each other. He finally feels free to express his love the way he craved to express it for years. I adore him.

"I lift Charles' head and bring his lips to my face. I kiss him with my wild passion. Our tongues confirm our love. We are of the same mind. I open my legs to take his glorious hardness into my velvety heat. His thrusts are beautiful. Our rhythm has perfect harmony. Now! Yes! I feel his flood! My vulva fills with his semen flow. It joins with my fluids. We experience conception-lust's ecstasy. We are beautiful together. We revel and laugh in our newly found freedom. We frolic shamelessly in our precious lust. We know we will be lovers forever.

"Charles is my dearest seduction conquest. I feel the indescribable intensity of his sweet, beautiful love. Our minds enjoy our endless copulations. Our bellies and loins join in pleasured revelry. We have become butterflies.

"When Charles and I make love, I feel new blood and new life surging through my body. My sense of nirvana assures me that everything about me and everything I do is honest and good. I know the Spirits have blessed me and my fornications. I know I am a highly *desired, beautiful woman. Every seduction experience I have ever had transforms me and renews me. But this experience is special. I tremble. My renewed freedom leaves behind all the troubles and cares of mundane earthly matters. My thoughts are completely at peace with my life choices. My whoring has made me into a complete woman; a better person.*

*"Being the consummate unrepentant whore, being the world's queen of intimate films is the right life for me. Any regret; any guilt or shame I ever felt falls away. I know I have been chosen to be as I am. Sexual intimacy refreshes me; reaffirms me. I thrive on it. It's my cathartic, wholesome gift from the spirits. All slights in my life become tiny, insignificant; then they disappear from my mind. I soar heavenward. I embrace my insatiable love of unbridled lust. I hear the chorale finale of Puccini's opera. It reverberates through my entire body. I tingle with a delirious, ever mind-expanding happiness. I flutter freely. I am finally free of morality! I am the immoral BUTTERFLY!*

# CHAPTER EIGHT

*Swimming can be hard. Standing on your head can be hard. Running marathons can be hard. Making love is simpler. Try it. (Rosemary Ness-Bitner, author)*

## EXOTIC BUTTERFLY

*"Charles helps me feel like a butterfly. My dear sweet Charles stays with me. Oh, he does! He lovingly, tightly holds me in our fervent intimacy, while I bounce and push and squirm. His tongue caresses and taps my clitoris in tune with my ecstatic mood the entire time. He holds his tongue into me; always gently, always lightly; and he moves in harmony with me while I clasp his head between my thighs. He loves joining me on my orgasm rides. He loves that intimate closeness feeling. I do so much love that he loves it. I love that about him.*

*"Oh, Consuelo, I go out of my mind thinking about my vagina romps with Charles' tongue. He's soooo wonderful! He gives me the most wonderful tongue love, ever! It's because he is such a sweet man. When he licks my vagina in the reverent ways he kisses me there, my heart sings with joy and hope for the entire world. I have a fantastic range of orgasms with Charles. Explosive eruptions; slow trickles; intermittent pulses; gush floods; surprise spurts; all of them, Consuelo! He's positively wonderful!*

*"Charles brings me through all of them. While he performs cunnilingus we listen to his music. My moods swing from wild, like a*

*lioness making a kill; to a patriotic woman making love to a sol-
dier; to the soft innocence of sweet loving intimacy's cuddling, loving
touches. Charles has educated his tongue. It brings out my full range
of feelings during orgasms. I love how he helps me express myself!
I love what he does for me! Ooohhhh! Mmmmmm! Those are the
best words to describe our love, Consuelo. It's simply profound! It's
wonderment! It's special! It's yummy, yummy!*

*"Charles is now a staunch advocate of Mrs. O' Dell's Modern
Morality Standard. And he's the happiest he's ever been in his life.
He is currently working with European adult film producers to have
me star in some productions. We'll be doing the shoots outdoors, in
Paris. French Gendarmes will block off all traffic while I'm filmed
making love on the Champs-Elysees. I'll be starring in two orgies;
one with six Frenchmen who discover me at a toga food fest in an
exclusive restaurant on top of the Eiffel Tower; and another at the
Louvre museum's Egyptian section where I will play a white slave
girl being thoroughly ravaged to exhaustion by six gorgeous Nubian
black men.*

*"My scripts for these films will be practically nonexistent. The
producers simply want my completely natural self, directing my own
performances with my partners; instructing them how to position;
where to insert; when to come; deciding when I give fellatio; where
I want the cameras positioned for close ups of my face and vagina
during my orgasms and cum flows; everything. I'll have complete
freedom to choose which penises to fuck and suck as my feelings
inspire me and spark my lusts. The producers mostly want me to be
my nympho crazed self. All they ask is that I be the most expressive
insatiable immoral whore I can possibly be.*

*"I'm wildly excited about this opportunity, Consuelo, especially
the film in the Louvre. I believe it will be the most breathtaking
film ever created. I intend to call it 'A Slave Girl's Sins.' I already
see myself in a white pearl choker, white pearl earrings and pearl*

studded, golden teddy belt; performing my finale. I'll receive the cum of three yearning penises onto my welcoming tongue while I fast twerk three fuck crazed penises in rapid succession, producing such an irresistible titillating intensity that those penises will all quickly release into my vagina.

"I intend to bump my booty so hard and so fast while performing Kegel squeezes that the penises inside me will release so quickly that their cum gushes appear to be cascading from an endless waterfall. Simultaneously, I'll squeal for joy, experiencing my shameless passion lust. I'll flaunt my debauchery. I'll lovingly kiss, lick, and stroke all six penises while smiling gleefully to the cameras. This film will demonstrate to my fans that I, unquestionably, love performing in orgies. This will dispel all thoughts that I perform them against my will. They'll see how I revel in uninhibited, sinful whoring. It will be fabulous, breakthrough intimate art; the pinnacle of shameless, pleasure-crazed whoredom. I promise you.

"I can't wait to start performing for the European market. I'm so excited I can barely contain myself. When we wrap the 'Sin' film, I promise you, Consuelo; I'll call you before I call anyone else. I'll send you a complementary copy of the film and I'll share every intimate detail of every portion of the shoot with you.

"I'm often seen with Charles when I'm in Europe. He's my liaison to European connoisseurs of intimate artistry. I love my new, Modern Morality Charles and his enthusiasm for the Modern Morality Standard. His generosity is boundless and unprecedented in my experiences. He's a changed man; so, free; so, loving. His mother now stoically watches European porn stars making regular visits to Charles' chateau. She never mentions what she sees. Charles controls his own life now. Her direct phone line to Charles remains unconnected.

"Charles is a whole new man, now; and with a whole new mind-set. He is on a revenge quest. He believes his mother's restrictive attitude about his sexuality stemmed from her religious indoctrination. He now blames religion for stunting the sexual growth of many young people all over the world. He does not want any other young people to be forced to endure the deprivation and humiliation which he endured. He now quotes a biblical phrase: That ye shall reap what ye sew. Charles feels religions have sewed self-serving disinformation about human sexuality and intimacy for centuries. He thinks religions are the cause of much of humanity's frustrations and perversions because they suppressed humans' natural sexual urges. He thinks the adultery commandment and the commandment about coveting one's neighbor's wife need to be repealed. And Charles intends to correct religion's repressive influence on human intimacy and restore human intimacy to its natural balance.

"He is committing half of him many billions to create what he calls 'A Second Renaissance.' He sees the First Renaissance as the Age of Enlightenment, the Age of Science, or the Age of Reason. He sees his 'Second Renaissance' as the Age of Humanity, or the Age of Intimacy. He is financing no fewer than five colonies: in Southern France; in the Bahamas; in the Colorado Rockies; on Carolina's Outer Banks; and in Vietnam. Each colony will be tasked to recruit porn stars, young women eager to learn pornography, and accomplished photographers and artists. The porn stars and artists will create stunning portraits of women in various poses, performing spellbinding, breathtaking, inspirational pornography. They will produce exquisite photographs, short films, and oil paintings of the most beautiful pornography ever created. And this art will be marketed through Charles' network of art galleries and film studios. Charles intends to be the push back force against his perceived evil forces of religion, which stunted his sexuality during half of his manhood. He intends to name his colonies after recognizable religious themes, such as: 'The Temple of the Immaculate Ejaculation; The Blessed Home of the Risen Erection; The Sacred Vessel Cup of

*Divine Orgasms; The Sacred Heartthrob of Intimacy; and The Risen Spirit Temple of Sacred Whoredom. Charles is a perfectionist and a very determined man. He asked me to be on his board of directors because, as Charles insists, he wants the most expert advice on pornography available; and where else could he get better advice other than from the most wonderful, most enthusiastic, most unapologetic, glorious porn star in the entire world! Of course, I could never say 'no' to Charles. He has such a splendid penis and he fucks me so beautifully. I would never do or say anything to discourage him from wanting me.*

*"And we are of the same mind set now. I've chased away every trace of the outdated morality that his mother once used to manipulate him. He thinks about morality and intimacy in the same way that Bob, Carl, Dominick, Marshawn, Fred, and Big Ed do, now. Like them, Charles has become a believer in 'Butterfly Morals,' He loves to make intimate love with me now, for the sheer joy of making love. Charles has become one of my most beautiful butterfly loves. I truly do love him. Naturally, I was honored to say 'yes' to Charles. He always gets what he wants. I'm certain his new venture will succeed. He sets high goals for himself and he accomplishes them."*

*"Goodness, Marty. Your European experience not only changed Charles; it looks like it will also change the world! Tell us more about Europe, please."*

*"With pleasure, Consuelo. During my times in Europe, when I'm not with Charles or posing for camera pictures and advertizing film clips, I have many fabulous experiences. Europe is my new, exciting world. Those Continentals are aficionados of love making and delicious intimate film art. I'd never had caviar eaten from my vagina or pate foie gras licked from my breasts before; nor had I ever had one lover hand feed me morsel bits of King Crab, dipped in melted fresh creamery butter, while stimulating my nipples; and while another lover ejaculated his flood stream of semen into my vagina; nor had*

*I ever sipped Champaign while one lover performed cunnilingus on me and my wine sommelier licked whipped cream from my nipples.*

*"Every experience was heavenly. The tabloids reported that my immorality had become the cause célèbre of continental erotica aficionados. They tailed me for photos. Some even call me 'The Fabulous Transatlantic Sex Goddess.' I'm also called 'The Notoriously Immoral Intercontinental Porn Goddess,' and 'Global Porn Queen.' Their tabloid accounts of me were, in every article, very respectful, even deferential; and always complimenting the artistic expressive beauty of my work. So, unlike American tabloids where I've been called names that a descent, respectable woman like myself can't repeat, the continentals' welcoming, accepting attitudes encourage me to learn all I can about their sexual peccadillos, so I can create even more spectacular porn; more erotic and more thought provocative than any porn ever conceptualized. I must shatter all taboos; leave nothing off limits. I especially want to do more threesome scenes that challenge the sanctity of marriage; and scenes that question the veracity of religious teachings. That's taking on a lot; challenging established mores. I know there's much more educational work that must be done. American mores need more examination and enlightenment; not less. The splendid beauty and positive societal benefits of intimate erotic film art must become main stream.*

# CHAPTER NINE

*If your beau takes your shoes off and licks your toes, you might have your ideal fella; but you'll need to give him directions. (Rosemary Ness-Bitner, author)*

## BUTTERFLY MINDSET

*"Marty,"* questioned Consuelo, *"Those descriptions were all so mouth watering. Thank you for sharing. I have here a write-in question from Marcus who states that he will be your adoring fan forever. He says he dreams of making love with you every night. He asks: What do you feel is the best part about making love with a new partner for the first time? Is it the initial penetration, or is it the orgasm? And, as a follow up question, he asks: 'Is there any one love scene that you remember as your favorite?' Could you answer Marcus for us?"*

*"Sure, Consuelo,"* answered Marty, *"Marcus, the act of making love has several components, or doors, that my feelings pass through. Each passage is equally beautiful and special. Initial attraction and foreplay are the obvious beginning of love making. When my partner first appears on set, he may be wearing tight breeches. I can see his bulge and imagine how wonderful his penis could be.*

*"Then, I get this huge empty feeling inside myself. It's a kind of hunger. I feel I must discover his penis and possess it for my pleasure. I must get him excited with foreplay. I must take his pants down and put my hands and my mouth on his wonderful penis. Then, when*

his pants are finally down and off, and his penis is fully revealed to me, I experience the awe of it. This feeling of awe never fails me. It floods over me suddenly, in a rush that pushes away all other thoughts.

"Then, slowly, very meaningfully, a feeling of reverence rises up from deep inside me. This feeling tells me that I must share it with the penis. Then, I greet the penis with my lips and tongue. This is our moment of splendor. I lick and kiss its head, assuring it of my adoration while I take its yearning eagerness into my anxious mouth. A fellatio love fest takes place between my mouth, lips, tongue and fingers, and our wonderful guest, the penis. This intimacy takes place in a separate part of my mind from regular conjugal sex. It's different; and somehow more endearing. There's no domination or submission about it; only adoration; and participants appreciation of the beautiful gloriousness of the deed, and honest love.

"As I begin to suck the penis and draw its strokes deeper into my mouth, I then draw my head back from it so that my lips glide over it with subtle downward pressure. As I do this, my feelings become dedication to giving the penis the fullest measures of pleasure I can possibly give it. My feelings become those of wholesomeness and goodness. I know the penis, my partner, and my fans love my sincere dedication to my fellatio artistry and my adult film star performance.

"I feel blessed to be who I am; to feel the incredible strength of my partner's penis inside my mouth; feel the penis's life blood coursing through its veins; straining with all its strength against my lips; knowing its experiencing my adoration of it and its incredible life force. I pause to behold the penis in my hands; to marvel at how glorious it is; how its coloration, whether a white or a colored man's penis, is a darker shading from my partner's skin's tone.

"I surmise that it is nature's way to focus my attentions on it; that my attraction to it and my desires to please it are all natural and good. It's nature's way of again drawing my face and mouth close to it; to adore the penis even more; to cherish this spellbinding time I'm privileged to have with it; to revere it as something holy, majestic, and wonderful; glorious beyond descriptive words. It's nature's way of assuring me that my passions and desires are natural and good; and that I must feel completely shameless and uninhibited about how I truly adore my partner's penis.

"My hollow emptiness lusts palpably. I hunger for his penis because my feelings know the penis is medicine for my nympho affliction. Only the penis, and it alone, can fill my emptiness. I feel I must make this penis my intimate friend. I again place my kisses on its head and shaft. This love I give with mouth and tongue, is love the penis always holds dear.

"My feelings then level off. They become a matter-of-fact, shameless joy about what I do with the penis. It's more than a get down to business sort of feeling. My feelings assure me that my immorality is good and beautiful; and that there is nothing wrong about what I am doing; but everything about the fellatio I am about to perform is wholesome, natural, beautiful, and good. I know I am being true to my beliefs and my natural self. Goodness and beauty describe what I do.

"The penis now knows I appreciate him and the wonders he will perform in my mouth and vagina. He accepts my fellatio without equivocating. We're united in our purpose. Nothing else matters. My mind knows only the penis. I will live with this feeling forever. It is so wonderful. I want Mr. Penis inside me; filling my emptiness; filling my soul; completing me as a woman.

"My lover and I may interrupt our fellatio and mouth kiss. We touch each other; feeling each other's bodies. This stimulates me. I feel wanted and desirable. I become more interested in my partner as a person, apart from him as my sex partner. And I think more and more about making love with him, I become warm and moist.

*You may hear me squeal and moan in my film scenes, as my nipples are pinched, sucked and tongue tapped. You may see me lift my pelvis to accept the joys of my partner's hand touching my vagina; letting him know I want him to appreciate me and love me, sexually. This part of my experience titillates and excites me.*

*"As I stroke his penis, I sometimes imagine it is a special kind of fountain pen that spurts endless streams of white semen instead of ink; and soon, oh so soon, it will be home inside my loving, waiting well; filling my emptiness with warm semen cream. I imagine I will feel semen shooting into me; first once; then again; and again, until I'm brim filled and overflowing with all the love my lover can give me. My breathing quickens. I feel anxious to move through lust's next opening door; penetration, his penis passing my outer vagina lips.*

*"I experience new sensations during this short phase. As I guide his penis into me and my lover's body presses against mine, I feel wanton. I am now becoming impaled by his penis; slowly at first; then rammed repeatedly and more rapidly by the wakened wonder feelings of deliciously wholesome, rising lust intensity. I'm speared by my partner's penis; fastened by it to my partner; captured by it to him, and I'm loving the feelings of our unity. I know I have captured my captor. I know he is loving his newly discovered captivity. I want to hold him close to me, forever. I don't want my captor to ever get away.*

*"My lips part with natural desire. I want to kiss his mouth and be kissed by his mouth. My eyes express my other worldly feelings in my far away gaze. I imagine green, pastoral hills and white sheep grazing. That's the wonderment of intimate sexual intercourse. I pray I'm pleasing his penis, as I feel it pleasing me. I silently pray that my partner's penis will stay firm and strong; that it will, will itself to pleasure me until I orgasm and beyond. I very much want this marvelous feeling, this feeling that only comes with the love of sex and the love of experiencing intimacy, to last long, and then longer*

*still. Actually, in all truth, I want this feeling to last forever. That's how much I love this feeling. That's how much I love to fuck.*

*"When you see me purse my lips with joyous wonder-lust, you know my ego is soaring. Notice that I'm in tune with my partner's powerful thrusts. I'm doing what my spirits and nature command. I know that being an immoral whore is wonderful and good; that my soul is in the right place; and that everything I am doing is blessed by nature's spirits. I'm in a beautifully good psychological place; my wonder place where I am truly me.*

*"Those who curse me and my behavior in the name of their god do not phase me or change my determination to excel at my erotica craft; not in the slightest way. They do not even give me pause. Their judgement values do not concern me. I'm totally nonplused by them. My own spirits are the only gods that matter to me. And they totally approve of and encourage everything I'm doing.*

*"I feel wonderful to be having straight, conjugal sex again. I reconfirm my commitment to the Modern Morality Standard, while sharing my partner's joys. I can tell he loves my body and that's he's totally into loving his intimate experience with me. I naturally meet his thrusts. Time stops for us. Our world stands still momentarily; and then it falls away. We share this feeling of our wonderment again and again. We know that what we are doing matters. We are creating beautiful intimacy. And nothing else in the world matters to either of us.*

*"Thoughts whirl through my mind during these initial euphoric moments of coitus. Does my partner love sex with me better than with his significant other? Will this begin a long-term relationship for us? Do I want that with him? I have those sorts of thoughts about all my porn partners. I often fall into love with them and with our love making. When that love happens, they become precious friends and special souls to me, from that moment on. My head shakes slowly from side to side. That's when I slip into my deepest mood.*

*I call it my savoring mood. It begins my transcendent journey into passion.*

*"A third door now opens inside my mind. It starts my crescendo. My coitus has built up to orgasm. I know my feelings are changing again. I experience this serene sensation where I'm cherishing our beautiful intercourse. I'm respecting how special our intimate love is. A flooding of feelings about how precious is our intimacy takes place, commanding all my mental energy; and joining our two souls. Something romantically beautiful takes place inside the film we are creating; yet m feelings are beyond the reach of the film.*

*"Perhaps, Marcus, your mind can appreciate what no camera can ever capture. It's how my mind processes my thoughts. Watch my face while I make love. Imagine you are my face. I hope you can then feel what I am feeling. I'm feeling beautiful. I'm fluttering like a butterfly; carefree. A kind of sheen crosses my face. Look closely. You'll see it. That's me. That's my serenity. That's me loving my lovemaking. That feeling you see is why I love performing my pornography. I hope you can share my feeling, Marcus.*

*"I feel like a butterfly, soaring up higher and higher through rising halls of beautiful delicious air, twisting and turning, rolling, and experiencing everything wonderful and beautiful all through my body. Lions and tigers and bears roar from behind my insatiable craven lust door. I'm in the throes of love passions in these spiritual moments. I experience a thrill. It's more powerful than a rocket's engines going full throttle up, blasting me higher and higher, away from confining earth into my open ended deliriously expanding, endless sexual nirvana. I know I am a glorious, unapologetic, shamelessly immoral porn star, creating my beautiful pornography. Then, it's happening! I'm given over to my passion. Passion takes control of me and my body. I love what I'm doing.*

*"Marcus, that's when you'll often hear me loudly screaming: 'YES! YES! Mmmmm! Mmmmmm! Yes baby. Yes, my love! Fuck*

me. Mmmmm. Fuck me harder. Yes. Harder. Mmmmm. So wonderful.' And then I often whisper: 'Would you like to come inside me? I want you to. Please stay inside me while you come. I want to feel your penis pulsing your hot semen inside me. I love that feeling.' I love saying those things to my partners while we're filming our love making. It's natural for me to say those things because I honestly feel that way. I'm a woman who doesn't hold anything back, Marcus.

"Marcus, I've become an incorrigible nymph. I have habituated myself to become completely immersed in the joys of intercourse. Sometimes, you'll notice, I break out laughing from the joys of my orgasms and I begin passionately kissing my partners. That's my wantonness leaving all boundaries of decency and expressing itself. That's me expressing my honest appreciation for the joys my partners' penises are giving me; how much I love the ways they are pleasing me. That's when my mind totally lets itself go. It happens when I become deliriously happy that I'm a totally immoral whore; that I can be completely uninhibited before the camera and be paid for being who I am; and that I'm thrilled knowing that my fans are watching my vagina experiencing an orgasm.

"It's this sixth sense I feel when I'm kissing my partner while I am being conjugal with him. It's knowing that my fans are imagining that their lips are kissing my lips; that their penises are stroking my vagina; that they are imagining that their penises are releasing their semen inside me, at the same time my partner is also coming inside me. This laughter release happens when my mind knows that everything about what I m doing, the immorality of it all, is so incredibly wondrous and beautiful; that I am blessed by the spirits and that they are pleased with me. I know that they love me for being a total whore. I'm confident knowing that I can do no wrong. I can only be my glorious self.

"I feel like enjoying my partner's beautiful vagina-pleasuring penis, forever. My laughter reflects my true bliss. I love kissing my partners while I'm having sex with them. Making love with a great partner and feeling his penis inside me is my ultimate high. I feel wildly sexual then. When cunnilingus is driving my wildness, I'm usually the one who orgasms first. My sexuality soars above the heavens during those orgasms. I give myself over to a rapture state.

"I have this feeling of ecstasy, knowing that my partner loves making love with me so much, that he'll pleasure my vagina's clitoris with his tongue; all the while knowing that my vagina has enjoyed the company of hundreds of penises before his oral sex with me. It's an immense thrill, knowing that he accepts me and intimately loves me for the total whore that I am; that he adores me for all the porn I've made; that he honors me for being uninhibited about my sexuality this way.

"Rapture and ecstasy are beautiful words, Marcus; but they don't come close to describing how I feel during my on-film orgasms. I feel like I'm doing something wildly beautiful; and I'm sharing my beautiful feelings with the entire world. I especially love twerking while having a huge penis inside me. I love feeling my naked body in rhythm with my partner's thrusts into my vagina. It's positively glorious. Its raw, lusty sexuality. I totally love the primal feeling I get while having sex that way; love that feeling of the penis probing deeply inside me. I experience a kind of out of my mind happiness.

"Marcus, it's just that I love having sex in so many different positions and with so many different partners it's impossible to describe all the wonderful feelings I have. There simply aren't enough words. That's why you have to watch me perform my porn in many of my different films. My mental state shows in my facial expressions. My eyes and smiles tell the world that I love, shamelessly love, being a totally immoral penis-obsessed whore; absolutely love giving myself over to the enjoyment of intimacy like I do.

"Sometimes you'll see me sublimate. That's when I'm imagining that those intimate moments will last forever. My mind gets totally *into the lovemaking then; and sometimes I squirt. I'm totally relaxed and in tune with my orgasm then. I just let myself go. It's wonderful. I feel blessed to be able to make love in such an open, uninhibited, natural, uncomplicated way. Porn is especially beautiful that way. It showcases my feelings; allows me a platform where I can express my innermost immoral soul in so many different ways. I love everything about my lovemaking while being filmed.*

*"My feelings are transported to another realm. I imagine I've suddenly become a beautiful butterfly. Everything is suddenly, completely, innocently beautiful, and wonderful; love flows everywhere around me. I float, immersed in lovemaking. It's infinite. It lifts me; holds me inside it; beckons me to flutter in it; enjoy it. And, above all, love myself.*

*"While my orgasm flows, my thoughts often turn to nature. I sometimes find myself wondering:*

*'Am I really any different than a flower being visited by butterflies and bees? People do not call flowers whores or think less of them for being visited by many bees; so how, I wonder, could anyone think I am less beautiful, or my life less meaningful than a flower's life, while I'm making love?'*

*"Finally, Marcus, I experience the beauty of my partner's semen entering me. I then have this overwhelming feeling of gratitude that I am blessed to be so honored, so graced to be performing this beautifully erotic act with my partner-lover. Sometimes my mind sees wild horses running fast, their hoofs churning the earth. They strain to come to me. Nothing can stop them. Their powerful hooves make the earth tremble. The ground literally shakes in my mind from the power of these imaginary horses. I feel pleased with my partner and immensely proud of him. He is my stallion. I am his mare. And he is having sex with me. He's my very own stallion for our film; but also, now mine; forever intimate with me. I ride him, hard and fast. I squeeze my legs against his sides and hold his mane.*

"He has become mine; all mine; my own magnificent, powerful stallion; my fierce, proud horse. His muscles and strength are boundless. We are running wild and free in our own world. Together, we escape from everyone. We run away with each other into our special secret moment. It takes place inside our minds, Marcus. The camera can't film this feeling, but you can sense it when you search my face. It's where my partner and I become incredibly close and so preciously intimate that no one other than the two of us will ever know how erotically beautiful it is. Only our minds know.

"In my films, I often shake my head at this moment while I'm moaning:

'Mmmmm. Mmmmmm.'

"My moaning tells you I am coming again. I usually come at least twice during intimate love making. I totally get my mind into it because I love having intimate intercourse that much. It's what I live for, Marcus; on film and off. What you see are my pleasure lusts exploding inside my shaking head, as I thrash from side to side. My mind becomes a million stars, all bursting open with twinkling starlight; lighting up the night sky.

"I simultaneously feel precious, intense love and gratitude for my partner. By making beautiful love with me, he becomes my connection to Earth. Watch closely, Marcus. See me hold his body tightly against mine? See me pulling him into me with my arms and legs? That's me, trying mightily to hold onto this moment of coitus, and never letting it go. That's me, cherishing our closeness. I'm trying desperately to prevent thoughts of separating; of ending our intimacy; of leaving our special intimate time together.

"Notice how I'm trying to block out the end of my beautiful feelings? I do that because I want my feelings to continue. I know the cameras are rolling; but I imagine we are alone, unseen. I know my nymphomania holds me in its grasp. I know I don't want to stop having sex. I never want to stop. But I know, at some point, we must stop; but I never want to stop after I make love. I imagine we are in our special place; in our other world; and there, we'll never stop loving each other; and there, everything will be beautiful, forever. I imagine the cameras aren't even there.

"The final door my mind passes through is my long, soft come down from my orgasms, Marcus. This is when my emotions turn sweet and spiritual. I recognize that I've performed a sacred act, which is what love making really is. I believe that, Marcus. I believe making love is more sacred than any religious service. I feel an immense inner satisfaction that I've shared my divine experience with another human.

"I think of myself as an angelic goddess for good. I believe I've brought beauty and goodness to the whole world. I feel filled with glorious immoral love making; like I did a holy thing. I know all that I have done and felt during our film's creation was good, because as humans, sex and love making is embedded in our DNA. We are a unique species that way. We are meant to make love and feel glorious about it. I feel my love spills out and flows over the entire world. I glow from inside myself with this radiant love.

"Then, Marcus, I feel I'm carried by loving hands, floating upon a peaceful endless sea with warm winds and soft breezes. Rose petals float down from the heavens all around me. Angels play peaceful music with their harps. I imagine that angels are kissing me. They tell me that I am their goddess. They take me to a shore where everyone knows peace and everyone loves everyone else.

"A warm sense of goodness, completeness, and radiance courses through my entire body. I hug and kiss my partner with genuine expressions of heartfelt love. I make a soft Mmmmm sound of contentment. It expresses my feeling when I know I've been wonderfully fucked. There's no other feeling that comes close to it. And I feel happiness and extreme pride for the beautiful film we just created. I think of my immorality as a special gift from the spirits, giving me *the divine privilege of bringing happiness and joy to the world. I feel thankful for whom I am. I'm grateful that intimate artistry is a venue people can enjoy in their human experience.*

*"Thank you for watching my films, Marcus, and especially for your interest in my feelings during love making. If you want to bring your own feelings closer to mine, pick any one of my films and carefully study my face during the four phases of love making. You'll notice the joy I feel during every phase of intercourse; and you should notice that joy expressing itself differently through the changes in my smiles; my lips; the lift of my eyebrows and cheeks. Those are all my natural expressions, Marcus. Studying them frame by frame will help you experience my same feelings, as the film takes you through the love making scene. And, if you can, Marcus, please consider my Premium Member Service. I'd love to help you personally experience the phases of my love making during our live sessions.*

*"And Marcus, my very favorite love scene is always the one I've performed last. I pride myself in continuing to perform better. Every time I perform an intimate film scene, I'm applying a technique that I learned before, only refining it to make it better, whatever that technique might be. It could involve my sense of timing, like how long I hold a penis inside me; how I move my hips to capture my partner's semen while my partner comes; or how long I stroke his penis and kneed his balls before I begin kissing and sucking his penis's head; or how I can better refine my tongue techniques on a penis's sensitive circumcision ring. It could be that I've learned, through my film studies, that I might twerk at a more enticing, erotic pace to create a greater sense of wonder for the camera. My improving techniques also simply reflect that I absolutely relish and enjoy the act of making love more and more, every single time I perform."*

Consuelo: *"Wow and double wow, Marty. Thank you. Here's another question. This is from Miss Sandstone, Marty. She says she's watched your films and you have inspired her to begin a career in making adult films. She says she's thought about this seriously for a long time and now she thinks she's ready to take the plunge. She asks your suggestions for overcoming hesitancy to perform before the cameras; and, she says she understands that choosing prostitution and film making will likely result in attracting many men who might want to become her lovers. She asks if that's been your experience and, if so, how do you manage to keep so many men's balls in the air (no pun intended, she says)? And she asks, do you have any advice or insights for her?"*

Marty: *"Yes, Miss Sandstone. You can expect that literally hundreds of men will try to find their way into your love life; and they will especially want to get their penises into your panties. I've discovered that the best way to keep your lovers happy or manage all those balls, as you put it, in the air is to hold two sets of balls in your hands and one set in your mouth at the same time. Tee Hee! No, in all seriousness, Miss Sandstone, men can become extremely possessive. You need to be careful from the outset of every romantic tryst.*

*"The best way to overcome your hesitancy about performing before the cameras is to be honest about who you are, what you're trying to accomplish, and making a beginning. Start by listing yourself on several dating sites. When you go on your dates, be honest. Tell your date that your ambition is to become a prostitute and a porn star, and ask him if he would please help you. Assuming he's handsome and presentable, ask him to have sex with you. After sex, ask him if he liked sex with you, and if he did, ask him if he could please have his friends call you. Slowly, but surely, through your dating, build up a list of those men whom you love to fuck. While you are building your book of lovers, join a web cam site, and offer video times of you preening, masturbating, and chatting with potential future fans.*

*"When you have decided on your preferred, suitable lovers, invite them to make some amateur films of you and them having*

sex. Make several one-on-one films; then graduate to threesomes and orgies. Make sure you capture the all-important explicit erotica scenes. You want these scenes to capture your smiling face and eager lips when your partners ejaculate into your mouth and your vagina. You'll also want to do some long running close ups of semen burbling on your lips and flowing from your vagina.

"Two more important things, Miss Sandstone: Make sure some of your partners are black men with really huge penises. There's something voyeuristic about a while woman taking a huge black penis into her mouth and all the way, deeply into her vagina. It drives some fans crazy when they see a massive black penis ejaculating into a white woman's mouth or vagina. It's a form of psychological atonement for all wrongs that whites inflicted upon blacks for so many years; at least I think that's what it is; a type of guilt release. Anyway, whatever the reason, fans adore scenes like that. So, give the market what it wants.

"Also, with your partners, go to a high-quality photo studio. Get at least two hundred still life photos of you performing explicit sex with your partners. Get shots of a huge black penis withdrawn from your vagina with white creamy semen flowing from your vagina and your smiling face displaying your open mouth with your tongue pressed against the back of your front teeth. That shows off your appetite for semen. Get extreme close-up photos of you licking your partners' balls and penises; and close ups of them with their tongues eagerly licking your vagina's lips while you hold yourself open, fingering yourself and smiling. Always smile a sincere, glowing smile. Because of the sex involved in creating an outstanding portfolio, you may need to book the photographer for several sessions over several weeks.

"Then, once you have your sample films and your photos, you need to approach the firms that produce high quality pornography. Call me. I can give you introductions to the best studios. You may *initially need to work for very little money or even for free to get your porn films established. Don't be discouraged. Love your work and remember, everyone needs to start somewhere. You'll see. You'll gather fans and followers.*

*"While you build your porn portfolio of films and photos, you may want to keep your regular employment. In today's progressive digital age, you have huge advantages that enable you to develop your parallel porn career. If you are a professional woman or if you work flexible hours or part time, you can begin by meeting your dates on line. Arrange with a friendly hotel or motel to meet your dates for sex. Insist on reasonable hourly rates; or, if you have privacy, simply invite your dates home, and fuck them there. I strongly advise vetting your dates before you take them into your home or before you go to their homes. At least meet them at a restaurant or bar. Get to know them. Vet them. Ask them questions. Make sure you are not booking intimacy with a bad hombre. Assess his ego. You do not want control freaks who want to possess you. You don't want to become a wife or mistress. You want to become a porn star, remember?*

*"The way to deal with strong male egos is to tell them up front that you are a businesswoman. Be sure of him before you allow him into your circle of lovers. That's why I recommend starting with male friends that you know. Then, when you are settled in with one of your lovers, you must give him all your love and attention, every single bit of it. Never withhold affection from him. Never hold anything back. Make love like he's the only man in the world and like you haven't had sex for months. Never speak to him about any of your other lovers.*

*"When your date time is finished, politely tell him that you need to be going to a meeting or an appointment. Never tell him you need to get to another man's bed or dinner date, or weekend away. Always keep your lovers concealed from each other. If he asks, politely tell*

*him you are meeting old friends for private, off-topic matters. That way, the man's imagination will take over. He'll assume he's your most important love and his ego will allow him to pretend your other lovers are not meaningful to you. He'll continue to love you. Trust me on that. Your lovers will ALL continue to love you.*

*"Now, if he's been your lover for a time and you learn that he's open minded about his relationship with you and about your other dalliances, you may want to feel him out about participating with you and some on your other friends in an orgy. Let him know you are working on becoming a porn star and you want to make explicit films and photos with him. If he says yes to that; well, then you'll have an ideal open and beautiful relationship with him. If he accepts and adores you for your aberrant behaviors, you have a true gem. Keep him close to you. Those sorts of like-minded lovers are the very best. My advice to you would be to cultivate as many of those accepting, open-minded lovers as you can and do orgies with them as often as possible.*

*"Experiment during your orgies. That's my best advice. Think of male semen like you would think about the base palate colors when you are painting something. Some men's semen is stronger than other's. Some men are more acidic; others are more mellow. Have several different men come inside your vagina during each of your orgy sessions. Some paint colors blend smoothly with others; other colors invade a competing color and clash with it; pushing it into a small corner of your color palate; still other colors will diffuse beautifully. They'll give you that: 'AHHH, SO SWEEET AND DREAMY,' feeling when you capture the perfect blend for the mood you want to express.*

*"Proper semen blending is a lot like color blending. Get to know how different combinations of men ejaculating their semen into you make you feel. Perhaps male A and male B and male C make your perfect blend for the mood you are in? Perhaps their combined PH*

valence makes your vagina feel all warm and creamy wonderful when you combine those three? And, if that's how you want to feel during that particular orgy; then by all means, make sure you have those three lovers participating with you.

"If, on the other hand, you want a tangy, acidic supercharged and itching for more sex feeling, you may wish to have more acidic males A, D, E and F ejaculating inside you. Perhaps that will help you achieve your lusty, ravishing 'Bitch in hot heat' mood? If so, make sure you include those particular males in your orgy plans. Always be honest with your partners. Tell them which men you want to fuck and in which order you'd like to fuck them, so that your vagina will feel the exact erotic sensations that you crave, throughout your entire orgy experience.

"You are responsible for creating the moods you wish to express in your films. Remember that. Your partners will understand that. Good partners will work hard with you to make sure they fuck you with the right sensuality and passion, and in the right sequence combinations at the right times. It takes practice. Don't be disappointed if your films don't turn out the way you want them to at first. Just keep practicing until you get the look you want. As you gain experiences doing lots of orgies, you will discover that, by changing your combinations of lovers during your orgies, you can run through an entire cycle of moods and send your emotions all over the place. And, that can leave you feeling totally drained, or 'all fucked out,' as I like to say. Try reaching that level. Then examine your work and compare it to your initial efforts. You'll notice your improvement. You'll appreciate your artistry. You'll feel wonderful.

"Always talk with your partners all through your orgy experiences. Remember, they are human, just like you; and they are there to please you. Let each partner know what you love most about him. Let him know how his semen feels inside you and whether his ejaculations are pleasing you; not just how warm they feel while gushing over your clitoris; but also, how their semen feels inside you, after that initial gush. Let your partner know whether his cum shot makes you feel dreamy; or if it makes you hungry to fuck him more; or if it inspires you to fuck a different partner; or, perhaps, to suck another man's penis.

"During an orgy is the perfect time and place for complete honesty. Don't be shy. You're becoming an uninhibited, shameless porn star, remember? Speaking candidly and truthfully during your orgies is the best way to forge honest, secure, long-lasting, loving relationships. That's how you build mutual trust and feelings of intimate love with all your partners. Those lovers will accept you for being a shameless unapologetic whore and they will absolutely, positively adore you for what you are doing; and for who and what you are. Remember: There is no shame in being a porn star. None. Adult sex work is a proud, humanistic, expressive, respected profession.

"Undoubtedly, you will develop certain love interests on your journey to porn stardom. Orgies give you the perfect opportunity to deepen those relationships. Make sure you include your favorite love interests in your orgies. Their participation will help them understand your need for sexual fulfillment. During orgies they'll gain an understanding about you that they never appreciated before. They'll come to know you as a complete, sexual woman. And here's the greatest benefit of including them: It's the afterwards effect.

"You'll notice it in their eyes. They will not be able to express it in words. When they see you in an evening gown or in your tennis outfit, they won't really be seeing you dressed that way. They'll be seeing you in your natural element of taking your pleasures. Their minds will go places they never went before. Each man will wonder whether, during your orgy fest, the man whose mouth was kissing yours, while he was thrusting inside you, is the mouth you'd rather prefer kissing; and when one was kissing you, were you perhaps hoping that another man, who was then thrusting inside you, would return to you later, that very evening, and plunge his lust into your vagina again? You see, the orgy will haunt your men's minds in this certain male way. Each man will become fiercely protective of you and very attentive to your needs and wants.

"When one of your orgy partners comes to pick you up on a date or when he beholds you across the room at a social event, look closely at his eyes. Study his feelings. You'll see awe and reverence that were not there before. Notice his certain inner gratitude that you allow him to be with you. You'll see it in his eyes. They will confirm that he has become attached to you. They will confirm that he has gained a deeper understanding of you. They'll reveal something profound and unshakable.

"They'll tell you that he has entered a whole new, deeper dimension of amorous feelings for you. You'll see respect, awe and profound adoration in those eyes that behold you; that, before, simply was not there. You see, in a way that's hard to explain, the orgy has elevated you. You are now in charge of your relationship with him. It's true.

"His eyes will tell you that he understands, accepts, and adores your soul in ways he could not reach before. You'll discover that your relationship with him has profoundly, wonderfully changed; deepened; become more intimate on this new, higher level of respect and understanding. You'll notice that your relationship has also attained a new, higher plateau in your conversations with him. He'll always want whatever is most pleasing to you, for you, because his soul will have joined itself to yours. It's hard for me to express in words how you will notice this transformation in your relationship. But you will notice it.

"Think of it as the male adulation effect. You'll have to live it and see it for yourself. Have your favorite man join you in one of your orgies. Tell him you need him to experience your joys with you while you perform in your porn world. Tell him you need to know he's comfortable that you perform porn and that he's pleased with you and proud to be dating a porn star.

"While he's on set, performing with you and your other partners, be your total uninhibited relaxed self. Laugh, banter with your partners. Love these moments and your experience. You will recognize the adulation effect in his behavioral changes after the orgy. You will have become his goddess. Notice how his face lifts and how his eyes smile when he beholds you from across a room. That tells you that his heart leaped at the sight of you. You will know that he is presenting his heart and his love for you on his silver platter.

"Notice the adoration in his eyes. Trust me about this. He will adore you. He will want you to perform more orgies and join you in them. He will go to every length and measure to please you and to ensure you are having your pleasures. That's part of his behavioral change. His reason for existence has now become to please you. You will have become his goddess.

"You may need to manage his adoration. When you become known as a porn star, expect several men to approach you at social gatherings, cocktail parties, and the like. They'll offer to bring you a drink or something similar to chat you up for your card or phone number. They'll likely seek to schedule a private rendezvous with you for any of a thousand reasons. This is natural male behavior. Hopefully, your love interest will accept it as such. Hopefully, you will not have attached to yourself a love interest who engages in cichlid-like behavior; chasing other males away. If he's going to conduct himself like a possessive fish whenever another male approaches you, you may need to dust him."

"Dust him?" Consuelo needed Marty to clarify her shorthanded terminology.

"Oh," laughed Marty, "I'm sorry. I mean to say you may need to put him in his place. Gently remind him that you are a woman of the American twenty first century; that your moral standards allow you considerable freedoms; that he was made aware of this when you first dated him; and that you will take your pleasures with *whomever and whenever you choose to take them. Inform him that you will not be owned, controlled, or dictated to; that he must accept you as you are or he must seek other waters to swim in. Be adult about this. Avoid making a scene. But insist on your autonomy and be clear about it. If this adult understanding does not materialize to your satisfaction, then you must throw him into the dust bin of past relationships that you no longer wish to have. If you do dust him, do not look back. Control freaks do not change.*

*"Always remember, Miss Sandstone, that you are the product you are selling. And, you are always selling yourself. That is why you cannot allow yourself to be controlled by a control freak. You must never stop selling. You are also your product's living advertisement. Package your product as beautifully as possible. Appearance counts, Miss Sandstone. If you need teeth, face and body work done, do not hesitate or put it off. Get those things done. A perfect mouth, midriff, tush, and sculpted thighs are essential. So, whatever the cost, bear it. Whatever the pain, bear it. Get your pearly whites pearly white. Get unsightly fat sucked out and excess skin trimmed off. Pain pays!*

*"Your boobs are usually your first noticed assets, Miss Sandstone. The boob is the first thing a baby male instinctively recognizes. It's his security, his love attachment to his Mommy; and his food. Psychologically, males never leave the female boob. That makes your boobs essential for attracting customers. Flaunt them. Sculpt them. Perfect them. Buy implants, if you must. It's not their size that matters most. You don't need nine pounders. Three pounders work fine. The key is how they present to your viewers and your porn partners. Make them as appealing and as appetizing as possible. Have their look perfected. Get them pointed straight ahead, like headlights announcing your presence. And have your nipples lilt upward so your areolas present themselves like cherries being offered up like tasty morsels on a plate, anxious and enthusiastic to be finger and tongue stimulated; begging to be sucked. Wear see-through sheer*

blouses and dresses that accentuate your beautiful nipples and your inviting cleavage. Magnetized males will flock to you. Men adore women's boobs. Much like babies psychologically, they will want to place their lips on your boobs and keep your boobs close to them.

"Attitude is everything for a working girl, Miss Sandstone. Always be proud of who you are and what you do. Your posture should be model perfect. Imagine a string pulling your head up, like you are a puppet. Pinch your shoulder blades together, not just when you stand and walk; always. When you walk into a room, get out of a limo, step onto a red carpet, or enter a foyer remember you must exude pride in yourself and what you do. You own the scene and all the eyeballs present. You are the center of attention. Males will eye you to assess their odds of a relationship. Women will either view you as a threat or a love interest. Keep the eyeballs on you by smiling with confidence and subtly passing your tongue across your lower lip. Your thoughts should message that you are the ultimate love goddess; and that you are available for sex, in the right circumstance and for the right price.

"All times are show-time for you. You'll be invited to escort men to social functions, for example. Are you there to ooh and ahh at the awards recipients? No, you aren't. Be gracious, of course; but you're there to attract additional select customers to your premium service. Have a few business cards that say you offer consulting service, interior decorating, image building or marketing. When your eyes notice a suitable man paying attention to you, flirt with him. Bat your eyelashes, pull your shoulders back a little; twist your torso, show off your beautiful boobs, and smile into his eyes. Let him know you're interested. Slip your card to him. Signal him. Let him know that you love to fuck and that your honey pot is available.

"When he calls, get him into the sack with you. Laugh; enjoy yourself; tease with him; be playful, and above all have fun while you seduce him and make love with him that first time. Declare you *want your life to be joyful and fun filled, and you're not the least bit inhibited or ashamed about it. In the fullness of time, let him know you're proud to be an immoral whore. Laugh and squeal when he kisses your nipples. Talk with him. Tell him you love the way he licks your vagina. Tell him you can't wait to get his big penis inside of you; and tell him you can't wait to know how you feel while he's making love with you.*

*"When he reveals his penis, make sure you lick it lovingly and passionately from the bottom of his balls, slowly, tenderly, adoringly, from his balls up his shaft to the tip of his penis; and then kiss the head of his penis like it's the most joyful moment you've ever experienced in your life; like you are in the presence of the most awesome thing you've ever seen. And, love, absolutely love, what you are doing. And, while he's making love with you, while his penis is inside your vagina, tell him you love how you're feeling; tell him you love how his penis feels inside of you. Laugh, giggle and squeal while you tell him how thrilled you feel. Remember, love making happens in the mind. Fill his mind with eroticism. Impart your passion for intimacy into his mind. And, above all, love your lovemaking. Be joyful and proud that you are making love. It's the very highest calling you have. Honor your calling. Love and embrace what you are doing. Never think that you are being immoral. Always think that you are divinely gifted and bestowing your holy intimacy upon your partner. Love performing intimate erotic scenes for the sheer joy and beauty of making love for its own sake. Love every second of what you are doing.*

*"If your partner or lover has a wife, simply ignore her protests and the controls she'll try to place on him. Tune out her moralizing cries. She is merely a child playing with dolls in her superficial world. Her husband doll was merely a prop to serve her illusions of security. How dare she oppose the inevitable victory of your immorality? Take her doll-husband away from her. Make him yours. He*

*wants to be yours. Remember that. Her marriage trap is what drove him to seek the comforts of a venal whore in the first place. And now, he's found you. Your ravishing wanton vagina will become his life-line; his understanding, accepting immoral savior from his righteous imprisonment. If you find yourself having moral qualms about what you are doing, I have this suggestion for you: Stop thinking about the man and his family. Instead, think only about his penis. His penis is his true decision maker. Stay focused on his penis. That's what's important.*

*"That's right; think that the man and his penis are two separate individuals with two separate sets of needs. You only need to care about your relationship with the penis. You want to become Mr. Penis's friend; his very best, truest, most loving, most understanding friend. Mr. Penis has a life of his own. He'll tell his man that YOU are his best friend, NOT the man he happens to be attached to. Your penis friend was endowed by his creator with his own set of inalienable rights, including life, liberty, and the pursuit of sex. As he first slides magically into your love channel, simply tell yourself that you are helping your little friend enjoy his favorite pursuit. Tell yourself, and him, that he's entitled to the wonders he's experiencing!*

*"When you think abstractly like this you will be more at ease with what you are doing. All your inhibitions and doubts about making love with another woman's man will evaporate; and, you will feel totally wholesome, natural, and good about what you are doing. Everything will be that much more joyful. All your inhibitions will fall away. And the other man, the large one that your penis friend is attached to, will also fall in love with you. He'll love you much more than his other woman; much, much more.*

*"Never fear that the man attached to the penis will forsake you. He'll cherish his time with you and your marvelous, iniquitous vagina. He's tired of the pretenses his wife holds him to; tired of smiling at people he inwardly despises. That's why his eyes first turned to*

you. Once you are in his mind, her efforts to hold him will fall short. He'll slip his leash. She'll redouble her efforts in the bedroom, but her efforts will be doomed to fail. Do you know why?

"Because he eyed you in the first place. That happened for a reason. His penis told him to go fetch you. When he saw you smile back at him, he immediately understood that his penis was spot on. You became the new exotic prize for that penis and man duo. You became their lust magnet. So strong is the hold their lust has upon their imaginations, there is nothing the wife can do to release their fixation grip. Too late! Their lusts for you will pierce the veneer of respectable civilization. The niceties his wife uses to wall them off from you will be rendered useless. Never fear. The man has already seen your films. He's seen your cunnilingus scenes. He already imagines tasting your sex. He already knows you are tastier than filet mignon or king crab legs sauteed in creamery butter. He already feels a desperate need to lavish your clitoris with loving tongue strokes, because he wishes his tongue to profess his adoration for your immoral, shameless pornography. But most importantly, his little friend, his penis, has already decided he wants you. His penis makes all the important decisions for himself and the big guy he's attached to. They have both chosen to seek intimacy with you.

"The man's affections are solely yours. They stem from his primal drive to mate with his passion object and pass on his genetics, perverse as that may be; because he knows you are on the pill and procreation with you is not possible. But it is the lust component of his procreation urge that causes him to obsess over you. After he has made love with you; when he sees you copulating with another man in your films, his lust urge will not diminish. It will increase. It will soar!

"His desires will actually be fanned into flames of passion. They will send him to higher passion heights than he ever thought were possible in his previously ordered world. His penis's thoughts and his *own thoughts will inevitably become indistinguishable. His limbic zone will experience a hitherto before unknown insanity. It's as if his heart became impaled with thousands of Cupid's arrows. He cannot extract these arrows from his heart. It's impossible to remove his passion lust for you. He suffers an indescribable torment that he cannot deny. Whatever the costs in money or relationships, he knows he must have you; no one else; only you.*

*"His wife will, predictably, battle for the mind and affections of his penis, but she will fail miserably against your barrier lust wall that he has already erected in his mind. Her attacks upon your lust wall will only result in disaster for her, like General Pickett's failed attack when he charged the Union lines during the battle of Gettysburg. She's simply overmatched by your vagina's superior position in her husband's mind. Your irresistibly wanton, immoral honey pot, offered freely in your incorrigible sinful shamelessness, is an insurmountable barricade wall she cannot surmount. All her attacks against you are doomed to fail. She flails against his mind's impenetrable limbic wall. It is an impossibly tall wall. It is a slippery wall, slathered with your KY jelly. She cannot run through the wall; cannot climb over the way; cannot persuade him to take the wall down and allow her back into his mind. You are inside his mental castle now; protected by his wall from her. Shoot your arrows down onto her. Pour your molten lead and fire onto her. Remember, his limbic mind is now yours. It wants you to get rid of her. Show her no quarter or mercy. Destroy her.*

*"Your profligate sexuality will leave the wife exhausted and shredded on the battlefield of sex. She will, predictably, deploy a scorched earth policy and retreat. She'll tell him your vagina is poisoned fruit. Laugh at her insults. You know that he knows your sex is delicious. In desperation she'll eventually throw him out of their home; keep him from his kids; whatever she can do to hurt him. Expect that, but don't let it bother you. He likes YOU; he loves YOU,*

*and he wants more of YOU. Add him to your clientele and continue making love with him.*

*"Above all, never feel sorry for her as she goes down in defeat. At their core of being, all people are naked savages. Never, ever, allow yourself to feel any guilt about who you are or what you are doing. Meek people do not get what they want from life. They do not inherit the earth. They get stepped on and crushed. Be willful about what you are doing; be determined to get what you want. If you have any doubts about what I am telling you, look to history for examples to guide you.*

*"Do you think the temple whores of Baal had any qualms about consorting with the husbands of the families that were paying tithes to the temple? Of course, they didn't. It was their pleasure to fornicate for power and wealth. They saw their whoring as their natural right. And, it was. Yes, we regard whoring as sinful and immoral; but that does not mean that there is anything wrong with it; or that it is somehow not natural and good. It is natural and good. The ancient pagans understood that and practiced whoring willingly, willfully, and with great reverence for their whores.*

*"More recently, do you think Bathsheba had any qualms about suggesting King David set up her husband to get slaughtered in battle, so she could whore with him and eventually marry him? Of course, she didn't! What she did was completely natural and beautiful; even sacred, and religious. They created a lineage of kings.*

*"You are also in good company when you consider Salome's whoring. She gave her incestuous favors to King Herod as his reward for decapitating John the Baptist, a man who chastised her whoring and made a nuisance pest of himself. She had every right to her pleasures and the Baptist had no business trying to preach morality to her, or to shame her in any way. After all, whoring was then and still is a glorious profession. Those are just two examples of how to deal with people who try to interfere with you.*

"You might also consider Cleopatra, who first murdered her younger brother to place herself in line for Egypt's throne; but, more telling, she was willing to exchange her favors to Caesar in return for his murder of her sister, thus removing all threats to her power. Has the world ever vilified Cleopatra for her whoring? No, of course not! She is venerated as a glorious queen, a goddess of her people, a splendid, spectacularly successful whore who met an unfortunate, tragic end. But you see, even to this day, the world venerates and loves her. Likewise, did Queen Dona Isabella have any qualms about fornicating in her magnificent palaces while outside the fortress walls the unfortunate people, whom she considered heretics, were being burned alive, screaming in the agony of their fiery deaths? Of course not. She never lost a wink of sleep over them!

"Isabella, through her reign and even now, is venerated as a near holy personage, inspired by God. There are monuments to her. She is spoken of as a glorious example of the power of womanhood; and yet, to have her way with the world, she likely poisoned her brother and half-brother; murdered millions of Jews and Muslims; and indirectly caused the murders of countless millions of Native Americans. Did she care? Did any of this carnage slow her ambitions or give her second thoughts? Of course not! How many men did she consort with when Ferdinand was away campaigning for her greater glory? Dozens? Who knows? She, not the people she destroyed, wrote the history of her times.

"Whores emerged from those world-shaping happenings as victorious heroines. Whores have played significant roles in shaping human destiny; especially those who correctly understood that their vaginas were powerful, persuasive assets. The Spirits have favored the progressive changes we whores have wrought. Be prideful of the determined, magnificent whores who preceded you, Miss Sandstone.

"Be determined, Miss Sandstone. Once you decide to become a whore, do not equivocate. Consider that the cameras are already on *you, Miss Sandstone. You already live in a surveillance state. Your cell phone, television, computer already record your every sexual experience. Creeps and perverts watch and hear everything you do. When your mind wraps around that reality, you will have no difficulty performing before cameras. You already are! What have you got to lose? You love sex, don't you? People already follow you. Shouldn't they pay you? Let the creeps hide behind their surveillance schemes. You can be open and honest.*

*"Being honest is right and beautiful. Do not let anything hold you back. Be confident. Whoring is an accepted, time-honored profession. Prostitutes are change agents. There's no shame in change. It's inevitable. Fornications and dalliances are mere expressions of human needs and lusts. Feel sorrow for no one. Your only duty is to yourself and your own betterment and pleasure.*

*"You will come to believe, as I do, that duty to self is what the spirits intend for humanity. We whores are catalysts for needed changes. Remember, it is lust for you that entices. Raw, unvarnished lust sells. Exude lust. You'll noticed your successes. They will shine in men's' eyes. Seize upon those successes. Remember, many wives are base creatures who plied sexuality to attract husbands. Dispatch pretenses.*

*"Civilization's niceties and cordial pleasantries are mere ruses designed to conceal the naked savagery which your opponent wives harbor in their souls. A wife is about ripping out material comforts for herself. Her children are mere pawns, useful foot soldiers.*

*"Think I'm harsh? Judgmental? Did some mothers deny their children at Auschwitz? Without hesitation, did they turned their backs on them and deny knowing them? Did some even help the guards throw their young onto trucks that were transporting victims to the crematoriums; then, offer themselves as prostitutes to the guards? Were those things true? Some say they were true. Who knows? But life is about survival, Miss Sandstone. Self-preservation is the core*

*driver of every naked savage, including your future wife-victim. She is no different than the Arctic fox that abandons her starving young to scavenge food for herself. The world is a dog-eat-dog place.*

*"This woman whose cushy lifestyle you are dismantling may do whatever is necessary to preserve her situation. Beware. She may harbor a capacity for savagery greater than your own. Take precautions to protect yourself; but never let her tears or empty threats stop you.*

*"My advice, Miss Sandstone, is simply this: Accept change. Civilization, as we have known it, is unraveling. We are besieged by plagues and terrorism, border invasions, unstable financial markets, cyber-attacks, and challenges to American world order. The times today are not really that different from the years before America's great Civil War. Our old social order is being uprooted and plowed under, like dead weeds in a field. Religion was a mainstay of the old order. Now, it is in retreat. Civilization is returning to its natural tendencies of six thousand years ago, and before; before religion forcibly imposed itself upon humanity's natural orderings.*

*"Society's old guard will cling to its old order. It symbolizes the status quo. Personally speaking, I have no use for religion. I believe society is in the process of sweeping it away. I view that as a good thing. I believe religion has done more harm to humanity than sex ever has or ever will. I think it will be a good, healthy thing to live in a non-religious, secular world. Some call me a communist for my beliefs about religion and morality. But I don't think communism describes my beliefs. Freedom and honesty describe me better than any label does. I don't believe in any political party, either. I only believe in human intimacy. I hope that makes sense. I'm being honest.*

*"Whatever your inclinations, Miss Sandstone, remember your duty is only to yourself. Your self obligation for your own preservation is to survive the great unraveling that is being thrust upon*

*you; and yes, prosper from it. I have shown you the way and the methods. Once you choose to become an erotic adult film actress you will also assume the mantle of prostitute. Feel no shame. Feel pride in your honesty while you create pornography. In our fast-changing world, prostitution is becoming widely acknowledged as an honorable profession.*

*"During the later centuries of the Roman Empire, prostitutes availed themselves of their opportunities to attained career satisfaction, riches, fame, and political influence. During the decline of America's empire, your opportunities will be similar. The Western world is fast becoming an immoral, craven heap. That is your opportunity. Become profligate. Survive society's descent into disordered poverty. Ascend to your throne of immorality. Morality and social norms are fickle and fleeting. But shameless immorality is permanent.*

*"You can help your own transition, Miss Sandstone. Think of yourself as an entrepreneur. Your body and sexuality are your assets and capital base. You can sell and resell a non- depleting asset, hundreds, possibly thousands, of times each year! your sales skills and proficiency improves with each sale. If sex addiction results, your partners will love you all the more for your addiction. The more you leverage your asset, the more you'll increase your profits. So, take advantage of every opportunity.*

*"Likely, you will experience emotional, even romantic attachments to many of your partners. These are similar to the attachments married women feel toward their husbands. Enjoy these relationships. If you feel honest love for a sex partner, that's perfectly normal. Feel no guilt or reservations over sexual relations or romantic love with other women's husbands. Those are merely normal, healthy ways to express your immorality and relate your feelings and desires to your male partners. Do not see your relationships as adulterous or tainted. Remember, you are a porn star!*

"You have fluttered away from your cloistered cocoon. Spread your wings! It's normal and healthy for you to be immoral and adulterous. Don't feel any guilt about it. You are now a free spirit. Your free spiritedness makes you more accessible. Your liaisons will confide in you, like many men trust their wives. Actually, you will be more trusted and more loved than your partners' wives. That's normal in illicit relationships.

"Some partners will fall in love with you to the point of obsession. And you will come to love them and take an interest in their lives, often knowing more of their intimate secrets than their wives know. Remember: you are a professional person. Maintain control of your relationships. Perfect your time management skills. Respect who you are.

"As a fledgling porn star, you will enter a portal that transports you into a new world. Accept your new world. Be unafraid. Your untapped new world is filled with opportunities. You will travel a passage, Miss Sandstone. It will take you into unimaginable realms of infinite pleasures and delicious guilt-free immorality. You will leave your present life behind and assume a new life.

"Unless you have an extremely understanding and supportive partner you will likely leave your old relationship. It's difficult and uncommon to live unconstrained in both worlds. With the right partner, it can be done; but ultimately, you and he will need to commit whole-heartedly to your career as an uninhibited porn star. He'll need to accept that you will have many intimate relationships and lovers. He'll need to love you and adore you for your immorality, without any reservations on his part whatsoever, if he intends to stay included in your life.

"As you traverse that passage you will discover you enjoy having sex with many different partners. Sex becomes addictive. Your mores will adapt. You'll want to experiment sexually with your different partners. Once you attain nymphomania, it will become very difficult to leave the business. Your addiction will cement your soul to it.

"Like a child becomes addicted to a video game, you will feel you can never have enough sexual experiences. But your addiction will be much stronger than the child's. The child will likely grow up and find new interests like sports or a romantic companion.

"But likely, you will never grow out of your addiction. It will strengthen as years pass. Younger men will hold increasing appeal. You will make compromises in your pay rates to perform with them. You will have no pride or shame about this adjustment because you love your work. Your addiction to sex must be satisfied. Old whores love sex as much, or more, than young whores. The quest for human intimacy never dies. Memories are revived and relived. Nymphomania never stops. It accelerates with time. Women still have orgasms in their eighties.

"So, Miss Sandstone, your career will defy retirement! Performers of adult films will become your new circle of friends. Be accepting of the choice you are making as you walk through that portal. Your thoughts and actions will be guided by overwhelming desires, many years afterwards. People you cared about in your past life will fade into meaninglessness.

"Crossing that threshold commits you to performing uninhibited shameless sex acts with a seemingly endless number of partners, in endless different localities, settings and positions. At times you will become exhausted from the physical demands of so much sex, especially if you offer premium member services; and yet, you cannot disappoint your fan base or your premium members. You must master time management skills.

"Your premium Members service will open new vistas. Almost imperceptivity, kindred emotional tendrils will reach out from both you and your members to one other. Those tendrils naturally connect and intertwine. People love connecting with one another.

Connections become bonds that tie lives together; theirs to yours. Tendril bonds strengthen with time and become stronger. They hold lovers close with the strength of steel cables.

"A love relationship is not a suffocating blanket. It's not a marriage; it is a sensitive and caring liaison. Enjoy it; hold it dear to you if it is useful and pleasing. Unlike a marriage you need not suffer the abuses of body and soul that many wives suffer. You will form many such tendril bonds with different men.

"You may have the great good fortune to rise into the top twenty rankings of all adult film stars. Work hard to make that happen. Make many films. Be innovative. Once you achieve that high level of success, powerful and wealthy men will seek you as their escort to exclusive social functions. I can explain this phenomenon.

"Within the limbic zone of many powerful men there resides a craving to be the number one, the best, and most accomplished. Being seen with a trophy porn star is, for many highly successful men, more prestigious than winning the Super Bowl or the Stanly Cup. Your vagina becomes their must-have trophy. They will move heaven and earth to win you. Watch bison, elk, rams, and hippos fight for mating rights. It's brutal. Males kill each other for the right to fuck. Alpha males are wired that same way.

"Once you are ranked among the top twenty porn stars on popular porn web sites, you have arrived. You will have entered the kingdom of trophy whoredom. That bestows high social status. At gala social events, like the Academy Awards, you will be noticed. My advice is to dress scantily at all gala events, partially reveal your breasts and your vagina. Remember: Sex sells. And smile confidently, knowing that you can bed every man who sees you. You'll be more in demand than the women who win the Oscars. I'm speaking from personal experience.

"When I walk upon the red carpet, I receive at least a hundred times more camera clicks than any non-erotic actress. I've seen *paparazzi contort and bend themselves into pretzels attempting to get that perfect tabloid cover photo; the one that looks up my dress or inside my cleavage. I get a thousand cat calls and whistles compared to the dozen or so the regular actresses get. Some people, including a few women, go crazy and rush the security lines just to touch me, or the dress I wear. The crowd goes positively nuts; pining, shouting, asking for my phone number. Security has to restrain them.*

*"Everyone loves to touch a trophy. Actresses get their trophies. They do their applause lines and take their bows; but top ranked porn stars, who are also invited to attend these events, are the real trophies. Trust me. The crowds will swoon over you. Unlike a lifeless Oscar, they'll go bonkers, head over heels in love with sexy, life-bringing you. Accept it. Understand why it happens. You make their hearts sing. Their joy is imagining what is possible in their own lives. The sight of you makes the boys' pricks rise and stand tall. An Oscar can't do that.*

*"Having you, scantily clad with your breasts and vagina partially revealed, on their arm, hugging them, is the ultimate male achievement. The most acclaimed Oscar winning movie actresses cannot hold a dim candle to the star power of your magnificent vagina. The man you are with knows all other men envy him. They will wonder how he is fortunate to have your luscious mouth and vagina lavishing your favors upon him, instead of them. Because the males' imaginations will remember the scenes you did in your porn films, you will naturally one-up everyone else, including the Oscar nominees for best actress. Once this recognition happens, you will become a cause célèbre, a beautiful, glorious sex morsel to be desired, savored, pampered, adored, celebrated, and worshipped. Notoriety attaches to you. Movie critics will whisper about your sensational immoral whoring, even though some of those people will have no idea about what they are talking about.*

"You will become involved in the social lives of wealthy, famous, powerful men. Think not of them as your routine customers, although they will be that, and more. Rather, visualize yourself as the center of their world, like a shining star with perhaps a dozen wealthy, powerful planets that orbit you and lust for you. You become their source of life. You will know their vocations, politics, tastes in food, culture, sports, and hobbies. It's a process whereby you become a well-rounded, highly cultured woman. Famous, rich, powerful men will, over time, reveal their lives to you. You become intimate with their souls. You unlock their innermost thoughts and feelings. This intimate bond is closer, dearer, and stronger than their bonds to wives, priests, or rabbis.

"Remember why this is, Miss Sandstone: It is because you, alone, own the key that unlocks their truths. Why? Because, you own their penises. Never forget that you own your men's penises for one single second. From that proper mindset comes the right behavior. Whenever you feel yourself uncertain about a situation, remember to ask yourself: What would most please my man's penis? Then, do that.

"Explore. Learn each planetary world. Each one will be different in many ways. Learn their differences by constantly exploring and probing. Let yourself go. Let your planets put on their displays for your enjoyment, You'll see. Your life will become a phantasmagoria of excursions to exotic places; yacht sojourns to uncharted secret hideaways; county fares, trade shows, operas, concerts, art museums, awards ceremonies; quests for fine dining at the finest restaurants; explorations that unlock each man-planet's secret goal obsession; cascading torrents of all sorts of musical performances and dances; shopping excursions that lavish fashion's latest wardrobes upon you; all mixed together with servants, cats, dogs and exotic birds tossed in as spice for good measure. As sun for your man planets, each will strive mightily to entertain, please, pamper and enrich you, because *you are his secret, sacred source of life and energy. All this comes true, Miss Sandstone. But you must understand why.*

*"The why is that all men psychologically need their mommies; and that attachment was broken when they were born. Through the vagina they came; and into the vagina they yearn to return, again and again, and again. So, you see, since they can't get their heads and bodies inside your magnificent, glorious vagina, they strive to do the next best thing. They seek to put the heads and shafts of their little best friends, their penises, into your welcoming vagina, as often as they can. Copulation is their psychological return to their source of life and energy. Copulation and cunnilingus are eternal forms of males' natural, healthy life worship. It fulfills males' very real, very deep-seated psychological need. So, happily see yourself as their adored, honored life force in your personal solar system of planetary worshipers. Above all, fuck them often and enjoy it!*

*"Other men will come and go through your gravitational field, like comets sail infrequently past a star. But, your stationary orbiters, your favored Premium Members will hold steady; circling you as the center of their lives, for months and years and decades, because they have attached their emotional lives to you. They need your warmth. They need those times when you awe them with your orgasm passion bursts; like solar flares shower planets with energy intensity. The emotional bond, the warmth males receive from your soul nurturing love making and your emotive bursts of passion rapture, creates a captivating gravitational pull that holds men predictably in your orbit. Your males had a natural need to please Mommy when they were babies. They transfer that need to please Mommy to the woman who becomes their love object. It's all very natural. Enjoy it.*

*"You will need to have available to you, on instant short notice, 'Muscle,' or body protection, for those times when a fan or member needs to be restrained from hurting you. Some men will sometimes try to cling to you for their every emotional need. These are*

the immature ones. They'll pester you with phone calls and letters. They'll tail you; and show up uninvited at places where they are not welcome. This is not love. It's obsessive madness. It's rare, but it happens. Control it. End it.

"And if you can't end it, have your 'Muscle' end it. Sometimes a man needs to be thrown against a wall and punched in the mouth. Don't feel sorry for them. They get over it. Choose your Premium Members carefully in the first place; and, probably, unpleasant moments will never happen. But they may occasionally happen. If and when they do, they are usually unexpected. So, be prepared for them."

Consuelo: "That's great advice, Marty. Here's another question from Chad. Chad tells us he's thirty-six, married, an international businessman who frequently travels to Europe. He says he's read the tabloid articles about your affairs with Marshawn and Dominick and how their wives claim you destroyed their marriages and how you are a creation of the Devil. Chad says he was taken by your replies to those two ex-wives; and especially your views about religion. He says he now questions his own religious beliefs. He says he now thinks of church as an echo chamber inside an insane asylum, where the organ bangs out songs with childlike rhymes and the priests spew incomprehensible tales of illogical, impossible past happenings. He also says he has seen several of your porn films. He cannot understand his own feelings; feelings he has never felt before; but they are recurring and extremely strong. Chad says he even falls asleep dreaming that he is 'Kissing your pussy' as if he's paying homage to his God. He awakens from dreams where he is holding you in his arms and making love with you. He loses his concentration at work, dreaming of kissing you and your fabulous vagina. He fears he will be sent to hell for eternal punishment for these recurring dreams he's having; but he doesn't know how to stop them and he's not sure he wants to stop them because he loves the feelings he experiences *while having them. Chad feels he has become obsessed with you. He is drawn to you like a moth to a flame. Despite your reputation as a fallen woman, hopeless sinner, and homewrecker, he feels this overpowering urge, this compulsion to approach you personally. But he fears if he does and is found out, he will face retribution from his wife and fellow churchgoers. He feels like his life stands positioned upon a cliff edge; and he knows he needs to jump off. But he is terrified of the unknown. He wants to know more about you. He thinks he may be hopelessly in love with you. He asks: Do you really believe the things you said about religion in those tabloid articles? And, do you think his questioning of his religious beliefs is normal? Have you encountered men in his situation before? Were you able to help them? Do you think this is just a passing impulse that he will likely get over? Do you think meeting you personally might help him resolve his conflict? And, if so, how might that occur?"*

*Marty: "Wow Chad. I feel for you. It sounds like you are at a crossroads in your life. Yes, Chad, those articles quoted me accurately. I am proudly non-religious, proudly promiscuous, and proudly immoral. And I am totally unashamed to live my life as an immoral porn star. By my ways of thinking, our society has morality completely misunderstood. Moralists, by my ways of thinking, are essentially hypocrites. Immoralists are essentially truth tellers. Immorality is honest, healthy and life affirming. And I think the world needs more people who feel about immorality the same way I do. I think its perfectly normal for a sane adult to question and reexamine their beliefs; especially when it comes to the ways they are choosing to live their lives.*

*"I have helped many men who have found themselves in situations similar to yours, Chad. After their thinking became adjusted to accept how normal it is to live an immoral lifestyle, the demons they wrestled with simply vanished. They discovered that change can be a very healthy, liberating experience. Many of these men whom I*

assisted were married, just like you, Chad. Most of their wives simply came to accept their husbands' new life choices. Many of those wives also adopted the new immoral lifestyle; and they became more accepting of their husbands; and these couples' married lives became less stressful. And, no, I do not believe what you are wrestling with is a passing impulse. I think your inner conscience, particularly your limbic mind, is urging you to seek what is normal, natural, and healthy. I think you are going through a process and you will resolve it in a way that gives you happiness and freedom. I think you will continue to be troubled until you confront it and resolve it.

"I'll be happy to help you, Chad. I think the only way you will ever resolve your dilemma is to find your dream. By that I mean coming face to face with your dream and actually living it, so that you can discover your own truth about what is right for you. And Chad, if your journey of discovery finds you 'Kissing my pussy,' and becoming intimate with me, I assure you, you will not go to hell. There is no such place, Chad. It is simply a fantastical creation of religionist control freaks. Fear not, Chad; for I bring you tidings of great joy: Hell does not exist, Chad. Honest, it doesn't.

"Chad, I'm willing to meet you personally to discuss your dilemma and try to help you resolve it. Perhaps we could meet in Europe? You could check my schedule with Jen's Inferno Decado Clubs website. This coming quarter I'm booked to perform live porn shows in London, Paris, Cannes, Barcelona, and Florence. I'll be doing an afternoon and an evening performance in each city for seven days. Perhaps you'd care to join Jen's club network or at least get a trial membership so we could meet at one of her clubs? You'll need to pass a test to make sure you have no communicable diseases and you'll need to pay a trial membership fee; but it's not a particularly onerous fee. We could meet for lunch; and, if you'd like, we could address your compulsion by experiencing shared intimacy. That real experience would give you a reference frame of comparison *between your religious beliefs and your attraction to me and my immoral ways. It might help you decide which life choice best suits you. And, should you choose to partake in my immoral ways with me, you could participate with me, as my special guest, in one of my live, on stage, porn performances. That might help you dispel your inhibitions and free your conscience of any guilt or stigma you may harbor about your compulsions."*

Consuelo: *"That's good advice, and a very generous offer, Marty. I hope you'll hear from Chad soon. Now, here are a few questions from Montrell. Montrell says he adores you and all your films. He mentions that he was intrigued by one particular scene where you were seated on a sofa next to your partner. You were kissing your partner while he stimulated you with his fingers. Montrell was fascinated by the way you moved your vagina and pelvis. He wanted to know what mood you were feeling in that scene and whether that same mood carried through the entire film, until when you were penetrated and when your partner ejaculated and when you sucked his penis afterwards? Montrell's second question is: Do you have different feelings when you perform in your live porn shows compared to the feelings you have while you are being filmed during a porn scene? And, Montrell's third question is: Princess Diana of Wales gave a lot to AIDS victims and to victims of mine fields. You are also a popular woman. Do you also give to charities?"*

Marty: *My goodness. Where to begin? Let's take them one at a time. Montrell, my feelings change throughout the entire seduction sequence. It's kind of like the ways that an octopus changes colors. Maybe I have something like a cephalopod's chromatophores in my nerve cells? I don't know. But my feelings change dramatically during the seduction phase, through to the coitus phase; and my come back down to Earth phase, afterwards. First, I feel this wonderful anticipation during stimulation. My mind races like crazy. I'm thinking how wonderful it is that my partner loves me and loves touching* my body and fingering me. My mind dreams of how thrilled I'll feel when his penis first touches my vagina's outer lips. Then, when his penis actually rubs against my outer lips, I know he's seeking permission to enter me. I feel so honored and privileged to be the recipient of his penis's desires. It's a hard to explain feeling; but it is definitely a different feeling. It's a wonderment sort of other-worldly feeling. It tells me I'm about to enter a special, wonderful world with my partner; like it's a sacred happening.

"Then, when his penis penetrates my inner lips, I experience another feeling. This is when I know that the two of us have entered into our private, sacred world; that I am one with him; and that we have entered into our eternal communion together. I have this overwhelming sense of adoration for my partner and his magnificent penis. It's when you often hear me voicing 'Mmmmmm' and 'Ohhhh,' and 'Ahhhhs' In my films. It's an appreciation for holiness sort of feeling; it's my awe of intimacy.

"Then comes the close intimacy of our bodies touching while we copulate in earnest; and I feel his thrusts inside my vagina. That brings out a revelry feeling inside me. I love all my feelings; but I know I'm sharing this feeling with my partner. It's like we have fallen into another world together; and nothing else and no one else matters. It's a selfish, possessive sort of feeling. It's ours! You'll often hear me whispering: 'I love you,' and 'Fuck me,' and 'Yes, yes, that's it, oh yes!' I think it must be similar to the feelings a cat has when it has all four paws wrapped around a ball of catnip. It's a type of euphoric pleasured madness that I never want to let go of; and I never want to stop feeling it. It's my: 'I love having sex' feeling; and my 'I want to keep fucking forever' feeling. It's the sheer physicality of making love and it's why I love making porn so much.

"Then, there are the wonderful feelings of orgasm. How can I explain them? While I'm coming, I'm a goddess in my heaven on Earth. I'm falling down an endless waterfall; riding on wild horses, *feeling them surging forward inside of me. I feel their amazing power; I'm exploding like the Fourth of July; and all these feelings of ecstasy and wonder are happening at once.*

*"Then, and this is often simultaneous with my orgasms, I feel his ejaculation of hot semen flooding into my vagina and over my excited, eager clitoris. That's like feeling lava from a volcano exploding inside me. I often go into orbit with my wild desires. I feel like I've conquered the world and I'm the most powerful and the most loved woman in my man's world. I thrust hungrily; pushing my mons pubis hard against his penis; trying to devour his entire shaft; holding it fast to my loving clitoris; trying to make sure my clitoris receives that same eternal closeness, that same intimate connection to his penis that my soul is feeling connected to his soul. It's my 'I want the two of us joined together forever' feeling. I want to capture every last drop of semen he has within him. I want it; it's mine. I don't want to share it with anyone else, ever. I want all of it.*

*"Then, my long, slow come down feeling comes. That's when I feel appreciation and adoration for my partner. That's when I feel like purring my kitten Mmmmm's, like I've become a satisfied kitten. That's why you'll see me in my films continuing to lick and suck my partner's penis, long after he has ejaculated. I have this nurturing feeling of wonder at how magnificent the male penis is; how much I loved what it did with me; and how wonderful it made me feel while it had sex with me.*

*"During my orgasms from cunnilingus I enter a whole different dimension, Montrell. You see, the penis tends to relax after it ejaculates; but the human tongue has no such limitation. It can continue giving pleasure long after I first orgasm while the penis usually begins to retreat. During cunnilingus you often see my hand grasping for something to hold on to; like a bed sheet or a fixture. That's me trying to stay grounded to Earth while my pleasures are soaring to the heavens. My other hand may be caressing my partner's head;*

*and even forcefully holding his head against my mons pubis, so his lips and mouth are firmly cupped to my vagina. You'll notice my pelvis thrusts against his face. That's me, trying to hold my clitoris over the fullest possible extent of his tongue. Yes, Montrell, I do crave the strokes of the human tongue over my clitoris. I'm being honest and shameless to tell you that.*

*"You see, Montrell, oral sex can go on pleasuring a woman long after a penis has spent itself. When I have a partner with the right mindset for oral sex, that is the most sensational erotic sex I have ever known. Orgasms repeat and repeat, seemingly endlessly. It's ecstasy on steroids. So beautiful; so enduring and unforgettable. I don't know how else to express myself about it except to tell you that I love it very much. And it brings out the deepest, most profound, trusting enduring connection with my partners. I think that's why so many women have relations with other women. Even now, many years after I graduated from WEX school, whenever I see my friend, Maria, we smile to each other in our special, knowing, guilt-free, loving way. Our eyes light up. Our smiles widen while our lips remain closed. Our breaths deepen. That's our girl-girl love signals communicating. That's the special silent connection of our minds."*

*"Let's see; Montrell's next question was do I feel different when I did live porn on stage compared with how I felt while making porn on set? Well, Montrell, you must be very perceptive. Yes. There is a huge difference in my feelings between the two venues. When I'm performing on set, I need to be aware of my spoken lines, my body positioning, and my lighting as well as my body positioning for the cameras. That creates a certain anxiety within me. You would think that, after making hundreds of porn films, that I would have gotten past all of that. But in truth, I haven't; and I don't think I ever will. Understand that, once I get into the mood of the scene, I love performing on set. I love knowing that potentially millions will see*

my explicit erotica and fall into love with me. There's no greater ego boost than that.

"But performing live causes me to feel a certain unique effect, which I call the 'Juice' effect. I hear my audiences whispering and saying their oohs and aahs; and I hear their clapping hands; and their shout outs saying: 'I love you;' and 'You're adorable;' and 'I want to kiss your vagina;' and 'Can I please come onstage and fuck you?' and 'Will you marry me?' Those instantaneous feedbacks; that audience participation, starts my emotive juices flowing. Typically, I'll notice one of my Premium members in the audience. Typically, he will be stroking himself while he's watching me performing a fornication scene's penetration.

"I'll smile enthusiastically to him and make eye contact with him; to let him know I'm totally into and loving my shamelessly wanton experience with my partner. Then, I'll smile my welcoming coquettish smile to him. I'll mouth kiss him from the stage; and I'll invitingly blow my kisses to him. If I sense that he's willing to engage in sex with me onstage. I'll ask him if he'd like to come and join me. Then, when he's joined me onstage, I'll peel down his pants and perform my most loving fellatio on him. That interactive, spontaneous intimacy drives my audiences wild. They love it. and then, of course, I will have sex with him on stage. And all during my interaction with my stage guest, I will frequently voice my:

'Mmmmm's, Ahhhhs, Ooohhhhs, and 'Yes's That's it's.' And my: 'Yes. Fuck me. Oh, yes, fuck me. I love what you're doing. That feels soooo good, baby. I love the way you're doing me, right now; just like that, Mmmmm; and my: 'Yes, of course I want your semen. I want all of it inside me. Yes. It's okay. That's it! Oh, how beautiful! Mmmmmm! I feel you shooting inside me. I love it. Ohhhh, Mmmmmm. Yes baby. Yes! How wonderful!'

"Nothing else quite compares with expressing beautiful live intimacy before my audiences. My partners love hearing it. My *audiences love hearing it and feeling like they are part of it; and I love saying it. Those precious, live intimate moments foster instantaneous communal bonding which a film set simply cannot deliver. I put my heart and soul into my live performances. I know they get people talking about what a shameless, uninhibited, sex craving nymph I am. It's priceless word of mouth advertising. So, I must tell you, Montrell, I do not prefer one venue over the other. I love performing in both venues.*

*"Let's see; your last question was about charity. Montrell, I don't believe Princess Diana ever made her tax returns public while she was alive, so I don't know whether or not she actually ever gave any of her personal money for those causes. I know she was instrumental in raising awareness and money for them, as well as gathering huge amounts of publicity for herself while raising that awareness. So, I can't address your question by way of comparisons between myself and the Princess.*

*"I freely admit, Montrell, I do not give money for charity. The government takes in so much money for so many things, I feel I am taxed to death already. I feel charities are just another hidden tax. Government progressives claim to have solutions for everything; so, let them take care of society's charitable needs.*

*"There's a lot of showboating and razzle dazzle connected with many charities; and there's that guilt feeling some of the try to impart to non-givers. I don't want to become part of that. I feel that when I liberate people from the confines of religion, I am doing a good, charitable deed. Those liberated people can send their monies to children with cancer or missing limbs, or to homeless people, or drug addicts, or disabled veterans, instead of to the Pope in Rome. They can even give directly to a needy person and help save a human life instead of helping that sanctimonious holy man buy more gold and artwork. My love of humanity is my charity, Montrell. I often think of myself and my work as a living charity. I can't help it if some*

Consuelo: *"Marty, here's a new question from someone who states that he is an independent film producer. He wishes to stay anonymous. He states that he has observed that porn is the fastest growing venue on the internet in terms of views, and that porn sales are the fastest growth area in terms of film downloads, while conventional film views and box office sales seem to be stagnating. Why do you, as a porn star, believe those trends are happening?"*

Marty: *"Oh, wow. I'm not a statistical analytical sort of person. There are probably a lot of factors driving this trend. But I think the main reason is that porn itself is changing. It's no longer just people screwing on film, like it was years ago. I've always had this personal theory that porn, when well produced and performed, is the ultimate art form. Let me explain that. Art, whether it's film or paintings, or writings, tends to touch and stimulate emotions. Take the Sistine Chapel in the Vatican's Apostolic Palace. Everyone who looks up at the Chapel's ceiling feels this overwhelming emotion, like they are in the presence of God. It's a profound feeling. Same with Leonardo's Mona Lisa. You look at it. You walk past it. Her face smiles. Her eyes follow you. She comes alive! She personifies a satisfied woman. Your heart leaps with happiness for her. That's art. That's the effect it has on peoples' emotions.*

*"Now consider conventional films; perhaps a love scene. Your heart strings feel the tugs of the love that the actors and actresses express in their words and the way they touch each other. You feel it. That's why you buy the ticket: to feel the emotions. So, take this emotive factor one step further. I think this will answer your question for you. In which venue does the viewer experience the greatest intensity of emotions, and why?*

*"Your answer must be in pornography; and here is the reason: Nowhere else can you, as a viewer, experience the ecstasy, the nirvana of love and joyous bliss that you feel while you're watching a great porn film. And here is the key to that: It is the porn star's*

*conventional film because in that venue, real orgasms usually don't happen. They are faked. One can write about orgasms, but it is not the same thing as seeing them in real life; nothing like watching a porn star actually experiencing them. You see, when the viewer observes the porn star's orgasm, the viewer is drawn into the porn star's emotive experience. The viewer experiences and relates to an intensity of feelings that is simply unattainable anywhere else in any other venue. Only by viewing porn can the viewer see the actress porn star performing with every organ of her body.*

*"The vagina is a highly emotive, expressive organ. It expresses nirvana, triumph, glory, and the intensity of intimacy when it orgasms. The porn star's body complements her vagina's expressions of its pleasure needs and its lust cravings. Conventional actresses' eyes, hands, lips, facial and head movements, while all wonderful and expressive, cannot hold a candle to the imaginative stimulations that porn stars' eyes, hands, lips, facial and head movements inspire while her vagina is experiencing the throes of her orgasms. There's simply no comparison to that telepathically delivered, intense, emotive rush. That rush, that flood of empathy, mirrors the same sensation of Sistine-like awe and wonderment. But it's even greater than that religiously inspired rush because it's personalized.*

*"What makes it so personalized? Because the female vagina represents life and its origin. That organ rivets the viewer's attentions to it. Viewers innately understand how important life's creation process is; how it's vital to the propagation of the human species. Sadly, viewers never see those same intimate expressions in conventional films. Those works can only hint at a woman's wonderous revelry during coitus. They fail to convey the rapture feeling that viewers only obtain by watching porn. To capture that feeling requires a real vagina experiencing a real orgasm with a real penis inside it. That's why ordinary film stars who do not do porn will always be at a*

*disadvantage and why the conventional film industry will continue losing market share to porn.*

*"When the viewer experiences the emotive intensity and majesty of the porn star's orgasms, the viewer emotively bonds with the porn star. He loves knowing she's experiencing pleasure. He realizes she is loving her experience. This identity with her, while seeing her orgasm, creates profound heartfelt empathy for her. The viewer feels her ecstasy. It's like seeing the Mona Lisa or the Sistine Chapel's ceiling presented to him; but it's a real, live human woman! The experience is greatly magnified, like it's on steroids; complete with alluring sound and lighting effects.*

*"It's the most complete, immersive, experience. Only actual sex can better it. The viewer's stimulation is overwhelmed. It's primal in nature; beautifully expressed. It rivets attention and captivates the emotive soul. It can also become highly addictive, especially if it fills a viewer's love void. It's much like alcohol, drugs, and nicotine that way, except it is the limbic mind's addiction to euphoria; not an addictive chemical substance. It's like a pleasing balm that sooths the limbic mind's emotive cravings, while delivering its fantasy experience. The empathy with the porn star effect causes many to fall head over heels in love with her. Viewers pay to share in her feelings of love and ecstasy.*

*"People also need something to believe in. They must feel that there is some higher power that is somehow greater than the powers they have within themselves. Religions seize on this need. They convince people that there is a God or variations of God; and they apply misogynistic ordered rules to create a structure within which people can express and outpour their beliefs. But I believe, as I look at the world today, that many people feel their religions are failing them. People are dissatisfied with their lot in life and with the stresses they endure to maintain their lifestyles. I considered these societal factors when I created 'CONSECRATION.' It's one of my most spectacular porn films.*

"The film begins with documentary clips. The clips show the pageantry of religious worship; the richness of our churches, synagogues, and mosques. The film pays particular attention to the majesty of the Vatican. Interspersed between the clips of majesty and riches we show documentary clips of children starving to death and dying in Somalia, Ethiopia, Nigeria, and on America's Indian reservations. We draw the stark contrast between unfathomable Papal wealth and unimaginable poverty.

"Then, through the use of holograms, we awaken a subconscious human reality. We show that the female vagina is the ultimate creation vessel. We contrasted the vagina as the symbol of life with religions' symbolism, which glorifies death followed by resurrection. We juxtapose an enlarged image hologram of my vagina upon an altar. My porn partners are dressed in religious vestments, bishts, kasayas, and kittles to represent leaders of several major religions.

"These partners approach the vagina hologram and lay their offerings of precious jewels and gold and silver before it. They also place all their religious identifiers; their robes, idols, symbolic relics, tiny hats, big hats, mitres, grails, goblets, and incense pots; everything that they use to accessorize their religious services, inside the enlarged hologram of my vagina. This introductory messaging shows religious leaders surrendering their trappings of authority to the creative powers of the female vagina. It is a powerful, suggestive introduction to the film's message.

"The film unlocks a thought in viewers' minds: If a religious leader pays homage to the female vagina, shouldn't I do the same thing? Seeing is believing. Monkey sees and monkey does are the film's subliminal messages. The viewer sees that the religious leaders who surrendered symbols of their beliefs to my vagina were not struck down by lightning; nor were their limbs torn asunder. No. They are all, perfectly, all right!

"Their god did not punish them for surrendering their power symbols to my voracious, insatiable vagina! No, their god did not do that. Nothing happened! What can this mean? The film keeps the viewer in suspense for a few moments as the religious men mill about, talking amongst themselves, trying to understand why their god has not punished them. Suddenly, out of a dry ice mist, I appear before the confused males. And, I am naked!

"These religious men, played by my porn partners now relieved of their religious accessories and relics, begin kissing my vagina's outer lips. One after another, they confess their adoration, saying: 'I love and adore you.' And, 'I honor your glorious powers of creation.' Then, accompanied by beautifully choreographed harp and violin music, they walk, as if in awe of my creation by conception power, into my hologram's enlarged vagina. After they have entered into my enlarged hologram vagina, they disrobe. The viewers' religious leaders have now become my porn partners.

"I reappeared, real and in the nakedness of my flesh. Then, with each of my different porn partners, I separately perform all manner of beautifully choreographed, erotic pornographic acts. After each porn partner ejaculates into my vagina, that scene is camera captured and shown as an enlarged hologram. My vagina hologram flows with semen. It occupies the full theater screen. I twerk-shake my vagina's triumphant fornications, spilling out copious volumes of semen. The full screen hologram close-up shows my vagina quivering and pulsating. Viewers see an abundance of life originating in my vagina and flowing from my vagina into the world. That is the film's profound message. Subliminally, the viewer recognizes that the vagina is 'du Monde,' or 'The World;' the origin of human life in the world.

"The film next cuts away to show my partners walking up a flight of stairs into a soft white light. There, I await each of my New

Morality converts with opened arms. They walk, individually, into my arms and embrace me and kiss me. Their ascensions symbolize their conversion; their casting off of their old ways and their rising up to embrace the world's new, immoral, whoring ways: the Modern Morality Standard.

"Then, each convert to immorality kneels before me and kisses my vagina one final time, before my full body image returns as a full screen hologram. Each porn partner stands and walks into my hologram's outstretched arms. I receive each of them and embrace them. They then they disappear into the hologram of my naked body, as if my immoral whoring has captured and absorbed each of their souls.

"Now converted to my immorality, they discover that real creation godliness is the female vagina. Their conversions to natural, religiously immoral, paganism are complete. The scene ends with my hologram walking with the formerly religious partners. We fade into a gigantic hologram of my vagina, walking through its waterfall of semen into the eternity of creation. Then the hologram fades away.

"The viewer next sees is the full screen image of my butterfly winged vagina. My vagina with its butterfly wings and my eyes behind it, now fill the entire screen. Then my vagina image becomes smaller, until it's only a life-sized butterfly on a full screen. The butterfly flutters over a field of flowers and fades into the distance, symbolizing that my vagina is forever on its fluttering quest; continuously seeking new converts to the Modern Morality Standard; and blessing humanity's return to honest, natural worship and the glory of nature.

"The film will open soon in theaters everywhere. It presents a choice for humankind. On the one hand there is the belief in salvation and life after death if one follows certain rules and seeks forgiveness from sins which one is somehow, inexplicably, born with. One *goes to HIM, brings offerings to HIM, goes through HIM and with HIM to get there.*

*"My new film presents a different choice. One comes to ME, brings offerings to ME, comes through ME, and becomes one with ME. Take your choice: the misogynists' fantasy fairy tale belief system way, or my visceral, touchable life-affirming way. Which way gives stressed out humanity its needed relief? Its Freedom? Its Self-confidence? Which allows a man to admit he'll never be perfect; allows him to let go; expects him to let go and walk away, and rewards him for starting over?*

*"The religious ways tell a man to have faith and be strong; to be charitable; to stand by the sick, the poor and the homeless. My way says save yourself. I tell men that it's perfectly okay to leave their wives when they drive them crazy with their demands and emotional problems; or when they tire of them and no longer want to support them. I tell stressed out men to jettison their families overboard, release themselves from their responsibilities and burdens; put their own happiness first and come to me; and I and my unapologetic, whoring vagina will help them through their difficulties. And everyone can just figure out something else.*

*"The choice between morality and immorality is a battle for faith market share. I am winning this contest. I am winning because the old religious ways are not working. Their belief systems have driven many people to desperation. My belief system offers relief and a way out; and a chance for a fresh start. I hope you'll see my new film. My vagina shows up beautifully in the full screen holograms. I hope you'll enjoy watching the film as much as I enjoyed making it. And I hope it gives you inspiration to continue your work. Pornography, well imagined; creatively produced and well-choreographed; beautifully, and lovingly performed, is the venue that best expresses and captures every one of the emotions that today's people crave experiencing. I hope that answers your question."*

Consuelo: *"Marty, is this a departure from your previous work? It seems like you are making a direct attack on organized religion, aren't you?"*

Marty: *"It may seem that way, Consuelo, but that is not my intent in CONSECREATION. I am merely trying to show that religions profess to help improve the lot of the poor. They will point to the things they do that have some effect and thusly justify their efforts to evangelize non-believers and convert them to believers. That and the moral structures they provide gives them their credibility and their claims to righteousness. CONSECRATION simply questions whether their efforts do any good; whether they are having a net positive effect, or whether they are merely perpetuating poverty by feeding existing poverty; and thereby creating more poverty. My theory, as I show in the film, is that by subsidizing poverty, the religions create more of it.*

*"The film is designed to make people think about their rationalization for practicing their religion. For many, the reason is that they believe they are doing good in the world. The film questions whether that presumption is true. It removes one of the reasons why some people chose to live a moral lifestyle instead of an immoral one. It highlights hypocrisy. It shows that, while religions tend to make people believe that they are helping the war on poverty, they actually make poverty worse."*

Consuelo: *"But you aren't saying that your immoral ways help the poor, are you?"*

Marty: *"No, not at all. I don't care about them; not at all. I think that by letting them suffer and die, they'll tend to die out and disappear. I know that's harsh. But it tends to make the problem of poverty go away instead of exacerbating it. My way is not hypocritical. It's brutally honest."*

Consuelo: *"But what about morality? Many belong to religions because of the moral structure religions provide. Are you also opposed to religion for that reason?"*

Marty: "*All three western religions have their roots in violence, murdering and pillaging, Now, many years later, they profess peace, so long as you find that peace within their construct. There is constant friction between the religions as they battle for market share and physical territory. The premise that religion brings morality is built upon a shaky foundation. CONSECRATION implies that one should feel no guilt about leaving one's religion and choosing Pagan immorality as one's lifestyle. It makes clear that worship of the female vagina is as valid as worshipping anything else. And the benefits of Pagan vagina worship are tangible and real. They are not abstract and theoretical.*"

Consuelo: "*Well spoken, Marty; beautiful explanation. I think you've explained it perfectly for our aspiring producer. Now, our aspiring porn star, Miss Sandstone, has two additional questions, Marty. She says she'd appreciate concise, unequivocal answers. Do you ever have regrets about any marriage you've destroyed? And, if you've had abortions, have you ever had regrets about having them?*"

Marty: "*No and no; concisely and unequivocally. I hope that answers your final questions, Miss Sandstone. Finally, Miss Sandstone, I wish you the very best for your success and happiness. I hope you will find, as I have, many healthy, wholesome, long-lasting friendships among the men and women you will meet in your new life. From your questions, I expect I'll be seeing you sometime in the future. Perhaps we'll perform together some day. If so, I look forward to meeting you.*

Consuelo: "*Thank you for those straightforward answers, Marty. Now, here's some questions from Kevin. Kevin asks: 'Marty, you are obviously an intelligent, sexual woman with a vast patina of romantic experiences and lovers. How do you avoid conflicts between lovers and complications with male egos? Do you have a 'Boss Man' or a reliable steady lover man who protects you, or do you have some other way to keep your life from going crazy?*

Marty: "*Those are excellent questions, Kevin. The way I protect myself is to have my member service carefully screen every man who wants to spend private time with me. Also, I arrange those sessions in a special hotel suite that is easily accessible by my security people if things start getting out of hand. I have a way of contacting them, at all times; and they will respond instantly if there's even a hint of trouble. Once I'm comfortable with a member, after I've had several private sessions with him, and the member wants to take our relationship further; for instance, if he wants me to spend a weekend with him, I'll usually agree to that. In those circumstances, my security people know who I'm with and where I'll be, always, so my risks there are minimal.*

*"And, yes, Kevin, I do have a steady lover. He's not a 'Boss Man' in the sense that my security people are. He's all about love. I'm with him at his place or mine every night I can possibly be with him. No matter how many lovers I've had in a day or a week, I always want to be with him."*

Consuelo: "*Why is that, Marty?*"

Marty: "*Well, two reasons I can think of right off the top of my head. It's not out of habit. I want you and Kevin to understand that. It's deeper than that. First, I know he loves me, for me; just me. I know that no matter how much I need to be away from him on my business trips he'll love me, for just being me, when I'm with him. He knows about how I lost my father; and I know about how he lost his, so there we have a common bond and a common need. When I'm with him I know it's not about business. Money never changes hands between us. It's just about the love we have between us; the shared times we have; the things we do together. We just totally enjoy each other*"

Consuelo: "*You said there was a second reason.*"

Marty: "*Yes, I did. Like I said before, it's not habit. But it is the physical manifestation of love. It's the penis factor.*"

Consuelo: *"The penis factor?"*

Marty: *"Yes, the penis factor. You see, in my profession I'm constantly experiencing sex with new partners, new positions, new settings, and so on. The directors are always trying to make things interesting. So, I'm continually having sex with different penises. Yes, there's a certain thrill about that, I'm the first to admit it; and I absolutely love making love with a brand-new penis for the first time. But, there's something very special about the penis that you know and understand. I feel lonely in a strange sort of way when I'm with a new penis, or even a penis I've partnered with many times before, when it's part of a performance I'm doing on set.*

*"You see, with my lover man, I never feel lonely. We know each other. There's love there, real honest love between us. I always know, or almost always know, exactly what his penis is going to do. I know when it's going to shove hard against my clit and make me come. I know when it's going to ram me hard from the doggie position, when it will push and bump against my cervix and shoot excitement all through my body; and I know when it's about to gush its wonderful stream of hot pasty cum inside me and heat me up and send me out of my mind with this feeling that assures me I am loved.*

*"There's something beautiful about knowing my lover's penis can be depended upon to make me feel wonderful and totally loved as a woman. I know how he'll hold me and tell me how much he loves me afterwards; and I know he's not acting for the camera. I know he means everything he says to me. And that means everything to me. And then there are the hugs and touches and cuddles we have afterwards while his penis shrinks inside me, before he withdraws it from my vagina. It's all so beautiful and loving, Consuelo. I love the predictability of our intimacy. Nothing compares with that. Nothing even comes close to that.*

*"We have that affirmation for each other. I think of it as my love trap. You see, Consuelo, the more secure I feel in his love the more*

confident I am about being an unrepentant, unapologetic, shameless whore; and, by the same token, the more whoring I do; the more films I make; and the more member partners I seduce, the more confident I feel that my lover will love me even more, for who I am. It's a continuous self-reinforcing cycle of beautiful erotic love and sex."

Consuelo: "Marty, do you ever tire of sex? I mean do you ever abstain for periods of time?"

Marty: "Oh sure, I think I'm normal that way. Often, I'll relax for a day or two or three, just to be alone with my thoughts; think about my goals, my relationships; be alone with my pet cat, that sort of thing. But even when I do that, there's this ember burning inside me. I feel it's constantly a part of me. It wants to burst into flame; and that flame is love and love making. It wants to have a man's lips pressed to mine. It wants his hands squeezing my ass and breasts, pinching my nipples; and it craves having his fingers in my vagina stimulating me, making me slippery hot for his penis, all the while he's kissing me.

"My inner ember is always searching for the fuel it needs, and that fuel is a lover and love making. When I find that, I feel myself burning with this unquenchable fire. It makes me want to make love until I'm exhausted from orgasm after orgasm. It's uncontrollable; and I love it when I'm in that mental space. I can never get away from sex for very long, Consuelo. It's on my mind constantly, even while I'm abstaining for a few days.

"There's also a restlessness inside me, Consuelo. I guess you could call it my spiritual destiny. It's my calling from something bigger than myself. It drives me to promote the Modern Moral Standard. I guess many would call it the Immorality Standard. I don't know about that. But whatever it is that causes me to have this inner drive to seduce; perform erotica on film; destroy conventional marriages; whatever it is, I feel this strong compulsion to continue doing promiscuous immoral things and my inner restlessness never allows me *to stop. So, I guess that's my way of explaining that even while I'm abstaining, I'm never truly at rest, mentally speaking. I'm always in quest of romantic erotica in some form or another.*

Consuelo: *"Have you thought about what drives your quest, Marty? I mean, do you have some goal that you hope to achieve?"*

Marty paused for a long thoughtful moment before she answered: *"Well, since you asked it that way, I suppose my ultimate goal is to eliminate religion, except for the ancient Pagan religion. I hope, through my work, that I'll do that. I think religions are too male-centric and too restrictive against human freedom. They were concocted by men who wanted to devise ways to control women, as their way of imposing socially acceptable domestic slavery upon half the human species. I think the world's peoples would be far happier and more ecumenical if the female vagina became the world's religion."*

Consuelo: *"Well, you certainly are making great progress towards your goal, Marty. I see religious attendance is in a downward spiral and progressive socialism is ascending all over the world, with few exceptions. And everyone has noticed your involvement in the Modern Morality Standard movement. Pagan temples are sprouting up everywhere. Tell us, Marty. What motivates you to pursue this goal of eliminating religion?"*

Marty, laughing: *"Oh, I guess going back to my childhood years I felt shut out and excluded by the religious types. But that motivation driver has kind of morphed into a much more powerful one."*

Consuelo: *"Which is?"*

Marty: *"Why, Consuelo, I'm surprised you need to ask me. It's the penises, of course. It's the joy of having sex with so many adorable loving penises, while I pursue my goal. It's all so natural and pleasurable. I am highly motivated. It's the wonderful, splendid penises I have the pleasures of meeting and making love with as a porn star; having so many delightful moments. Every day of my life I wake up* knowing that I'll have a wonderful new experience while doing my part to set the world free from religion."

Consuelo: "Well, good luck with your goal, Marty. Marty, here's a new question from Jillian. She asks about your film 'DAYNIGHT CREATION,' the one that won the Felatio Film of the Year Award. She is giving serious consideration to creating her own explicit erotic films as her full-time career choice. She says, and I'm quoting her here:

'Marty, DAYNIGHT makes me dream at night. I find myself imagining I'm performing blow jobs on my male friends. That film takes my heart and lifts it to a higher place. I loved it so much that I've seen it twenty times already. I can't imagine a more divine experience for myself than sucking off two men simultaneously, like you did. I could tell by the intimacy that came through the film that you really, honestly, loved both men. My question is: Could you please explain the techniques you used to make that fabulous scene possible?'

Marty: 'Sure, Jillian. I'm thrilled that my film inspired you to perform more fellatio. My compliments to your ambitions! I think they are wonderful. The film was my idea and I was the mastermind of its production. Its underlying psychological theme is that the races must find ways to remove societal barriers and come together. Human intimacy can accomplish a great deal to help us get to know each other as humans with human needs. I put a great deal of thought and work into the film. It takes dedication to create anything successful and an outstanding, memorable porn film is no exception. Technique was the key to this film's success. I had pads placed under the sheets where my two partners lied. Their bodies were positioned on their sides with, their penises placed only a few inches from my face. That positioning raised their bodies and penises three inches higher than my head and my mouth.

'This elevation difference was the crucial key to the success of the film. I understood that nothing should compromise the erotic focus *of the film. I placed a small pillow under the curvature of my neck to support my neck and head. The pillow cover matched the color of the sheets so it's indistinguishable from the sheets while the cameras were shooting the film from above my head. Through this elevation scheme, I made sure that my neck and shoulder muscles were always relaxed while I performed my dual fellatio. You've no doubt noticed from the joyous expressions on my face that my concentration and enthusiasm was unwavering. That look of awe and joy is natural for me. I naturally feel that way when I'm around a penis; and especially while I perform fellatio. There's no hint or pause to suggest that I was uncomfortable at any time. All the viewers could see from my facial expressions how enthused I was to be sucking two fabulous penises nearly simultaneously; and how immensely I was enjoying myself. The cameras were, at all times, positioned directly overhead or only slightly off perpendicular. That way, the viewer couldn't see shadows that would reveal that my partners' penises were elevated. That elevation made it convenient and effortless for me to turn my head from Josh's penis to Marshawn's, and vice versa, without expending more effort than moving my head.*

*"As you may imagine the greatest challenge was to have both Josh and Marshawn ejaculate simultaneously onto my lips and tongue. My director was ingenious here. He placed virtual video headsets on both my partners while we filmed. You'll remember, the entire film was focused on their penises and my face and mouth. No other body parts were shown. It was important that Josh and Marshawn stayed aroused and primed to ejaculate. We solved this by having a continuous stream of my most erotic porn scenes playing in an endless loop in their video head sets. Neither Josh or Marshawn could see the other. We kept all distractions away from them; and focused all their thoughts on having sex with me.*

*"We wanted their limbic minds completely immersed in endless visions of my explicit eroticism. We understood that whenever*

*a man sees endless film clips of a woman being a totally shame-less whore, he naturally becomes aroused, and stays aroused. So, while I was sucking Josh and Marshawn, they were simultaneously watching me making love with many different partners, having multiple orgasms, performing in several different orgy scenes, and having fellatio with other partners. The idea was to have their minds completely beholden to receiving oral sex from an uninhib-ited, shamelessly immoral whore. We wanted Josh and Marshawn experiencing maximum erotic stimulation; while simultaneously, psychologically bonding with me and my need for eroticism; with both men falling further into love with me, as their most adored, incorrigible, glorious, revered, shameless whore during the entire time I was sucking them.*

*"Getting our ejaculation sequence perfectly timed required con-stant communication and practice. Each partner spoke aloud when he was ready to shoot his cum. When one was ready before the other, my producer told him to hold back from ejaculating until the other partner was ready; and then when both men were about to peak simultaneously, my producer commanded them to both let go; and they both ejaculated. Now, as simple as that may sound, we needed to work on our timing for seven different afternoons, five days apart from the preceding afternoon's shoot, to capture their ejaculation timings perfectly.*

*"My partners needed that recharge time and tons of protein, vitamin E, Lycopene, Ginseng, Nettle, Pygeum, Saw Palmetto, and Goat Weed to bring their semen reservoirs up to fully charged. My producer kept them at his house between shoots, and stuffed them with steaks, prime ribs, and bushels of raw oysters. He also injected their male sacs with a prescription hormone that more than doubled their normal semen production. My producer is a perfectionist. He insisted that both of them be able to shoot off massive loads of cum every time they ejaculated. He wanted to capture a Niagara Falls*

*effect coming out of both penises. He gorged Josh and Marshawn with protein for breakfast, lunch, and dinner; so, their penises had maximum strength and hardness.*

*"We paid them not to perform with any other women during this period. We wanted both of them, at all times, fresh, fully charged, and totally focused on having their penises sucked by me; and by no one else. I can't recall ever sucking penises that were harder or more fully charged with cum than those two were over that five-week period. When my producer believed both men were ready, we filmed. I sucked them and kissed their penises' heads while they watched me performing explicit erotica in their headsets. Their minds were overwhelmed with images of my vagina engaged in intercourse and my lips sucking penises.*

*"Then, when they both said they were ready, I speeded up my hand strokes and my lips' sucking on their penises' heads and increased my lips' down presses along the tops of their shafts; and then, predictably, they came. Well, even with all the communication, one penis would come slightly before the other, so we decided to do it all over again. That was fine, understand, because I absolutely love performing fellatio, and I wanted to achieve simultaneous ejaculation perfection.*

*'When we finally achieved our perfectly timed ejaculation release, we wrapped the film shoot. During the wrap, my producer dubbed out all the verbal communications between himself, Josh, and Marshawn; so, what the viewer sees is me performing sensational felatio on two different penises: One black and one white, for essentially one entire hour; and me bantering with and praising the two penises, while hand kneading and giving mouth and tongue stimulus to their balls; and climaxing the film with that voluminous simultaneous eruption of cum from both those penises onto my adoring lips and welcoming loving tongue. It was masterful timing. And the visual effect was wildly erotic.*

"You also noticed how I continued kissing both penis heads; and how I lovingly sucked both their shafts long after the eruptions, until I drained every drop of cum from both penises and they went completely limp. And I hope you saw how I frequently displayed my tongue in different poses to capture the explicit erotic sensation of semen on my tongue and in my mouth. And, I'm sure you noticed how I let my head fall back while the penises continued spurting semen into my mouth. That's tradecraft, Jillian. It comes with experience and the mastery of performing many fellatios. I Wanted my viewers to feel the same triumphal empathy that I felt in that moment; that I wished this flow of cum into my mouth could go on forever. I hope you caught that expressive wish in m facial expression. Notice also that, for the first and only time in the film, I caressed my partners' balls with my hands and fingers. I was again applying my well-practiced tradecraft, Jillian; communicating through my loving touches to their most sensitive body parts that I sincerely wanted them to give me everything they had.

"I have this thought while a man is ejaculating, Jillian:

'Here is this gorgeous man, giving me all of his life essence. I must honor him by taking all of it into me; otherwise, I am actually rejecting his offering of his life. I cannot refuse him. I must let him know how much I appreciate him; how much I want all of him.'

"Then, at the end of the film, you'll notice I gave my signature, innocent school girl smiles to the cameras while mouthing my seductive kisses, inviting more penises to come visit me for fellatio. That's my tradecraft again, Jillian. It's my goodbye to the camera and my fans, until next time. I want them to see me as the sweet, innocent, loving, cuddly girl next door, who also just happens to love intimate sex and fellatio; and who is anxious for them to come by and visit with her again, soon.

"We're creating a follow up film with the same underlying racial unity theme, Jillian. It will open with ten men playing pick-up basketball; five whites playing five blacks. The game ends and the men are sitting around, laughing, and talking together. One of them remarks that they had fun and he wishes there were more things they could do to have fun together. I happen to walk by in a micro mini. I overhear him. I chat with them; tease them. The film's finale has me taking cum from all ten of the basketball players. There's a great deal of innovative technique involved in this production. I think you will find it spellbinding. I can't discuss it until after it's been released, but I encourage you to see it once it's available. Until then, I'll let your imagination fill in the details.

"A stand out successful film needs both a talented director and an erotic performer who loves her work. While performing in my films, Jillian, my mind is on the beauty and passion of erotica the entire time. I think, beyond the technical aspects of the DAYNIGHT fellatio film, Jillian, it became so successful and achieved record downloads because it captured so beautifully how much I truly love performing explicit erotica. The message I would impart to all aspiring porn stars is that, within the deepest recesses of your mind, you must commit yourself to absolutely, completely love your work; love the romantic intimacy of sex; and love the unashamed dignity you have within yourself for committing yourself to a career of performing explicit erotica. You must put your heart and soul into every motion you perform, in every scene you perform; no exceptions. That's what it takes to become a stand out star in this business; and, that's how DAYNIGHT won the award for best fellatio film, Jillian.

Consuelo: "Marty, that was beautiful and very informative. Here's a theological question from Peter. He says it's okay if you don't want to answer. He knows it's sensitive. He asks: Do you believe in God?"

Marty: "Oh wow, Peter. That one gets into my head. The short answer is yes and no. Let me explain. I think the world was essentially pagan before the time of Terah, Abraham, and Sarah. I read *scripture differently than the way the religions teach scripture. I try to take the mystic out of scripture and replace that with my common sense. So, I think Pagan Terah was the father of Abraham and Sarah; and, being pagan, I think Terah was doing Sarah. I think Abraham was also doing Sarah.*

"So, here you have a fabulously beautiful, sensuous woman. She's having incestuous relations with her father and her brother. Well, something got tense there, in that ancient land of Ur; and Sarah told Abraham that she was tired of a controlling old man who couldn't please her anymore, done with his mitzrayim (controlling ways). She wants to be a free spirit; free to conjugate with whomever she desires and with as many partners and as often as she desires; plus, she enjoys the finer things of life. And she appreciates that her sexuality will be highly prized by those who can afford her. So, Sarah told Abraham to take her to Egypt where she could get it on with Pharoah and his princeling sons. Abraham became her dutiful pimp. He devised a way to get her in front of Pharoah. A deal was struck. Sarah did Pharoah and his sons for some time; until she got paid half the wealth of Egypt. Then, Abe and Sara left with their gold, silver, jewels, and cattle; enough seed money to start the Hebrew tribal nation.

*"Well, here's where the story get's into my theology. While in Egypt, Abraham noticed that the males ran everything. They worshipped one god, Ra. Monotheism stuck in Abe's mind. It was a way for him to gain control over Sara. A while later, Abe told Sara he was going to take their son, Issac, up a mountain, build an altar and sacrifice him. He said God told him to do this. Now, Sara was okay with it because pagans did child sacrifice. But, when Abe got Issac up the mountain, he concocted this story about God telling him not to sacrifice Issac. Instead of killing Issac, according to Abram, God showed him a ram in a bush and told Aram to substitute the ram for Issac. That's the departure point in history, where the Hebrew*

*tribe stopped being pagan and became monotheistic. Christianity and Islam followed the Hebrews and adopted their own homilies to explain their religious practices.*

*"Well, here's the thing, Peter. I do not believe in any of the Abrahamic originated religions. I'm still a believer in paganism, where nature and the universe are my spirit god; and where worship is all around me. For example, when a butterfly pollinates a flower and takes its nectar, that is a holy worship happening. And when a penis gives semen to a vagina, and a vagina takes in its sperm, that is another holy worship happening. I believe the glory of nature is holy; and the female vagina is the most sacred worship place in the universe. And I believe prostitution and pornography are making a huge societal resurgence because they are natural expressions of human freedom and nature worship. I hope that helps, Peter."*

*Consuelo: "Thank you ever so much Marty. That was very enlightening. Here are some final questions. They are from Harry, who says he's your most devoted fan, ever. He states he has been a devoted church goer for his entire life; however, he would gladly trade eternity in heaven for eternity in hell if he could only hold you in his arms and kiss you and love you for just one hour. His first question is this: Why is it that, when I watch your films, I feel I am seeing elegance and while I see other erotica stars, I feel I am simply watching boring and, or, barnyard animals?*

*"Harry also asks whether you sometimes have doubts about promoting the new Morality Standard. He wonders how someone with such a pure, innocent face can be so sinful, so casually immoral, so uninhibited and carefree about making love with so many different partners. He notes that you seem to be a throwback to the pagan whores of heathen antiquity and wonders how you can reconcile that mindset with modern religious values and society? He also has a question about your performance in your Immaculate Conception film. He wants to know why you held your arms out to your sides or*

over your head every time you settled your vagina over a new penis? Was that scripted; or was it spontaneous?

"Finally, Harry asks how a woman as intelligent, articulate, and beautiful as yourself came to become a porn star? Why not a movie star, a television personality, or a woman who works in a profession like law or medicine or politics? And Harry asks if you have any regrets about choosing porn as your career?"

Marty: "Your first question notices my state of mind, Harry. When I walk onto a set my thoughts tell me it's a great privilege to be there. I think, at all times, how the spirits blessed me to be able to perform as I do. I honor my privilege. I try to make my lovemaking the essence of elegance. There are traps in the erotica film business, Harry. Some women fall into the trap of becoming automatons. They mechanically suck penises without putting feeling into it; or they lie there without expressing any feelings while their pussies get pounded. They become human robots. They'll be replaced by actual robots someday and they'll have no future in the business.

"Another trap is hubris. That's when a woman believes she's the most gifted, hottest body to ever grace a film set. That attitude shows. It repulses viewers. People want to see a woman who loves what she's doing and who loves her lovers; not a woman who wants you to think you are lucky to be seeing her.

"I try to avoid ever having that hubris attitude, Harry. I never take anything for granted. For example: My vagina. I go to great lengths to ensure that my vagina is always appealing to my partners. I wax frequently. I keep myself scrupulously clean, always. I experiment with the most enticing fragrances. I consciously try to make my partners' oral sex experience with me a delightful pleasure that they will always remember and cherish.

"When I cradle my vagina over a partner's face, I want him to remember the delicate softness of my vaginal lips; the enchanting wafts of my scents; and the delicious tastes of my orgasm juices. I *want him to hold fast in his memory how beautiful, delicate, and divinely sumptuous his experience was. I want him to revere that experience; enjoy it infinitely more than eating his mother's apple pie or a hot fudge Sunday.*

*"When we finish, I want him to feel like he's experienced something wonderous. I want him to feel like he's a butterfly that has had the great fortune to discover the world's most delectable flower. And savored its nectar. And, with rapture in his heart, he'll yearn to return and partake of my delicious nectar, again and again.*

*"In my own personal journey, Harry, I've come to understand that the spirits placed me here on Earth to discover the meaning of love. I believe they want me to propagate that understanding as best I can. I see myself promoting the New Morality Standard as its gifted spiritual change agent; obeying the will of the spirits; trying my best to help make humankind more civilized and more perfect through human acceptance of sexuality.*

*"I do not believe that what I do is evil; hence, I feel no need to apologize for what I do, or feel any shame in my behaviors. I believe that, while I perform, I'm sharing a holy experience with my viewers. If my interpretation is wrong, then I believe the spirits will nonetheless love me and forgive me. And, while I know I must eventually die in this life, I believe the spirits will reincarnate me and give me new lives, forever.*

*"If the spirits love what I'm doing in this life, I feel certain they will reincarnate me so I can continue my commitment to whoring in my future lives. If there is a little man with a long white beard, who sits on a throne in heaven somewhere, then I guess I'm screwed and I'll be remanded to hell; because, I certainly do not intend to ask him for forgiveness. I'll tell him to his face that I am pleased and content to remain immoral and unforgiven, because I firmly believe his different religious paths are the wrong paths for me. Actually, Harry, I whole heartedly believe that I am the living embodiment of*

*a long lineage of reincarnated temple prostitutes from that beautiful humanistic era of Pagan prostitution worship. I think it is my purpose on Earth to restore the glorious, sensuous religious traditions of female 'Creation by conception' worship.*

*"So, Harry, everything about my performances, from my make up to my wardrobe, to the way I move and gesture; and especially how I must revere and hold precious my intimate times with the penises I'm performing with, I absolutely must at all times be appreciative of how blessed I am to perform as I do. You see, Harry, I do not see myself as a Victorian woman whose duty it was to please her husband and bear his children; nor do I see myself as a vessel for a man's pleasures to be used and abused as he pleases. No, I see myself as a woman who has evolved beyond those stereotypes. I'm on a mission to bring more love into the world. I'm a catalyst for humankind's advancement toward acceptance of human needs.*

*"Thus, I am a thoroughly modern woman. I am committed to the New Modern Morality Standard. That means I am committed to experiencing my own pleasure for my pleasure's sake; and no one else's. Pleasure is my goal. It is an end in and of itself. Staying true to that that mindset is a comfort to me. In my film art I portray how beautiful and elegant it is to give oneself pleasures of the explicit, erotic kind.*

*"I help my viewers see how beautiful intimacy can be. I show them with my explicit interpretations why the Madonna Mona Lisa is smiling in her portrait; why she was so pleased with herself and her love making. I show the world that women's roles have changed from child bearing, drudgery and servicing men's urges. I show that a modern woman's place in the world is to enjoy pleasure; to please herself. I use my sexuality to make the entire world a more uninhibited, perfect, and equal place.*

*"I advocate that there's nothing wrong or shameful for a man to consort with prostitutes; rather that consorting is actually a form of*

historic human need expression for creation by conception worship. That's why you see my work as elegant, Harry. That portrayal of love and elegance comes from my deep spirituality. You see that in my films. There, I challenge righteous morality with my immoral, intimate artistry. I strive to make every film more beautifully erotic, more pleasing to my fans, than my last.

"You ask if I ever have doubts about what I'm doing. No, Harry, I don't. Critics say I promote anarchy, but I don't. I promote an alternative to drivel blather spew. My alternative is real and honest. It is not based on fairy tales. It is not grounded in a scheme to control peoples or nations. It is a choice for those who seek awareness of who they are and who wish to acknowledge their human needs.

"Change can feel like one is being tumbled about a bit, like a rolling stone in a flood stream. I understand that; but, Harry, I'm merely a representative of that onrushing wave of change. It is a relentless, cleansing force. I feel it in my soul. I express it when I perform. It is changing civilization as we know it.

"You see, Harry, I believe the elites of our world intend to depopulate our planet and replace the human species with robots. Elites see most of us as replaceable bartenders, waiters, waitresses, mechanics, bus drivers, pilots, maintenance workers, and on and on. They think we are useless polluters. They want to eliminate us to save the planet. They want the planet to be their utopian, environmentally friendly playground. They've already started with sex robots, Harry. But the things they can't replace are human feelings of caring love and sensuality. Try finding feelings in a robot. Sharing honest feelings and love requires another human.

"So, Harry, by promoting the new Modern Morality Standard, I'm saving humanity from extinction. You see, Harry, if a woman chooses to become a highly talented prostitute with no moral compass whatsoever; and one who, at the same time, can provide honest love and love making skills to other humans, she will likely have an important role in the new elite-centric world. Prostitution, whoring, and explicit erotica film making will be highly compensated, honored professions. Women who follow in my footsteps have extremely promising futures. Likely, many will become elites themselves.

"Women who choose traditional careers will likely be liquidated. At a minimum they'll be forced into vaccinations that de-sex them so their lineage goes extinct. I believe vaccine programs are trial runs to desensitize the populations so they will willingly accept secret substances that de-sex them and cause them to die or fail to reproduce.

"Elites, jetting about in their private planes, will not need these people. And, in our emerging immoral world, the elites will feel no stigma or guilt about eradicating useless surplus people. Ridding the planet of non-elites will be considered a desirable, humanistic social goal, analogous to the way Hitler murdered people with disabilities. Wholesale liquidations of non-elites and non- elite populations will be applauded, possibly even made into gala spectator sports, like the gladiator games of the ancient Romans. The progressive socialists will likely form elite killing battalions to hunt down and eradicate non-elites.

"Ultimately everything will settle into something better and more beautiful than what we have now. Society will adjust to the Modern Morality Standard and become the better for it. But one must do all one can to prepare for these changes that will come, which is why I encourage young women to seriously consider careers in prostitution. Their lives and their families may depend upon them making that intelligent choice. So, Harry, I will continue creating films while not harboring doubts in my mind; but with honest, deeply held conviction in my soul.

"Why did I end up in porn was another question, Harry. Well, I assure you, I did not end up in porn. I willfully chose porn as my career. It was a conscientious, willful choice. You see, Harry, each of us has two minds, the conscious mind, and the limbic mind. The *conscious mind is the everyday dog-eat-dog mind. It is filled with goals, deadlines, demands, stresses, and expectations; things we must do to please others; asses we must kiss to get ahead; compromises we must make to get ahead; drudgery we must do; ladders we must climb to pay our dues and fit into an acceptable norm.*

*"Well, I didn't want that for my life. I wanted to work within the limbic realm of my mind. I wanted to experience pleasures as much and as often as possible. I wanted to enjoy the freshness of new intimate relationships and express love and feel loved by many new and interesting partners; and form strong emotional bonds with them; essentially, get to know their essences as human beings. Love and making love appealed to me. It still does and it always will.*

*"So, Harry, I did not just end up in porn like I was some kind of failure everywhere else. I figured something out when I was still in high school, Harry. I could choose to marry some man who my family would approve of, a man who went to the same church they went to and believed the same things they did. I could choose to make them happy with my choice. But that choice would not make me happy. It would not be me. I understood early on that life does not just happen for someone. It's not about luck and what happens to you. It's about the choices we make.*

*"And I made my choice. I made the choice that I knew would make me happy. I wanted the choice that would empower me and value me. And more. I wanted the choice that enabled me to destroy those sorts of people who would chastise me for my unfortunate childhood experiences. Thinking introspectively, Harry, I wanted validation for who I am as a human being. I suppose that was the naughtiness in me, Harry; that inner urge to get even; to not let it go; to not turn the other cheek; to destroy a few bitches; whatever.*

*"Harry, I wanted my career in porn. I wanted it with all my heart. I sought it out. I love my career. It is not work for me. It is never ending experiencing of joys and enjoyment. It's very fulfilling.*

*I love who I am and what I do; all of it, including the performances I do and the marriages I've ruined; all the bad girl aspects of it. I hope that helps answer that question.*

*"About the way I held my arms out or over my head each time I lowered my vagina over a fresh penis in CONCEPTION: Well, Harry, that's my girl thrill factor letting go. No, none of those arm throws were scripted. They were all spontaneous. They were my natural joy of having a fresh, hard penis suddenly inside my vagina, replacing one that had just ejaculated. It's that thrill that starts inside my vagina and surges inside me until it feels like it is going to blow off the top of my head. It's like the ultimate feeling of success for this girl, Harry. Getting a new, fresh, rock-hard penis in my vagina is kind of like turning on a light switch. It's positively electrifying; thrilling beyond anything that words can express.*

*"I love that feeling, Harry. My nymphomania responds with joy that I can not contain. I allow myself to express myself. I must express that happiness. I must let it out. I'm feeling that beautiful wonderfulness of beginning to fuck a new, fresh; loving, vagina-pleasing penis. It's the whore within me letting myself go, Harry. It's my raw, human feeling. It's the whore that I am, rejoicing; feeling reaffirmed; feeling blessed in my worthiness to fuck a new, wonderful penis. Thank you for that question, Harry.*

*"The simplest way to answer your question about how I can be so sinful, so carefree and casual about my immorality is to examine yourself, Harry. Think about how you feel while you are having an orgasm, Harry. You love that moment, don't you? Well, I'm the same way, Harry; only I can orgasm much more frequently than you can. And why shouldn't I? Why shouldn't I enjoy the greatest pleasure that there is in life as often as I can? I guess that's the best way to answer your question, Harry; by a question of my own. As far as how I can behave like a heathen Pagan goddess? That's easy for me, Harry. My limbic mind rules my morals and my*

*choices, not my programmed, civilized mind. It's a choice, Harry. I choose sybaritic pleasures instead of the civilized world's religious constraints.*

*"When I perform in orgies, you often see me lying upon a bed with my head over the edge and my legs spread. I'm happily sucking the penises of two partners; men are by my sides, kissing my nipples and massaging me; and partner after partner is ejaculating into my vagina. While I perform this way, I become the modern-day Whore of Babylon. What I am doing is not evil or sinful or dirty or disgusting. It is divine, beautiful and a holy obedience to the call of eternity; of life; of human need and human love.*

*"Here's what the religious types don't want you to understand, Harry. There's nothing evil or dirty or sinful or ungodly about what I'm doing with my partners. I'm not trying to emulate the religious types with their holy robe garbs and their kabuki services. They can perform their majestic ceremonies; they can spew their mumbo jumbo speak about some illogical fairy tales and hocus-pokus riddles; and then they can demand their ten percent of your income to support their grand charades.*

*"They can expect you to believe that, long, long ago, sticks turned into snakes; a raised stick parted the seas; stone tablets were handed from a god in the sky to human hands; another man changed water to wine, made a blind man see, made a dead man walk; arose himself from death after crucifixion, walked around and kibbitzed with other men, then ascended into the sky; that another man split the moon into two, multiplied quantities of food, got on a horse, and rode the horse to heaven.*

*"Really? If you believe that stuff, what won't you believe? Do you also believe that the moon is made of green cheese? That you can buy the Brooklyn Bridge for a nickel? Religious types insist that you believe their stories and romantic riddles. Fine, believe them if they give your mind comfort.*

"But I choose not to believe any of them. I do not wear fancy robes and perform elaborate ritual ceremonies. I do not use a fancy building with lots of image statues for my stage settings, either. I perform simply, honestly, and naked. There's a purity and innocence in being naked. I like the way naked feels. It feels free; natural; uninhibited. I love to freely whore. I'm guiltless and conscience free. You see, Harry, my Pagan services appeal to a different dimension of the human mind, the limbic dimension. It's not the serenity and peaceful balm that the conscious mind receives from ordinary religious services. It's altogether different.

"It's that sudden longing you feel in your chest, that passion throb that causes your limbic mind to block out everything else except your animal lust. It's that other voice in your mind that suddenly comes alive and tells you that you'll do anything, give anything, forsake everything and everyone, if only you could have the honor of joining me onstage and making love with me. It's the voice that tells your penis to stand up and get hard; that your purpose for living is to love and make love; and it commands you to abandon all other thoughts. It's emotive feelings that you cannot experience at conventional religious services. Harry, I allow my pleasure-seeking limbic mind to chart my path forward; and I don't look back. I have no desires to change who I am. I look forward to doing more than I've ever done before. Yeah, Harry. I'm willful. I'm a girl on a mission; and I'm gaining converts. I'm returning Pagan beliefs to humanity. I'm unchaining limbic minds. Paganism is my chosen venue.

"Paganism is a valid alternative to the spewers of fairy tales and riddles, Harry. Being a Pagan whore lifts my heart. I love performing fellatio and copulating with two huge penises simultaneously. That's an example of what you'll see at one of our rituals. I could do that all afternoon with six or eight different men taking turns with me. I feel completely free and natural while I'm doing them. You'll notice how free and uninhibited I feel by how I banter with my partners. That's the real me, Harry. I can't get enough of those sensational feelings that I have while I'm into intimacy and performing fellatio. That's because I know that I'm giving honest human love and freedom to those who seek it.

"I and my partners are performing a new form of worship devotion. Actually, we are reviving an ancient form of worship devotion. It's timely for our modern culture, Harry, because we have birth control and abortion services available now. We need not worry about the disastrous consequences of our human pleasure worship. We only need to affirm human love for each other and ourselves. It's a profoundly spiritual and glorious experience, Harry. It's the ascendancy of limbic spirit essence above the stresses and obligations of every day. It's refreshing and soul cleansing. It helps people believe in themselves and in each other. I'm proud of the services that I facilitate with my partners. I love whoring, Harry; totally love it; totally adore the penis I'm sucking and the one that's pleasuring my vagina; can't ever get enough of it; never want to stop. That's how much I love it. Call me a Pagan whore if you must call me anything, Harry. I'm honored. The only regret I have, Harry, is that I didn't start my porn career sooner. If I had known then what I know now, I believe I would have already performed in an additional hundred films.

"Thank you for your questions, Harry. And, Harry, your flattery made me feel appreciated and wonderful. Please call my Premium Member Service. I'd like to meet you. You are more than welcome to have your hour with me; and you are welcome to participate in one of our rituals."

Consuelo: "And thank you for those insights, Marty. They were profound and beautiful. Now I have a question of my own. It's about how your mind perceives morality and how you use your mind to seduce a man. When you said you imagined you were holding your composite wife's head between your thighs, you didn't exactly say how you imagined you destroyed her. Could you elaborate about *that? It sounded like you were reliving a deliciously naughty experience. Hearing you describe your emotions while you imagined drowning her made my blood churn with excitement and awe about those wicked thoughts you expressed.*

*"Your wickedness made me wet, Marty. It sounded so passionate; so naughty. I and my readers all applaud your sincere commitment to the Modern Morality Standard. Can you tell us more about your most wicked thoughts? Could you elaborate for us just how you think about your planned marriage destructions and how you bring them about?'*

Marty: *"Sure, Consuelo, I'll enthusiastically do anything and everything I can to advance the cause of immorality. Hopefully this will encourage and embolden your readers and give them some ideas.*

*"Often enough a married wife seeks to explore her sexuality. My typical experience has been that she's a well to do suburban housewife with a fantastic household income. She's home alone often and she's bored with her country club socializing and her bridge clubs. She feels put upon to make social appearances with her husband. Basically, she's climbing the walls and going out of her mind. There's no excitement in her life. Her natural promiscuity tells her she should experiment a little and discover new things. She hears that the men in her social circle have seen my films. She figures her husband has seen my films and would love having sex with me. She sees my work and admits she has her own desires and cravings. She wants her pampered poodle lifestyle; but she also wants intimacy with me.*

*"The couple invites me into their home. I quickly make her comfortable and teach her the joys of cunnilingus. I make sure she experiences the most fantastic orgasms she's ever had. She discovers a whole new world when my tongue connects our limbic zones through her clitoris. She experiences that new, mind-expanding dimension.*

*"Her oral sex with me becomes addictive. She feels her whole world opened and expanded. She loves me and becomes infatuated*

with my vagina. I'm very patient and loving. I want her addicted to my love making. I soon receive regular invitations to their home. She adores my vagina like it's her secret goddess. It's always accessible to her. My immorality helps her feel comfortable and guiltless. She loves connecting with me. She freely reciprocates oral sex. She loves using her tongue to stimulate my clitoris. We establish a complete relationship. We laugh and talk openly and honestly about our sexuality.

"We freely and unashamedly release our orgasms, gushing into each others' mouths; and we love our relaxed feelings about the totality of our love making. She becomes totally uninhibited with me. We tumble freely and often into lesbian love. This is different for both of us than love with a man. It's more understanding; more emotive; more tender; more caring; more everything. And, it's profoundly beautiful. It's liberating and addictive. Our love making becomes a form of worship. We attain a subliminal adoration for each other. I can sense when a woman loves me.

"I feel an inner sense of guilt growing inside myself. I know what I must do. In a way I hate myself, but I know I will do it anyway. My dilemma is that I pity her as much as I love her. She does not understand that I offered my gift of sex to her as my modern-day Trojan Horse. She idolizes my whoring and loves kissing my sex. She relaxes her defenses, unaware I'm about to betray her trust. She opened the gates to her home and welcomed me inside. Now I'm part of her home life and free to do as I please. I know her marriage fortress is vulnerable. I'm safely inside her kingdom, imbedded in her marriage. I know her routines, preferences, family finances, prejudices, everything. While I suck and make love with her husband, she applauds; enjoying watching us orgasm together. We erotically exchange her husband's semen, kissing each others' mouths. I'm family.

"I changed her former monogamy into a pan-amoral lust fest. Profligacy and whoredom cement our triangle. Our triangle bond is strong. It absorbs and dissolves her marriage bond with her husband. Within the inseparable union of limbic conjugal love my intuition tells me when my bond to her husband becomes stronger than his bond to her. I knew my bond with her would become disposable before I introduced myself to them. Easily made, easily discarded was my intent for that bond all along.

"Realize, Consuelo, my goal from the outset was to annihilate her marriage; sack her household wealth; and convert her husband to my premium member service and the Modern Morality Standard. When the moment is right, I unleash my forces. I attack her without mercy. It comes when I am alone with her husband in their kitchen or bedroom. I know her guard is down. Perhaps she is in repose, like a sleeping Trojan, completely unaware of my treachery. She is defenseless.

"Then, I pounce. I draw my body tightly against her husband's. I French kiss him. My lips and tongue infuse him with the most overwhelming sincerity I can summon. My soul amplifies the intensity of my passion by placing one hand on the back of his neck and my other hand on his penis. When I rub his penis, he cannot mistake my desires for mere playfulness. He must know this is something more intense, more profound and life changing. There can be no doubt. I overwhelm his senses with erotic seduction lust. I press my breast against his chest and lift his hand to my bosom. I make his limbic zone command his thoughts. I French kiss him while I squeeze and stroke his penis, I tell him:

'I love you. I want you to get rid of her. I cannot stand to share you with her anymore. I want us to be alone for days and weekends and weeks, kissing you and making love with you, without her. I want to have unimaginable sex with just you. She bores me. I'm tired of her. She's disgusting. Get her out of my life. Get rid of her. We don't need her. She tries to chaperone us. She tries to keep me from feeling totally free with you. There are so many naughty things

*I want to do with you, for hours and hours; but I need you to get rid of her. I can't stand her being around us.*

'If you want your penis in my hot, slippery pussy every night, having sex with me all night long, you'll do as I ask. You'll get her out of our lives. You know I'm what you want. You know you want a total whore and not a housewife. Admit it. Leave her. Separate. I don't care how you get rid of her. I just don't want her around us anymore. Go to my hotel suite and stay there where I can be with you all day and night. Do as I ask. Do it for me. Divorce her. Get her out of my life. I insist that you do this, for me; for us. I hate the sight of her. She has to go. Tell her your marriage is over. Tell her you love only me. Tell her that there is no longer any room in your life for her.'

*"While I say these conspiratorial things to her husband, I imagine deliciously evil thoughts. I imagine the wife is nearby. I imagine she is dumfounded, spellbound by what she hears, thinking I could not possibly betray her this way. I know this is my chance to destroy her. I reveal the true nature of my predatory viciousness. I imagine pulling my dagger from its concealed sheaf and plunging it deeply into her heart. I twist it, tearing her heart apart while I smile at her, murdering her and the love she believed that we shared. She reels from her shock and horror. My dagger slices her stomach open and disembowels her. She stares, traumatized in horrified disbelief. I shove her corpse to the floor.*

*"I am remorseless and proud. I imagine defiling her dead body to make her husband prove his love belongs to me alone. Her corpse serves as my pillow as I brazenly position my triumphant tush comfortably upon her chest. A tidal wave of jubilation courses through my murderous blood. Her husband's responding kisses, the earnest passions I feel from his tongue, tells me he's reading my thoughts. Our inner souls unite in our shameless treachery. He approves of my vicious deed; and he loves me for it.*

"The sincerity of his lips, the intensity with which they press against mine tells me he would murder her in real life, if I demanded that. I now know he is just as bored with their marriage as she is. I smile at her husband. I press my upper body closely against him. I guide his hand up, under my skirt, lifting it higher and higher over my thighs; up until I bring it to rest upon my vagina. I push his two fingers into me. I want him to feel my hot slippery wetness. I want him to stimulate me into a frenzy state for love making. I French kiss him again. My renewed passion fervor lets him know this is no mistake or game. I communicate through my body that the words I spoke are exactly what I want. I offer him the way to change his life. I show him my wonderful world of immoral pleasures is his for the taking. He does not pull away from me. His mind joins mine. We are anxious to enjoy our lust. I know his passions for me are stronger than any love he ever felt for her. I feel his want.

"My legs spread widely as I pull him down to me. My hand guides his penis to my welcoming home. I'm wet and slippery hot; anxious to meet his thrusts with my own. I love feeling his penis entering me; more this time than all those times before this moment. This time signals a profoundly deeper meaning than those before times. This time celebrates his acquiescence to change.

"We surrender ourselves to the natural forces of destruction and creation. They sweep over us, unite our bodies as our sweet thrusts begin. We are lost in erotic romantic love. We become passionate animals, obsessed with love making. He is no longer her husband. Dissolving the marriage is now just a matter of time. The details are left to lawyers with their paperwork and formalities. My arms hold him to me as he thrusts inside me. My vagina's silky-smooth warmth guides him to unimaginable pleasures. We make wild frenzied love on top of the wife's imaginary dead body. My mind races. Is her soul still alive, I ask myself? Does it feel love for me in my debauchery;

*knowing I'm removing myself from her life? Does it know I've closed the door on her life and opened a new door for my own life? I smile, then close my mind to that thought.*

*"I feel incredibly beautiful. I have achieved completeness as a woman and a seductress. I've performed a glorious deed. I struck a blow for freedom and immoral lust! My implied promise of endless passion lust cleaves her husband's commitment to me. I ignited a sybaritic fervor, greater than he ever imagined was possible. With every thrust of his penis, with every spurt of his hot pasty semen over my clitoris I become more certain that the monies from his wife's accounts will soon be redirected to my own. As I feel myself becoming enriched by my debauchery, I imagine she is becoming a discarded, crumpled husk; no longer a lovely flower.*

*"Every loving hot semen pulse furthers her destruction. We love what we are doing. We are rebirthing honest immoral love; passionate love. We kiss, we laugh; we frolic with uninhibited abandon. We enjoy defiling her. Our evil riot is hilarious. Our beautiful sybaritic evil delights us. Her naivety is our contempt. Husband and I are together in mind and purpose now. We discover eros; intense, romantic love. Her end justified my means. We feel good. I upended her world. I, instigator, feel accomplished and proud of my deed. I enlisted her husband as my accomplice; that elates me. My ego soars. My daydream ends.*

*"But my daydream had its desired effect. It filled my kisses with wanton passion. My lust was communicated to her husband. My thoughts magically passed from my mind to his. We experienced telepathy on a dangerous level and WE LOVED IT! His imagination applauded my imaginary deed of murder. He LOVED me for it. He loved imagining that we made love on his wife's dead body. He adored my treachery and my debauchery. Our minds and purposes are now united. He swears that he wants only me. He confesses he*

*has read my mind and that he will get rid of her. He tells me that he loves me. I know he is truthful. I know that, while I have not actually murdered her, I have accomplished her devastation.*

*"I know she will suffer endless agonizing nights knowing that he is with me, knowing that I have betrayed her intimate trust. Her mind will wrestle during torment maddened nights knowing her husband's penis rocks cradled, inside my amorous, shameless vagina. She will wonder how I could betray her after the love we shared. We both knew it was beautiful; but I always knew it had to end. Now my deed is done. I have him. He's mine. She may plot revenge against me, possibly even murder; but she will fail.*

*"I have my security people. They will protect me, keeping their eyes on her while I make love with her husband. I'll be safe. In a sordid way, I'll also be mocking her life; but I won't care about that. A girl has to know her priorities. Her husband's penis is my priority. I can't feel guilt or shame about whom or what I am. I remind myself: I'm a whore. I'm an unrepentant, guiltless, amoral whore. She didn't understand what she was dealing with. Too bad!*

*"He will go through divorce hell. I'll love him for that. I'll reward him. I'll drop to my knees, fondle his balls, and perform exquisite felatio. I'll deeply love what is happening in his awakening mind. I'll adore him. I'll love sucking his beautiful penis. I know I will suck him often in the future, and love having sex with him even more after these precious moments. I know I will suck away every vestige of his love for his wife while I swallow his semen. Sex does that for a man. It's a finality of sorts; like when you see the guard change at Buckingham Palace. The old guard is gone, replaced by the new guard. Then, I'll smile my most delicious sinful smile of cherubic, childlike innocence. My eyes promise him endless felatio and erotic romantic love.*

*"My plan was brilliant. My vagina lured his wife into complacency and devoured her common sense. It annihilated her marriage.*

*Her comfortable married life was doomed the moment she invited me into her home. My lust consumed her husband. He became mine, only mine.*

Consuelo: *"Oh, Marty, you are so deliciously naughty! I love how your mind works! I have often looked into your warm inviting eyes and imagined that you had a certain irresistible magnetism, but I had no idea you could be so delightfully clever and so beautifully evil! You really are quite the vixen, a real promiscuous she-devil! I've gotten moist while listening to how husbands actually leave their wives for you. They leave everything to be with you, don't they?*

Marty: *"Consuelo, they leave for themselves, for their freedom. I simply show them the way forward, the path they can take, so to speak; and the beauty of total freedom. I help them see that immorality and decadence is their pathway to escape their prisons of Victorian morality. I know how marriage, religion and politics structure peoples' lives and keep them enslaved. I've met and seduced many men whose lives were so organized and regimented that they didn't have time to stop and ask themselves if the life they were living was what they really wanted. Whenever I sense a man has those sorts of frustrations and time constraints in his life, I know it's time to kiss him and place my hand on his penis; and follow that initial suggestion with fellatio and love making as soon as possible. I sort of see myself as a woman on a rescue mission. I understand that marriage and religion are time honored institutions. I don't question that. But what I do question is the hypocrisy of so many millions who pretend to live their lives as marriage and religion prescribes them to be lived; when in fact, they do not want to live them that way.*

*"That dichotomy makes a person uncomfortable with their truest nature. They are being deceptive to their true souls which causes them internal strife and emotional distress. That's the insidious power of the institutions of marriage and religion. It's hurtful to the natural internal needs of so many millions of people. But I show*

*people how they can take their power back. Power is never freely given back. Once some people and institutions have established power over others, they never willingly give it back.*

*"Several men I've seduced have had to suffer through church counselling sessions with their wives. The churches and the wives never like to lose their man to me. They see the man as a sheep in their flock. I see him as a human who is free to do as he pleases. Be with me; or leave me if you wish. It's the man's decision. I admit that I do use sex as a means to keep a man attracted to me. But I never tell him that he needs to stay with me. People can always take their power back. Power has to be taken. No one ever gives you your own power. Human nature doesn't work that way. Freedom is everything. This is why I feel so wonderfully shameless and unapologetic about being a totally carefree, immoral whore. That is my natural truth about myself. That is how I live my life. I am at peace with my truest nature.*

*"As a porn star, I celebrate helping people express their yearnings. I flaunt my whoring at established morals. I introduce millions to the New Modern Morality Standard through my dedication to erotic romantic pornography. I help millions discover their courage and their right to take their own natural power back, without feeling guilty about it. I release them from the institutionalized psychological bondage that has been imposed upon them since their childhoods. That's why I have many fans. Millions love me. Millions want to make love with me; and millions use my films to work up the courage to call a prostitution service. Yes, I make it easier for them to call a beautiful, loving whore who will understand their need for freedom; and who will make love with them; and who will be there for them when they choose freedom over oppression.*

*"A whore's vagina is the pathway to freedom for millions. It is a legitimate, honest choice and an escape from their yoke of mental slavery. That choice should always be respected and honored as a*

*person's natural right. Some people will kill for the vagina they want. That is usually the result of extreme emotional distress, like possessiveness or fear of the unknown. It happens all too often. But why should it happen at all? All one needs to do is make a call or click on a web site for a beautiful understanding vagina. Why suffer stress when there's such an easy alternative? How many men with sexual addictions would be spared the conviction for sex offenses if the government provided free or subsidized prostitution services? How many murders would be prevented? How many families would be spared turmoil? What's wrong with decriminalizing natural human needs? I represent freedom. I spark that freedom quest that resides within every human. That deep desire for freedom is humanity's most precious thing.*

Consuelo: *"Thank you, Marty. I loved your explanation. I'm sure Marcus, Kevin, Jillian, Harry, and Miss Sandstone also appreciated your insights. Marty, my producers tell me you have developed an exciting new product for your on-line store. Is it a complement to your BDSM line or something to help a woman's man keep it up for her? Could you tell us about that, please?"*

Marty: *"Oh, I think they are a little confused, Consuelo. I was telling them about this exciting creative product line that I and my product producers have developed for the youth market."*

Consuelo: *"Children? Seriously, Marty, are you going to market porn to children? What gave you that idea?"*

Marty: *"Oh, absolutely, Consuelo. We see youth porn as a huge, untapped market. We're taking our cues from the religious market. As a child, church bored me and terrified me. I was frightened by the thought that, every year, this poor man had to get crucified for my sins. I didn't think I did anything so bad that some guy needed to be killed for it. As you know, the religious types begin to indoctrinate children as soon as the children can speak. They don't make excuses for the brainwashing they do. They just assume it's their right to do* it; to pound their dogma and homilies into malleable young minds. I thought there should be a counterweight to the religious brainwashing. Well, we intend to offer a young impressionable mind freedom of moral choice so that the young impressionable child, with proper adult guidance of course, can decide what is the appropriate belief system and the most appealing career options she wishes to explore."

Consuelo: "Well, this certainly sounds innovative. Can you tell us more about what you're offering the youth market?"

Marty: "Sure, Consuelo. As I've said, we're very excited about it. My product engineers have replicated the female vagina while it is experiencing sex and orgasms. It's made to be carried around, like a small suitcase. It has a clear plastic see through side, so the child can see what happens inside the vagina while a penis is fornicating with it. It's a very elaborate, realistic showcase, complete with tiny feather-like rubberized feelers that simulate the sensations of a penis rubbing inside the vagina. It also has a scaled model clitoris that causes flashing mauve, soft green, and pink lights to come on automatically. The lights illuminate the penis with inviting colors. Tiny squirts of water spray inside the vagina while the penis rubs over the clitoris, simulating what the vagina does while it is having an orgasm. Each product has a push button and a joy stick that the child can manipulate. When the button is pushed, the vagina contracts around the penis and squeezes it, just like a real vagina does. When the joy stick is maneuvered, it causes the vagina to thrust, gyrate; and pitch and yaw on the penis, exactly like a real vagina does while an adult woman is enjoying sex.

"Each product comes complete with rubberized latex penises; and each penis has an apparatus attached at the back, which simulates a male's testicles. And here's the most exciting thing about these penises. Each one has a little compartment on the top of it, into which the child can put whipped cream and salt. Each battery powered penis vibrates at different speed options. They all pulsate, much *like real penises do when they ejaculate. So, if a little girl wants to get a sense of what sex is like, she can turn on the switch that activates her toy penis. It will pulse and thrust like a real penis. It will swell up and get very hard.*

*"And, here's the feature that will really help the product sell, Consuelo. When the little girl puts her mouth around the head of the penis and squeezes her mouth tight on it, the penis will shoot its salt flavored whipped cream into her mouth, much like a real penis does. Each penis comes complete with a three year's supply of dehydrated whipping cream and salt; and each penis is detachable from the vagina box. So, if the little girl wants to use her penises as dildos, or if she wants it to shoot its whipped cream into her own real vagina, she can use it to do that."*

Consuelo: *"Very creative, Marty. How many penises come with one of your Vagina Toys?"*

Marty: *"We'll be offering three versions of the Vagina. We're going to call it 'The Vagina.' There will be the 'Porn Star' model. That's the basic starter toy, mostly for girls in elementary school. It will have three penises, sized five to seven inches; about what a young girl might discover in sexual encounters with boys her age. The intermediate model will be called the 'Porn Queen' model. It will have six penises with sizes ranging from five inches to nine inches; about what a girl in high school might discover in boys her age. The deluxe model will contain twelve penises, including three enormous black penises. The six enlarged penises in the deluxe model will be ten to eighteen inches in length. All of the deluxe model penises will have the capability to shoot two to three times more cream than the intermediate and starter models. We're calling our deluxe model the 'Porn Goddess.'"*

Consuelo: *"My goodness, Marty. You really are going to tap a new market with this! How soon will it be available in you online store?"*

Marty: "We're going to try a different marketing strategy for this product, Consuelo. It will not be offered through my online store. It will only be available through our franchised network of liberal female elementary school teachers. Sales will be via multi-level marketing teams. We feel the students will naturally trust their teachers more than they trust their parents. So, our marketing strategy will emphasize benefits to the teacher for attaining her sales goals. It's a high commission sales program. We'll designate one teacher per school. A teacher can easily achieve three times her salary income by becoming one of our program reps. We'll also have prizes for sales success, including things like free BDSM products and trips to Hawaii.

"Each teacher will be given a sales presentation kit so she can demonstrate the Vagina Toy to her students during her sex education classes. She can illustrate for her students how the vagina experiences its orgasms, how a woman feels during her orgasms, and how the penis can ejaculate into the female vagina or into a partner's mouth. She can even use her own vagina and the penises from the Porn Goddess model to make her student demonstrations live and realistic, should she so choose. She can also demonstrate how a girl can use the penises in her Vagina Toy as standalone dildoes to give herself orgasms. Trust me, Consuelo, these penises are much better and much more realistic than the top-of-the-line dildos that women typically purchase in sex stores. The teacher can also use the penises to demonstrate the best techniques for girls who are interested in learning how to perform fellatio.

"Once our franchised teachers have demonstrated that they are qualified to sell the product, our teachers can then offer our Vagina Toys in their exclusive franchise territories. We've designed our sales offerings and price points so that a teacher who dedicates only a half hour of classroom time per day should easily be able to double or triple her annual income. As an added sales incentive, we are offering *a free promotional code to each student who buys a Vagina Toy. The promo code will enable the student to download, for free, any five of my porn films, including my Premium Orgy and Premium Threesome films.*

*"We encourage the teachers to get the students to use their promo codes to purchase all my different porn films and swap and share them amongst each other; and to form 'after class' porn clubs. And, as an extra incentive for sales, we are including three free annual subscriptions to your Wonderful World of Intimacy Magazine, for each school library. And, we'll be advertising our Vagina Toy in your magazines to help penetrate the youth market through cross marketing with your magazine marketing staff! Sounds exciting, doesn't it?"*

Consuelo: *"It sure does, Marty. I can't wait to purchase a Vagina Toy for my own daughter. I know she'll just love it! Are you working on any other product offerings for your new distribution channel?"*

Marty: *"Well yes, we are, Consuelo. We assume the Vagina Toy will be wildly successful. If so, we will be following that offering with another. It is in the prototype phase; but My engineers have shown me the basic model and it is very exciting. We're thinking we'll call it the 'Duster Miss.' It will be a scaled model of the female uterus. Inside the uterus there will be a small clump of material stuck to the uterine wall. This represents a fetus that has attached to the wall, which is highly undesirable for the sexually liberated young girl. The Duster Miss will have a tube that goes through the vaginal opening and locates the simulated fetus. Then, the child operating the Duster can flip a switch and the Duster sucks out the problem fetus. The objective of the Duster Miss toy is to eliminate a young girl's fear of becoming pregnant if she chooses to have sex with boys.*

*"We would like these young girls to feel liberated and free to experiment sexually with the boys that they like, should they choose to do that, without ever being fearful about becoming pregnant.*

*We're trying to help them understand that pregnancy is their choice; and, if they don't want to be pregnant, then there's nothing wrong with simply vacuuming out the fetus. We make it seem as simple as vacuuming up a clump of undesirable dust off a floor.*

*"Our marketing strategy for 'Duster Miss' will include on-site visits to schools by myself and other participating porn stars. We'll go into the classrooms and give talks about career opportunities in prostitution and porn. We'll assure the young girls that we, ourselves, have had occasions to have our uteruses dusted to remove unwanted fetuses; and we've all quickly gotten over it and continued having fun filled, sexually active lives. Essentially, we'll be endorsing the 'Duster Miss' and encouraging sexual freedom for young children. We'll also be available to sign autographs for the children and for any adults that come to our presentations."*

Consuelo: *"Gee Marty, aren't you concerned that some parents might object to you going into elementary schools and advocating sexuality and a career in porn?"*

Marty: *"No, I'm not concerned in the slightest, Consuelo. I feel I'm successful in my career. I set a positive example for girls that want a similar career path and I feel I owe it to my community to give something back. I think I'm no different from these sports stars that go to schools to give talks to kids; to encourage the young boys to try out for football, that sort of thing. I want to eliminate the double standard that young girls are forced to tolerate. On the one hand, NFL football players, representing a tax-payer subsidized monopoly, are invited into schools to give motivational talks and advocate for football, which is a sport that can cause brain and bodily injury; on the other hand, women who advocate careers in sex work, face hellfire opposition and banning from schools.*

*"It's a perverse, discriminatory double standard and it needs to be seen as such. Men must stop controlling women's bodies and life*

*choices. Morality must be a matter of individual choice. Women should not be subjected to male-controlled religious morality. Belief indoctrination from birth to grave is the opposite of freedom of choice. It's impressment into belief servitude for perpetual cash extraction. It's institutionalized psychological brutality.*

*"Religions are comfortable with brutality. Look no further than forced conversions, religious based wars, the inquisitions on the Iberian peninsula, the horrific genocide of Americas' Ethnic Native Peoples, and the Israeli-Palestinian conflict. Religionists use brutality to enforce their mandates on the powerless. Look at the Salem Witch Trials; Muslim dress codes for women; discrimination blocking women from the rabbinate and the priesthood; the servile status of women in many religious based cultures; the horrible practice of intubation. We must ask ourselves: Why is this second-class treatment acceptable? What's the logic? Who makes these decisions? Why do the decision makers have the right to make these decisions? Who benefits from their decisions, and who is harmed? And, what kinds of humans are we to tolerate these abuses of other humans?*

*"Religions' methods of garnering market shares of belief systems can be physically and mentally inhumane. You wouldn't try to make a dog believe it is a cat; or make a boy believe he is a girl, would you? Some nut hatch people will do that. But it's immoral, inhumane, and wrong minded. A religiously immoral lifestyle, or a Pagan lifestyle if you wish to call it that, is a perfectly valid, sensible free-will choice. Every woman should be free to make that choice of lifestyle. Men may try to take a woman's free choice away from her. That's immoral. She should not be coerced. It's her life. It's her body. She is not owned by anyone or by any religion."*

Consuelo: *"Bravo, Marty. Well said. That's the Marty we all know and love; fearless advocate for freedom of choice. That's why we all love you so much, Marty. Now, we're all excited to learn more about what you've been up to with your life and your career, lately. How did you manage your transition from the subtle European porn culture you learned at Cannes to the more raucous American culture of Las Vegas in such a short two-week period? Can you help us navigate that? Especially, how you and Dom became such a popular item? You must know that you are the rage of all the morning talk shows."*

# CHAPTER TEN

*When a man pours his heart out to you, you have a choice. You can listen sympathetically or simply kiss him, put your hand on his penis; then tell him to be quiet because you want to move things along. (Rosemary Ness-Bitner, author)*

## CONVERSION

Marty: *"Of course, Consuelo. After making my Cannes connections I felt widely respected and loved. I was recognized in exclusive European circles as a highly sophisticated, cultured, privileged courtesan. I had experienced all sorts of erotic titillations, and my immorality was championed by those who appreciated exceptional sexual talent. Europeans are very open minded and accepting of whores, especially notorious porn stars who use discretion and discernment about their availability, and who travel seamlessly in the most elite circles. Dom told me never to think these sophisticated men were paying too much to be with me. Money is no object for them when it comes to having relations with a woman they want. He assured me that his circle of wealthy European connoisseurs adored uninhibited shameless prostitutes; that they all had a dark side and that they all loved their immoral pleasures.*

*"Many men told me that experimenting with me was their ultimate pleasure. And I soon found out that my money demands were never questioned. That would be considered impolite by these men. My exorbitant premium member prices were no obstacle. They paid*

*my asking price, gladly. And they were all perfect gentlemen and delightful lovers. Dom explained these Continentals were excellent marketers that knew exactly what they were doing; and that they would reap many returns on their money. Dom assured me that I had conquered Cannes. He declared me the most highly desired whore in all of Europe. I was so pleased with myself. After our rounds of the casinos, he suggested we get some fresh air.*

*"That's when the Paparazzi went crazy taking photos of the two of us lying on the beach. We were touching, and kissing; walking arm in arm; kissing with lingering soul kisses; sharing food and feeding each other in the casino restaurants. And there were pictures of Dominick on his knees before me, smiling up at my face, his lips one half inch from my transparent bikini bottom. Those photos made it appear that Dom was salivating, about to untie my bottom, remove my skimpy napkin triangle and kiss my vagina. My hands were on Dom's curly mop. My back was arched and my head thrown back. I was laughing, realizing that Dom wanted to go down on me again, right there on the beach, in front of everyone. Definitely a lover feeling the passion! That's Dom. Dom melts me into a puddle of desire when he kneels in front of my vagina like that. He knows he can have me anywhere he wants me.*

*"After making over four hundred erotic films I thought I knew everything about male lust that any woman could possibly know. I couldn't have been more wrong. Dom and I were lying on the beach at Cannes. I was into one of my long foreplay moods. I was in my bikini with my top off and my flesh pressed closely to Dom. We were French kissing and my hand was inside his trunks, lazily stroking his penis. Sometimes I love doing that for a whole hour, just to drive Dom crazy to make love. I like lying my head on his massive chest while I touch him. I imagine that he'll soon wrap his massive arms around me and squeeze my body against that massive chest. I love feeling I'm about to be dominated.*

"Confident anticipation tells my blood that Dom will soon sweep me into his strong masculine arms. I imagine being ravaged by Dom in his beast mode; him thrusting into my vagina so forcibly that I scream with endless pleasure, knowing that I, woman, am cave man Dom's love slave. I was thinking those thoughts when Dom opened to me and explained his innermost feelings. I never appreciated the transformation he went through while falling in love with me.

"Dom explained his transition. Before he watched my films, he felt like a lowly caterpillar. Now that we were lovers, he could clearly see what he was before. Like so many other caterpillars he went to church every Sunday and took communion with his wife. His mind ate the milkweed of church dogma. He happily munched away, mentally; eating teachings of idol worship in the forms of statues of saints, the Virgin Mary, the cross, and Jesus. He accepted, without any objective thought or analysis, church teachings about the miracle of faith.

"But, after watching my films, he saw the beauty of love and creation within my work. He watched films of other porn stars, but they left him feeling empty. Then, he started watching my films. He told me it was a different experience. Images of my vagina performing with penises stayed firmly fixated in his mind. Every time he watched my erotic love scenes, he wanted to see more.

"He became so obsessed with my smiling face and my insatiable, penis craving vagina that he couldn't stop thinking about me. He knew it was only a matter of time before he would call me. He knew we were fated to become lovers. He told me that my love making and the way my vagina seemed to quest after my partners' penises made him realize that I was an exceptional whore; the most desirable porn star he had ever seen.

"He told me that he obsessed over how my vagina seemed to throb while cum flowed out of me; like my vagina felt compelled to continue with intercourse; that my vagina yearned for even more sex. And that's why it quivered and throbbed like it did. He realized he could not deny me. His manliness felt summoned. He would lay awake nights wishing he could bury his face in my vagina; respond to its need. He intuited that once he gave me an orgasm with oral sex, he would cherish me as his most beloved woman and would never leave me. He believed the two of us were fated to do great things together. He was certain we would become lovers.

"Before he even called me, he had decided that he would dedicate his life and his fabulous wealth to pleasing me. He would make it his mission to show the entire world realize what a sensational, immoral whore I was; and how my erotic films were the most sensational intimate artistry ever created. When he watched white cum paste flowing from my vagina, he told me that adoration overcame him. He was so smitten by those images, that he wanted me to have the most handsome partners and fabulous penises that any woman could ever want. He confessed that he had become entranced by my vagina. He couldn't get it out of his mind; nor did he want to. He wanted to experience intimacy with me, for real. He nearly went insane, agonizing over making that first call.

"He realized that my film art honors life's creation process. He no longer saw me as an immoral woman. He didn't care that I had other lovers. He concluded that my films were creation art; Pagan-like; touching human consciousness; taking humanity beyond questions of morality. He had an epiphany: That there's no difference between the rightness of a religious life and the rightness of a immoral life. Love and human happiness were all that mattered.

"That's when he decided to join his life to mine. He needed to find me and come to me. He could no longer obsess about life after death. He rejected the dogma that my porn films were evil; something breathtakingly beautiful could not possibly be evil. He decided my immoral ways were wonderful and good; not evil.

"He had a transformative dream. He imagined he was in a bedroom with two beds. His wife was lying there naked on one bed and I was lying naked on the other bed. We both opened our legs for him. He imagined that his wife's vagina was dark and dangerous, like the deadly, radioactive Fukushima reactor. He dreamed that if he kissed her poisoned waste, his flesh would melt and his bones would crumble into powder. He imagined dying an agonizing, painful death.

"Then, he looked at my vagina. He imagined kissing it would be like gorging on a delicious cream puff; only warmer, tastier, and juicier than any cream puff he'd ever eaten. He'd be happier than he'd ever been; and never able to eat enough. His dream progressed.

"As he began cunnilingus, my vagina became like an overflowing bowl of juicy peaches. He began eating them. Each one was more delicious than the previous one. He was eating from this juicy fruit bowl; never getting full, always craving more of the tasty peaches inside my bowl, always thirsting for more of my copious peachy juices. He was acquiring a taste for my vagina's peaches. It became obsessive. He couldn't explain it. It was the way my pheromones interacted with my scents; the way I welcomed his tongue while he stroked my clitoris; how I naturally enjoyed it; all those things.

"He imagined he left his worries and cares inside me; like how he previously laid his problems at the foot of the cross. He discovered eternal happiness and endlessly beautiful sex by letting go of all his cares; surrendering himself while keeping his face and tongue deeply inside my peach bowl; swallowing my peachy juices and eating my delicious fruit, forever. His lips and cheeks dripped with juices from my delicious peaches. He rubbed my juices all over his face. He loved my peachy tastes on his lips. He never wanted to remove my delicious tastes from his cheeks or lips. Wearing the taste of me on his lips and cheeks became a badge of honor for him.

"Then he awakened. He realized he adored my vagina. He told me he was so smitten by my vagina he couldn't think of anything else. He resolved to watch every one of my films because seeing how I loved sex freed him from all his cares.

"The more he watched my films, the more he loved watching them. My erotica became a self reinforcing obsession for him. The more he watched me making love, the louder he heard the voice of this unexplainable force calling to him from deep inside himself. He arrived at a profound understanding. He realized he couldn't resist my invitation to immorality, any more than a caterpillar can resist nature's call to enter chrysalis.

"He admitted to himself that he had to contact me. He needed to come to me. He instinctively knew he had to leave the life he had. He followed this instinctive compulsion. He wrapped himself in my immoral lust chrysalis. Coming to me; immersing himself in my immoral lust was essential to his survival. He obeyed his instinctive command to leave the life he knew and surrender himself to his new life. This was a natural calling which no religion or social construct could oppose. He could no longer be the man he was. He was speaking the truth.

"Dom told me it became time to enter human chrysalis. His old ways of thinking about sin and lust became mentally liquefied jell. He would absorb his new, freedom- loving way of thinking into this jell, much the same way a caterpillar absorbs its old body into its new, liquefied form. Every time we made love, within Dom's mind a new nervous system and a new way of thinking about life was taking place; as within the caterpillar's liquefied body its nervous system is reborn. A reincarnation process happened within Dom's persona: A desire for freedom was born!

"During these nights of our beautiful lovemaking, Dom experienced his chrysalis and rebirth. He had these spontaneous bursts of real, colorful, refreshing thoughts. He no longer thought about life in the ways he had before. Epiphany after epiphany struck him like a series of lightning bolts. Then, like before hurricane force winds, the *ignis fatuus*, that delusional flame of illusory hope which the Church has dangled before its believers for millenniums, simply blew away.

"I beheld Dom's transformation. Poof! Just like that, his will set itself free of admonitions and contrived fears. I could feel his freedom. It was palpable. His life was no longer hobbled by theological dogma. He discovered freedom of relationship choices. He turned away from the Church's 'Jesus is God' messaging. He was finished with the Church's gospel teachings, prayers, and creed. He asked himself the same objective critical questions that he had asked himself years before, when he questioned his belief in the Tooth Fairy. Then, he deleted the church from his will and made me his sole beneficiary. Immorality became Dom's new God. And his new God was alive; embodied in me and my flesh. He welcomed sin loving, promiscuous porn star me, into his life. No longer did he feel any duty to placate his wife or pay homage to her beliefs. And I joyfully obliged him. I flooded into his new life and became the center of it.

"Dom continued to be a good father and provider to his children, but he could no longer be with his wife. His feelings for me precluded that. He ditched her. He threw away his old soul and embraced his new soul. He emerged from chrysalis and fluttered above everything he once thought was important. He saw the world fresh and new, from above now; no longer as a lowly, unseeing, crawling, pedestrian caterpillar struggling on Earth's surface. He fluttered with me, far away from all the old things, especially his wife. He wanted to copulate with me; flaunt our love like two carefree, amorous butterflies; dancing in the sunlight; knowing no shame or regrets. He desperately wanted to cavort and sin with me; savor his lust for me. He wanted to be head over heels in love with me; and yes, he wanted to make love with me often, and in every position imaginable. He wanted only me; me forever; and, then, he wanted more and more of me.

"He wanted escape from all his past behaviors. He didn't want to crawl. He wanted to fly and flutter freely. He felt like a newly minted

Monarch Butterfly, searching for a meadow of fresh flowers. He wanted my vagina's delicious nectar; not his former diet of boring, tasteless milkweed. He wanted to shout his new feelings to the world and proclaim his new love by holding me in his arms, in the sunlight. He did that. He proclaimed his love for me before the entire world. He wanted everyone to see us together, as a romantic couple in love; and he wanted to share his joy with the world. That was Dom being Dom; bold; expressive; uninhibited; proud. And there we were in Cannes. Cannes fascinated him. He loved the place.

"He wanted to kiss me on Cannes' beaches and in the casinos. There, he would express his feelings of happiness and celebrate his release from bondage. There, he would reject the life that no longer made sense to him. There, he would express his gratitude to me, a profligate, notorious porn star, for saving him from morality. Dom believes our love is eternal, and that the two of us have attained nirvana. He professes that his devotion to me will never waiver.

"Now, instead of taking weekly communion with his wife, Dom enters my holy of holies. Whenever we're together, he reposes his head between my welcoming thighs. There, between my butterfly wings, he performs his new communion ritual with my wonder of life. Instead of his tongue receiving a wafer, Dom's tongue prefers my clitoris. He savors my immoral vagina. He no longer ingests the symbol of death. He rejects the glorification of death. Dom cherishes life. He kisses life. He savors life; clings to life; and worships life. In my vagina, Dom finds peace. Dom is free now. He's like a butterfly dancing in the sunlight. He enjoys his new life. He loves it. Dom's renewed faith in life has renewed his strength and purpose, like a butterfly gains sustenance while drinking nectar from a flower. Nature, Dom, and I have become one.

"I'm pleased that Dom bared his soul to me. His penis and tongue commune with my unconditional love. Before he explained his metamorphosis, I didn't fully comprehend how my intimate erotic art sweeps away the confining kamatz of stale thinking. I'm pleased my work freed Dom's mind. Dom is free of guilt and shame. Before, when he was with his wife, he was a pretender. I understand that. But he's unburdened now. Freedom is the foundation rock of his new belief. I find the new Dom refreshing and exhilarating. He's a joy to be with.

"There in Cannes, between the many times we made love, Dom proposed we collaborate on our erotica clothing line and our motion picture venture. Dom provided the millions of dollars. I provided my intuition and my commitment to star in at least ten full-length feature films, performing explicit, intimate scenes with multiple partner-lovers.

"Dom opines that adult film stars are more honest, believable performers than women who perform in "straight" films because we have discarded our inhibitions. He believes my love scenes will resonate with the public because I'm not acting while I make love. I'm my uninhibited self; my immoral, lust-loving, shamelessly joyful me! Teee-Heee! We're excited to show the world that Dom's instincts are correct. I can't wait to begin filming. I'll feel energized and loved, knowing that hundreds of millions of men will see my upcoming full-length films!'

Dom's marketing insights were brilliant. He detected the soft breeze of changing morality and opened doors for that soft breeze to enter and play. He produced twelve full-length feature films with Marty starring in intimate romantic roles. His three thousand big screen theaters debuted Marty's dazzling erotica at a time when the country was reeling from disease, economic strife, and the collapse of the Dollar's buying power. Movies, alcohol, and drugs were still affordable. People were polarizing into warring political factions: those who advocated secular liberalism and those who clung to their religions and traditional family values. Everyone escaped to Dom's theaters. My fan base swelled, setting new records for film and merchandise sales. Dom's cash registers rang nonstop. We had hit the jackpot.

Dom took his next big step. He used his growing fortune to acquire political influence. He supported secular candidates for positions on school boards and city counsels. He backed his chosen candidates for mayors, district attorneys and judges. He acquired ownership control of important print, television, cable, and social media outlets. Then he ushered the soft breeze of immorality into schools, the courts, and America's homes. Political leaders got paid; and they fell into line. Dom reasoned that humans were morally the same as many other species; natural selection would lead humanity forward. The strong would flourish; the weak would wither away.

Curriculums were changed to include immorality and prostitution. These new subjects were taught to children. Municipal, state, and federal governments passed ordinances granting tax free incentives for temples of prostitution. Judges ruled increasingly in favor of dismissing prostitution offences and imposed harsh sentences upon those who interfered with prostitution rituals and upon those religious types who desecrated the New Morality Temples. Advertisers for religious services were shunted to media time slots where viewership was small. Ads for the New Morality Temples were aired in prime time. A morality changing revolution quietly took root and grew.

Based upon the pronouncements from these Temples, secularists soon dominated America's inner cities. Mandates were issued which sought to create the ideal, humanistic society. Only those who professed belief in the immoral teachings of the Temples and practiced the New Morality faith were deemed worthy citizens.

Those who refused to tithe to the New Morality Temples were deemed unworthy to belong to this new progressive society. These people were *selected* for disposition. The soft breeze of immorality grew in strength. It became a destructive, gale force wind. The wind strengthened into a hurricane. It lifted families and communities off their moral foundations and swept away all undesirable elements with its cleansing force. The day Marty was consecrating a New Morality Temple, this progressive force was busily enforcing its latest decree.

Marty had approved a local chapter's new temple. The congregation had acquired a church building. The tabernacle, which formerly held the Eucharist, was replaced by a golden, ruby jeweled butterfly, fashioned after the bauble that Marshawn had given Marty. The stained-glass windows of saints and prophets had been replaced with stained glass images of past years' most famous porn stars. The windows were reminders of immorality's relentless path forward. The congregants beamed with pride. Marty, the biggest name in all whoredom, was here to approve their work.

Today, Marty herself, the Supreme Goddess of Immorality, presided over this magnificent new temple's admission ceremony. Three exceptionally handsome young men and three beautiful young women, dressed only in flowing robes of silken gossamer fabric, proceeded down the aisle, accompanied by Marty's favorite melody, the Ave Maria. They bowed before Marty, recited their respectful lines of submission to immorality and loyalty to the Temple; and then consummated their 'marriage' to The New Morality Standard. All six took turns kissing Marty, performing cunnilingus with her; and, for the young men, ejaculating inside her vagina. Prostitution service rituals for the entire congregation followed the admission of its six new members.

While Marty blessed one young woman who was blissfully sucking two new converts' penises, a spectacle of a different sort took place only a few blocks away. The uniformed, Undesirable Peoples' Patrol rounded up all peoples deemed unworthy to live in the New Morality Society: Homeless, disabled, mentally handicapped, persons with criminal records, veterans and aged people were detained and herded into cages. Homeless tent villages were scraped from sidewalks and city parks. These peoples' tents and all their possessions were taken to open pits and burned. Protest cries were silenced by clubbing. These Deplorables were not allowed to disturb the indoctrination rites at the newest New Morality Temple. All misfits were rounded up.

Attractive children under the age of four were placed in a special bus. They were taken to the Temple to begin their years of service and indoctrination into prostitution. Older children and adults were declared superfluous, incorrigible Deplorables; and scheduled for disposal. Marty selected a Deplorable hater named Barking Hillbilly to manage the disposal process. Barking Hillbilly was chosen from among over a thousand progressive socialist applicants because of her unique qualifications. She was an avowed Cloward Priven communist who hated all religions with unbridled passion. She was a highly successful, accomplished murderess. Laws and ethics never got in her way. She had connived and thieved her way to political power; and regardless of how wrong headed she was, she never doubted her convictions. And, she was devoid of conscience and was ruthless; perfect for her role.

The Disposal Squad received its official orders. Deplorables were loaded onto cattle cars and transported to ocean terminals. No food, water or sanitation was wasted on these people during their transit. At terminal piers they were loaded into cages. The cages were hoisted aboard ships. The ships took these people-cages fifty miles out into the ocean, out of sight and sound. Barking Hillbilly did her best work when she knew no one could observe her. A few Deplorables were selected for bait chum. Barking Hillybilly used her trusty machete to hack wounds into her hapless victims. She then pushed these mortally wounded Deplorables off the ship's fantail. Predictably, bloody water attracted hundreds of sharks. Ships cranes next hoisted their Deplorables cages up and twenty feet away from the ships. Then, the trap door floors of these crates opened, spilling their human cargo into the ocean.

The ship moved slowly forward during its Deplorable disposal process, leaving the drowning Deplorables in its wake. Sharks understood the routine. They trailed the ships. Barking Hillybilly took her position on the ship's fantail. She practiced her marksmanship by shooting the helpless Deplorable survivors. Her blood sport attracted more sharks, resulting in spectacular feeding frenzies. Barking Hillybillly roared in laughter at the plight of the Deplorables. Back on land, Barking Hillybillly was given awards for efficiently eliminating Deplorables. She was a frequent guest on talk shows and starred in a reality TV series, where she portrayed, not a cold hearted murderous, blood thirsty bitch, but a soft, cuddly, all inclusive, warm hearted, loving, family-oriented woman.

Religious leaders decried Marty's erotic films, stating they were a bane on morality. Priests, rabbis, imams, and pastors decried whoredom's shredding of society's social fabric. They urged their congregants to avoid seeing pornographic films, especially films starring Marty. But their pleas only increased the demand for Marty's films. The religious leaders urged opposition to the New Morality Standard and the new temples. Parents went to school board meetings. They demanded banning Marty's sex education series. Alarmed citizens across America urged civic leaders to ban all books mentioning Marty and all her films. Zealous committees were formed. They searched out books about Marty's life and the New Morality Standard. They shamed people who had the books and publically burned the books. A software company was hired to prevent computers from showing Marty's films.

The resistance of these moralists did not go unnoticed. Secular liberal spies from the New Morality Order Network took down peoples' names. Political and religious dissenters were rounded up and held in prison cells and removed from society by the Disposal Squad. The dissenters were herded into Barking Hillybillly's human cargo cages. The Disposal Squad and Barking Hillybillly's murder sport did the rest. The hurricane wind of immorality spared no one.

Despite efforts to block Marty's message, burn books about her, and prevent her intimate artistry from polluting their families and communities, Marty's sales continued their meteoric increase. She and Dom rode a transformational social juggernaut. Depressed people turned to whoring to escape societal stress. Prostitution services experienced mushrooming demand. Orders issued by the governing counsel of the New Morality Temples became the law of the land. Whoring and prostitution were ruled desirable, socially beneficial activities worthy of tax-exempt status. Religious institutions of all sorts were deemed divisive; and therefore, subjected to heavy taxation and licensing fees. Churches that could not pay the new taxes and fees were confiscated by the New Morality Council. These church properties were converted into temples of prostitution worship.

Society became like a snake eating its own tail. After all the Deplorables were expunged from society, a cry arose from the Deplorable Disposal squads that their volumes of disposable humans were declining. They feared unemployment, which could make them eligible for Deplorable status. They lobbied their masters in the counsels of the New Morality Temples to declare more people deplorable so that their employment could continue. Academic studies were done. Cost benefit measurements were analyzed. After deliberation, it was determined that racial discord was not productive to the New Morality Society. Therefore, one race needed to be eliminated.

Blacks were chosen for elimination rather than Native Americans because blacks tended to live in inner cities and Natives Americans tended to be more dispersed. The efficiency of rounding up Blacks tipped the committee's decision to eliminate them next. The supreme council of Immorality voted to eliminate all Blacks. But, Marty, as presiding chair of the Immorality Council vetoed the committee's decision. She gave an eloquent, impassioned speech about Marshawn and her many black orgy partners:

'*These black men are beautiful. Their bodies are extremely attractive. Whoring with a black penis is an exceptionally gratifying sexual experience. A woman's orgasms are more spontaneous, more thrilling, longer lasting, and more memorable than orgasms with white penises. These black men perform necessary, vital services to the temple prostitutes and must, therefore be exempt from the council's decree.*'

And she challenged the committee to think more deeply about their decision. She charged them to consider that there were elements of society that felt a bond or a need for one segment of society, even though others did not. She ordered them to be sensitive to the needs of others in their new Immoral Global World Order. She charged them to think of ways a given group might benefit society.

Black males were Marty's perfect example. She spoke of the benefits of healing the racial divide. She advocated new fornication programs, to be administered by the temples. These programs would pair more white women with black men, so that white women would learn the ecstasy of copulating with blacks and their magnificent penises. She told the Council it would be a travesty to whoredom and hedonistic pleasures if these splendid men and their magnificent penises should be lost.

The whores who managed the New Morality Temples were in complete accord with Marty's position. They petitioned the Council that black males must be exempted from the Council's order. They stated in no uncertain terms that, without black penises, their harmony and psychosocial well being would be adversely affected and their prostitution performances would suffer. Depressions might ensue and prostitutes might need to cancel services for lack of enthusiasm. Their petition was signed by every whore from every temple. Similarly, several Council Members objected to having attractive black females included in the Disposition Order. A secret vote revealed that over half the male members consorted regularly with black females; and three members were married to black females. The committee conceded that its original order was overly broad.

Accordingly, the committee modified its order. Only obese black females were deemed Deplorable. All black males were spared. A new sex education program was authorized. It ordered white females to prove they had familiarized themselves with the joys of copulating with black males, including that they attended a paired weekly vacation for multiracial breeding instructions. The goal of the program was to create a new hybrid race of highly sexualized, uninhibited, immorality-loving people.

The revised Disposal order was made, stamped official by the Immorality Counsel, and given to the Disposal Squad. Black women were given a nationwide obesity test. Those categorized as obese were sent to the Disposal Squad. The machinery of the New Morality Standard again ran smoothly.

The Progressive Immorality Counsel next ordered the committee to schedule a review of other groups for classification as Deplorables. The list of groups to be reviewed included Baptists, Jews, Muslims, Native Americans, reconsidered for a second time, religious Lutheran and Evangelical Protestants and Catholics, all obese white people, all persons with IQ's below 100 and all with IQ's above 150. The committee decreed that people too stupid to follow committee orders as well as highly intelligent people, who might question committee orders, should all be eliminated.

Like a category five tornado, Marty's New Morality Standard ravaged everything it touched. Buildings, cars, planes, and fixtures were spared, but families and individuals who did not conform to the 'new normal' standards were not spared. People cowered in fear of the inquisitions and the squads. No one dared raise their voice to oppose the new order, less they be labeled Deplorable. Marty's immoral whirlwind was glorified. Her tireless promotional efforts earned her the Presidential Medal of Freedom, awarded by Hilly-billly, the nation's progressive leftist president. Who was mentally incapacitated and who vacationed 99% of his time in office.

The President honored Marty for freeing so many Americans from the shackles of marriage. Marty was also awarded honorary degrees from twenty prestigious universities for her highly compensated, provocative speaking engagements. From her lectern she extolled the fabulous career opportunities in prostitution work; and she followed her lectures with live fornication demonstrations.

Applications to join Marty's burgeoning support staff flooded her office. Licensing agreements, promotional contracts, advertizing placements, documentary films about prostitutes in the New Morality Network, the network's extensive servicing reach, all required organizational skills and management. Dom oversaw the business aspects of Marty's enterprise. Together they reordered the social fabric of America.

Dom noticed that more and more women were avoiding their religions and entering the intimate artistry field. Prostitution services were ordered exempt from all inquisition programs. Tax exempt status was granted to the New Morality Standard temples and the earnings of all their affiliated prostitutes. Their work was considered a charitable, necessary social good. Other religions lost their tax-exempt status. They were considered obstructionist institutions that caused social discord and racial divisions.

The Deplorable inquisitions programs managed by the secular liberals terrified many women and frightened them away from religious services. The crushing economy forced many others to sell their precious metals and heirlooms, their homes, and prized possessions. The New Normal Economy, the dishonest money economy, squeezed the life out of these women and kicked them in their guts. They took the priceless treasures that their mothers handed down from their grandmothers and great grandmothers; and sold them for a pittance. Parting with these items separated these women from their souls, parted them from their sense of right and wrong, and shredded their childhood beliefs. They were now divorced; their husbands had all gone off with whores. Many of these women had only their bodies left to sell.

Less orthodox women were more nuanced trend followers who realized that fornication and immorality were waves of the future. They searched their consciences and admitted to themselves that they were perfectly willing to expand their sexual horizons. The prospect of careers in prostitution titillated them. Dom saw these winning trends. He hired these women, the downtrodden and the adventuresome, and assimilated them into his prostitution networks.

He astutely avoided aligning himself with people who sought to heal the nation's divisions; nor did he cast his lot with those who suffered from the great disparity of wealth. He dismissed losing causes. At his core, Dom remained a clever businessman. He marketed to those who could afford what he and Marty were selling.

He doubled down on his alliance with Marty. It was his easiest decision. She was a proven money maker. She was a fabulous, agreeable business partner. She proved a fountainhead of new ideas that profited from the destruction of morality. She was also a sensational, creative sex partner. Besides her business attributes, Dom truly loved her. He adored everything about her; especially the ways her immoral mind worked.

It was Marty's idea to dispose of the Deplorables in such an efficient ocean absorbing manner. She was a modern-day Queen Isabella, joyfully murdering the millions who dared to oppose her. Dissent and differing opinions were not tolerated. Marty's decisions caused real estate values in Temple neighborhoods to rise. It became fashionable to live close to the Immorality Temples. They became safe neighborhoods. She and Dom bought up neighboring real estate and rode those appreciating values higher. It was Marty's idea to train young children as temple helpers. They were free labor who would grow up knowing only whoredom; believing it was the only true religion. It was the psychological antidote to religious schools. Marty's creativity inspired Dom. They believed they could transform American society.

In swift succession Dom and Marty produced no less than thirteen big screen films featuring Marty in orgy settings. These were themed around the holidays. Marty dressed as Christmas Elf, Easter Bunny, Halloween Witch, Patriot maiden, Native American Princess, Queen of England, Pilgrim woman, cheerleader, weather forecaster, secretary, news anchor, congresswoman, and retail store clerk. One hundred of the most handsome men with the most impressive penises were selected from thousands of applicants to perform with Marty. The films' orgy scenes were breathtaking tributes to spectacular erotica. The films were all box office sensations. Dom leveraged the most salacious hundred still frames from the new erotica extravaganza into a highly successful sell through campaign.

Individual frame shots and collage prints of Marty's orgy scenes were produced and published as calendars, backings for greeting cards, posters for sale, and licensed to artists for royalty interests in oils, etchings, and reproductions on all sorts of mediums. Countless images of Marty's gorgeous waxed, plump pink vagina, oozing creamy semen from hundreds of ejaculations; and as many pictures of adoring penises' ejaculating into her welcoming mouth were omnipresent in public view. The cigarette and fast-food industries could only wish they had half of Marty's branding success.

Dom understood impulse purchases. He struck Licensing agreements with the top twenty nationwide marketers of prostitution services, allowing them to position their ad tags before, after, and selectively during highly evocative, explicit, erotic segments of Marty's films. He purchased all rights to past Oscar award winning films for best actress and had them remade with new actors and actresses; and with Marty playing the role that won best actress. In these revised film versions, the scenes played by the Marty were extended and extensively rewritten to include scenes of explicit erotica. The remade films far surpassed all their previous box office records. There were all sorts of sell through products, from calendars to dolls, to fashion wear, hailing Marty's success as the world's most accomplished actress ever, across all genres and venues.

Marty became national phenomena. She rode the crest of immorality's tidal wave that swept the nation. Her wave of relentless unapologetic whoring dislodged many marriages from their foundations. Whores became celebrities. They ruled the new normal world order. At first, Marty's tide receded as concerned groups sought to ban her films and her message, as well as the books that hailed her spectacular success. But, the national craving for more of the luscious sex goddess could not be held back. Tsunami-like, her sales and popularity flooded back in wave after wave, stronger than ever. Her salacious pornography overtook civilization with a vengeance. Marty's consistent message of immorality's freedom and her erotically addicting films drowned her demoralized enemies in an endless deluge of sin.

Millions of men and women hailed Marty as the world's most glorious porn star, ever. Countless images idolized her. Photos of Marty with penises in her mouth and vagina, licking partners' balls, stroking penises, receiving cunnilingus and multiple simultaneous insertions from several penises flooded the public's consciousness. Her smiling face assured all doubters that her immoral ways were preferred social conduct.

Dom understood that most humans are crowd followers. And he milked that trait. The subtle message underlying the ads was that there was a righteousness and a wholesomeness about this sensational, cherubic, innocent appearing, all American whore-goddess. Temple priestesses preached that Marty's example showed everyone the correct religious way to honor the spirits of creation. Something profound was happening in the public psyche. Psychological chains were snapped; traditional mores were shredded; and old beliefs were plowed asunder. People rejected morality and flocked to immorality. It was the humans' herd instinct thing, the 'be part of the crowd' thinking at work. It was living proof that few people could think for themselves. People no longer felt any stigma about idolizing a profligate whore. Marty became the object of a national love fest; a modern-day golden calf.

Marty changed the morality of America. Men left their families to consort with prostitutes on a scale never before imagined. Women joined the ranks of whoredom's prostitutes and embraced their new vocations with great optimism. Paganism became accepted as a bona fide religion. Pagan temples sprang up all over America. The new Pagan religion took full advantage of recent U S Supreme Court decisions which allowed religious expression in public places and government buildings. School teachers, who practiced Paganism, held religious ceremonies in their classrooms during after school hours. Children of all ages attended these ceremonies. There, the children observed their teachers practicing oral sex, prostitution worship, and orgies. As part of their religious indoctrination, children were invited to join the adults. In schools and activities groups, children were taught how to view moral issues the same way porn stars did. Dom and Marty created props and instruction materials that described the sensual feelings when penises and vaginas join together in sex.

Compliments to Marty's vision, Paganism achieved full parity with mainstream religions. Pagan religious indoctrination was offered to children of Pagan temple parents, complete with prostitution rituals. Many children persuaded their parents to join the new Pagan temples because these children preferred Pagan religious indoctrination to conventional religious schools' indoctrinations.

While America's divorce rates skyrocketed, families disintegrated, and morality and religious memberships plunged to new lows, Dom and Marty reaped vast fortunes. Pagan ordered inquisitions targeted other religions. Members of Christian churches, Jewish and Muslim Temples perished in Barking Hillybillly's pogrom genocides, while Dom and Marty garnered fabulous wealth by confiscating the gold and silver holdings of religious malcontents. Religious leaders of all persuasions were crucified, hacked to pieces, and burned alive, in retribution for those same methods used to propagate religion's grip on the world's peoples' during millenniums past.

Public government buildings took down the Star-Spangled Banner. They flew flags of Red and Black, symbolizing America's national allegiance to Pagan anarchy. Prostitution services flourished. Experienced prostitutes were appointed to national cabinet positions and high ranks in the nation's armed forces. Marty and

Dom aligned their Immorality Movement with the leftist American Progressive Socialist Party. After Barking Hillybillly's Anti-Deplorable Party won the next national elections, they changed the party's name to the Now New American Marxist Party. Marty was named the honorary Secretary of Education. That cabinet department's function was to indoctrination the nation's youth about the wonderful benefits of the Modern Morality Standard.

Children were sent to Prostitution Academies and taught from Marty's Syllabus of Immoral Whoring. At Academy camps, young girls were taught how to fornicate in many different positions from Kama Sutra pictorials and trained in techniques for sucking penises by their adult supervisors. Girls from each age group were given awards and prizes for excellence in promiscuity, fornication, fellation, and erotic expression posing.

America became the world's whorehouse. Except where it survived in remote Appalachian Mountain enclaves, family values withered and died. Some bible belt, bourbon drinking holdouts insisted on clinging to their bibles and their guns. They were targeted as purveyors of dangerous disinformation. Pagan militia groups were periodically formed to hunt down these outlawed pro-religious renegades and eradicate them.

Dom continued his raptured fascination with Marty. He loved her; always placing her interests ahead of his own. But he could not understand how her employment with David produced a benefit to her. He tried several times to persuade Marty to leave David and work exclusively on their branded merchandise promotions, but Marty always refused. Marty never revealed the nature of her relationship with David. And Dom could not persuade her to change it.

Once while making love, Marty told Dom in no uncertain terms that David was her tried-and-true friend; that she felt a duty of loyalty to him; and that she would not leave her position at the

Firm. She insisted on living her dual lives. She also refused to leave her relationships with Bob and her other lovers. Dom was told that he was her business partner and one of her lovers; but that he had no exclusive rights to her body or her time.

Dom suspected there was some sort of nefarious connection that joined Marty to David, but he thought it best to set the matter aside. He never mentioned David's name to Marty again. A true businessman, he accepted those things that he could not change. He moved his business dealings with Marty forward, accepting her as his partner on her terms. She and Dom eagerly planned the gala promotional introduction of their new, Premium Bikini line.

More to come.

*Beware Barrack, that silver-tongued sycophant panderer who falsely promises an end to struggles. He is our modern-day Trojan Horse; sinister, dangerous as Priam's horse. He is inside our gates. Like the devil's termite, he undermines our foundations and our walls. My characters represent the fruits of his destruction. Shun them. (Rosemary Ness Bitner, Author)*

# PREVIEWS OF
# TROPHY BUTTERFLY

"But what is U expecting of me, Bob? How am I supposed to love her? Am I expected to brush her hair, massage her neck and shoulders, kiss her mouth, and perhaps suckle her nipples; maybe stimulate her vaginal crown with my encouraging fingers, while she's copulating with the man who is the love of my life? What humiliations, what mental tortures am I expected to endure?" . . . . . . . . . Chapter One.

'Close your eyes; remember. You were pampered. Every day the young altar girls massaged your body with oils; coiffed your hair; cleaned and polished your fingernails and toenails. It was the morning of special offerings. The temple matron had just freshly shaved your vagina's mons with her sharpest obsidian blade. Then she salved and anointed your sex with her prized gardenia scented salve and lilac scented oils, in preparation for your fornication rituals. Remember?'
'Yes, Miss Iniquity. I remember now.' . . . . . . . . . . Chapter Two.

"That is the mystery, Big Horse. I have asked myself that question a thousand times and I cannot come up with any rational answer to it. The relationship that she has with David is, I think, the key to everything. But it is disguised from everyone, even you; even from Susan, I think." . . . . . . . . . . . . . . . . . . . . . . . . . . Chapter Three.

"We couldn't wait to walk those few steps to our room. That would take an entire minute and we could not wait that long. We had to do it now. Right now. Dom was so intent about having me that I knew he had to be in love with me. Nothing else mattered. Love happens like that. We both knew it was happening. He had lust rage. For me. For my body. For my vagina. When he hiked my skirt, I felt hot fire run wild through my blood. Volcanoes popped and spewed hot lava inside me . . . . . . . . . . . . . . . . . . . . . . . . . . . . . . . . . Chapter Four.*

*"Well, changing my feelings between the men I love is the same as that, like changing the TV channel from one man to another. I just love the man I'm with; and while I'm with him, I forget the other men. It's very easy for me to do that, mentally, once I start kissing and making love. My shrink assures me that having a variety of lov-ers is excellent for my mental health . . . . . . . . . . . . . . . Chapter Five.*

*"After the sun had set and we sailed into Weems Creek past the Naval Academy's Trident Point, I looked at the Academy's huge gray stone buildings with those green copper roofs; and do you know what I felt I was seeing for the first time, after all those other times that we had sailed past there?"*

*"No Marty, what?"*

*"Death, that's what." . . . . . . . . . . . . . . . . . . . . . . . Chapter Six.*

*"Some were saying that I was the reappearance of biblical Belial, the princess of wanton depravity. Some cursed me for being iniquitous, in my godless pursuit of mammon wealth; soulless in my profligate sinful debaucheries. But I felt something else happening within me."*
*. . . . . . . . . . . . . . . . . . . . . . . . . . . . . . . . . . . Chapter Seven.*

'When that woman shouted out to her husband to stop fornicating with you, complaining that your cost was twice his required tithe, you pointed to her as your defiler; and you caused her to be hacked to death, dismembered, and disemboweled. Do you remember?'

'Yes,' answered Marty's mind, 'I remember . . . . . Chapter Eight.


"So, my clever daughter has figured out how to make the illegal, legal?"

"That's right, Dad. Aren't you proud of me?" . . .  Chapter Nine.


"In Spain, Portugal, the Netherlands, and several other European countries, incest is perfectly legal, Father." . . . . . . . . . Chapter Ten.

*Well, dear readers and listeners, in BUTTERFLY MORALS, book nine of THE SECRET BUTTERFLY SERIES Marty revealed her spiritual destiny was to advance the Modern Morality Standard. She enthusiastically embraces whatever advances her immoral crusade, including mass murder. Dom converted to the immoral ways of the new standard and discovered erotic nirvana with Marty. Mmmmm. Dom couldn't get enough of her, could he? Did you like the way Dom and Marty dazzled Las Vegas on their historic promotional tour? I hope you did. We glimpsed human behavior in the throes of limbic passion, didn't we? What sort of times were those times before the modern religions took hold; when people believed in sex goddesses? What did people believe in back then? How did they behave toward their goddesses and toward each other?*

*Rosemary reveals her dark fantasy about human sacrifices. Should we believe her; or should we believe the biblical version? Why the Apis bulls? What purpose did they serve the ancient Egyptians? Did Moses's passions for Baaleezebelle really induce him to forsake his wife and kids to the Nile crocodiles? Marty tells all as we live her fictional fantasy with her.*

*In our next book, TROPHY BUTTERFLY©, book ten of THE SECRET BUTTERFLY SERIES, an apparition appears to Bob. It delivers a foreboding, chilling message. Let's discover whether Bob can ignore the apparition's message. That takes courage and the strength to know yourself. Can Bob resist the apparition? Can he do anything about it? How could the apparition possibly know of which it speaks?*

*I'm Minna Morinette, your audiobook narrator. Come flutter with me as I take you on Bob's mind-bending trip back in time; back to the days of Moses, Egyptian fertility rites, the birth of religious pornography, and the early creation struggles of humanity's first experimentation with the unnatural notion of monotheistic religions.*

www.ingramcontent.com/pod-product-compliance
Lightning Source LLC
Chambersburg PA
CBHW051305300726

48976CB00002B/269